Beyond the Palace

BEYOND THE PALACE

SARA ELIZABETH GOODMAN

Cover images by Jordan Goodman and Sara Elizabeth Goodman

For Uncle Jules
Thank you, and I miss you

1

If you ask Laura, she'll say we first laid eyes on each other on December 8, 2002 in Charlotte, North Carolina, as Bruce Springsteen was playing "Backstreets." She'll ignore that the song is actually about a breakup and that even that far below the Mason-Dixon Line, December 8 is by no means part of the "soft-infested summer" that the song takes place in. But she'll say that we became friends. If you ask Laura.

Like everything she would tell you, there is some truth in that, I guess. The first time we talked to each other was months earlier and the first time I saw her was right before the show started in Washington, DC on August 10 of that year. Second show on the tour. She was a couple of rows ahead of me, a little to my left. I'm sure that I thought she was pretty, but I don't remember specifically paying any attention to her before the show. I only remembered her at all because she caught my eye during the song "Bobby Jean." She never took her eyes off of Bruce, and she watched him with a look of absolute wonder on her face. Then a tear rolled slowly down her right cheek, hesitating slightly before it slipped past her upturned chin and slid down her neck. She didn't wipe it away or show any sign that she knew she was crying. Somehow I never got rid of that image. That was two months before I ever even talked to her, but she was just etched into my mind.

If I had to pick the moment when my life so drastically began to change its course, I would have to start there.

I was three years out of college and was working a decently-paying desk job in Washington, DC. Not particularly exciting, but I was sort of the office whiz-kid and was already in line for promotions. A few months earlier, I had moved into an apartment with my girlfriend of the past two years, Katie, who taught second grade. I hadn't spent all that much time thinking about it yet, but Katie had been dropping not-so-subtle hints that she thought the time was right for us to get engaged. I wasn't quite ready for that then, but I definitely assumed that we would eventually. Because that's what you did after you moved in with someone. Everyone knew that.

By the standards that I had held up until then, which I suppose had been ingrained in me since my birth twenty-five years earlier, my life was going exactly where it should be going.

And I was happy.

I thought.

That is to say, I didn't realize that I could have more or even that I wanted more. I hadn't yet asked the question of what I wanted my future to look like. I just assumed it would follow the general pattern that my parents' generation had set. Katie and I would get married, have a couple of kids and then—well, I didn't really know what came next. But it seemed like the right idea. Most of our friends were coupled off at that point, and it was the same plan we all had.

Therefore, it hadn't yet occurred to me that I wanted out.

Laura changed all that.

Looking back, I can't imagine that I would have been happy if I had stayed with Katie. It would have been like my life ended before I even got the chance to really live it. Although, if I never met Laura, maybe I could have been happy with that life. But after I saw her, I knew that my future lay down a different path.

It wasn't even that I was interested in meeting Laura when I first saw her. I still had a girlfriend and, pretty girl or not, I'm no cheater. What impressed me so much was the emotion I saw in her. She understood the music. And she was moved by it to the point of tears. Yes, I would later learn the reason that she had cried while listening to that song about saying goodbye, but right then it didn't matter. Seeing her made me realize, for the first time, that there were people out there who could love what I loved and understand the things that meant so much to me.

Katie and I had met through mutual friends in college. We hung out in the same places and were attracted to each other. But nothing happened until after we graduated and started running into each other most weekends. Those run-ins were accidental at first, but soon we started arranging to hang out. And then somehow we were dating. I don't remember specifically asking her out, especially not on the set date that we celebrated twice as our anniversary, but we did well together and I liked having her as my girlfriend. We didn't really have all that much in common, but that doesn't always matter that much in the beginning. And then it gets comfortable and that's why you stay. It's easy. But watching Laura's reaction to Bruce's music, I realized that this girl, who I had never seen before and would probably never see again, was more capable of understanding me than the girl who I lived with and thought that I wanted to eventually marry.

Watching the tears glistening on Laura's face, I thought about Katie, who had laughed when I asked if she wanted go to the concert with me.

"Are you kidding?" she asked. "All he sings about is cars and depressing stuff! I can't imagine a worse way to spend a Saturday night!"

I remember looking at Katie like I was seeing her for the first time. Bruce had always been a big part of my life. *Born in the USA* was the first tape I ever bought. *Born to Run* was the second. She was trivializing the music that had shaped the person who I grew up to be. What right did she have to do that?

Just as Laura's eyes never left Bruce's face, my eyes stayed on hers through that song. And I recognized, in those three minutes, that there was much more to life than what I currently had. That image of Laura, standing there, watching Bruce so intently that she didn't notice she was crying, became a permanent reminder of what I wanted but didn't have.

Of course, it's easy for me to say now that I realized all of that in three minutes, but it wasn't quite that simple. It was really just the catalyst for me realizing that something bigger was wrong. And I didn't act on it immediately, but after that, I started to notice that life with Katie might not be what I wanted after all. It took me several weeks to fully reach that conclusion, but I started to chafe when I realized that most of Katie's conversations centered around her seven-year-old students. Yes, it was great and noble that she was a teacher. But for Christ's sake, did she think I really cared if Derek put paint in Kayla's hair? And it started to drive me nuts that she didn't enjoy anything deep. She refused to finish watching *Fight Club*, one of my all-time favorite movies, because it was "just about fighting." She preferred soap operas and Oprah to music. She even liked the Ravens over my beloved Redskins because she preferred purple to burgundy. And she was proud of her color-based allegiance! Early in our relationship, I had thought these quirks were kind of sweet and innocent. But by the end, I had begun to realize that there was a lot in life that was just a little over Katie's head.

I was listless and started snapping at her when I got annoyed. I felt guilty for doing it, which only meant that I felt worse around her and snapped at her more. I hated going to work because I felt like I was trapped in my own life, but going home was worse because I felt more trapped by Katie. Which wasn't remotely fair, because I had made my own choices. But I couldn't be unhappy without resenting her for making me feel that way. I was listening to more Bruce music than ever, both because I was going through concert withdrawal and because his songs seemed to be about what I was going through. They were about getting out on the road and finding that "moment when the world seems right." About finding that person who you can *really* fall in love with. And Katie just wasn't that girl. Not for me.

I felt awful about it, but I had to leave. I know Katie was completely bewildered by the change in me, and I wish I could have given her a better explanation than I did. But I had to get out.

I moved out about a month and a half after the show in DC.

While they couldn't fill the void that I felt in my life in a permanent way, I realized that the concerts gave me something that nothing else in my life had ever been able to provide until then. It was indescribable, but I had to keep going back. I knew that I wasn't the only one who felt it either, because I had met a lot of people on the reunion tour two years earlier who had followed Springsteen for more years than I'd been alive. So while some of my friends told me that I was crazy for spending seventy five bucks per ticket for multiple shows on the same tour, I needed more. At the end of September, I drove to Chicago to see Bruce again. Then the next week, I went to Philadelphia to visit my little brother, Mike, who was in medical school up there, and we went to that show together. Our dad always listened to classic rock when we were kids, and he took us to our first Bruce show as a family bonding thing in 1999. I appreciated that, because it meant that Mike understood what I got out of the shows. But he didn't have the time to go to many of them with me. Apparently, unlike college, in med school he was actually expected to go to class.

Mike knew about Laura already, because I mentioned her when I tried to explain the Katie breakup. I could tell he didn't really understand though; Laura herself had nothing to do with my decision to leave Katie, but she represented what was missing to me.

When I saw her for the second time, outside of the arena before the Philadelphia show, I didn't recognize her. Her hair was still long but now it was red. Like Bruce's wife, Patti Scialfa, I remember thinking. She was in the parking lot of the sports complex, drinking beer out of a can, and laughing at something one of the men she was with had said. She was with three older guys, all about forty to fifty years old. As she laughed, she put her hand on the arm of the tallest of the group, who was wearing a very old *Born to Run* tour shirt, and she said something that made the three of them laugh. I admit that I found the situation odd. *Born to Run* guy's shirt looked old enough for him to have gotten it at a show on the 1975 tour, and there was no way that Laura was old enough to have been born yet in 1975. I figured that maybe he could be her father. But it sure didn't look like that was the case.

I wanted to talk to her, although I had no idea what I would say even if I got the chance. "Thank you for making me realize that I wanted to dump my girlfriend" would probably be just the littlest bit creepy. And nothing else seemed important enough to interrupt her conversation. So I gave up, both for lack of anything intelligent to say and because, based on how absorbed she seemed by the men she was with, I was clearly half the age of someone she would be looking for. But as it turned out, I didn't need to worry about an opening line.

"*They*'ll know I'm right!" I heard as we walked by. "Hey!" she called out. "You two!" I turned my head, positive that she couldn't mean me, but unable to not look. She had broken out of the group and swayed toward us. I stopped walking as she reached me.

I thought she was pretty in Washington. In Philadelphia, I realized she was gorgeous. In my first really good look at her, I wasn't sure that I could have spoken to her if she hadn't come up to me first. She was impossibly thin, and in her high heeled boots, she had to have been almost six feet tall, no more than two or three inches shorter than me. She had the most fascinating eyes I had ever seen, and I would later spend hours unable to sleep as I attempted to determine their exact color. Before that moment, I had wanted what she stood for. But looking into those eyes, I wanted her.

"Only a fan *young* enough," she said, shooting a wicked smile over her shoulder to the man in the *Born to Run* shirt, "to still have his memory will know I'm right about this." She turned back to me and asked, "Did Nils and Patti actually play on the *Born in the USA* album? Not the tour, because I know they were on the tour, but was either of them on the album?"

"Nils joined when Little Steven left, which was after they cut the album," I replied immediately. "Patti..." I hesitated. I wasn't sure. Someone was doing some backup on that album, but was it her? Traces of a frown started across Laura's face. She was starting to think she had picked the wrong guy. *Think!*

"No!" I said as soon as the answer hit me. "She was in the video for 'Glory Days' but she wasn't singing, she was just playing the tambourine because that video was the actual album version, and she wasn't on the album. The first studio album that she sang with the band for was *Tunnel of Love.*" I looked at her in triumph.

"Impressive," she said seriously, meaning it. Then she visibly lightened, looked back over her shoulder and, saying nothing, batted her eyelashes rapidly at the group of older men.

Born to Run guy looked amused. "Alright, babe," he said with a smile. "You win. As always."

She turned back to me. "Got a cig?" I handed her one and fumbled with my lighter while she put the cigarette between her lips and waited. I lit it and she winked at me, the faintest hint of a smile across her lips, then she turned and walked back to *Born to Run* guy without a word or look back. He put his arm around her waist, his hand resting just a little too low for me to keep believing that he could be related to her. I followed Mike into the concert and willed myself to not look back at her, because she hadn't looked back at me. I almost succeeded.

The next time I saw her, and the first time that we actually introduced ourselves, was at the December 8 show. So you see, there is some truth in what Laura would say. I got to the General Admission line for that show at about 8am the day before the show, after driving down with my friend Joe through an ice storm. We got our wristbands for "the pit" as the area right in front of the stage is called, and were told when to check in for roll calls. We killed most of that first day in Charlotte hanging out in our motel room.

After one of the last roll calls on the day of the show, Joe and I crossed the street and headed to the venue, just to check it out. And there, right next to the "General Admission line will form here" sign, she was. Her head was down and she was digging through her purse, an unlit cigarette hanging from her lips. Alone.

Philadelphia was two months earlier, but I was still thinking about her. Since then, I had gone to shows in Cincinnati, Greensboro, and Atlanta. And even though I knew there wasn't a chance in hell that she would be at any of those shows, I looked for her. I had no idea what I would say if I found her, but I wanted to see her again. And maybe, I hoped, she would have ditched *Born to Run* guy and have started liking younger guys by the time I did.

When I finally did see her, I wanted to go over to her like James Bond and light her cigarette before she even realized I was there. It would have been the perfect way to begin a conversation. But she looked up, startled, as I approached. Then a look of relief spread across her face as she saw the lighter in my hand. She cupped a purple-gloved hand around the flame as I held it, then took a quick drag and surprised me by moving in to kiss me on my cheek. "You're an angel," she sighed breathily near my ear, then pulled away and took another drag. As she exhaled she said, "I swear I was about to start rubbing two sticks together to get a light!" Then she smiled and tossed her hair, which had fallen forward in her search through her purse, back over her shoulder. It was brown again, like the first time I saw her in DC, with thin blonde streaks laced through it. It made me think of the line in Bob Dylan's "Tangled Up in Blue," when he's wondering if the girl's hair is still red. She started to turn around and I panicked, realizing that I hadn't even said a word. I had to talk to her this time.

"You were at the Philly show, weren't you?" I asked desperately, hoping that she would remember me.

She turned back and studied my face, which was, I think, the first time she had actually really looked at me as more than a provider of trivia answers and nicotine. "Ye-eah," she said slowly. "Have we met?"

"Sort of." *Please don't think I'm stalking you.* "I said you were right about Patti and Nils both joining the band after *Born in the USA* came out." She looked like she remembered the situation but not me. "I gave you a cigarette." *Idiot*, I thought. She was going to walk away. I knew she was. But then she did something incredible. She laughed. The same clear light laugh that I had heard in the Philadelphia parking lot.

"So when I die of lung cancer, I can blame you for encouraging my smoking habit?"

"Sure," I said with a grin. "I'll take that blame." I introduced myself, extending my hand. She considered it for a second before deciding to shake it, as if it was a completely foreign gesture that she had never seen before. Then she pulled her hand back and took the cigarette out of her mouth. A faint, pink ring of lip gloss circled it as it came away.

"Laura," she said with that irresistible smile that I had seen when I answered her question correctly in Philadelphia. She glanced over at Joe and he introduced himself too.

"So," I began, for lack of a more interesting conversation starter, "where are you from?" It could have been anywhere, considering the five-hundred-plus mile range of places where I had now seen her. But she was from DC. Just over the line separating Maryland and the

District and, I calculated, only about fifteen minutes away from my post-Katie apartment. She had driven down for the show, like Joe and I had, and she was there alone. But, as she told me with another flash of that smile, she was never *really* alone when she was in a crowd of other dedicated Bruce fans.

"Well, you're my cigarette savior already, of course," she said, tilting her head and looking up at me mischievously. "But you'll be my hero for the day if you've got beer." And her hero I was, because Joe and I had a cooler in the car, which felt incredibly lucky as she probably would have wandered off in search of better-equipped admirers if we hadn't had anything to drink. We stood in the cold parking lot, playing a mix of concert tracks out of the open windows of my car, drinking beer, shivering, and talking about the shows we had seen.

I don't think I have ever been as grateful to Bruce as I was in that moment. I wouldn't have known how to begin talking to this girl under any other circumstances. Hell, like I said before, I'm not sure I would have had the guts to talk to her if I had just seen her walking down the street, or in a bar, or anywhere other than at a Bruce show. But there's an immediate bond between all of the "tramps," as fans who travel all over the country for shows are known. Some guy even wrote a book on the subject, called *Tramps Like Us*, with a full chapter devoted to the pattern of a conversation between any two tramps meeting. I saw it on a shelf one day at Barnes and Noble and before I knew it, I had spent an hour in one of the plush chairs with it. What amazed me was that all of the conversations that I'd had in ticket lines, in parking lot tailgates, in stadium seats, even in line at Best Buy to get *The Rising* the day it came out, all followed the pattern laid out in the book.

I found all of this out later. When I tried to talk to Laura, however, I thought I was being ridiculously original. Which, I would discover later, was all a part of Laura's charm. She could be manipulative and malicious. But when she felt like it, she could put anyone at ease, and make him feel like he was the absolute most important and witty person on the planet while he was talking to her.

In the first hour of our acquaintance, I learned that this was Laura's eighth show on the tour, but that DC had been her first Springsteen concert ever. The show in Buffalo the night after the Philly show was the best setlist she had seen yet because it had "Tougher than the Rest," which she said would be her wedding song if she ever got married, leading right into "Lost in the Flood." *Born to Run* was her favorite album, followed closely by *Darkness on the Edge of Town,* and *The Wild, the Innocent and the E Street Shuffle.* According to her, "Sandy" was the single most beautiful song ever written in the history of the world, although life as we know it would not exist without the songs on *Born to Run.*

I also learned that her eyes were a color between brown and green and that every time I decided they were brown, I would realize that they were green, and every time I decided that they were green, I would realize that I was wrong again and that they were brown. She always had a cigarette in her hand, but seldom actually smoked it. She had no problem drinking beer from a can, which so many girls do, and she kept up with me fairly well without ever showing the effects of the alcohol. The ring of lip gloss on her cigarette was duplicated on each beer can that she drank from, yet her lips never seemed to lose that luminous shine. And she had an opinion on absolutely everything. Joe was mildly impressed. I was smitten.

Our persistence in line paid off because of the extremely cold weather and the three of us wound up about five feet from Bruce's mic, which is the only way to experience the show. After that, real seats, no matter how expensive or good they are, can never compare.

A little more than halfway through the show, we heard the opening notes of "Backstreets," an underplayed but phenomenal track off *Born to Run.* His first time playing it on the east coast during that tour, and therefore our first time hearing it. At the opening line, Laura threw her arms around my neck and breathed into my ear that I must be good luck and that this would be our song.

We had been officially acquainted for six-and-a-half hours at this point, so we weren't *just* meeting, but as you see, there is some truth in her saying that we met as Bruce sang "Backstreets." Laura never lies. She just tells her own version of the truth. It's maddening, it's unfair, and it's impossible to decipher. It's Laura.

2

After the show, we went around the corner to a bar. Our throats were sore and our voices hoarse from cheering. It gave Laura's voice a sexy, husky breathiness, like when you call someone and can tell they've just woken up. But there was no sign of sleepiness about her as we rehashed our favorite moments of the show. I had never met a girl who understood music the way she did. She knew every beat of every song. She knew when they had changed arrangements for this tour. She picked up on it when Clarence, Bruce's saxophone player, who was already in his sixties, was a little slow to jump in on "Darlington County." She said the new arrangement of "Dancing in the Dark" changed the whole meaning of the song. That it showed how far Bruce had come in his life since he wrote it. And she was absolutely right. About all of it.

Laura finished her second beer, pulled out a new cigarette and waited for me to light it for her, which I did. "Well," she said, "I'm heading to Columbia for tomorrow night's show." She hadn't mentioned the next show earlier in the day, and the way she announced it made it sound like this was just a spur of the moment decision. She stood up to leave and started to walk away without a goodbye. Then she stopped and turned back, and she looked surprised to find us still sitting. "Aren't you coming?"

I looked at Joe and raised my eyebrows. I was game. "I've gotta get back for work tomorrow," Joe said slowly. He had been up for road-tripping to one show, but he wasn't the kind of fan who would spend the money for two in a row. And we'd driven down in my car.

"I'd love to," I said apologetically. "But we drove down together. And I don't have a ticket. But maybe I can call you—?"

"You didn't answer my question," she said, cutting off my feeble attempt to get her phone number. "I don't have a ticket either. We'll worry about that later." She brought her cigarette near her mouth, then paused and lowered it without inhaling. She looked right into my eyes and asked, "Are you coming with me?" with an emphasis on *you* and *me* subtle enough that I could have imagined it, but I hadn't. She knew I would say yes before I did. Laura turned to leave. I looked at Joe and he nodded slightly, mouthing the word "go." So I tossed him my car keys and I went.

I couldn't tell whether I should expect her to drive a hot sports car or a beat up pick-up truck. I felt like she could have gone either way. As my best friend, Melanie, would later tell me, if I knew anything about fashion, I would have known that it couldn't have been a pick-up truck. But I didn't recognize her leather jacket, purse, and boots as being designer stuff. All I knew was that she looked incredible, and it didn't occur to me to wonder how she had the money to wear such expensive clothes at her age.

When I saw her car, however, I wondered.

Instinctively, I thought back to the group of older men I had seen her with in Philadelphia and asked myself if they had something to do with the car. Because I really had trouble believing that a twenty-five year old had a job that paid well enough for her to have a BMW M3 convertible. Call it a hunch.

But I kept my mouth shut.

I threw my backpack in the backseat, which was littered with various brands of empty cigarette packages, half-empty water bottles, and a couple pairs of shoes. Laura dropped her cigarette on the pavement without stubbing it out before getting into the driver's seat. She buckled her seatbelt, put the key in the ignition, then turned to me with an expectant smile and asked if I knew how to get to Columbia.

I started to laugh. I couldn't help it. It was too insane. I was in a car with a woman I had just met a few hours earlier, about to drive a couple more hours for a concert in a city that we didn't know how to find. And what would we do if we even managed to make it there? We had no tickets. This was far from normal behavior for me. Driving 350 miles for a concert was a pretty rare occurrence, one that I wouldn't have done for anyone but Bruce. Not even for Bob Dylan. But here I was, in quite possibly the oddest situation that I had ever encountered. And she didn't know how to get to Columbia either.

Laura started to laugh too and it dawned on me that she might not be okay to drive, as it was pretty late, we had been drinking before the show, I hadn't seen her eat much, and she just had two beers in about an hour. But she reached across my lap, still laughing, and opened the glove compartment. It was pristine. There were three maps, a roll of quarters, a small flashlight, a toothbrush and travel tube of toothpaste, both still in boxes, and a car cell phone charger, wrapped neatly around itself. It didn't fit with what I had seen of her so far, and it definitely didn't match the rest of the car. This was a responsible person's glove compartment. One a father would pack for his child's first road trip.

She reached in and took the bottom map. They were even arranged in North to South order. She saw me looking and shut the glove compartment forcefully. I looked up at her, surprised, and caught the slightest hint of a scowl on her face. But she quickly erased that and I was distracted by the way she seemingly accidentally brushed her hand against my leg as she opened the map. Pulling off her gloves, she turned on the car and music flooded the enclosed space. Without looking, Laura reached automatically to turn it down to a level that would allow conversation. She unfolded the map, studied it for a minute, then handed it to me.

"You're going to have to be my navigator," she said. "Since it's dark out and all." I looked at my watch. It was almost 1am.

"No problem," I responded, and I watched as she traced our route with a perfectly manicured, blood-red nail. It was pretty straightforward.

Soon we were on the road, this strange girl and me. "Take the wheel for a sec," she said once we were on the highway and I complied. She unhooked her seatbelt and leaned way into the backseat, giving me a flash of her flat stomach. When she re-emerged, she was holding a plastic bag with half a dozen apples in it. She pulled one out for herself and offered the bag to me. I took one, inwardly chuckling over the idea of this girl driving me down an unknown road and offering me the biblical fruit of knowledge. I went to Sunday school every week as a kid. It was funny.

I still consider that car ride to be one of the best times that I have ever had. It was exhilarating. We had the anticipation of another concert in just a few hours, open road before us, and no plans as to where we would sleep. But we were going anyway. I had never felt so free.

And Laura. Laura was like no one I had ever met. She changed somehow once we were alone in conversation. Or maybe it was the time, as the very early hours of the morning have an intoxicating effect that lower inhibitions nearly as well as alcohol does. My college roommate used to have a theory that the best way to hook up with a girl without getting her drunk was to be alone in a room with her after 2am. "Foolproof," he always said. I wasn't that sure. Laura didn't lose her inhibitions exactly, but she was softer. And just talking to her alone for even two minutes made it suddenly very clear that she was incredibly intelligent and well-educated. She could name all of the members of the Rolling Stones (not just Mick Jagger and Keith Richards) as well as all the members of the Grateful Dead. But she didn't just know music, she knew literature and art and astronomy, and though she didn't have an opportunity to prove it that night, she claimed she could change a tire too.

She didn't smoke a single cigarette on the drive, not even when we stopped for gas. Instead, she pulled another plastic bag from under my seat and would dig out a lollipop every half hour or so, although she kept the empty stems in her mouth for a while after each candy was finished. It answered the question of why she always had a cigarette but seldom smoked it and why there were the discarded boxes of about ten different brands of cigarettes in the backseat, whereas serious smokers selected a brand and stuck to those. It wasn't the nicotine she craved, but something to hold and gesture with.

I asked her what she did. "Besides follow Bruce?" she asked with a slow smile.

"Besides that," I said, somehow not sure that what she was about to say would be the truth.

She hesitated briefly, as if deciding what to tell me, then shrugged the slightest bit, keeping her eyes on the road. "A little of this, a little of that."

"Ah," I said, nodding knowledgeably. "You're a drug dealer."

She laughed heartily. "No. Guess again, Sherlock." I looked her up and down and she smiled over at me.

"Movie star?"

Laura scrunched up her face. "God, no. I'm no actress."

"I thought every little girl wanted to be a movie star when she grew up."

She thought for a second. "Some of us wanted to be princesses and ballerinas," she said. There was a pause. She still hadn't answered my question.

"Then are you a princess or a ballerina?"

"Neither," she said, shaking her head in mock sadness.

"Are you a spy?" I asked after another pause. She laughed again.

"Me?"

"It would explain the secrecy. And the hot car."

"I'm not a spy." She hesitated, then looked over at me. I met her eye. She quickly looked back at the road. "I guess I'm sort of a freelance photographer."

"You guess?" When she said it, I could tell she wasn't lying, but she sounded oddly unsure about her own job. And would photography pay well enough for that car?

"Well, I—it's more of a hobby that I get paid for sometimes."

"Oh," I said, not quite sure how to process this. "Do you have a real job?"

She glanced over at me sharply. "That is my real job."

I dropped it. "What kind of photography do you do?"

She shrugged again. "Whatever catches my eye. I've got a couple of magazines and newspapers that call me for stuff sometimes. Most of it's just for me though."

"What magazines and newspapers? Would I have seen any of your work?"

She looked at me again, this time like she was checking to see if I was actually interested before she deciding to reply or change the subject. Apparently I passed the test because her tone softened some. "I just started doing a little concert photography. I got a couple of pictures published in *Rolling Stone*. Not Bruce though. Obviously. I've done some work for the *Post* recently."

"*The Washington Post*?"

"Yeah."

"Wow," I said, truly impressed. I didn't know what photos went for, but she was shooting for some serious publications. Maybe that *could* pay for the car.

"It's not much," she said, with a raw honesty that was new in her voice. She sounded vulnerable. Or maybe it was just the time of night. "It's not like rocket science or curing cancer or anything."

"Because being a ballerina princess would have been so meaningful."

She looked over at me and I smiled, which seemed to be the right response because she smiled sheepishly back. "What do you do?"

"Have you seen *Office Space*?" She nodded. "That's about it."

"Well, what do you want to be when you grow up?" she asked.

I laughed. "You mean this isn't it?"

"No," she said, shaking her head. "Like when you grow up, grow up."

It was my turn to shrug. "Can I say rock star?"

"If that's what you want to be. Do you play an instrument?"

"Nope."

"Sing?"

"Not well."

"You're probably out of luck then, honey."

I shrugged again. I knew I wasn't joining a band any time soon. "What about you? What do you want to be when you grow up?"

Laura hesitated. I got the feeling that she knew the answer but didn't quite want to say it. "I—I never quite figured that one out." She laughed softly. "That's probably why I don't have a real job." And even though I had given the least realistic answer possible and even though I liked my job, I knew what she meant. Was what I did for a living actually what I wanted to *be* when I grew up? I didn't think so. But I didn't really know what I did want either. I'm still not sure that I know the answer to that one now.

We found Columbia and followed the signs to the USC arena. Judging by the volume of North Carolina, Virginia, Maryland, Pennsylvania, and New Jersey license plates that we spotted on cars we had seen on our drive down, several other people were doing the same thing that we were and had come down from the Charlotte show as well. There was something magical about so many people doing the exact same thing we had just done. They felt the power of the show and *needed* to feel it again. Just like I did. Just like Laura did. We were part of something bigger than any normal concert crowd. We felt like we were the tramps

Bruce sang about in "Born to Run." Everybody was out on the run that night. And so in our first night spent together, Laura and I were far from alone.

Some fans who were more rabid than us had apparently raced straight there after the last show without stopping for the beers that we did, so our position in the pit line wasn't nearly as good as it was the previous afternoon, but the line hadn't reached 300 yet, so we were sure we would be in the pit. We were told to report back at 6am for the next roll call. With only a couple of hours until then, we decided to nap in the car instead of trying to find a motel so that we could begin our ticket search among the people who showed up for the roll call.

I won't lie; it was not the best night's sleep that I've ever had. Laura and I climbed into the tiny backseat, which was better suited to groceries than people, and she leaned her head into the crook of my arm while we shared a crocheted afghan that had been in her trunk. It was cold, but sweet. Laura's hair, which common sense told me would smell like cigarette smoke, smelled clean and slightly like peppermint. She actually helped keep the cold at bay. Most thin people can't provide much warmth, but she did. And the way she just leaned into me without any pretension or timidity; it was like we had known each other all our lives.

I half woke up when Laura moved away from me. It was still dark out, but the sky was just beginning to lighten. I closed my eyes again, unwilling to wake up after so little sleep. I heard her moving around in the car and forced my eyes open a tiny bit to see what she was doing. I woke up all the way, however, when she took her shirt off. She was facing mostly away from me, but I could see the curve of her right breast in its lacy black bra. My eye traced the path up over her shoulder and down her back, where her hair hung down past her bra strap. She folded the shirt that she had been wearing and placed it in a small duffle bag on the floor of the backseat, and pulled out a different shirt, still black, but with a glittery post 9/11 New York City skyline on it. She pulled it over her head and twisted her hair up into a ponytail. Next she pulled out a mirror compact, which she placed, unopened, on her knee, and some cold cream, which she rubbed under her eyes and then wiped away. She pulled out mascara and applied it without even opening her compact, which was still resting in her lap. When she finally opened it to check her reflection, she seemed to like what she saw because she winked at herself. Then, she angled the mirror at me and saw me looking at her in the reflection. She closed the compact and turned around. And she smiled.

"Come on," she said. "We've got tickets to find!"

"What time is it?" I asked, trying and failing to suppress a yawn as I climbed out of the car after her.

"Almost six. We'll go for the roll call, then find someone who's got extra tickets."

"Do you think anyone will?"

She shrugged. "*Someone* will."

We went back to where we had put our names on the pit list the night before and waited for them to call our numbers. By the end of the 6am roll call, we had moved up several slots as a handful of people, probably exhausted from the drive from Charlotte, had failed to show up. The next roll call was at 10am and we were warned to be on time or suffer the same fate as the people whose places we had taken in line.

As there were no scalpers to be seen yet and the ticket office would not open for another hour, I turned to Laura to ask what was next, but she held her finger against my lips to silence me. Most of the crowd was dispersing in the same general direction and Laura inclined her head to say we should follow them.

When we were walking a little ways away from everyone else, I leaned in and asked her quietly what the plan was.

"We don't want the people in line to know we don't have tickets," she warned. "We could lose our place then."

"Then how do we get tickets? The only people here this early are the people who were in line."

"I've got this," she said. "Trust me." And God help me, I did.

She took my hand and pulled me along to catch up with a group of three men who were walking a bit ahead of us. She dropped my hand as we approached. "Hey guys," she said, as if she had known them her entire life.

They stopped walking and turned to look at her. They were probably in their early forties, two with graying hair, one with a baseball cap covering his. "Hi there," one of them said, and she smiled broadly at them, angling her head down slightly to give them impression that she was looking up at them, even though none of them was taller than her.

"So I need some help," she said, then paused, baiting them to ask with what.

"What can we do for you?" one of them asked.

"Well, two of my girlfriends called me last night and they want to come to the show tonight. But they don't have tickets. Do you know anyone who has any extras?"

"I've got a couple of seats," the man in the baseball cap said. "They're in the nosebleeds, but they're in the house at least."

"Thanks," Laura said genuinely. "But I'm going to try to get them GAs if possible. I know they can't be in the pit with us because they weren't here to get on the list as early as we were, but they've never been that close before."

"I think I know someone with a couple," the first man said, pulling out his cell phone. "Hang on."

Laura smiled seductively. "I *knew* I asked the right guys," she said.

The man held up a finger indicating that she should wait when his friend answered the phone. "Mike," he said. "You still have those extra tickets?" He listened, then gave Laura the thumbs up. "I've got someone here who wants them. We're still in the parking lot right now. Where are you? Uh huh. Row G. Your car? Okay if I send them over now? Great. Thanks buddy." He closed his phone. "He's got a white Acura over in Row G. Other side of the lot. Can't promise he'll sell them to you at a good price though. He's kind of a douche about scalping sometimes."

"You're the best!" Laura said. "Thank you so much!"

"No problem," he said. "Glad to help."

"What's your number in line?" Laura asked him. He was about 20 people ahead of us and she told him our numbers. "Thanks again," she said. "Maybe we'll see you in there tonight." And with a wink, she turned back to me and started walking toward the far side of the parking lot. I followed.

"Good work!" I said once we were a safe distance away.

"That was nothing," she said.

"How much are you willing to pay for the tickets?" I asked her. I'd gone as high as two-and-a-half times face value before. And while I wasn't happy about it, I'd be willing to do that for this show with Laura.

"Face," she said. "Not a penny more."

"So if this guy's asking more, we find someone else?"

"Nope," Laura said. "These are our tickets."

"But how—?"

"You'll see," she said. "Just let me do the talking."

We spotted the car we were looking for in Row G, which was nearly deserted, and as we approached a man stepped out of the driver's side. "Hi," Laura said. "Are you Mike?"

"I am," he said, sipping coffee from a paper cup. "And I'm guessing you need some tickets."

"That I do. I'm Laura."

"Nice to meet you."

"You too," Laura said, smiling. *No chance*, I thought. *This guy's not losing money he could make off someone else just because she's hot.* "How much are you charging for those tickets?"

"I was going to try to sell them for three-hundred each. But you seem nice. Two-fifty."

Laura laughed. "Honey, I can't afford that."

"Then I'm sure you can buy some cheaper seats from someone else."

Her face absolutely fell. The smile was completely gone and she looked crestfallen. Which was, if anything, even more heartbreakingly beautiful on her. "I guess you can't help me," she said sadly and started to turn away. She looked back at him over her shoulder and smiled despondently. "Thanks anyway."

"Hey," he said grabbing her arm. "Two-hundred each?"

"I can't," she said sadly. "I wish I could." She turned back to me. "I guess we won't be in the pit tonight after all."

"One-fifty," he said. "That's as low as I'm going."

"I can pay face value," she said, biting her lower lip slightly, then releasing it. God she was sexy.

Mike sighed. "You're killing me here."

Laura's voice rose hopefully. "Does that mean you'll do it?"

"Got any reason why I should?"

Laura pursed her lips slightly but smiled with her eyes. "You mean other than the fact that I'll absolutely love you for the rest of my life?"

"Yeah," he said dourly, but he was fighting off a hint of a smile. "Other than that."

"No reason at all." She wasn't *quite* flirting. It was something else. I don't know how to explain it. It's something that only girls can do. And I'd never seen a girl who could wrap any guy around her finger as quickly as Laura could. If I had been Mike, I would have given her the tickets for free already. Hell, I'd have given her the tickets, and then paid for her drinks all night! I was impressed that he had managed to hold out as long as he did.

He contemplated her for a moment and she smiled sweetly at him. "Shit," he said finally, under his breath. "Yeah, all right. I'll do it."

"You're an angel!" Laura exclaimed and she hugged him, planting a loud kiss on his cheek. "Honestly, darling, you're my hero!" I tried not to let that bother me. She had called me her hero yesterday. But that was yesterday.

"Yeah, well," he stammered gruffly as he pulled the tickets out of his back pocket. Laura reached into her purse and handed him the exact right amount, including the Ticketmaster fees. She must have set the money aside earlier to have it all prepared. Mike grumbled something about Laura robbing him blind.

"You did a good deed, sweetie," she said handing me both tickets and turning to leave.

"I think you and your boyfriend there owe me a drink after the show," he said.

Laura turned back around. "Who said he was my boyfriend?" she asked playfully, then took my hand again and started to walk away. "Thanks again, love!"

Once we had walked away, Laura smiled in smug satisfaction. "What an asshole," she said.

"What do you mean? He sold us the tickets at face value."

"He wanted to sell them for three hundred bucks! He's not a real fan," she scoffed. "*Real* fans don't try to cheat other fans."

I shrugged. "I guess not. But I'm impressed. How did you know that would work?"

She shrugged. "I didn't *know* it would. It just always does."

And she was right, as over the next ten months, I would see her perform this trick at least a dozen times, with the only change being the substitution of Jesse or Steve or Greg for Mike. I could tell when she was moving in for the kill when she started using multiple terms of endearment. Honey, darling, sweetie, angel, love. No one lasted through all of them.

She squeezed my hand. "Come on," she said. "I just saved you two hundred dollars on that ticket. I'll let you buy me breakfast to thank me." And I laughed. It was easy to see why the man she had been with in Philadelphia had said "as usual" when she won. Who could say no to her?

Later, I would learn she had been wrong. We didn't need tickets yet to be in the pit line. Then again, she was almost never wrong. Maybe she knew that and told me not to tell anyone because she thought it was more exciting to act like it was a secret. But I knew that even if I asked her about it, she would stand by her assertion that we couldn't let people know that we didn't have tickets. It was one of those quintessentially Laura things that made being with her both exhilarating and infuriating. If she decided something was true, even just for her own amusement, then it was. And whether she was just wrong or trying to make our overall experience more fun, it didn't really matter in the end. Being around her was exciting. And when I thought about it later, I realized that I didn't necessarily want to know the truth.

3

After the show, which was fantastic, I quickly realized there was no way that we could drive home that night. We had gotten maybe four hours of sleep the night before and while the initial energy burst of the show would keep us going for an hour or two, it was not going to get us back to DC.

"I think we should get a motel room for the night," I said, as we headed back to the car.

Laura suppressed a yawn. "Not up for a nine-hour drive right now?" she asked with a smile.

"Oh, *I* am, but you looked a little tired."

She nodded with an exaggerated motion that reminded me of a little kid. "You're right, I am. Let's get a little out of town to find a place. It'll be cheaper and easier to find a room."

We found a Motel 6 off the highway, pooled some money, and checked in. I watched over Laura's shoulder as she signed the register "Mr. and Mrs. James Anderson." The night clerk handed us a key without looking at the name she had given and directed us toward our room.

"Why'd you give a fake name?" I asked as soon as we were out of the office. I had only ever seen that in movies. She giggled. It wasn't her normal laugh, which I already knew so well. This was childlike, and I thought of the way she had nodded when she admitted she was tired. Was she younger than I had thought she was?

"Always wanted to," she said with a devious smile. "I mean, how often do you get a chance to give a fake name when you check into a motel room with someone? It's fun." She was right. It felt illicit, like we were having an affair or were on the run from the law.

The room only had one bed. I hadn't thought to ask for two. Didn't all rooms come with two unless you asked for one? It would have looked strange if I had asked anyway, considering that Laura had said we were married. Of course, I had hoped we would share a bed that night, but I definitely did not want to seem like I was planning on it.

"Do you want me to ask for a different room?" I asked, figuring I had a better shot with her if I was a gentleman about it.

"Why?"

"Well. Um. Because...there's only—the one bed."

"It's okay," she said. "We can share. I don't bite, and I don't think I snore. And all we're doing is crashing for a few hours before we drive home." That last part answered my unspoken question.

She tossed her bag on a chair and took off her boots. She then turned away from me, pulled her shirt off over her head and swapped it for an old concert tee. Next she removed her jeans to reveal a black lace thong that matched the bra I had now seen twice. I looked away quickly when she turned around. I guess she saw me look away and when I looked back there was a hint of confusion in her eyes. "You don't mind, do you? Jeans aren't exactly comfortable to sleep in." I shook my head, trying not to stare at her. She unhooked her bra and pulled it off *Flashdance*-style through her sleeve as she asked the question. She grabbed her toothbrush and headed into the bathroom. I used the time to take off my jeans as well and contemplate the situation.

What on earth was she playing at? Who did this kind of thing? Was she nuts? Or was I crazy for being here with her?

She came out and climbed into bed. I shut off the light and joined her. She was on her side with her back to me. There was no move that I could make and to be honest, at that point, I wasn't sure I wanted to. Yes, she was one of the most beautiful women I had ever seen in real life. Yes, she was intriguing. Yes, I wanted her. But I didn't know enough about her yet. If she really was crazy, getting involved would be more work than it was worth. But there was something so sweet about her. She was trusting. Or else she thought she was tough enough to take care of herself. It wasn't very smart though; getting into a bed, with no pants on, with a guy she had met twenty-four hours earlier and expecting nothing to happen. I mean, I guess she figured I was safe because nothing happened when we slept in the car, but this was—different. But she was clearly not a stupid girl. So what was her story? What was it that made her do all this? And why chase Springsteen? I knew why I did it, and I knew that she loved the music and the lyrics and the magic of his live shows, but why go to all this trouble? What was missing from her life that she was filling with the thrill of the tour? What was she looking for that she found on the road?

I didn't know the answers to any of those questions. All I knew was that I wanted to stick around long enough to find some of them out. And the way to do that was to be a little patient. And so I stopped worrying and went to sleep.

The first thing that I noticed when I woke up was that I was alone in the bed. I didn't sleep very well, because I hadn't spent a whole night with anyone since leaving Katie, and I hadn't shared a bed in a non-sexual way in years. So I had that uneasy, platonic bed-sharing sleep, where you have to make sure you don't roll over and try to cuddle with your bedmate in your sleep, or worse, fart. Meaning that as soon as I started to wake up, I became instantly aware that I was alone, and I bolted awake, with a sudden certainty that she was gone and I was stranded in South Carolina.

But then she laughed.

She was sitting on the windowsill, one bare foot on the sill and the other dangling off the side. Her toenails were painted a bright red to match her fingernails. Her hair was wet from the shower but pulled back into a ponytail again. There were two empty Diet Coke cans on the motel desk, with a third can in her hand. Her tired, childish giggle from the night before was gone and this was the hearty laugh that I could have recognized anywhere by now. "Worried I'd ditched you?"

"No," I lied, leaning back into the pillows and yawning. "Just worried you'd gotten breakfast without me."

"Liar. You thought I'd taken your wallet and your pants and stranded you here like in a bad movie."

I smiled. She was adorable. "Nah, you're all talk."

Her smile faded and she raised her eyebrows in bemusement. Had I said something wrong? She turned to the window and took a sip of her Diet Coke. When she turned back to me, whatever it was that she hadn't liked was gone, and she sparkled again. She reached over languidly and took a small throw pillow off the armchair, then with a suddenness that caught me off guard; she tossed it at my head too fast for me to catch it. "Get dressed," she said, laughing again. "Let's get out of here."

The end of a road trip is almost always an unpleasant affair. When you begin the trip, you're filled with this sense of adventure and the anticipation of what's going to happen. You know that you're about to be at an incredible concert, or the beach, or Mardi Gras, and at that point, the trip can be whatever you want it to be. The beginning of a trip is an endless array of possibilities. But on the way home, one of two things happens: either you're exhausted and just want to get home as quickly as possible, making the drive seem interminable; or there's this sadness that the fun is over and all that you have to look forward to is your real life again. And a long drive home with just that knowledge can be rough. Coming home from the Philadelphia concert had felt like that, as had the Cincinnati show, and each time that I was on the road home from a show, I wound up promising myself that I would go to another one soon to take the edge off of that post-concert depression.

There are exceptions, of course. There was the trip home from Florida freshman year of college when Mel, Eric, Angela, and I played an impromptu 3am game of "strip pididdle." I don't even remember the specific rules that we came up with, but it involved hitting the ceiling of the car and yelling "pididdle" whenever we saw a car with a burned out headlight. Mel was winning and still had her bra and panties on because she was driving and therefore was less distracted by the nudity around her and spotted most of the cars first. She did not, however, spot the cop who pulled us over. Or maybe she did and thought it would be funny, because she hadn't wanted to play in the first place and her passengers were all completely naked by then. That ride home was definitely more exciting than the trip there.

In this case, however, the way home *was* the beginning of the road trip. Yes, these two concerts were over. But there would be more. I had no doubt of that. There was an electricity between us, a promise so crisp I could feel it. And what's more, I had found a girl to share this passion that had taken control of my life. My girlfriends had always nodded when I said Bruce was the best musician in the world, then gone on to say that they were partial to Dave Matthews or Tori Amos or, in one brief and very unfulfilling case that I shudder to even remember, N*Sync. The horror.

Laura seemed, that day, to be the kind of girl who I had only ever dreamed that I could meet.

She had XM radio in her car, which we listened to the whole way home. There were controls on the side of the steering wheel, and she changed the station decisively as soon as a song displeased her, which happened frequently.

"Not a big Peter Gabriel fan?" I asked, as she switched away from the second song of his that we had encountered.

"No," she said with a distasteful scowl. "I absolutely cannot stand him."

"Not even 'In Your Eyes'?" Laura shook her head. "What do you listen to other than Bruce?"

There was no hesitation here. "Pretty much just classic rock. Some alternative. I hate all that hip hop crap. Dylan, of course. Anyone who claims to love music and doesn't listen to Dylan is an idiot. The Stones, same thing, if you don't listen, you're not really a music person. Clapton, but his unplugged stuff doesn't really do it for me. Petty. Pink Floyd. Dire Straits. Jackson Browne. Counting Crows, I love them. The Wallflowers. And The Who, of course. Stuff along those lines." She looked over at me and I was smiling. She had just named the majority of my music collection. She smiled back. "Got anything to add to the list?"

"Pearl Jam," I said definitively. Laura nodded. "REM," another nod. "And the Eagles." She raised an eyebrow. "Well you have to give me 'Hotel California' and 'Take it Easy.'"

"Well, yeah," she said. "But Jackson Browne wrote 'Take it Easy' and gave it to the Eagles."

"He did?"

"Yeah, I heard an interview with him on one of the XM stations the other day. He was saying that there's actually a corner in Winslow, Arizona where people stop and stretch their legs because there's nothing else in the town. That's why he wrote that part of the song." I decided right then to sign up for XM radio and I had it installed in my car the next week.

"You can't forget the Beatles," I said. "If we're talking about classic rock."

"The Beatles are good, but they're more pop. Not rock. The Stones were the better *rock* band of the sixties."

"But the Beatles were more iconic."

"Yeah, but the Stones were edgier. Still are."

"They have to be edgier, half the Beatles are dead. And Ringo's part of the remaining half."

Laura laughed. "But the Beatles are *such* a cliché."

"They weren't when they came out."

"I know that. And it's not their fault that they're a cliché now. But they are. Like I'll give them that they were original when they first came on the scene, and I respect that a huge amount of what we listen to now is built on their foundation, but everyone and their mother copied them until they can't sound remotely original anymore."

There was a slight pause.

"Who's your most humiliating musical obsession?" she asked.

"What do you mean?"

"I mean, who do you secretly, totally, and completely love that you're ashamed to talk about?"

Here I hesitated. I had an immediate answer. But it was pretty embarrassing. "Who's yours?"

She laughed. "Wow, it must be bad. But I asked you first."

Okay, moment of truth. "Journey," I said. Then held my breath.

For a few seconds, nothing. I started to breathe again. Then she exploded into laughter. "Journey?" she asked incredulously. "*Journey?*"

"What?" I asked defensively.

"Like, 'Don't Stop Believing,' Journey?"

"Yeah."

"Oh man," she said, still laughing. "I didn't think it'd be *that* bad. I mean, Journey? Are you really being serious?"

"Well, who's yours?"

"Mine?"

"Yeah, who do you secretly listen to? If you're going to bust my balls about Journey, I need some ammunition to do the same to you."

She smiled sweetly at me. "Well I don't exactly have balls to bust," she said. "But I've got two people. Although neither is even *close* to as bad as *Journey*."

"Come on, who are they?"

"Bon Jovi," she said. "Which really isn't that bad at all. And Billy Idol."

"Billy Idol?" I asked. "And that's supposed to be better than Journey?"

"Yes," she said. "Billy Idol is hot."

"Bleached blonde hair and weird punk piercings?"

She shrugged and grinned sheepishly. "Whatever. He's still hot."

"And Bon Jovi?"

"Well you know how I love those Jersey rockers." I laughed. She was right. Neither was as bad as Journey, but knowing who we secretly listened to was a great icebreaker.

I remember watching her as she drove. I had noticed when I first really talked to her that she was fidgety, but in the car it seemed to increase. Maybe it was just magnified by being in such close proximity for such a long drive, but she seemed incapable of sitting still. She drummed her fingers softly on the steering wheel, and shifted in her seat, sometimes bringing her left foot onto her seat and reaching her arm around her knee to steer. I thought, and later found out that I was right, that she would probably be one of those people who constantly jiggled one of her legs when she was sitting down. Those people usually annoyed me. A lot. But in Laura, it was cute and quirky.

I didn't know what she had studied in college or where she grew up or what her parents did. She managed to keep the conversation away from those topics. And when I flat out asked what her parents did, she didn't answer for a long time. "They're gone," she said eventually. That was a conversation killer. I said I was sorry and asked how they had died, but she didn't want to talk about it and changed the subject. I didn't know quite how to handle that topic anyway, so I was just as happy to move on. We didn't talk about much of anything specific except for music, so most of what I knew about her was pieced together from how she acted and her opinions on other things.

She didn't have any identifiable accent. If anything, it was a little New York, I thought, but I couldn't quite put my finger on it. She discussed things in such an intellectual way that I thought she could have been an English major in college. Or something obscure like Art History. She was smart enough to have had a real major, but I had a feeling she hadn't studied anything useful. She mentioned college once, so I knew that she had actually gone, but she didn't seem to want to talk about anything related to where she had come from at any stage of her life.

It was weird. We were so at ease together that it felt like we had known each other our whole lives. We had those conversations about nothing and everything that you can only have with people you already know almost everything about. I've never had that with anyone so immediately. But maybe Laura fostered that kind of conversation to avoid talking about anything real.

For lack of a better word, she was fun. And I was fun with her. But it didn't feel real. I had seen this girl, rearranged my whole life based on seeing her cry at a concert, and now I was in her car, laughing with her. And by the time she dropped me off at my apartment, we had plans to drive to two more shows the following weekend.

For the first time since I saw her crying in DC, I felt like my life was heading where I really wanted it to go. Even if I had no clue where that was.

4

"Wait, explain this to me again."

I sighed. My brother had said the same thing when I told him about meeting Laura. But Melanie was my best girl friend, and girls are always better when you want to talk about other girls, which meant that I had to tell her about Laura.

Mel and I had been friends since freshman orientation for college. We experimented briefly with dating that first year, before both realizing that we were much better as friends. For the past six years, she had been involved off and on with a mutual friend of ours, and although she didn't know it yet, he was planning to propose sometime around Christmas. Mel had, of course, already heard about the amazing girl I had seen at the two concerts, but she was too practical to put much weight in my first two encounters with Laura. "Did you talk to her?" she had asked. I said not really, and Mel changed the subject. So after my adventure in the Carolinas, I called Mel and met her for lunch the next day.

"Her name is Laura, and I met her at the Charlotte show, then drove down to South Carolina with her for the Monday show, and drove back home with her."

"And she's the same girl that you met at the other shows?"

"Well, we didn't really *meet* at the other shows, but yeah, she's the one I told you about before."

"And you spent two nights with this girl and all you really know about her is that she loves Bruce, may or may not be insane, and kind of works as a freelance photographer?"

"No. I mean, yes. But no. I know more than that. I liked her."

"Wait, I'm confused. Did you sleep with her?"

I sighed again. Maybe telling Melanie about Laura was a bad idea. But I always told her about girls I met. She was my only window into decoding crazy girl behavior. And I knew that she had been worried about me since I left Katie. "No, not like that. We basically napped in her car that first night, then we got a motel room the second night, but just slept, no funny business." Melanie looked skeptical.

"What's she look like?" she asked.

"Gorgeous."

"And you didn't sleep with her?"

"Mel! I didn't sleep with her."

"Did you want to?"

"Well, yeah."

"Then what happened?"

I tried to explain the situation to her. It wasn't like that. It was about the music.

"I don't know," Melanie said. "I feel like it's weird that she drove to an unfamiliar city with a random guy—"

"I'm not random!" I protested.

"—just to go to a concert, then spent two nights with him, and drove back with him from South Carolina. I mean, she doesn't know you're not random. For all she knew, you could be an axe murderer!"

"Maybe she's a good judge of character?"

"Then why'd she invite *you* to go with her?" she asked with an evil smile. I threw a French fry at her, which Mel ducked as she started to laugh. "Seriously though, I feel like there's something off about this girl."

"You haven't even met her."

"And I don't need to! Normal girls are more careful than that! A normal girl doesn't go on a road trip and sleep in the same bed, even if it's fully clothed, with a guy she doesn't know at all!"

I grinned devilishly. "Well, under your criteria, she may still be normal then." Melanie arched her eyebrows and I started to laugh. "She wasn't *fully* clothed; she definitely wasn't wearing pants the night we were in the motel!" This time it was Melanie's turn to throw food at me, but she threw the roll that came with her salad, which she had no intention of eating anyway because apparently carbohydrates are the root of all evil in our society. This is why I need Mel. Without her, I would never have known that carbs are the devil. But I personally have no problem with them, so I caught the bread and took a bite.

Mel just laughed at me. "Well, what kind of underwear was she wearing? Please tell me it was at least granny panties."

"A gentleman doesn't tell." She raised her eyebrows again, not needing to say anything. "Black lace thong."

"What's today's date?" Mel asked abruptly, grabbing a spare napkin and digging through her purse.

"What?"

"Today's date."

"Ummm, the eleventh?" She uncapped a pen that she had pulled out of her purse and started to write on the napkin. "What are you writing?" She didn't respond. Finally she finished writing and handed it to me. Beneath the date, she had written, "Melanie says this girl is going to be trouble."

"Hang onto this," she said.

"Why?"

"Because she's going to be trouble, and I don't want to have to say 'I told you so.' This way you can remember that I told you and I have proof if you choose not to believe me. But this girl is going to be bad news."

"You don't know that."

"I do. Call it intuition. She's trouble." She paused. "When are you seeing her again?"

"We're driving to Ohio and then Indianapolis for the shows on the sixteenth and seventeenth." Melanie just shook her head.

"Do you have tickets for those shows?"

"No, but we didn't have tickets for the Columbia show when we decided to go either." Melanie just shook her head.

"Trouble."

5

Laura called me two days later, the day of the Albany show.

"I wish we were going tonight," she said immediately, without saying hello. "But even if we left now, we wouldn't make it on time."

"I know," I said. "One of my friends from college is up there and is going. He said he would call me from the show."

"Do you have a speakerphone?" she asked immediately and I replied in the affirmative.

"DSL?"

"Cable modem."

"Same thing. I'll be there at eight." And with that, she was gone. No "do you have plans?" or "can I come over?" For all she knew, I could have had a girlfriend who lived with me. Although I guess she figured that if I were really taken, I wouldn't have gone with her in the first place. Or slept in a bed with her. Even platonically. That's the kind of thing that girlfriends just don't seem to like you to do. But then again, Laura had no idea. I could be the kind of guy who cheated. I could be married for all she knew.

With anyone else, I think I would have been amazed at the rudeness of inviting herself over. But with Laura, it wasn't rude. She assumed that I would want to share the call from the concert with her, and as I would find out later, she had something to share with me as well. Maybe she even knew that I wanted her there. Maybe she wanted to be there and didn't care all that much if I wanted her there or not. Whatever the case though, I did want her there. I hurried to call Lee and told him to call my apartment line instead of my cell phone when he called me from the show in Albany so that I could put him on speakerphone easier.

At seven, I started checking my watch every two minutes. By my thirtieth watch check, there was still no sign of her. She had said eight, right? Suddenly, I wasn't quite sure why she was coming over. What were we going to do? Sit around and wait for Lee to call from Albany then try to hear what we could of the show? I was nervous. It was one thing to spend time with her when we were going to a concert, although truth be told, I was nervous about going to the next set of shows with her too. We hadn't planned to go together last time, it had just happened. This felt distinctly date-like. But with the unsettling lack of any type of date agenda, or even any confirmation that she was remotely interested in me. I hadn't been on a real first date since meeting Katie more than two years earlier, and this felt much stranger than a real first date. There was no dinner-and-a-movie situation, or even a casual meeting in a bar or coffee shop. She was coming to my apartment and we were going away together this weekend. But I didn't know what any of that meant.

It was too bizarre to know what to expect or how to handle it. I needed a beer. Did I have time for one before she showed up? Was it weird to be drinking one already when she arrived? She certainly had no problem drinking with me in North Carolina, and I certainly needed a drink. But I shouldn't have worried, because I had finished that first beer long before she showed up at 8:17. Exactly five minutes before Bruce took the stage in Albany.

"Hello, darling," she said as she kissed me on the cheek then breezed past me into the apartment, a six pack clinking merrily in her hand. My grandmother was the only person I had ever met who could call people "darling" without sounding stuck up and weird. That brought the grand total of people who could pull that off to three, Audrey Hepburn being the third, but I think she's dead.

And the way Laura said it didn't feel remotely like when my grandma said it. Which was a very good thing.

She stopped a few feet past where I was still standing in the doorway and spun around to face me. "Do you want to give me a quick tour or should we save it for after the show?"

"After the show?" I asked. *What show?*

She nodded and smiled. "We're going to watch the setlist. We just need your computer and a stereo."

She was so excited. I couldn't help but smile back. I wasn't completely sure how we were going to do this, but I would play along. She hadn't steered me wrong yet. "Well, here's the abbreviated tour," I said as I walked backwards past her, imitating a tour guide and gesturing that she should follow. "This is the lovely hallway, leading to the kitchen and the living room, where you'll find the stereo." She followed me into the living room and sat on the sofa.

"Nice," she said genuinely, settling the six pack onto the coffee table. I liked her approval.

"I'll get my laptop."

"And a bottle opener!" Laura called after me as I headed into my bedroom.

I set up the laptop and Laura directed me to go to Bruce's website, which had a message board with threads devoted to the setlists of the shows each night. We found the discussion thread titled "Albany setlist watch," and as Laura hit refresh, someone posted that Bruce and the band had just come onstage. "Perfect timing," she announced gleefully. She rummaged in her purse, pulled out a chrome CD wallet, jumped up, and headed to my stereo. She pulled out a disc and put it into the CD changer.

"It's from the Charlotte show," she said with a huge grin as she turned the volume up and the opening strains of "The Rising" filled the room.

"Our show?" I asked loudly over the music. She nodded. "How'd you get it so quick?"

"I know a guy," she said with a shrug, and I didn't ask who he was.

"Will you burn me a copy?"

"Already did," she said. "This one's yours. I've got Columbia for you too." She held out the CD wallet. I opened it and folded up inside was a list of what was on each disc. There were eight discs total and a space for the one that was currently in my CD player. Two more from the Charlotte show, three from the Columbia show, and three from the Philly show. All labeled with a red Sharpie in her distinctively sloppy handwriting. I pulled out the first disc of the Philly show and held it up questioningly. She gave me a slightly shy look.

"You were there," she said simply.

She had brought another, bigger CD wallet with her as well to cover any rarities that Bruce played as we kept up with the concert. Someone on the message board would post what song was being played, and Laura would find a version of it, almost always live, for us to listen to. She had a version of everything that he played except two songs. One of them I had an mp3 of. The other was a Chuck Berry cover, which neither of us had a version of, but because he closed the show with it, we were fairly satisfied with what we had. It didn't come close to being at the show itself, but because we wanted a substitute, it was a fun way to spend an evening. She said she had done this for all of the shows that she hadn't gone to since this tour started. But, she quickly told me, she never posted on the website. Like she wanted to make sure I knew that she wasn't the kind of person who would post on a fan forum. I didn't care either way, but I wondered if she was trying to impress me. She said she checked for updates almost every day, but from how quickly she changed the subject, I couldn't tell if she was lying or uncomfortable with the idea of posting.

She also had the episode of the Conan O'Brien show from Wednesday night when Bruce was on. I had meant to tape it, but I was so exhausted from the trip the previous weekend that I had fallen asleep before it came on and missed it. My friends all thought I was the biggest Bruce fan on the planet; I wondered what they would make of her.

"So," she began, leaning back after we had exhausted her six pack, quite a few of my beers, the concert, and the Conan tape. "Columbus and Indy." Pause. "The last two shows until the end of February."

"That's a depressing thought," I mused solemnly. "Makes sense now why there are so many suicides over the holidays."

Laura went into a fit of laughter. "Bruce-icides," she choked out eventually, which made me laugh.

"I wonder if he would add more shows if he knew how many lives he could save with them!"

Laura nodded. "We should sneak backstage and tell him."

"Yeah, I can picture it now, 'Bruce, if you play every day, you can end holiday-related suicide attempts.'"

"Hey, maybe he'd be into it."

"Maybe," I said. And then there was silence. We still didn't know each other well enough to have completely comfortable silences. It wasn't uncomfortable, but it wasn't quite cozy yet.

"I'm going to head out," she said finally, gathering up her CDs and separating them out from mine. "Oh," she stopped and looked at me. "One thing we have to clear up first before I can go to any more shows with you."

She's got a boyfriend, I thought. Or is a lesbian. Or something else that's going to completely ruin how great this night was.

"You're not one of those guys who wears a Bruce shirt to a Bruce concert, right?"

I would be shocked if my relief wasn't completely transparent to her. "No," I laughed. "I wear my concert shirts to the gym."

She drew the back of her hand across her forehead and sighed in exaggerated relief. "Thank God. I can't stand it when people do that. It's like in my top five pet peeves." I remembered seeing her in the Philadelphia parking lot with *Born to Run* guy and wondered if he was the reason this behavior annoyed her. But I didn't feel right asking about that.

"What are the other four?" I asked. "I mean, I ought to know, just to be on the safe side and make sure I don't accidentally do any of them."

She thought for a second. "People who make those little air quotes when they speak. And people who say random words in French to try to sound smarter. And people who say 'it's me' when they call someone. I mean, what the hell is that? If you know who the person is, they don't need to say 'it's me,' and if you don't know who it is then that doesn't tell you anything. Ridiculous." She paused. "How many was that?"

"Only three."

"Hmmmm. Oh! I've got another one: men who wear Speedos to the beach."

I shook my head. "Bastards."

Laura laughed again.   "Well, I'm glad we're on the same wavelength with that," she said. "Otherwise, this would never have worked." I wondered what "this" was, but knew I would sound like a girl if I asked. There was another silence.

"Should I bring anything for the road trip?" I asked finally.

"You've got a cooler, right?"

"Yup."

"Wanna bring beer to tailgate with?"

"Sure."

"Then we should be fine. I'll bring some bootlegs."

"How many have you got?"

"All the shows I've been to plus a bunch from the seventies and eighties that I kind of—inherited. Thank God for CD burners."

"Thanks for burning me copies of the shows we were at." She shrugged and headed for the door. It was like she didn't like me acknowledging that she had done something nice for me. She had done the same thing when I thanked her earlier for bringing beer. I didn't want to not say thank you for stuff, but it elicited silence on her part. It was strange.

I followed after her and wondered if she was okay to drive, but I didn't ask. With anyone else I would have. If she had asked me to list my top five pet peeves, people who drive drunk would be on there. I lost a friend in high school that way, and I would rather be the designated driver than see one of my friends not make it home. But I couldn't quite bring myself to ask her. Besides, she really seemed fine. She reaffirmed what time we were leaving for Columbus, kissed my cheek, and was gone.

I could smell her perfume in my living room when I went back to throw out the beer bottles, and I dreamed about her that night.

6

I didn't wake up when my phone rang, but when Laura nudged me. "Your phone's ringing," she said softly. It took me a minute to remember that we were in Indianapolis. We had driven like hell after the Columbus show, gotten ourselves on the pit list for Indy, then checked into a nearby motel for a few hours of sleep before the next roll call, which wasn't until 7am. I glanced at the motel clock. It was 3:13am. Pretty much exactly when you get home if you catch the last Metro from the bars in Dupont Circle or Adams Morgan. I didn't need to calculate any of that right then; I knew what the 3:13 call meant. Someone was drunk dialing. Usually it was Mel, in a giggly drunk mood. Or crying if she and Eric had just had a fight. And Katie used to call me after the bars before we lived together, if we had gone out separately.

I rolled over and looked at the caller ID. Shit. It was Katie.

I hadn't really heard from her since the breakup. I had sent her an email saying when I was going to move my stuff out, and she wasn't there when I showed up. We had broken up nearly three months ago by then. This was going to be ugly. It would either be a crying, "Why did you leave me?" call or an angry, "I can do better than you" call. Either way, I had no intention of answering it. I hit the volume button to make the ringer stop, mumbled a sleepy apology to Laura, and closed my eyes again. Laura didn't ask who it was, and I was grateful. Now wasn't the time to explain about Katie. We weren't exactly at the point in our relationship where we were talking about exes.

Ten seconds later, the phone started ringing again. I hit the volume button again. And it rang again. "Shit," I muttered, climbing out of bed. I turned the ringer off and grabbed my jeans off the chair. It had stopped ringing by the time I climbed into them but started again immediately. I went out into the hallway and answered it.

"What do you want, Katie?" I asked, groggy, annoyed at being woken up after such a long day, and *really* pissed off that she was calling me when I was with Laura. Not that she could have known any of that when she decided to call. But some of the old irritation toward her flared back up.

I could hear her crying before she even said anything, which made me feel a little like an asshole, but I was still too aggravated to really care. "It's been more than two months since I've heard anything from you at all, and you don't even say hello?" she asked through her sobs.

"It's three o'clock in the fucking morning," I said, but without malice. "Are you okay?" I knew how she would respond as soon as I asked it, but I honestly meant the question purely in the physical sense. Like had she been in a car accident, or was her building on fire? But I should have been more specific.

"No, I'm not okay!" She was crying so hard that it was difficult to understand her. I waited until she got enough control of herself to talk.

"Katie," I said. "Calm down, Katie." She mumbled something unintelligible. I rubbed my eyes hard and blinked in the harsh fluorescent lighting of the hallway. "I can't understand you when you're crying that hard." I heard her take a few deep breaths, and finally she started talking.

"Why didn't you answer your phone?"

"I was sleeping." She started crying harder at this. "Katie," I said again.

"With who?" she asked spitefully. *Wow, she must be really drunk*, I thought. That didn't sound like the Katie I knew.

"Alone," I said, but I hesitated a little too long for her.

"If you were alone, you would have answered the phone sooner." She was right, but I wasn't about to tell her that. If I was alone, I probably would have answered that first ring, exhausted or not.

"I'm tired, Katie. It's been a long day. And I'm in Indianapolis."

"What are you doing there?" I sighed. I wanted to go back to bed more than I could ever remember wanting anything.

"Bruce is playing here tomorrow night. We—I saw him in Columbus tonight then drove here."

"We?" she asked. "*We*? If you're alone, who's 'we?'" Fuck. I did not need this right now. I slid down the wall until I was sitting on the worn, orange carpet, my head leaning against the thickly-textured floral wallpaper. This place must have been seriously trendy in about 1976. If Laura had enough money for that car, why were we staying in a shit hole like this?

"I'm here with a friend, Katie. Just a friend." It dawned on me that this was true, although I didn't like it. I still wasn't telling Katie the full truth, but it made me feel a little better to know I wasn't technically lying to her right then.

"Were you with her when we were together? Is that why you broke up with me?" I sighed again. No, and yes, but also no, would have been the real answer. But that wasn't an answer that I could give her.

"No."

"No, you weren't with her then or no, she's not why you broke up with me?"

"Neither."

"I don't believe you."

"Katie, what do you want me to say?" She started crying really hard again and said something completely incoherent. "I can't understand you."

"I said I want to know why you left me."

I didn't know what to tell her. There wasn't any one answer to give, and certainly not one that I hadn't already given her the day that I told her I was moving out. "It just wasn't working."

"Yes it was! It was for me." Oh God. How much worse was this going to get? I didn't say anything for awhile, just sat there listening to her crying. I deserved this, I told myself. She had still loved me when we broke up, and she had no idea that I wasn't happy, therefore I deserved this. Of course, that didn't mean that I planned to listen to much more of it.

"I'm sorry," I said eventually, slowly, fumbling for the words. "I am. I wish it could have turned out differently. But I wasn't ready for where we were going."

"Maybe you'll be ready soon?" she asked.

"No, honey," I said as gently as I could, realizing even as I said it that I shouldn't be using any of Laura's terms of endearment here. Nothing that would give Katie hope.

"Then you just didn't want to be with me?" she asked between sobs. I didn't respond for a little while.

"Please don't think of it like that."

"Well I don't see you being too afraid of being with *her*." I stared at the flowers on the carpet and realized that Katie just wasn't going to see reason tonight. Possibly ever. Looking back, I should have been far more sympathetic. But it just wasn't in me anymore. Not for her. I didn't feel anything for her by then. Except a mild annoyance, which probably had more to do with having been woken up from such a deep sleep to deal with this. But I decided that I was finished, and there wasn't anything I could do but tell her that.

"Katie, I'm done with this conversation."

"You mean you're done with me." *I was done with you three months ago*, I thought unkindly.

"We broke up. I'd like to think we could be friends. But not now. We need time first."

"Friends?" she spat out. "Are you actually, really saying this to me?"

"Look, you're drunk, I'm tired, and this conversation is over. Don't call me like this again."

"Fine!" she yelled. "I won't call you again at all!" And she was gone. I sat there with my head in my hands for a few minutes. That was ugly. I honestly hadn't wanted to hurt her, but there didn't seem to be any way to get around it unless I stayed with her. Which I couldn't do. It's like Tom Cruise said in *Cocktail*: "Everything ends badly, otherwise it wouldn't end."

Eventually I picked myself up and reached into my pocket for the room key. And then realized I had left it on the desk in the room. Perfect. Just fucking perfect. I knocked gently on the door, and a few seconds later, Laura opened it, wearing just an old, very worn Bruce T-shirt. It was from the *River* tour, and I wondered briefly whose it had been. She would have been about two years old at the concert that the shirt was from. She looked at me, blinking into the bright light of the hall, but didn't say anything. I followed her into the room, tugged off my jeans and climbed back into bed, desperate to get back to sleep and put this behind me. But I was awake by then.

I lay there for a while, feeling guilty and looking up at the faint shadows of the rough, gravely textured ceiling. Then I gave up. Laura had said she was an insomniac. "Are you awake?" I asked softly, hoping that if she was asleep, I hadn't just woken her up. It felt like a long time before she responded. But it's impossible to tell time in the dark.

"Are you?"

"More than I want to be."

I heard her bed creak as she sat up. "Me too."

"Is this what insomnia is like? Being awake at 4am?"

"No," she said. "This is waking up once and having trouble falling back asleep. Insomnia is not falling asleep every night."

"Must be hell."

"It is."

"What do you do when you can't sleep?" She was quiet. I was about to ask something else, to try another tactic, when she responded.

"Keep trying anyway most nights. Sometimes I read or put on music."

"Does it help?"

"Not usually."

"What about pills?"

"I have Ambien and Halcion."

"Do they work?"

"Sometimes. But it's worse than just not sleeping when I take them and they don't work." I could just barely see her outline in the dark. Her eyes glowed softly like a cat's, picking up the tiny bit of ambient light that never leaves cheap motel rooms.

I sat up in my bed too. "This sucks. I'm completely awake."

"Close your eyes," she said. I assumed she was going to give me some sleep tip, but she turned on the light next to her bed. Then she laughed at me. "You can open them now." I did and my eyes didn't have nearly as much trouble adjusting as they would have if I had left them open. I blinked a couple times and smiled at her.

"Now what?" Laura got out of bed and went over to her bag. She rummaged around, then climbed over her bed and came to sit cross-legged on mine. I tried to not be obvious about being able to see her underwear. I would love to say that I succeeded. She didn't seem to notice though, because she grinned at me and slapped a worn deck of cards, held together by a ponytail holder, onto the bed between us. I couldn't help but smile again. This girl was great.

"What's your game?" I asked. "Poker? Gin?" Laura shook her head at these. "Go Fish?"

"Egyptian Rat Screw," she announced.

"That sounds like a bad drink." She gave me a look that made me stop being a smartass. Besides, it had the word "screw" in it. Maybe there was nudity involved. "How do you play?"

"It's like War with an attitude," she said and proceeded to explain the game. It seemed complicated at first. And there wasn't any stripping, at least not in her version of it. I wasn't quite alert enough to be good at slapping doubles, which was part of the game, but it turned out to be fun once I got the hang of it. Pretty mindless, unlike poker, which did make it perfect for a sleepless night.

"Okay, so other than the Beatles and the Stones," she said as she dealt the cards for our second game, "because I know we're not going to resolve who's better tonight, who's your favorite rock band of the sixties?"

"The sixties? Easy. The Who."

"Oooh," she said. "Good answer."

"Who's yours?"

"Well I was going to say the Animals but The Who is a *much* better choice."

"Yeah, it doesn't get much better than *Tommy*.'"

"Definitely. Remember in *Almost Famous* when the sister says to listen to that with a candle burning and you'll see your future?"

"Yeah."

"We should try that."

I laughed. "Does that answer make up for the whole Journey thing?"

She grinned. "No, but it's a start."

I don't remember what else we talked about specifically. Mostly about music and a lot of trash talk about each other's playing. And we laughed a lot. We played until just after 5am. I was finally tired enough that I felt like I would be able to sleep again, but I wasn't quite ready to stop playing. I was enjoying her company too much, even though we were both starting to yawn. Eventually, Laura put down her cards and crawled over to the top of the bed. She got under my covers and looked up at me. "Do you want to go to sleep?" I asked her, feeling stupid. She was in my bed, and I was asking if she wanted to sleep. Granted, there were quite a few other things that I was hoping she would rather do in my bed, but she looked tired, and I was exhausted. She nodded and lay down with her head on one of my pillows. I reached over and shut off the light between the beds and settled back in next to her.

I did think it was a little weird that she wanted to stay in my bed with nothing happening. But I wasn't going to complain. And I was so worn out that I was pretty sure I would be unconscious enough to not even notice her there within a couple of minutes.

I was right. I didn't wake up until I heard the ancient pipes clanging as she took a shower.

7

The next week felt longer than a year. Christmas was coming up quickly, and it would be my first without Katie in three years. Not that I minded. But the idea of spending Christmas at home with my parents at age twenty-five was more than a little depressing. And even more depressing was the fact that I had no idea when or if I would see Laura again.

She got quieter and quieter as we drove closer to home on the way back from Indianapolis. I knew why. We didn't have any more shows until almost March. And the idea of January and February with no Bruce, with nothing to look forward to, was enough to make me quiet too. And we hadn't exactly specified when we would see each other again. Laura left it by quoting what Bruce said at the end of the show, "Be seein' you further on up the road." I looked across the seat at her. Her face was completely unreadable. She didn't quite make eye contact.

"I'll call you this week," I said. She cocked her head and looked at me as if to ask why, but she didn't say anything. Finally, she smiled a grim, forced, ghost of a smile and nodded. I didn't know what else to say, so I got out of the car. By the time I reached my front door and looked back, she was already pulling away.

Everywhere I went, everything was covered in Christmas decorations. My apartment became my one haven from all of the cheerful commercialism. The only sign of Christmas that I had was the Santa hat that I had gotten in the pit in Indianapolis with Laura. I put it on one night and laughed at myself, remembering how much fun we had when Bruce sang "Santa Claus is Comin' to Town."

I wanted to call her practically all day, every day. I would wake up at 3am and know that she was probably awake. I knew that I could even call her and say I couldn't sleep and she'd get it. But I wasn't sure what I would say after that. And I kept remembering the look in her eyes when I told her that I would call her. She didn't want me to call. And I think I probably wouldn't have called her at all, no matter how much I wanted to. At least not until I had something Bruce-related to say, as that would be sure to grab her attention. If nothing else, I thought that I would hear from her when the tour picked back up. If she hadn't found someone else by then. But waiting another two months? I didn't know what I should do.

Luckily, I didn't have to decide. My cell rang at work on the Friday before Christmas. I knew it was my mother calling again to try to convince me to stay over at her house on Christmas Eve, and I was ready to ignore the phone. But I glanced at it as I turned off the ringer volume. It was Laura. I should have guessed that it could have been her. Everyone else who called me would have known to call my work phone. But Laura didn't have my work number.

"What's your email address?" she asked as soon as I answered with an enthusiastic, "Hey!" No hello from her, and there would be no goodbye. Not ever.

"Work or home?" I asked.

"Where are you now?"

"Work," I paused. "Must be nice not having to go to an office on weekdays!" She laughed a little.

"Yeah, well, it gives me more time to pursue my outside interests."

"Like Bruce?" I asked.

"Be nice," she warned. "Or I won't send this email." I smiled. I had missed her this week. It was stupid, because I had only known her for two weeks. But I had still missed her.

"Send it to my home account," I said, and gave her the address. "I can check it from work."

"Okay," she said. "Doing it now."

"What is it?"

"You'll see," she said. "Just a little Christmas present."

Christmas. Right. She wasn't being serious, was she? It wasn't like a real present, right? We had only known each other two weeks. Nah. Couldn't be. It was an email. I mean, getting me a present after two weeks, that would be a little weird, wouldn't it? It wasn't like we were dating. Yeah, we had slept in the same bed a few times now. But we were definitely not dating. We hadn't kissed or anything.

"Anyways, call me later. Tell me what you think," I almost missed what she said, because I was that far along in my little paranoid, Christmas-present contemplations. By the time I had completely registered what she had said, she had already hung up, and the phone was quiet in my ear.

I logged into my email. Two new messages. One from my mother, titled "Christmas Eve." Surprise, surprise. The second, from SandyGirl0704@aol.com, with no subject. I laughed. One of my coworkers, Grace, was walking by wearing an overly decorative red and green sweater, and she glanced in at me with her eyebrows raised, making sure that I wasn't laughing at her. I shook my head slightly, and she kept walking. If I had to predict an email address for Laura, I couldn't have come up with a better one. It was from her favorite song, "4th of July, Asbury Park (Sandy)." And of course she wouldn't put a subject line. It would be like saying hello or goodbye. There wasn't any text in the email either. Just a link. I clicked it and waited for the page to load.

It was a video of Bruce singing "Santa Claus is Comin' to Town." It wasn't from a show that we had been at, but he was wearing a Santa hat like at the Indianapolis show. I turned the volume up as far as I figured I could without pissing off all my coworkers, even on the Friday before Christmas, and watched the video. A couple people walked by my door and smiled indulgently, hearing the seasonal music. But I didn't care. Laura was thinking about me too.

I decided to wait until I was on the way home to call her back, so I read the email from my mom before I watched the video again. She started with the general holiday small talk. What her work party had been like, what she had bought for my dad and brother, etc. Then she launched into her request.

"Are you sure I can't convince you to come home for Christmas Eve? I know I've been pestering you a lot about it but I just hate the idea of you being all lonely in that new apartment of yours now that you and Katie have split up. I know you only live a little ways away, and I know it's silly, but it would be so sweet to have both of my boys home for Christmas like when you were little. Please think about it.

Love,

Mom"

Let Guilt-Fest 2002 begin. What was it about the holidays that turned parents into guilt machines? My mom only wanted me to come home because she felt guilty that I would be alone, and she was passing that on by making me feel guilty. I mean, Mike was only going to be staying with our parents because he lived in Philadelphia now. If he lived closer, there was no chance that he would be spending the night at home. And if I got out of staying at home that night, Mike would probably try to crash on my couch too so that he could go out later that night with his high school friends.

I briefly let myself imagine what it would be like if I were actually with Laura. My mother wouldn't be trying to get me home then at least. Then I realized. Laura didn't have parents to go to. And she didn't mention any other family. Ever. She could have had some stashed somewhere, but if she did, it seemed like she would mention them in some context, especially because she was an orphan. But there had never been one word about family. Meaning that if she had any relatives, she clearly wasn't that close to any of them. Finally the real guilt kicked in. I was sitting there feeling annoyed that my mom wanted me to go home for Christmas Eve when Laura probably didn't even have a place to go for Christmas Eve at all. Then again, was I even sure she celebrated Christmas? She could be Jewish or some Eastern religion. Buddhist or Hindu or something like that would probably be a good fit for her. Although to be honest, she didn't seem like the type who would believe in God or any kind of real organized religion.

Should I invite her to my parents' house for Christmas Day? I wouldn't have to spend the night then, and my parents would be thrilled to welcome someone who didn't have any place to go. But would she say yes? Was it weird to invite her? Should I ask my mom first or just ask Laura if she wanted to come?

All of a sudden, I was a nervous wreck. I didn't actually want to ask her to go to my parents' house. But I felt like I should. Stupid Christmas guilt.

I waited until I got home. And then I waited another hour. I had a beer. Then another. I popped open a third and finally was ready to call. Well, as ready as I could be.

The phone rang four times. I was about to hang up. I may have been ready to call her, but I was *not* ready to leave her a message. But then she answered. She had waited just long enough for me to be off guard. I started to sputter out a hello, reminding myself not to say "it's me," no matter what. Not that she gave me an opportunity to do that anyway. I guess caller ID has done away with the need for real phone greetings these days anyway.

"How cute was that?" she asked immediately. She was a little out of breath, like she had been running for the phone.

I hesitated a second. The video. She told me to call her about the video. Duh. This was fine. "Adorable," I said. What had I been so nervous about again?

"I thought you'd like it."

"It takes a little bit of the edge off the whole Bruce-withdrawal thing."

"I know, I'm suffering here. This week has been hell."

"Same," I agreed. There was a pause and the oddness of our relationship struck me again. I couldn't invite her to my parents' house. I didn't know anything about her except for the Bruce stuff. Well. Okay, I knew a ton about her. But I only knew the things I had observed. I knew how she could pull her lip gloss out of the pocket in her jeans that it permanently resided in, then open and apply it with one hand. I knew the difference in her smile when she was actually completely delighted by something and when she was faking it. I knew the look that crossed through her eyes for a split second right before she avoided answering a question that she had no intention of answering. I knew a lot. But I didn't know the stuff that you could make small talk out of. I didn't even know if she had any siblings. An aunt, an uncle, a cousin. Or a boyfriend for that matter. Although, I honestly believed there was no boyfriend in the picture. There couldn't be. She would have mentioned him in some way. And he would have objected to her spending all that time alone with me. Maybe she had some huge network of friends with whom she would be spending Christmas. But then why was she alone at the concerts? If she had that many friends, someone would have gone with her. Unless she wanted to go alone. That was possible. But then why include me? And I had never heard her mention any people who were unrelated to her fascination with Bruce before.

But I had to ask her about Christmas. It was the reason I had called. But I could ask what her plans were before I actually invited her anywhere. It was an easier start.

"Listen," I began. "What are you doing Christmas Eve?"

Silence. I pictured that look I knew so well by now darting across her eyes. I wouldn't get a real answer.

"Christmas Eve?" she asked, but it wasn't really a question. "Drinking." I laughed. It was the answer that I should have expected from her. Evasive, and it didn't give me any real information. And I realized that she wouldn't want me to invite her to some family thing. I don't even know how I knew that exactly, but I did. But that didn't mean I couldn't see her.

"Do you want some company?" Another pause. Longer this time. "We could make our own concert or something."

I love how a smile can spread across someone's voice as easily as it can across a face. She replied coolly, but I knew which smile she was wearing. "Okay," she said.

8

"I don't mean to nag," Mel began, ever so tactfully over happy hour drinks, "but when do I get to meet your girl?"

"Never if you're going to keep calling her that."

"Just bring her to the engagement party."

I sighed and took another sip of my beer. I wanted to ask her to go to the party, of course. But I hadn't been able to get Laura to do anything that wasn't Bruce related yet. I did try, in an admittedly half-assed way, after Christmas. I asked if she wanted to get together for New Year's. But I copped out before she could answer and added that we could do what we did on Christmas and listen to a bootleg of a show from New Year's Eve. She agreed, which led to a few more Bruce dates since then, but we hadn't done anything else. I think part of it was that I wasn't quite ready for a rejection from her, but another part of it was that I wasn't sure that I was ready to introduce her to the rest of my life yet. "I just don't think she'd come."

"Would you stop being such a girl already?"

"Look, Mel, it's complicated—" I stopped. She was looking at the ring again. It had been almost a month since Eric proposed. And *I* was being the girl?

She slapped her hand down on the sticky table. Then, because it was Mel, she quickly removed it and wiped it on her napkin with a small "ew." I just looked at her. "I've got it," she said with a sheepish grin.

"Okay."

"When are you seeing her next?"

I looked at my watch. "Um, three hours?"

"Okay," she said, starting to put her hand back on the table but thinking better of it. "I'll just come back to your place, and be 'picking something up from you' when she gets there."

"Isn't that suspicious?   Plus, I wanted to take a shower."

"Not if you don't make it suspicious.   I can be borrowing a movie or something. We'll pretend I just got there.   And whatever, I can entertain myself while you shower."

I shrugged. "Are you sure she won't think it's weird?"

"Look, would it be weird if I actually really was over at your place randomly?"

I thought about it. "I guess not."

"See?" she said beaming. "It's perfect."

I nodded.   "Just don't call her my girlfriend or anything."

She gave a half salute, her engagement ring sparkling in the dim light of the bar.

And I had thought I was nervous when Laura was coming over other times to hang out.

Jesus.

I showered. I shaved. I didn't cut myself. I tried to not be a complete idiot. Mel picked out a DVD that she just "had" to borrow that night.   Finally, I heard Laura knocking at the door.

Mel stayed on my sofa. She had said that she would be on the way out when Laura came in, and I looked at her. This wasn't part of the plan.

"You going to answer that?" she asked in a sugary voice, with a raised eyebrow and a moderately wicked smile.

Fuck. I made my feet move toward the door. Mel could be pretty damn brutal on the girls I dated. And I wasn't even dating Laura. Which meant all bets were off. I mean, I knew that Mel would be nice to her no matter what because she knew how I felt, but I had seen girls get catty around each other before for no reason at all except that some girls just rub each other the wrong way. You just never knew when two girls would absolutely love each other or hate each other. And with most girls, it was either one extreme or the other.

I was pretty sure they would be okay together. But I just didn't want anything to get awkward between us. It was all hanging in this strange balance. Clearly there was an attraction on both sides. I think. But so far, there hadn't been anything out of a friendly context. True, we had been spending a lot of time together, even in the interim before the tour picked up. But it wasn't like a normal friendship or a normal early-dating period. It was unique and special. But we hadn't brought any other people into the equation, and what if Mel upset the balance?

Deep breath.

I opened the door. "Took you long enough," she said, leaning in to kiss me on the cheek. I loved the already familiar smell of her perfume whenever she was close to me.

She breezed past me, a six-pack of beer in her hand, before I could warn her that Mel was there. She got down the hall to the living room and stopped short with a surprised "Oh!" Her head turned back to me questioningly and there was something new in her eyes. Something I didn't recognize. But I didn't have time to wonder what it was.

Mel had jumped up and was coming over to introduce herself. I was behind Laura, but I stayed close. "Laura, this is my best friend, Melanie. She just stopped by to borrow a movie. Mel, this is Laura." Mel extended her hand. Laura hesitated so briefly that I don't think anyone but me could have noticed it, handed the beer off to me, and shook Mel's hand. She towered over Mel, who stood about five-foot-three in heels. Laura seemed gigantic by comparison.

Here it came.

But Mel was, as promised, on her best behavior. "I'm so happy to finally meet you," she said with a genuine smile.

Laura nodded awkwardly and crossed her arms in an uncomfortable gesture that clashed with everything I knew about her. The "finally" echoed strongly with me. I had been afraid of this. We were all still standing in the doorway of the living room.

Then, Laura surprised me. She uncrossed her arms, forced a smile that didn't look too strained, and asked, "You're the one who just got engaged, right?"

Mel's face lit up. Laura had picked the exact perfect topic. "On New Year's, right after midnight." Laura knew that already, of course, as she had been with me when I got a phone call from Mel at 12:08, screaming that she was engaged. Laura and I had been listening to Bruce's New Year's Eve 1980 show that night and were already outrageously drunk by midnight.

"Can I see the ring?" Mel was only too happy to oblige. Laura pronounced it beautiful, and Mel launched into the most abridged version of wedding arrangements that I had heard from her so far.

I remembered exactly why Mel was my best friend when, less than five minutes later, she said she had to be leaving.

"You *will* come to the engagement party, won't you?" she asked Laura. I held my breath. This wasn't part of the plan. Then I looked at Mel. I had misunderstood her. She wasn't there to meet Laura. She was there to get her to the engagement party. Sneaky, but she was doing it for me. Which was sweet, but it made me no less nervous.

"I—um—" Laura, for once, was at a loss for words. She looked at me helplessly. I shrugged slightly in terror and gave her what I hoped was an encouraging nod.

Mel looked at me, then back at Laura. "Good," she said, not waiting for a real answer. "It's next Saturday."

"I—" Laura began to protest.

"I've got to run," Mel interrupted smoothly. "But it was so nice to meet you, and I can't wait to see you next weekend!" Laura just nodded weakly.

Mel winked at me from the door and gave me a goofy thumbs up when she saw Laura wasn't watching her leave. I scowled at her in return, and she laughed softly as she let herself out of my apartment.

It wasn't until the next morning that I figured out what the new look was that I had seen in Laura's eyes when she first saw Mel there. It was fear. Fear of what, I didn't know. It couldn't be because there had been another girl in my apartment when she first walked in. Could it? But then what was it that she was afraid of?

I waited until nine the next morning before I called Mel for a post-mortem. I knew she wouldn't be awake yet, but I had been up since seven and couldn't wait any longer.

It wasn't that I specifically cared that much if Mel liked her. I mean, it would be nice if she did, especially as I kind of hoped that Laura would be around for awhile. But more than that, I wanted Mel's take on the stuff about her that I couldn't figure out yet. It was really why I had agreed to let her meet Laura.

And she showed me, once again, just why she was my best friend. She answered the phone at nine, knowing exactly why I was calling.

"I am so good to you," she yawned into the phone. "Just know I wouldn't drag my ass out of bed for anyone else."

"Yeah, yeah, you're the best. But what did you think?"

"She's absolutely drop-dead gorgeous." For a second it sounded like she was going to say more, but she didn't.

"But?" I asked finally. No response. "Mel?"

"I don't know," she said finally. "I can't put my finger on what bothered me. She was very polite; she asked the right questions, she said the right things. There was just something—off."

"What do you mean?" I knew what she meant though. It was exactly why I wanted Me's analysis of her. I was hoping someone else would be able to spot what I had been seeing. But I realized I could identify it better than Mel could. It was that it was impossible to tell who she really was. She could be devastatingly tough in most situations, completely unshakeable, but she couldn't even kill a bug. She was never afraid of being alone, but "made friends," as she put it, with random people everywhere she went. Of course, all of those friends were a means to an end. Someone to sell us tickets, or save our position in the pit at shows, or a place in line, or bring us drinks. Not real friends. Except for me. I still didn't know what it was that made her want to keep me around. Yet seeing Mel sitting in my living room seemed to be the only thing I had witnessed so far that could make her uncomfortable.

"I don't know," she said again. "I really can't figure out what it is. It kept me up for a while last night. But I couldn't quite put my finger on it. She's coming to the party though, right?"

"I didn't mention it again." I wanted her to come and I already knew that if I brought it up, she would figure out a reason why she couldn't go.

"You idiot, I did that for you!"

"I know. I'll try to get her there."

"I think she'll go. She likes you."

That certainly got my attention in a hurry. "You think?"

"Definitely. Did you see the look on her face when she saw me? She was *jealous*."

"I don't know," I said, more thinking out loud than disagreeing with her. I could see the look on Laura's face in my head, but it wasn't one that I would label as jealousy. Jealousy was when she talked about Bruce's wife or the girls who he would pull up on stage to dance with during the eighties. This was something different.

"Whatever," Mel said. "I think she was jealous. And if not, she should have been."

"Thanks." Pause. Normally there wouldn't have been room in a conversation with her for a pause, but Mel had, after all, just woken up. It was very different from my conversations on the phone with Laura. Then again, I knew Mel's entire history, meaning that there was always something to say. With Laura, conversations were still very utilitarian.

"Oh yeah," she said finally. "I know what I meant to ask you. You said she's like a photographer, right?"

"Yeah."

"But just freelance? Like once in awhile?"

"Uh huh."

"What else does she do?"

"Nothing that I know of."

"Then her family's got money?"

"She doesn't have family. Her parents are dead and she's an only child." I knew what she was getting that. That had bothered me too, of course. Money never seemed tight with her, and I knew she only shot for publications when she felt like it. The older men I had seen her with at the DC show and in Philadelphia flashed through my mind again, but I didn't want to suggest the sugar daddy theory to Mel. "Why?"

"Because unless she buys the best knockoffs on the planet, that outfit cost about the same as my wedding dress budget."

"What? No way. She was wearing jeans and a t-shirt!"

"Yeah, but that was all serious, *serious* designer stuff. The jeans were Diesel, the shoes were Manolos, I don't know who made the jacket but it was incredible, and her purse was a Marc Jacobs."

"Mel, I have no idea what any of that means."

She sighed. "Okay, the jeans were *at least* two-fifty, the shoes at least four-hundred, I'd be shocked if that jacket was under a thousand, and the purse was at least fifteen-hundred, and that's if she got good deals on all of it. So like I said, she either gets the best knockoffs in the world, or she's not taking pictures for the money."

I was speechless. Mel was a slave to fashion magazines, so I was sure that she knew what she was talking about. But if she did, that meant that one casual outfit for staying in and listening to music on a Friday night cost more than three thousand dollars. *Three thousand dollars*, I repeated in my head. It was absolutely mind-boggling. What twenty-five-year-old non-movie or pop star had the money for that? How was that even possible? I had basically been working off the theory that her parents had left a decent amount of insurance money, because I didn't want to believe that she actually had an older man who was paying for her lifestyle. The guy who she had been with in the Philadelphia parking lot didn't look rich enough for all this though. Did she have more than one guy supporting her? Even thinking about that, picturing the man in the *Born to Run* shirt touching her, made me feel slightly nauseous.

"You still there?" Mel asked.

"Yeah," I said quietly, trying desperately to flush that image out of my head.

"Anyway, she's got money from something." Mel laughed. "Hey, maybe she's got a sugar daddy!"

Thanks, Mel.

9

"Melanie said you've got a new girlfriend or something?" Eric asked as we were heading into the gym.

"Ooh, then I can call Katie now?" Chris asked with a malicious grin. I ignored him. He wasn't serious.

"She is definitely not my girlfriend," I said. And this was definitely not the conversation I wanted to have right then either. Eric hung his keys on a peg and I selected one next to his. Number twenty-eight. February 28 would be the first show of the next leg of the tour. We were prepared this time and already had tickets.

"You getting some at least?" I shot Chris a dirty look and he started to laugh. "That's a no then. So yeah, in other words, she's his girlfriend!" Eric started to laugh at this as well.

"Thanks guys."

"Oh come on, who is she?"

I hesitated. They were going to meet her at the engagement party if Laura came with me, and I still hoped she would. If I told them what the situation was now, maybe I could stave off any embarrassing questions at the party. But then again, the less I said, the less it would seem like I really liked this girl. Which meant they wouldn't say anything too bad in front of her.

"Just a friend."

"Ohhh, I see, it's *serious*," Chris crowed triumphantly.

"Yes," I said. "A serious friend."

"Have you seen her naked yet?"

I hesitated the slightest bit too long. I hadn't seen her naked. In her underwear, but not naked.

"All right, Romeo, it's about damn time! Is she hot?"

They weren't going to let this drop. Fine. "Hotter than any girl you've ever been with."

"Hotter than Lindsay Kramer was?"

"She makes Lindsay look like that mutt that used to hang around outside the frat house."

"Holy shit. Well, good work then." This was one of those moments when I really appreciated just how much Eric and Mel deserved each other. There are few people in the world who will actually be happy for you instead of jealous when you find something good, and Eric and Mel are two of them. The only two I know, in fact.

"When do I get the chance to try to steal her?" Chris on the other hand, was more the typical friend. A blast to hang out with, but not someone to discuss girl troubles with. Ever. Chris's idea of an ideal relationship was a girl who would sleep with him, leave immediately after, and never call him unless it was for sex. Amazingly enough, he was still single. Although apparently he made good first impressions because he seemed to have a new girl on his arm just about every weekend.

"Um, yeah, never," I said with a sense of finality. I wasn't particularly worried though. Chris would definitely try to flirt with a girl of mine, but Laura would chew him up and spit him out. She wasn't one to fall for random cheap lines. And Chris wouldn't be smart enough to try to use a line from a Bruce song on her.

"You bringing her to the engagement party?" Eric asked.

"Working on that one."

"Is it bad taste to steal your friend's girl at an engagement party?" Chris grinned maliciously.

Eric and I laughed. "Yeah, probably," Eric said. "Besides, Mel would murder you if there was any kind of disruption."

Chris shuddered. "I can't believe you're getting married. Don't do it, man, for our sakes!"

"Don't worry baby, Mel knows you're still my first love," Eric stroked Chris's arm in mock affection. "She knows she can't begin to compete with you."

"Gonna be a really short marriage if you're going gay."

"Going?" Eric asked.

Chris was laughing almost too hard to speak. "Asshole," he said finally. "How can you make fun of someone who makes fun of himself so well? It takes all the challenge out of it!"

It was funny, but with the subject firmly off of Laura, suddenly I wanted to talk about her. God, I must be falling for her. I was acting like a high school girl with a crush.

"If I get Laura to the party, you can't say anything about her being my girlfriend," I ventured. Eric looked surprised that I brought her back up, and I realized he had deliberately steered the conversation away from her for me. Oh well.

"Hey, if she's as hot as you say, I'm not promising anything," Chris said with a smirk.

"What's her story?" Eric asked eventually as we headed toward a weight bench and he started piling weights onto the bar.

I shrugged slightly. "What do you want to know?"

"What's she do?" He motioned for me to spot him.

"Freelance photographer," I said as Eric lowered the bar close to his chest.

"What's she look like?" he puffed.

"Thin, great body, really pretty face, dark brown hair, great eyes, amazing legs, she's really tall. You know that old actress from the seventies? Sophie Landau?" Eric nodded slightly, but Chris shook his head. Eric put the bar back and sat up, a little out of breath, then held both of his hands out in front of his chest, asking if she was the one with the rack. I smiled a little and nodded and Chris exclaimed that he knew who we were talking about. "She looks a lot like her. Thinner, though."

"Sounds good to me," Chris said. Eric climbed off the bench and Chris sat down. "Get her to come to the party."

"Yeah, we'll help you out."

"Yeah, I'm not that sure your help would actually—well—help!"

"Well how long have you been dating her?"

"We're not dating."

"Okay, how long have you been not-so-platonically hanging out?"

"Since December 8, but it *is* platonic."

"You know the date and what she looks like naked. It's not platonic." I sighed. He had a point.

"I like her." All my cards on the table.

"Then what's the problem?"

"I don't know. There just doesn't seem to be a moment to make a move." *And I like her too much to make a move and have it flop*, I added in my head. "It's a strange dynamic."

"Stop being a pussy and just kiss her. If you forget where you go from there, I can draw you a diagram, lend you some porn, etc." Nice to know I could always count on Chris to be subtle. Eric was laughing again and a couple of girls standing by the free weights to our right were staring, clearly they had heard Chris and didn't approve of the vulgarity.

I looked at them apologetically and the girls both smiled a little, then looked away quickly. Chris, at this point, noticed them and raised his eyebrows at me. They were cute, but I shrugged my shoulders. Laura might not be my girlfriend, but in my mind, I was already spoken for.

"Jesus!" Chris exclaimed when he saw that I had no intention of making the slightest bit of an effort with the other girls. "You're not even hooking up with her at all, and she's already got you completely whipped? You need to dump this girl quick."

"You're an asshole."

"I know," Chris said with a grin, "but I'm doing this for your own good."

"Eric, help me out here," I figured he would understand. After all, he was actually getting married.

But it was Eric's turn to shrug. "I don't know. If you're not getting anywhere at all, it's time to move on. I plan to be able to live the single life vicariously through you guys for a while, and if you're acting like you live in a monastery, you're no help."

Not going the way I wanted it to at all.

"You'll see if you meet her. It's not that kind of a relationship. We're friends."

"Then what's the matter? Grab some other girl now." Chris said. "They're like busses anyway, if you miss one, another will come along in a couple minutes!"

Eric laughed loudly enough for half of the people at the gym to look over at us. "Can I tell Mel you said that the next time we have a fight?" he asked when he got himself under control. "I don't need this shit from you, because another bus will come along soon!"

I started to laugh picturing Mel's reaction to this sentiment. It was no secret that Chris was not her favorite person in the world. Maybe it was his comment that Eric was "throwing his goddamned life away before he had a chance to start it," when Chris heard they were engaged. Maybe it was the fact that he told her (only half-seriously— I think) that he was planning to get Eric a hooker for the bachelor party. Or maybe it was the time he got really drunk sophomore year of college and threw up in one of Mel's shoes after hooking up with her roommate. On Mel's bed. Who knows with girls? But clearly his bus comment was not going to go over well. If I had said it, I would have gotten a dirty look, then a laugh. But girls just have no logic sometimes.

"Can I be there when you tell her that? Or better yet, Chris, you should say it to her. Because she'd kill you, and I think enough people would want to see you get your ass handed to you by a girl that we could sell tickets. In fact, Eric, you can pay for the whole wedding plus buy a house out of the profits from that fight."

Chris laughed at that as well. "Hey, that's fine, as long as we have the fight in a ring with mud, or better yet Jello or something like that. It's all good." He turned to me. "Hell, bring the girlfriend along, I'll take her on after Mel, 'cause even covered in Jello and getting my ass kicked by a girl, I'm still a better option than you."

I smiled. "You know what? Go ahead and try to get with Laura when you meet her. I dare you. I'm going to enjoy seeing her shoot you down."

"Shoot me down? I don't think so. You forget, I'm one charming motherfucker."

"Charming, douche bag, same thing. Either way, she won't go for it."

"All girls go for me," Chris looked at Eric after saying this and saw the look on Eric's face. "Oh, you both know that Mel only *pretends* to hate me because she knows you'd be jealous if she said how she *really* feels. And I just don't hit that out of respect for you." With anyone but one of us, Eric would have gotten angry at any guy who talked about "hitting that" with Melanie. But we had all been friends too long for anything we said to be offensive. Eric took his lead from me.

"I know all about that. In fact, you know what? I'm giving you a free pass. Go nuts."

Chris smiled benevolently. "Oh, you know I wouldn't do that to you, I'm just fucking around."

Eric grinned wickedly. "Come on, I want to see what's left of you after you make a pass at Mel. I'm betting the police wouldn't find enough body parts for anyone to be able to identify you. Even with dental records."

I secretly thought the same thing would happen if Chris made an attempt with Laura and I smiled. I wouldn't normally try to compare Mel and Laura, but they were both tough and I liked that. You wanted to take care of them because you knew they didn't need it. They would never be clingy or desperate. They would never ask you for help with anything. They would never admit that they were wrong. And it was that self sufficiency that drew me in. In Mel, it hadn't been as big of an attraction for me, but it was part of why we were such good friends. And I knew that was part of what had hooked Eric about her and what hooked me about Laura. She could take care of herself. She didn't need anything from anyone. And therefore, I wanted her to need me.

Katie was sort of the damsel in distress type. She would break down over little stuff. If she got a flat tire, she would call me instead of AAA. If we needed a plumber, I had to make the call. Before we lived together, she made me come to her apartment in the middle of the night to kill a bug for her a few times. She had made it worth my time, but it was still something Laura would never have done. Laura would have found a way to toss it out of her house without killing it, and she never would have mentioned it to me. Katie didn't go anywhere alone. Ever. She had to have a posse of friends around her to shop, or go to the bathroom, or even the grocery store. Laura didn't seem to have many friends only because she didn't need anyone. Katie's insecurities drove me insane. She would flip out if I even looked at another girl. Laura would never in a million years do that. Laura was a balm on the irritations of the relationship with Katie. She was independent. I didn't have to save her; it was more like we were keeping each other company while we saved ourselves. Maybe it was more than that, maybe we were helping each other save ourselves. My relationship with Katie was exhausting and all-consuming. With Laura, it was easy. Yes, it was impossible and I wasn't sure that I would ever get her, and I wasn't always sure that I wanted to. But we fit each other. And even if I knew nothing else about how she felt about me, I knew that Laura knew that as well.

Discussing her with my friends, I realized that I definitely did want to bring Laura to the engagement party. Before, I had said I would try because Mel had asked me to, but I hadn't known if I was ready to introduce her to my life. I had been keeping her just as separate from my life as she had been keeping me from hers. I didn't want her with my family at Christmas. I wanted to spend New Year's with her, but just the two of us. I wasn't ready to share her, to expose her to the rest of me yet. She was something holy, something that I was keeping away from reality in order to keep it pure. But she could stand her ground. And even if my friends said anything to throw her off, she could handle it. She wouldn't run, I realized. She would laugh and reply with a witty comeback. True, there was still something in her eyes I couldn't read, some sadness in her that was holding her back from who she wanted to be, but she had gotten through it, hadn't she? She would be fine. And realizing that, I saw that there wasn't anything to be worried about in bringing her to the party.

10

Once I decided that I wanted her there, the only remaining problem with bringing Laura to the engagement party was that I had no idea if she would actually go or not. We hadn't discussed it after she left my place on Friday night. But I knew that if I called to ask about it, she could, and probably would, say no. And I didn't want that. So I called Mel for advice.

She eventually came up with the plan that got Laura to the party. Nothing ever illustrates to me how large the gap is between men and women until I see how easily a woman can manipulate someone. It wound up being ridiculously easy, but I would have never come up with her plan. I gave Laura's cell number to Mel. Mel sent a message through voice mail, without actually calling Laura, so that there was no chance of her answering the call and therefore no chance for her to say no. She said what time I would pick her up and that it was dressy-casual (whatever the fuck that means—Mel just told me to wear khakis and a dress shirt but no tie); she didn't leave a return number and told me not to answer my phone until I picked Laura up. I was positive that Laura would call me, but I hoped that her hatred of leaving messages would win over her desire to avoid coming to the party. But Laura, perhaps understanding the ruse, didn't call. And so I went to pick her up at seven the night of the party.

I had never been invited into Laura's house before. I had picked her up once before, but she had been watching for me that time and came outside as soon as I pulled up. We had only ever hung out at my place.

But when Laura was nervous, as I would later learn, she ran late. I didn't expect to make it up the walk. I even rang the doorbell. And then waited long enough to wonder if she was actually home. Maybe she was out so that she wouldn't have to come to the party. I could see her doing that. It would be the same as her not answering any questions that were too personal. She wouldn't flat out say that she didn't want to answer a question, and she wouldn't flat out say no to the engagement party. But she would probably be willing to non-confrontationally sidestep something that she didn't want to do. My finger was on the bell to ring it a second time when she flung the door open.

I had slept in the same bed as her. I had seen her without makeup on. I had seen her in her underwear. But somehow seeing her in this half-state of readiness was more intimate. It was—well it was cute! She would hate to hear me calling her that, as she subscribed to the school of thought that puppies were cute, not women, but it's what she was when she opened the door. She had one shoe on, the other in her hand, no lipstick on, and she had chunks of her hair wrapped around large Velcro rollers on each side of her head. The hand not holding a shoe had an open beer in it and the match to the one earring she was wearing.

"Hold this for a second, will you?" she asked immediately, thrusting the half-drunk beer at me and putting the earring in, then putting one hand on my shoulder while slipping on her other shoe. She then turned and started walking down the hallway, her heels clacking noisily on the hardwood floor, leaving me standing in the doorway. I shut the door behind me. "I'll just be a minute," she said, hurriedly over her shoulder. She stopped after a couple of steps, came back to me, reached for her beer and took a deep swig. Finally, she seemed to actually see me standing there. "Do you want a beer?"

"Sure," I said, trying not to laugh. She wouldn't like that right now.

She started to walk off again. Then stopped. "Oh," she said turning to look at me, realizing I had never been there before. "Um. Kitchen's downstairs. It's on the right, you can't miss it. Beer's in the fridge. There's hard stuff in the freezer. But yeah. Beer in the fridge. I just need a couple more minutes." She was talking just the slightest bit too fast.

I said okay and headed down the stairs. Fifteen of them, carpeted in a creamy off-white that made me wonder if I should have wiped my feet at the door. I can admit that I was curious. This was huge. I wanted to see what I could learn about her from her home. It was a two-story townhouse, and you entered from the upper level, which was clearly where her bedroom was. The downstairs opened up into a large living room, with, as she said, the kitchen to the right, as well as a hallway under the upstairs hallway that seemed to lead to another room and bathroom.

Looking at the living room, I thought about what Mel had said about Laura and money. First of all, the townhouse was about ten times the size of my moderately-sized apartment. And my place was furnished in Ikea and hand-me-downs from my parents. Not that there's anything wrong with Ikea. It just didn't look like Laura had ever been there. Her house was anything but the typical post-college apartment.

The centerpiece of the room, along the far wall, was clearly the entertainment center. She had a huge, wide-screen plasma TV mounted on the wall, with some serious speakers and an equally serious sound system, complete with a turntable that looked ridiculously out of place with the modern electronics. A closer inspection showed surround sound speakers carefully camouflaged in the room. Two were mounted on the wall, but painted to match it and one was green and hidden in a plant. Set up to be perfectly positioned for the television were two huge black leather sofas, with an expensive-looking glass coffee table in the middle. Several potted plants dotted the room, and a few prints from artists I didn't recognize decorated the walls. I thought of the single framed poster that I had hanging in my entire apartment, which only had a frame because my mother had come over with it, put it in the frame, picked out a spot for it, and made me hang it while she stood there. An impressive record, CD, and DVD collection lined nearly all of one wall.

I didn't really think anything of it until later, but something was missing that I had seen in all other girls' rooms and apartments. There were no pictures of Laura with friends or family. Mel's apartment was littered with photos of her with everyone she had ever cared about. You couldn't turn around without seeing a picture of her on vacation, or at a graduation, or a party, or the beach, or a bar. The only common element was the huge smile on Mel's face and her arms thrown around whoever else was in the picture with her.

I started over to the music and movie collection when I heard a large thump from above me and Laura's voice uttering a mild profanity drifted down. I jumped as if I had just been caught snooping, although I hadn't really gotten a chance to yet, and I figured I had better just get a beer and head back up.

The kitchen was remarkable too though. Chrome, light wood, and deep gray granite, with a real ceramic-tiled floor. No linoleum or Home Depot cabinets for Laura. And unlike the mess in her car, it was spotless and looked too pretty for cooking. Not even a rogue refrigerator magnet or pot holder broke the unblemished surfaces.

Maybe Laura thought the kitchen was too pretty for cooking too, because there wasn't anything in the massive chrome refrigerator that could be cooked. Lots of beer, a couple bottles of wine, Diet Coke, yogurt, cottage cheese, apples, carrot sticks, lime juice, and olives. It certainly explained why she was so thin, if this is what she lived off of. No eggs, milk, or butter even. And I would bet that the lime juice was for margaritas and the olives for martinis. I took a bottle of beer and peeked quickly into the freezer. At least she was human. Along with all of the alcohol bottles, she had the requisite pint of Ben and Jerry's ice cream that all women keep for emergencies. Chubby Hubby. Unopened. But there.

I heard another thud above me and, as desperately as I wanted to poke around, I knew I should go back upstairs. I wanted a chance to see her bedroom anyway.

I followed the light coming out of a room off the upstairs hallway. It was a very grown-up looking house, so far, I realized. But it was impersonal. I had really thought that her house would just scream of her. She seemed like that type. But it was decorated like she was trying to hide any traces of herself. Or like she'd hired someone to decorate everything as neutrally as possible, which was more likely. Everything was black and white and chrome. It felt—well—sterile. I couldn't picture her sprawling on that sofa and watching TV or painting her toenails. The idea of her baking cookies or even making toast in that kitchen just didn't seem to work.

Seeing her room was a relief. This was more Laura. It was well-lit, with yellow-painted walls. Her bed was queen-sized with a black wrought-iron frame. A black and white comforter was accented with red pillows and red sheets. One of the walls was decorated with framed Bruce albums arranged in a rectangle three albums high by five wide. A massive mirror hung over her dresser, where Laura stood, applying her lipstick. She had fresh flowers in several different vases throughout the room. There was a TV in here too, also a flat screen, also mounted on the wall, but smaller than the monstrosity downstairs, and a stereo, complete with turntable, up here as well. A walk-in closet and a bathroom opened up off one wall. Large framed black-and-white pictures adorned the walls in here, and I wondered if she had taken them. The light scent of her perfume filled the room. There were unlit candles littered around the room, and she had two empty beer bottles on the dresser next to her, as well as the one she was drinking out of. *Three already?* I thought.

She looked at me in the mirror without turning around and smiled slightly as she dug through a jewelry box, eventually pulling out a silver necklace. A picture on her nightstand, leaning next to a steep pile of paperback novels, caught my eye, as it was the only thing resembling a personal picture in her whole apartment. It was of a young child, about five or six, and it had to be her. Her face was the same. She was lying on a wall in front of the Eiffel Tower, vamping with an innocent smile, as only a child can, in front of the camera, while an adult couple, their faces turned away from the camera, gazed toward the tower itself. I wondered briefly if they could be her parents. But if so, why were they standing away from her instead of posing in a family picture?

Laura must have seen me looking, and, although I didn't see her face, I knew what expression crossed it. First, that slightest look of annoyance, like the first night we met, when she caught me examining the contents of her glove compartment. Then she would hide that quickly and set her face in an appealing smile, which was all I saw when she swayed over to me. She turned her back and raised her arms around her neck, holding the ends of her necklace out to me. "Would you?" she asked.

She lifted her hair and offered her neck to me and I hooked the clasp, loving that she had asked, knowing full well that this was a girl who knew how to fasten her own necklace. But Laura was an expert at changing a subject, even before a disagreeable topic was raised. And she knew that asking for help with something like that would distract me enough to keep me from asking a question she didn't want to answer. And of course, it did.

Laura never looked more at ease to the outside world than when she was secretly incredibly nervous. She didn't fidget. She didn't talk too fast. Every move was perfectly graceful and elegant.

Which is exactly how I later figured out that she was, in fact, nervous about going to the party in the first place. Even in the car, there was none of the rapid-fire chatter that occurred when she was excited or happy. Her hands rested perfectly still in her lap. She didn't play with her hair, or smooth her dress, or constantly cross and re-cross her legs. I had noticed, of course, that Laura was always in a state of constant motion, but I hadn't realized just how much she was usually moving until she no longer was. But of course, she had already had three drinks to get her going. We always drank a lot together, so I didn't think too much of it. But later, I realized it took that much alcohol to get her to be comfortable that night. To be able to be as charming as she was.

I'd be lying if I said that she nervous because she was starting to fall for me. She had her own reasons for being uncomfortable going into a party where she would be an outsider among a tight-knit group of friends. I was hopeful at the time though. Liking me was the only reason that I could come up with for her being nervous, and it was certainly the only reason I could come up with for her actually making the effort to go to a party that she was nervous about going to. Later I would know better, because Laura seldom does anything to please other people. She had her own reasons for forcing herself to go. And her own reasons for making sure she was the most charming person there. And she succeeded.

She took my arm as we approached the restaurant that Mel's parents were hosting the party at, as if it were the most natural thing in the world for us to be walking in as a couple. Until she did that, I hadn't been concerned about anyone raising questions about our relationship, because clearly Melanie would have prepared people for it. But with her holding my arm, what else could people assume? But she smiled at me. And I couldn't worry when Laura smiled.

Once we walked in, I felt her hand tense slightly as she took a really good look around. Not at the room, but at the people. She didn't know a soul other than me and Mel, and apparently that was what she had hoped for because her grip loosened and she smiled more easily. I loved watching the reactions of people whom I had known for years when they saw me walk in with her. She was easily the most beautiful woman in the room. The looks on my friends' faces told me that they were impressed. But the response from the girls was better. Laura was clearly a formidable opponent to them. Most of the girls started self-consciously adjusting their hair or clothes when they saw her. It was as if as soon as they saw her, they realized they were in a shadow. I don't know if Laura picked up on that. I mean, I have a theory that all girls do know when they have that effect. Like Marlon Brando's character said in that movie. You know, the one that you watch in high school when he yells "Stella" as loud as he can. He says he's never met a woman who didn't know that she was good looking without being told. Girls notice everything else about other girls, so they have to notice when they're making them jealous.

For the most part, she stayed by my side. And miraculously, no one asked how long we had been together or anything else that would require awkward explanations. I reminded myself to thank Mel for that one later. But Laura was at the most charming that I had ever seen her, and she enchanted everyone who talked to her.

At one point, Mel dragged me off to say hi to her parents, and Laura wound up in a conversation with a couple of my college friends. I looked at her apologetically, but she was fine. I was close enough to hear most of their conversation; she laughed at their jokes, and I could see that she had instantly won them over. Unfortunately, these two friends had girlfriends. And the girlfriends were Mel's sorority sisters. Not the nice ones. I saw trouble coming as soon as they looked across the room and saw their men talking to Laura. Emily nudged Carolyn, whose eyebrows came together quickly, and the two of them went immediately to Jason and Steve's sides.

Carolyn asked Laura if she had come with me. Laura said yes. Then Emily asked how long we had been seeing each other. I held my breath. But there was no way to go rescue her without being fairly rude to Mel's parents.

Laura, however, didn't need rescuing, and she didn't hesitate in her reply. She said "not *too* long," with a smile, and tried to steer the conversation back to where it had been before the girlfriends attacked.

"Well it *couldn't* have been *too* long," Carolyn said with a truly vicious smile.

"No, of course not," Emily joined in. "Because he just broke up with Katie."

"And you know how these rebound relationships work," Carolyn said quickly.

"Not that we're saying you're a rebound girl, of course!" Emily added, feigning sympathy. "But you know how guys are with this stuff. And they were living together after all."

"Yeah, it was really serious. We just want to make sure that you're being careful."

"We would hate to see you get hurt because he's on the rebound."

Laura took a sip of her wine and smiled a slow, sexy smile that I hadn't seen before. Then, in a lower voice that I had to strain to hear, she said, "Oh, I know all about that," although she didn't even know that Katie existed. "But I'm really just with him because the sex is *so* incredible. I absolutely can't keep my hands off him." She finished her wine and winked at Jason and Steve over the glass as they gaped at her. "So if you'll excuse me," she said and walked toward me, setting her empty glass down on a table. Then she crossed behind me and came around to my right side, leaving her left hand behind me, where she rested it on my ass, as Jason, Steve, Carolyn, and Emily all watched. And without missing a beat or moving her left hand, she extended her right hand to Mel's mom, saying, "You *must* be Melanie's mother, she looks just like you!" They introduced themselves and Laura gushed, both about Mel and the party, while Carolyn and Emily dragged their boyfriends away in a huff.

When Mrs. Hawkins excused herself to go talk to her sister and Melanie's father went to get another drink, I finally had Laura to myself for a minute. "That was awesome," I whispered. She shrugged but kept smiling.

"I couldn't help it. Sorry I had to molest you a little there in the process."

I put an arm around her. "You can molest me any time you want to."

Laura laughed. "I'll keep that in mind."

It hits you very suddenly when you're falling for someone. I don't believe in love at first sight. It's a process. I know that. But it still creeps up on you and feels sudden. I knew I was interested before. But standing there with her at that party, I realized it had happened and was a done deal. This was the girl for me.

Of course, I wasn't about to tell her how I felt. Jesus, I hadn't even kissed her! Realizing it and wanting to tell the person are usually two completely separate moments. And after the drive home that night, I wasn't sure that I would ever have the chance to tell her, nor that I necessarily wanted that chance.

Trying to keep track of how many drinks Laura has at an open bar function is a lost cause. Especially because she has to be wasted before she even seems the littlest bit drunk. And I mean wasted. It's easy to calculate at my place, because I can just subtract how many drinks I had from how many we drank total. But otherwise, it's hard to tell sometimes if it's really her talking or if it could be the alcohol. Sometimes I think that she pours out half of her drinks, then just says stuff that she knows will mess with my head. That's one of the things about her that I still haven't figured out completely.

She was radiant that night as we left the party. She leaned into me slightly as we waited for the valet to bring my car out, pretending that she was cold. And it *was* cold out. But that wasn't what she was doing. And I knew that, although I think that she thought that I bought the cold explanation. I like to think I saw through her more often than she thought I did. If that makes any sense.

I opened the door for her and she beamed up at me as I shut it. My pulse quickened slightly. I didn't want to let myself hope, but I thought, *maybe tonight.* Maybe what? Who knows? But maybe.

We talked about the party for a little while. Then Laura took the conversation where she wanted it to go. And horrified me.

"So," she began, innocuously enough. "How long do you think Mel and Eric are going to last?"

"What?"

"Well 'till death do us part' is just so passé! What do you think their real expiration date looks like? A year? Two? Ten?"

"Are you seriously asking this?"

Laura smiled innocently. "Of course. Don't tell me you believe they'll last forever."

I started to get angry. Which was, of course, her goal. "Of course I believe that!" But did I? Did I really believe someone my age could make something that would last *forever*? Forever. That's a scary word.

She laughed at me. Not with me. That's not her style. She laughed at me. "That's so *sweet*," she said, still laughing. "No, really, it is! But come on. No one stays married anymore."

I didn't think it was funny. "My parents are still married. Mel's parents are still married. Even my grandparents are still married."

"That's different," she said, waving her hand in the air. "When they got married, you had to stay married. It's just not done now!"

"I think you're wrong," I said as coldly as I could, completely forgetting my earlier realization. "They're in love."

Laura started to laugh again.

"What?" I asked. "What's so funny about that?"

"Well the whole idea of 'in love,' for one thing!"

"What's wrong with love?" Who the hell *was* this girl?

Laura smiled sweetly. "Nothing's wrong with being *in love*. It's a pretty idea. Like heaven. And Santa Claus. And the tooth fairy. But it's not *real*. It doesn't exist."

"How can you say that?"

"Oh I don't mean that *love* doesn't exist *at all*. Mothers love their babies, kids love puppies, I love my hair stylist, et cetera. It's that whole *true* love thing that I don't believe in. There's no one person you're meant to be with. It's bullshit."

"That's the stupidest thing I've ever heard." Laura raised an eyebrow. "I mean, how do you explain all these people falling in love and getting married then?"

"Easy," she said. "We tell ourselves that we're in love because we're terrified of being alone. That's people's biggest fear. It's not the dark, or flying, or public speaking. It's being alone and not having anyone to carry on our memory. So we find someone who we think we can tolerate for as long as possible and we decide that we're in love."

I didn't know what to say. I was flabbergasted. Did she really believe that? Could she? Finally, for lack of anything else to say, I told her, "That's the saddest thing I've ever heard."

Laura shook her head. "It's not sad, it's pragmatic."

"You'll never get married then?" Laura didn't say anything for a little while.

"No," she said finally. "I'm not saying that I guess. I'm just going to see it for what it really is and not try to sugar coat it."

"Maybe you've just never been in love."

She shrugged. "Have you? Really?"

I started to say "yes, of course." But I couldn't quite say the words. Laura looked at me. Why couldn't I say it? I felt dirty all of a sudden. Earlier that night, I had first thought that maybe I loved Laura. No, there was no maybe when I thought it earlier. And what about Katie? Clearly I had at least thought that I loved her. But I still couldn't say that I had ever really been in love.

"What about Bruce?" I asked eventually, needing to break the silence, change the subject, get her to talk about something that I knew she was passionate about. That she felt a real emotion about.

"What about him?"

"Don't you love him?"

"That's different, silly," Laura laughed, but there was no malice this time. "Bruce is the exception to the rule."

I couldn't sleep that night. Did she mean it? Or had she been trying to get a reaction out of me? Could she mean it? Why couldn't I say that yes, I had been in love? Because I had. Hadn't I? But if I had, wouldn't I be able to say it? Was I scared of being alone? Was she? And what about what I had realized earlier? If I loved her, shouldn't I have been able to say that I'd been in love? Could she be right?

I didn't talk to her for a week. Didn't want to. No, I'm lying. I wanted to. But it was such an innate desire, like wanting to breathe or sleep or eat, that I could want to talk to her and *not* want to talk to her all at the same time. The one thing that I did know, however, was that I needed to get her out of my system a little before I could talk to her again. Because how can you be in love with someone who doesn't believe that love exists?

11

Of course, Laura didn't call me for a week either. I told myself that it was really my choice to not talk to her for a little while, but it would have been easier to believe if I had been able to not return one of her calls. So even though I didn't want to be the one to call her first, I knew full well that I would have to. I had no idea if I would ever see her again otherwise. Because while I knew she liked having me around to go to concerts with, I also knew that she would have no problem going to them alone again, if it came to that.

I thought about it on Friday. My cell phone practically taunted me from my desk. I signed onto AOL Instant Messenger too, because maybe she would be online. I could IM her instead of calling her. That wasn't quite as much of a capitulation. Right?

But no luck. She wasn't on IM. I would have to call. Fine. I could do that. Right now in fact. I opened my phone.

Just need to push that send button.

Any second now.

Just one little button.

Maybe I should wait awhile.

I mean, what was I going to say? Okay, to be fair, I was probably just going to see if she wanted to do our usual. Listen to bootlegs and drink beer until we fell asleep in my living room. Why was this so hard?

I didn't call.

I met Mel, Eric, and Chris for happy hour in Bethesda after work. I was the last to arrive, and Mel had a beer waiting for me by the time I got to their table. Chris and Eric were on their second, while Mel was nursing her first. I downed that first beer quickly to catch up and ordered a half-price burger.

"Your girl," Eric said, nodding at me. "Hot." Mel gave him a sharp look, which he ignored. I shrugged.

"Seriously hot," Chris added. "Are you fucking her yet?"

"That is ridiculously sexist," Mel protested.

"This from the girl who says feminism is for ugly chicks," Chris retorted.

"I'm a girl, I'm allowed to say that."

"And that's not a double standard?"

"No," Mel said, smiling.

"Fine." Chris turned back to me. "Have you two begun the process of participating in consensual sexual intercourse with each other yet?" I laughed. Until it became clear that all three of them were expecting an actual answer.

"Um..." I said, trying to come up with a way to say no that wouldn't sound totally lame.

"She told Carolyn and Emily that you were," Mel added, ever so helpfully.

"I know," I said finally. "But we're not. Carolyn and Emily were being bitches and that was her way of fending them off."

"That's the saddest thing I've ever heard," Eric said, holding up his beer and four fingers to the waitress to signal that it was time for another round.

"How long have you guys been hanging out again?"

I thought for a second. "A month and a half."

"That's not that bad," Mel said.

"You're in the friend zone," Chris said, shaking his head. "It's not going to happen at this point."

"That's not necessarily true," Eric said. "Mel and I were friends for like a year before we hooked up."

"That was different," Chris argued. "You were part of a group. They're just hanging out on their own and nothing is happening. They've stayed in hotels together and nothing has happened. They've gotten trashed alone together and nothing has happened. If you're in a room together drunk and nothing is happening, it's not going to happen." He turned to me. "Sorry man, fact of life."

"Eric and I drank together before anything happened," Mel said. "And now we're getting married!" Eric smiled at her and Chris rolled his eyes at me.

"Um, Mel," I said, knowing I was hurting my own case. "You were dating me before you started dating Eric. That's why nothing happened. He wasn't going to make a move on someone I had dated."

Mel looked a little sheepish. "Oh yeah. I kinda forgot about that."

"Thanks."

She laughed. "Whatever, I still think there's hope here. We're not in college anymore. There are different rules now." She looked at me. "And she likes you. She wouldn't have bothered with Carolyn and Emily if she didn't." I shrugged. I didn't really know. And I didn't want to get my hopes up. If I didn't talk to her soon, it definitely wasn't happening. "When are you seeing her next?"

I shrugged again. "I'm not sure."

"When did you talk to her last?"

"When I dropped her off after the party."

"Are you going to call her?"

"I don't know, Mel."

Mel shook her head. "You're such a dumbass. Just call her. She likes you." I gave her a skeptical look. "Do it," she said firmly.

I said I would. I trusted Mel's judgment. She had never steered me wrong when it came to girl advice. But I wasn't quite ready to call. Even with the happy hour beers in me.

Chris said that Joe and some of the other guys were heading downtown that night to hit some of the bars around Dupont Circle, so I went home to take a nap before meeting up with them. I woke up to the sound of someone knocking at my door. It was a little after eight pm. I had set an alarm clock for nine. My room was dark and pulling myself out of bed wasn't easy. I wished I had left a light on. I wouldn't have napped as well, but it's almost impossible to wake up from a nap at night once it's totally dark in the room.

I felt like death as I dragged myself to the door. What made me think that napping after happy hour was a good idea? I always felt worse than I had before. And who the hell was at my door? Did I misunderstand? Were the guys meeting me at my place? If so, this was awfully early to go out.

But it was Laura. She had never showed up unannounced before. And it was kind of a strange move considering that we hadn't talked in about a week and I was clearly annoyed at her the last time we saw each other.

She laughed when she saw me. "You look like hell," she said. "Did you forget how to shave?"

We were still standing in the doorway. I wasn't quite awake enough to both process an insult and be polite enough to invite her in. I wished I had taken a shower instead of a nap. "I was waiting until later."

Laura smiled and rubbed my scruffy cheek. "But you didn't know I was coming over," she said as innocently as possible and I smiled. I couldn't help myself.

She held up a six-pack of beer. "Are you going to let me in or are we going to stand in the doorway all night?" It was just about as close as Laura would ever come to apologizing in all the time I knew her. When she realized that she had stepped the littlest bit too far over a line, she would give me time to cool down and then just show up. She wasn't one of those girls who spent hours on the phone; she only called when she needed to tell me something and was off the phone within about two minutes every time she called. But she knew better than to wait for me to call her after a disagreement. And she didn't want me to call her. She wanted to just pretend that nothing unpleasant had happened. And after not seeing her for a little while, that was exactly what I wanted too.

That night began a pattern for us that would last for the better part of a year. Almost every weekend when we didn't have a concert, Laura would show up at my door with beer and her latest bootleg acquisition. I teased her that she was in the "Bootleg-of-the-Month Club," but it was more like bootleg of the day. She seemed to have amassed thousands of them. She found shows from different years of whatever the current date was and sometimes we would go through two in one night. If we stopped after one, we listened to other classic rock albums, on vinyl when we had them, settling for CDs when we didn't.

It meant I almost never went out with my friends on the weekends anymore, but I didn't miss that. I saw them for dinner pretty frequently during the week. Chris, Eric, and Joe all went to my gym and I often went there with them after work. Mel and I met for lunches and happy hours. They still called me to go out during the first couple months, but after awhile, they knew that I was going to say that I was seeing Laura and they eventually stopped asking. I tried to make sure that I went out with them at least once every few weeks, but the times between those nights gradually stretched into months. And they were slowing down in going to the bars during that period anyway. Mel and Eric were planning their wedding and trying to save money, and both Chris and Joe started dating girls that spring, although both relationships had ended by early summer, so I doubt my absence was felt that strongly.

Every few weeks, I would realize that I wasn't getting anywhere with her. Or decide that I didn't want to. Sometimes, I actually believed that we were strictly just friends. Other times, I realized that my feelings for her weren't healthy when they weren't being returned and I would try to get past the idea of ever having a romantic relationship with her. So I went out with other girls. But they all paled in comparison. It wasn't even that I found anything wrong with them. I just couldn't justify sustaining a relationship with anyone who couldn't hold my interest the way that Laura did.

I hadn't learned how to say no to Laura, and I didn't yet want to. I loved that she would show up just before the time when Bruce would have gone onstage if we were at a show. I loved spending that time with her. I loved discussing the music. I loved how she understood me, and how, even though she didn't share that much, I understood her. And most of all, I loved her.

After I left Katie, I did some of the typical, post-breakup hooking up. And two of the girls who I met during that period were willing to stick around as "friends with benefits." No strings attached. I didn't want anything more from them and I was clear about that up front. And as far as I knew, they didn't want more from me either. Maybe they were in a similar situation, wanting someone they couldn't have. Maybe they hoped I would become interested if they fooled around with me often enough. But when either seemed to be getting too attached, I stopped calling for awhile. They got the message. I didn't talk to Mel about them, because I knew she wouldn't approve. But it's not the same for girls. Yes, in a sense I was using them because they took the edge off of the Laura situation. But they knew what they were getting into. And they still weren't saying no.

Besides, Laura and I didn't talk that often during the week. The odd Bruce-related email or IM here and there. But our relationship was based on our face time, be it in a concert audience, Laura's car traveling to a show, or in my living room listening to a show from before we were born. Maybe that was for the best, because it meant we didn't get tired of each other. I was always left wanting more, and I think she was too, even though I always felt that it was her who was keeping the distance between us. But maybe she did that on purpose. Because it meant she could also always be left wanting more.

12

February 28, 2003.

At the end of December, when the first leg of the *Rising* tour ended, it felt like the end of February would never come. It sounded like the longest period of time imaginable. Two full months without any concerts. And in December, I didn't believe that it was possible that Laura and I would still be talking by February. What would we do for two months without our Bruce fixes?

Well, we solved that with the bootlegs, and we finally survived to the next leg. Bruce was only playing a handful of shows before going to Europe, but everyone at the shows and on the message boards, both on Bruce's official website, and the much better one we had found, www.Backstreets.com, said that a stadium tour was in the works for the summer. So we knew Europe would not be the end. We bought tickets for five shows within a span of a week and a half. My first thought when my alarm went off in the morning wasn't wondering how many days were left until the weekend, like it had been since high school, but instead I woke up asking myself how many days were left until the twenty-eighth.

We drove to Georgia for that first show, skipped the shows in Texas and Florida, headed to Richmond on March 6, then drove straight from there to Atlantic City for the show the next day. We went back home for March 8 and 9, then up to Rhode Island on March 10, and from there to Rochester for the March 11 show. I worked fourteen-hour days on both March 8 and 9 to make up for the work that I had to miss when we went to the shows. But it was worth every second of it.

I didn't know what to expect. From me and Laura, that is. I knew that Bruce, of course, would be superb. And he delivered. But I didn't know if the novelty of a road trip would have worn off now that we had spent so much more time together. She had stayed over with me in my bed. No, nothing happened, but still. My bed was more intimate than a hotel room bed. And nothing had happened. Would being together on the road have the same adrenaline rush that our concert-going had when we'd first met the previous fall?

It was better.

We had more to talk about now. I wasn't nervous around her. We knew what to say to make each other laugh, and we had jokes that only the two of us understood. We were actually friends by then, whereas in December, we were strangers. And we got to feel like we were doing something impetuous and crazy because we were still following Bruce all over the east coast. True, for Laura, it probably wasn't that extreme, as she didn't have a job to take off from, and I got the feeling this kind of behavior wouldn't be all that out of the ordinary for her. But it was for me. Five shows in twelve days. It was like I had been in a daze for the first twenty-five years of my life. But this? This was being alive. And I loved every second of it.

Two stints of two shows in a row also gave us more of a feel for our day-to-day routines. Laura certainly wasn't lying about being an insomniac. I always fell asleep before she did, and she was always awake before I was. I started to wonder if she ever actually slept. There were a lot of little endearing things that I wouldn't have guessed about her. When I would turn on the television and flip through the channels looking for the news or SportsCenter, Laura perked up at random things. She loved *The Simpsons*, but didn't look up once when *Friends* was on. *Sex and the City* was apparently worth watching, but she would tell me to shut off the TV when I had the news on. And she loved any ancient history stuff on the Discovery Channel. If I mentioned it, she would immediately feign disinterest. But she paid attention when I paused on those channels. Once I noticed that, I started leaving them on for longer and longer. If it was American history, she couldn't care less. But anything with mummies and pyramids or shipwrecks or any religious symbolism and she was absolutely riveted. She never asked me to change the channel back if I switched away from it, but she would look up from whatever she was doing when those shows were on. It was nerdy but cute.

She read before she tried to go to sleep, no matter how late it was. Always paperbacks, which she positively devoured, dog-earring the pages to mark her place. She read quickly and had widely-varied taste as well. One day it was a book of short stories by Raymond Carver, another day Jane Austen's *Emma*, then the third Harry Potter book, then *Sister Carrie* by Theodore Dreiser, then *Bridget Jones' Diary*. Heavy duty literary stuff, mixed with pop culture. Which, in essence, was Laura as well.

When I woke up in Atlantic City the morning of that show, Laura wasn't in the room. We had driven up the night before in order to get onto the pit list and we figured it was better to kill a day in AC than Richmond anyway. The women had big hair and tapered-leg jeans and the men had mullets in both cities, but at least in Atlantic City, there was gambling.

Her stuff was all still in the room, so I figured she couldn't have gone far. I debated calling her, but decided to take a shower and get dressed first. Maybe she had gone to a casino. And if I was dressed, at least I could meet up with her and it wouldn't look like I had needed to call her the second that I woke up.

When I got out of the shower, I heard her moving around the room and was relieved. But I took my time. I shaved and brushed my teeth and pulled on boxers and my jeans. Then I headed out into the hotel room.

She was sprawled on the chair in the room, completely engrossed in Edith Wharton's *The Custom of the Country*. She had on sleek Adidas running pants, a fleece sweatshirt, and a pair of Nike Shox. Every part of her outfit matched: dark grey and black with red trim. A thick headband lay on the table next to her, with a pair of thin fleece gloves and her MP3 player. Her hair was pulled back into a ponytail, and her nose and ears were slightly red from the cold. She didn't seem to notice that I was standing there for a minute, then she marked her page, set the book down, and looked up at me. I raised my eyebrows at her in an unspoken question, but she didn't say anything.

I shrugged, pulled a shirt out of my bag, and put it on. "Are you done in there?" she asked. I nodded. "Good," she said. "I'm dying for a shower."

"Where'd you run?" I asked. I had no idea she was a runner. I mean, I figured she had to work out to maintain a body like that considering how heavily we drank, but she never talked about it. Plus, I wasn't sure she actually ate when she wasn't around me because of how skinny she was and how little food I had seen in her fridge. Then again, she didn't talk about the books she read either. Her hobbies, other than Bruce, just didn't manage to come up in conversation.

"Along the boardwalk," she said cheerfully, as she untied her shoes and peeled off her socks.

"How cold is it out today?"

"I don't know," Laura said. "Not too bad. I mean, it's cold, but once I get going I don't really feel it."

"Do you run a lot?"

She shrugged. "I didn't do that much today. Probably about five miles."

"Wow."

She didn't say anything, but stood up and pulled off her sweatshirt and the Under Armour top that she had on underneath it, leaving just a black sports bra along with her matching pants. I looked away when she turned to look at me, but it had to be pretty clear that I had been watching her take her shirt off.

"I'm going to take a shower, but then let's go get some breakfast before we head over to the line," she said, pulling her hair out of its ponytail. "I'm starving today."

This was pretty usual for Laura I soon realized. She ran almost every day from what I could tell. I brought sneakers and running gear with me when we went to Rhode Island, and I asked her before we went to sleep if she was going to run in the morning. She said she didn't know, so I told her that I would go with her if she woke me up. But she didn't wake me before she went, and I didn't mention it again. It was just as well. I figured that I should do some running on my own before I was ready to go running with her. I didn't want her to see me all out of breath.

13

There seems to be some unwritten law of dating that states that when you really don't want to look like an asshole in front of a new girl, a girl who you didn't treat that well in the past will show up and make you look like an asshole. If you've only ever been a jerk to one girl, well then that girl is going to pop up every single time you're dating someone whom you want to impress. And if the girl you're trying to impress has trust issues, which I (well, Mel) decided that Laura had, that encounter is going to be particularly ugly.

In other words, I really should have known that I was going to run into Katie at some point when I was with Laura. I should have known it had to happen. But I didn't. I kind of figured that the drunk phone call when I was in Indianapolis would be the end of it. It didn't occur to me even after Melanie's sorority sisters brought her up to Laura at the engagement party. Katie just was not in the sphere of my thoughts anymore. And I couldn't have imagined a situation in which the two of them would ever meet because they lived in completely different worlds. Katie wasn't likely to show up at my apartment or at a Springsteen show, and in those days Laura and I didn't go many other places. Running into her just never crossed my mind as even the slightest possibility.

The E Street Band did a quick trip to Australia, went out west, and spent all of May and June in Europe after that run in early spring, leaving us with an ocean of time between the handful of March shows and the beginning of the Giants Stadium stand in the middle of July. So we did what we could, and held setlist concerts in my living room.

We couldn't do them in real time, of course, due to the time differences, but we started them at real time for us. Using the websites, we saw what time Bruce came on locally and would start our show accordingly. It gave us time to find the rarities and make sure we had every song he played. For the couple of shows in California and western Canada, where we could do it in real time, I wired my laptop through my stereo so that we could work with my MP3 collection and didn't have to dig through CDs. Laura loved the inventiveness of that, and I loved that I had managed to impress her with something so hopelessly geeky. I got to feel like I had impressed her so rarely that I reveled in the moments when I knew that I had.

We took turns reading the comments off the message boards of what Bruce said during the shows. And we drank. A lot. On our lighter nights, Laura would drive herself home around two or three in the morning. Most nights, she stayed with me.

I still couldn't explain her though.

When I first met her, I thought she was crazy. But she wasn't noticeably crazier than any other girls I knew, and in fact, she was much more sane than most. My next theory was that she was incredibly trusting. That definitely wasn't it. Maybe she was just didn't care what happened to her or what she did. Except she clearly *did* care. I'm not sure I'll ever know what it was that drew her to me in the first place, but we were connected now. And I loved that she was unlike anyone else I'd ever known. I had started to feel like everyone else I knew was cut from the same mold. Laura couldn't have fit that mold if she tried, which loaned my life a feeling of freshness that I hadn't realized was lacking until I met her.

I think I had kind of accepted that it was probably too late for anything romantic to happen, despite how I felt about her. I knew that I was stuck in the friend zone. I didn't give up hope exactly, because there was something about her that kept me from doing that. I knew that we were more than friends because I had a connection with her that I'd never felt with anyone. Not even Mel. It was like we were together in every way but sex. Which, yes, is the most important way to determine if you're together. Everyone who knew about us thought I was crazy because I was sticking around without anything happening, but I was willing to wait it out a bit longer. It was okay, somehow, no matter what. Even if nothing ever came of it. Even if friends was all we could ever be. As long as I was with her, it was still okay.

We had slipped into a comfortable place together. To not be together as much as we were would have been unnatural by then. For both of us.

I didn't realize I was out of beer the night that it happened. I always made sure that I had an extra case on hand. And she almost always brought at least one six pack with her, if not more. But she didn't that night. And when Laura went to my fridge to grab a drink, she called to me from the kitchen and I went in to see what she needed.

"You've only got three cold beers. Where's the next case? We should stick it in the fridge now." I went to my pantry to get a few and pulled out an empty box. *Idiot,* I thought to myself. I should have checked. But I was sure that I'd had more. Did we really drink *that* much last weekend? Apparently we did.

I looked at the clock on the microwave. It was only seven-thirty. I checked the freezer. A third of a bottle of tequila and an almost empty bottle of Jagermeister. About two shots worth of the Jager. Not great supplies, but the tequila would probably be enough to do the job. I held up the bottle of Cuervo toward Laura. "We've got this." Laura made a face. "Well it's still early," I said. "We've got time to go get some beer." She was already zipping up her jacket by the time I finished my sentence.

It was really one of those situations when the fates just align against you, because I always went to the same beer and wine store that I had been going to for years. No particular reason. It wasn't cheaper, and it wasn't closer.

It's like a local supermarket. You go to the one you like. There was a beer store that was a little closer to my apartment, but it smelled like the Vietnamese restaurant next door to it. So when Laura asked where the closest store was, I directed her to my favorite.

Laura shot me a worried look as we pulled into the parking lot.

"You okay?" I asked.

She put the car in park but left the engine running and turned to face me. "I think we need to talk," she said. *She's got a boyfriend*, I thought immediately, although I knew that was crazy. Unless he wasn't local. It could be long distance. Maybe it wasn't that bad. Maybe she was way younger than I thought, and she wasn't legal yet so I had to go buy the beer. Not that I believed that was it for a second. Oh God. This was going to be bad.

"What's up?" Okay, that was good. I didn't sound too worried. Very nonchalant.

"You know I really care about you," she began. "Which is why I have to tell you this." I held my breath.

"I think we have a drinking problem." I looked at her for a second, while that sank in. Then we both started laughing.

"Yeah, we definitely have a drinking problem," I said. "We've got nothing at home to drink!" Laura kept laughing and shut off the car.

"I totally had you scared," she said as she climbed out of the car. I followed her.

"Oh, whatever," I said, but I was still laughing.

"Come on, what did you think I was going to say?"

"That you were out of cash and I had to buy the beer."

She rolled her eyes at me playfully as I held the store's door open for her. "Bullshit. You should have seen the look on your face."

"You're right," I said. "I thought you were going to tell me you were on the run from the law and you were secretly only fifteen and not old enough to buy the beer." The two guys working the cash register looked up as I said this, and they both glared at us. "We're just kidding around," I said to them. "We're both legal." This started Laura laughing again, which made me start laughing again. They eyed us warily, which I knew meant that both of our IDs would be carefully scrutinized for about an hour when we went to pay. For some reason, people who sell booze have very little sense of humor about that kind of thing.

Laura followed me back to the store's refrigerator case. "They don't trust us," she stage whispered, indicating the clerks who were still watching us. "Think we should steal something?"

"I'm not bailing you out of jail," I said.

"You so would."

"So wouldn't."

She pouted. "Jerk. You really wouldn't bail me out of jail?"

"No," I said. "I'd miss the start time."

She smiled. "Good call. I wouldn't bail you out right before a setlist watch either." I put my arm around her shoulder.

"And that, *mon ami*, is why we have such a truly special relationship," I said, using the French specifically to piss her off because it was one of her self-declared top five pet peeves. "We understand each other."

She looked at me with a fake scowl. "You're such an ass."

"And you're a bitch. Therefore, it all works out in the end."

She laughed. "You're right. Let's go get drunk." I smiled and pulled two cases of cold Miller Lite out of the refrigerator. I turned toward the checkout counter and ran smack into Katie as she rounded the corner of the aisle. If it had been Laura, I would have seen her over the row, but Katie was only five-foot-two and didn't clear the top. And to make matters worse, I dropped one of the cases. It didn't break, miraculously, but made enough noise to wake the dead.

"Oh," she said, her face turning completely white. I reached down to pick up the case of beer, and Laura came to stand next to me.

"Smooth move," she said, then looped her hand through my arm in a playful gesture, misinterpreting what she was seeing. Then I guess she noticed the awkward silence between me and Katie and, still holding onto me with her left hand, she held out her right to shake Katie's. "I'm Laura," she said.

I cringed. Laura had to pick this moment to be sociable with people who she thought were my friends? Katie didn't say anything, and she didn't shake Laura's hand. She just stared at us. Laura raised her eyebrows and lowered her hand, but kept her grip on me. She might have misjudged the situation at first, but she certainly wasn't going to back down. Not Laura.

It had been about seven months since I moved out. But somehow it was the first time we had seen each other. I was sure that Katie would be okay by then. I mean, it was seven months later. I had to believe she was. But the first time running into the person who dumped you, especially if it had been out of the blue like it was for her, is rough.

"This is Katie," I said finally, as if that would explain everything. It was vague. I couldn't remember if Mel's friends had said her name to Laura at the engagement party or not. And the odds of her remembering that were slim. But I hoped it would work because not explaining who she was would make it seem to Katie like I already had. Then she could feel like she was important enough to have been discussed already. But Katie still didn't say anything. She was dressed up, and I wondered for a second if maybe she had a date tonight, and that could be why she was buying the bottle of wine that was in her hand.

I didn't know what to say or do. I desperately did *not* want a Katie meltdown scene in front of Laura. But we couldn't stand there in the beer and wine store forever. Someone had to move first. And I was scared that if it was me, Katie would lose it.   Eventually Laura broke the standoff.

"Well. I guess I'll just go wait for you in the car. Okay, sweetie?" she asked me. I cringed again at the "sweetie." Laura smiled and kissed me on the cheek before she walked past Katie, turning over her shoulder to say, "nice to meet you," in a far too sugary voice.

Katie's hands were shaking.

"How are you?" I asked once Laura gone, knowing that after her gross misinterpretation of the situation, asking that was way too little too late. Okay, Laura didn't know who dumped who. And she must have thought that she was being snubbed when Katie wouldn't shake her hand. But that was mean. She probably didn't intend for it to be as mean as it was. Because Laura's just not that cruel. Not intentionally. If she understood the situation, she wouldn't have done that. But it was still harsh.

Katie shook her head a little, like she was snapping herself out of the shock of seeing me. "Fine," she said, sounding anything but fine.   "So.   That's the new girlfriend?"

I shook my head. "She's not my girlfriend."

"You could at least tell me the truth," she said, her voice just a little too shrill. "I'm not going to freak out or anything. I knew about her before and all. Emily told me."

I sighed. I just couldn't get into that. "I've got to go," I said. "I'll call you. We should get dinner one night. You know. And talk and stuff."

Katie bit the inside of her lower lip. She always did that when she was upset. "You're not going to call. If you haven't called since you moved out, why would you call now?"

Why do people say things like that? Of course I didn't want to call her. But it was what you said. I was just trying to abide by the normal social conventions. There was no need to call my bluff. I shrugged. "If you don't want me to call, I won't, I guess."

"Do whatever you want," she said. "I don't care." But her hands were still shaking.

I leaned down and kissed her on the cheek. "I'll call you," I said, and headed toward the counter to pay for the beer.

But I never called her.

And Laura didn't ask me a single question that night. Which made me love her even more.

14

"Is Laura coming?" Mel asked.

"I haven't asked her."

"Are you going to?" I hadn't really thought about it. My birthday was the next Friday. April 18. I would be twenty-six years old. Officially in the latter half of my twenties. And we were celebrating in the same way that we had celebrated all milestones since we turned twenty-one, meaning that all of my friends and I were going out and getting ridiculously drunk.

"No," I said eventually, forced to finally think about whether Laura should be there or not. The night we ran into Katie was the deciding factor. She wasn't part of my group of friends. I would love for her to be there. But it meant more effort on my part because I would have to worry about her interacting with everyone. I mean, she would be fine. But I didn't want to have to spend the evening wondering if she was having fun, or what she thought of my friends. I didn't honestly care that much what they thought of her. Because I knew how I felt. I cared if she liked them. What if she didn't like them and judged me on that?

And, more importantly, I didn't want to get drunk enough in front of her to risk saying anything that could give away how I felt. And my friends were notorious for buying me shot after shot after shot on my birthday.

Mel was looking at me funny. "What?" I asked.

"Nothing," she said. "Where do you want to go Friday night?"

"Happy birthday!" everyone yelled as we took our fourth group shot of the night. We were at Madhatters in Dupont Circle. Danny, the bartender and manager, had done Mel and Eric's mortgage, which meant that the tab for the night would be cheaper than if we had gone anywhere else. I was on my sixth drink total. Eric had promised to keep up with me shot for shot. We had done that for each other every year since we met during our freshman year of college. It was one of those bonds that proved how deep our friendship was. Real friends will drink until they puke with you on your birthday. Twisted? Yes. But we all need a friend who will do that.

And a friend who will do what Mel did. Because Laura walked into the bar a few minutes later. "What are you doing here?" I yelled over the music, after she kissed me hello and said "happy birthday."

"Mel called me," she yelled back. "You didn't tell me it was your birthday."

"I didn't think you'd want to come," I said, the alcohol making me more honest than I probably would have been otherwise. I glanced over at Mel, who was standing with Eric, Chris, and Joe in a huddle by the bar watching us. Chris waggled his fingers at us in an exaggerated wave when he saw me look over, and Mel slapped his hand down and said something sharp to him that I couldn't hear. Eric started laughing and turned to the bar, either because he was laughing too hard to keep watching us or to order more drinks.

Laura shrugged, but smiled. "Mel's pretty persuasive," she said.

"You're telling me! I've been dealing with her for almost eight years now."

Eric walked over with three shots in his hand, Mel following close behind him. "One for the birthday boy," he said, handing me one, then giving one to Laura. "Hello again," he said amiably, and kissed her on the cheek in greeting. Mel did the same.

"I'm so glad you came!" Mel said to her. Laura smiled a little awkwardly.

I noticed that Mel wasn't holding a shot. "Where's yours?" I asked.

She shook her head. "I'm done for a little while."

"Wimp."

"I had four already and I'm like one-third your size!" she yelled. "Do you want me to have to go home by midnight? Cause when I leave, Eric is coming with me."

I laughed. "That's what you think. He's my date tonight."

"That's right, baby," Eric said. "Now let's take this shot!" He raised his glass and Laura and I clinked ours with his before draining them in a smooth single gulp.

"When's the next show?" Eric asked Laura.

"Not until July," Laura said, shaking her head sadly.

"Ouch," he replied. "That sucks."

"I know," she said. "It's brutal." Pause. "So have you two set a date for the wedding yet?"

"September twenty-seventh," Mel chimed in. "It's at this awesome church right by Georgetown."

"Have you found a dress?

"I'm still looking. I think I know what style I want, and I found a few that are close, but I mean, it's my wedding dress. I'm not going to settle until I find the perfect one." Laura asked all about the honeymoon plans and colors and bridesmaids dresses and flowers and all kinds of other details that I wouldn't have thought about in a million years. Eric and I left them talking wedding details and went to get us all another round of drinks at the bar, although Eric ordered a plain Diet Coke for Mel.

"Oh, get her a drink," I said, because at that point, I was feeling no pain and figured that everyone should be drinking.

"Nah," Eric said. "She doesn't want it yet. And she's probably going to be taking care of both of us later tonight. We need someone to be responsible so we don't have to."

Chris and Joe walked back over to the girls with us and I handed Laura another shot, which she took with me.

"How's it feel to officially be old?" Chris asked.

"I don't know yet. I'll ask you in a month and a half when you catch up," I said.

"Shut the hell up, both of you," Joe said. He had turned twenty-six in January.

"Please," Mel said. "We're not old until we're thirty. And I, for one, am not turning thirty." She turned to Laura. "Back me up here. It's all about stopping at twenty-nine." Laura smiled.

"Screw twenty-nine, I may be stopping at twenty-five."

"Well how old are you now?"

"Twenty-four," she said. "Part two." We all laughed.

I think I was on drink number ten or eleven when she told me she had to leave. I thought about asking why. But I didn't. I wasn't quite drunk enough to ask that. She had been there for about an hour, and that was one more hour than I had expected to see her for. "Okay," I said with a cheerfulness that I didn't have to fake after that many drinks. I was genuinely happy that she had shown up at all. "Thanks for coming!"

"No problem," she said with a smile. "Happy birthday." She kissed me on the cheek and walked to the door without looking back. I watched her go, then went to get another drink.

"Are you alive?" Mel asked the next morning. And by morning, I mean two in the afternoon. Eric had been right. Mel wound up taking care of both of us, and I had passed out on their couch sometime around 4am.

I groaned as I sat up. "I'm not sure." If I was, that might not be a good thing. She handed me a glass of water with a straw in it. There's a reason she's my best friend. I moved my feet to make room for her, and she sat down on the end of the sofa.

"How bad is it?"

"I've felt better. But I'm pretty sure I've felt worse too."
Eric stumbled out of the bedroom wearing just his boxers.
He lurched over to the fridge, got himself a glass of water
and collapsed onto the love seat. He took a deep sip, then
held the glass against his forehead.

"Good morning," Mel said, trying not to laugh. "And
how are we feeling today?"

"I hurt," he said, then looked over at me. "Dude, you're
like a brother to me. But I think we might be too old to
drink that much and live."

"We're not too old. Our livers are just too damaged."

"It's bad when you need a transplant at the ripe old age
of twenty-six," Mel said.

"Maybe we should start having kids soon," Eric said.

Mel and I both looked at him like he had grown three
heads. "What?" she asked at the same time that I yelped,
"Not yet!"

"Where else are we supposed to find me a new liver
that'll be a perfect match?" Mel hit him on the head with a
throw pillow. "Ow," he yelled. "Nice way to treat your
fiancé when he doesn't feel well," he said. We laughed,
even though it made my head throb. I drank some more
water.

"Where did Laura disappear to last night?" Eric asked
when we stopped laughing. "She was there, then she was
gone."

"She just said she had to go."

"Did we scare her off?"

"I don't think so," I said.

"So why did she leave?"

"I don't know." Mel wasn't saying anything. "What do
you think?" I asked her.

"I thought it was rude."

"Mel," Eric said in a warning tone at the same time that
I asked her why.

"I mean, it's your birthday, and she shows up for like
ten minutes then bails?"

"She was there for longer than that," Eric said. "She had at least three or four shots with us."

"I thought it was cool that she came at all," I said. "Thanks for getting her there."

"I don't know," Mel said. "I mean, okay, it's great if you think that it was good that she was there. But I feel like if she really cared about you, she would have stayed longer. It was your *birthday* after all."

"But he didn't invite her," Eric argued. "You did. Maybe she wasn't sure that he wanted her there because he didn't tell her about it."

"Please, it was obvious he wanted her there."

"Thanks," I said sarcastically.

"You know what I mean. I just didn't like it."

"You don't have to," I said, and closed my eyes. "I liked that she was there." I looked back at her, but she was looking at Eric, who was shaking his head at her and the two of them had some conversation with their eyes that I wasn't a part of.

"Okay," she said finally, when she looked back at me. "I'm glad that she showed up for you, even though I think she should have stayed longer. Better?" Eric was watching me.

"A little," I said. "But it would be a lot better if you wanted to make me some post-birthday breakfast." Mel laughed.

"And me," Eric said. "Because I'm feeling kind of abused. You did assault me with that pillow while I was suffering from a hangover."

"You two better be glad I love you," she said.

"We are," we replied, as she got up and walked into the kitchen.

15

I was surprised when I heard someone knocking at my door. It was a Thursday night and I had been absentmindedly watching *Friends*, nursing a beer, and deciding if I wanted to bother going down to Dupont Circle to meet up with Mel and Eric at a bar. I was tired and dragging myself off the sofa wasn't looking too likely. Of course, I hoped it would be Laura at the door, and she was really the most likely candidate, as anyone else would have called before they came over.

She leaned on the door frame when I opened the door instead of just walking in. Her head was tilted down and she looked up at me with mischief in her eyes. "Are you in a gambling mood?" she asked in a sexy voice.

"Why? Do you want to go back to Atlantic City?"

She smiled a slow smile. "Close. Asbury Park."

I frowned. "Is there gambling there?" I knew it was Bruce's adopted hometown. The place he actually wrote "My City of Ruins" about because it was falling apart, although casual fans thought he really wrote it about September 11. Half of his early songs had references to places there. I had never been, but I was pretty sure there were no casinos there and I wasn't getting the gambling connection.

"No. Southside is playing the Pony tomorrow night." Southside Johnny was one of Bruce's friends from the early days. Of the songs on his first few albums, about half were written by Bruce and the other half by Little Steven, Bruce's lead guitar player and best friend. And the Stone Pony was Mecca to Bruce fans. It was a little seaside bar where Bruce showed up fairly often to play, but had only actually been on the bill about twice in its history. Legend even had it that he met Patti there.

"Do you think Bruce will show up?"

Laura shrugged. "That's why it's a gamble."

"What do you think the odds are?" Laura reached into her back pocket and pulled out two tickets, which she fanned out in front of me, a huge smile spreading across her face.

"Two to one?"

How could she know that I would say yes so easily? She had either bought the tickets a while ago to give them time to arrive in the mail, or else she had gone to a Ticketmaster outlet today, which I didn't think was that likely. Either way, she knew I would say yes long before she told me about the show.

"What time do you want to leave?"

"Well, the drive's about three-and-a-half hours, but let's spend the day there. I wanna check out all the Bruce sites. How's nine?"

I didn't exactly think my bosses would love that I was starting my summer of taking days off to go to concerts so soon. But there wouldn't be another local show until July. And I needed a fix. And what Laura didn't know was that it wasn't a gamble. Even if Bruce didn't show up, for me, a trip anywhere with her counted as a win.

We couldn't have picked a much nicer day to spend in a convertible. After the ten-hour drive from Indianapolis and eight-hour trip to Atlanta, three-and-a-half hours was easy. One long concert bootleg would get us the whole way there. But Laura packed a shorter show and a mix CD that she had made, which was composed entirely of songs about Asbury Park. I called her a nerd for doing that, but she glared at me, and I dropped it. She was more sensitive to that kind of insult than I would have thought. Call her a bitch and she would laugh. Call her a dork and she got annoyed. Go figure. She put the mix in as we turned onto Asbury Avenue, and I realized she must have used a map to compile it, because it was in order of what we drove past first.

Asbury Avenue brought us into the city itself. I had taken over driving after we stopped at a rest stop on the New Jersey Turnpike, but Laura told me to pull over as soon as we saw the Palace Amusement complex looming on the horizon, its cracked and peeling green façade rising abruptly out of the flat seaside landscape. Commanded is a little closer to what she actually did. I thought she wanted to get out and walk around, so I looked for a parking lot, but she told me that the side of the road was fine. We had only seen a couple of cars on the road since coming into town, so I obliged. Laura hopped out of the car practically before I brought it to a complete stop. She ran around to the driver's side and opened my door before I could open it. "I want to drive the circuit," she said, excitement showing in every curve of her body. The circuit was no longer really a circuit by the time we got there in 2003, as the water purification plant at 8th Avenue effectively closed that end of it, but we had heard Bruce's stories from concert bootlegs. In the 1970s, four one-way streets formed a sort of hangout/racetrack through town, where girls would "comb their hair in rearview mirrors" and the boys tried "to look so hard." The Palace was a crumbling landmark from Bruce's songs, a testament to his city of ruins. But the circuit was where you could still find the Bruce from *Born to Run* and *Darkness on the Edge of Town*. Driving it was something that we knew he had done. And I knew that Laura would want to give me a chance to drive it too, so I had no problem letting her take her turn first.

She pulled the car into drive and took us slowly down Asbury to Ocean Avenue, where we passed the Casino. She had timed her mix almost perfectly. The next song was "Sandy," which was about the attractions on the circuit and the beach. We made our way past the rotting hulk of the Casino, which had been an arcade with an arm that jutted out onto a pier in better days, but that part had long since washed away. We could see the boardwalk to our right, and the legendary Stone Pony to our left. Past a bizarre, rusted, half-finished high-rise, past Lance and Debbie's Wonder Bar, which Clarence once owned, past the Howard Johnson's, orange and space-age looking in its un-maintained 1960s splendor. Convention Hall rose up on our right, by far the nicest building in town, which wasn't saying much. Facing the end of the circuit, we turned down 7th Avenue to Kingsley Avenue, and again Laura's mix proved perfect, as the opening line of the next song was about driving down Kingsley and deciding to stop for a drink. Laura looked around in wide-eyed wonder. She drove us down to where we had started and then we switched seats and went back around the same course, this time with me driving. After a full lap, I looped back to park near the Stone Pony so that we could walk around and explore the town.

Laura usually left the top of her car down with the windows up on nice days, and this certainly qualified. Her car had a strong alarm system, and no one could really reach anything with the windows up. But Laura started putting the top up before I could even suggest it. This didn't look like the kind of town where it was smart to leave anything remotely accessible if you ever wanted to see it again. Not that there was anyone around to steal anything. We got out of the car and I walked immediately around to Laura's side. It was creepy. We hadn't seen a living soul yet. It looked like no one had lived there for about twenty years. The only signs of life were a few old, dilapidated cars parked near the Pony.

Laura dug into her purse for quarters to feed the meter and I fished two out of my pockets. Laura inserted one with a dull clink, then peered at it.

"Shit," she said idly. "Broken." She looked at me and shrugged. "I'll move the car." I looked around. There was a sea of empty spaces and the meters looked older than us. No flashing red lights to show which had expired here. Laura started to climb back into the car, but I stopped her.

"Let's find a working meter first," I said. I went to the one next to the one Laura had tried. It was expired. I put a quarter in, but nothing happened. I tried the one next to that, and again, nothing. Laura started to look amused. She tried the one on the other side of the car. Looked at it curiously. Then tried one more.

"They're all broken!" she exclaimed. "Does that mean we can just park here?" I looked around. Even the asphalt of the parking lot looked older than dirt. Stringy grass sprouted up in large clumps all around and a rainbow of brown and green broken bottles glittered in the sunlight.

"Yeah," I said finally. "If we get a ticket, I feel like this place needs the money more than we do." Laura smiled weakly and nodded. I don't think she had expected it to be quite this bad. We knew it would be fairly rundown, or else Bruce couldn't have written a song about it that would later be used to describe New York after September 11. But we hadn't imagined the level of devastation that we actually found there. We didn't know how dead a place could feel.

I felt disappointed too, but I wanted Laura happy again. "Let's go exploring." She nodded again and hooked her camera strap across her body as we set off toward the Palace of "Born to Run" fame. An exceptionally seedy-looking motel stood on the corner of Kingsley and 2nd Avenue. Laura stopped and stared at it. I turned and looked at her while she worked out whatever she was thinking. Finally, a huge smile spread across her face. I turned and looked where she was looking. A battered sign read "The Flamingo Motel."

"Do you see it?" Laura asked. I looked more carefully. It looked like the sign had fluorescent lights along the looping words once, but if they had been there, they were long gone now. Pink, fluorescent lights, I would assume, to go with the Flamingo part. She watched me expectantly, but I shrugged. I didn't know what she wanted me to see.

"What if I said 'Flamingo Lane'?" she asked, hinting. *Flamingo Lane?* A line from "Jungleland." Off *Born to*

Run. The two lovers "take a stab at romance" and vanish "down Flamingo Lane."

"Oh!" I said as I realized what she was getting at. Flamingo Lane wasn't a *street*. Disappearing there meant getting a room at this motel. It was one of the many things that both of us loved about Bruce. His songs were poetry. If you didn't look deeper, Flamingo Lane *could* be a street somewhere. If you did, the story became a love affair, with the sax solo acting as the un-vocalized verse that represents the culmination of that passion in this little dive motel. But it doesn't matter that it's a dump, because to them, it's beautiful; it's not a motel anymore, it's a whole world that they can disappear into.

Laura beamed at me. "That is just the coolest thing ever." She took my hand and pulled me across the street. "We have to check this out!" But the Flamingo, like just about everything else in town, was closed. Laura's smile faded quickly.

I did have an ace up my sleeve, even though I hadn't expected to have to play it that soon. I leaned down to whisper into her ear. "We're less than a couple hundred feet from where Bruce will probably be tonight." She smiled again and turned back to face me. She looked at me for just a second too long, her face a little too close to mine. I hesitated. She pulled back, kissed me noisily on the cheek, then turned away to walk down Kingsley toward the Palace. If she had stayed a second longer, would I have had the nerve to kiss her? Would she have let me? Doubtful, but I couldn't help but wonder. She was halfway down the block before I realized I had better catch up. Maybe she would have let me kiss her. But there were still no guarantees that she would wait for me when anything involving Bruce was at stake.

The Palace, once one of the largest arcades in the country, was hardly more inviting than the Flamingo had been, as it was closed down in 1988. It was hard to believe, but it had gone way downhill since Bruce shot his video for "Tunnel of Love" there. A chain link fence surrounded the building, keeping vandals and teenagers out. There was barely even any graffiti on the peeling, faded paint; almost as if Asbury Park was so deserted that there weren't even enough people there to vandalize an abandoned building. Instead, only the weather desecrated this once unmistakable landmark of the Jersey shore. Even the words on the street sign at the corner were faded and missing a letter. We walked around the side of the long-since empty building, reading the attractions advertised on the side in reverent silence. Laura stood in the middle of the road to take pictures without even needing to worry about traffic. The only moving car that we saw since arriving in town passed us as we walked down Kingsley toward the lake that separated Asbury Park from Ocean Grove, which was an entirely different universe. Ocean Grove was populated. Booming. Rich. Alive. Yet one block away, Asbury Park was as decimated as if a bomb had been dropped on it. We both turned to look at the car as it passed. It was the first sign of life that we had seen.

I personally thought that would have to be the worst of it. But the Casino had trees growing inside of it. Literally. Trees. The roof was torn off in some storm in the 1980s and never replaced. The carousel, which had once been world-famous, was sold off piece by piece and the space around it turned into a skate park before the entire building was shut down. By the time we got there, it was completely boarded up, and the only windows that weren't broken were too high to reach with rocks or even BB guns. The remains of the pier hung perilously over the edge of the beach, guarded by a lone "No Trespassing" sign, which I doubted would have been enforced if people who wanted to trespass ever showed up. Nearer to the edge of the pier, only the frame of the roof remained, with big patches of blue sky visible through the broken windows. Plant life was clearly thriving in that end of the building, but the windows were higher there and there wasn't a chance of getting a peek inside without a tall ladder.

An empty paint bucket stood near some of the lower windows and I turned it over. "What are you doing?" Laura asked. I climbed onto the bucket.

"Seeing if there's anything inside." I grabbed the ledge and pulled myself up enough to see inside. She watched me expectantly as I looked in. But there wasn't anything exciting to report back. I climbed down and shrugged at her. "Do you want to see?"

She nodded and climbed up onto the bucket, but wasn't quite tall enough to see, so I picked her up. I held her while she snapped a few shots of the inside through the broken window, and when I put her down, we wandered around to the boardwalk side, where an entire panel of windows was missing and the foliage inside was clearly visible.

Turning away from the Casino on the boardwalk, a ramp to our left led up to nowhere. It just ended about ten feet off the ground. I looked from there to the beach and touched Laura's arm to get her attention. "There are some people, at least," I said, pointing toward the beach. Laura looked relieved. The beach was pretty deserted, but a handful of people had also played hooky from work (or maybe in a town like this, they didn't have jobs to skip out of) and were scattered along the shore, enjoying the beautiful day.

Laura had started down the boardwalk and when I looked at her, her jaw dropped open. "Look! It's really there!" she almost shouted, pointing toward the Convention Center. She was pointing at a tiny white shack, which was barely noticeable, but a serious attraction for a Bruce fan. It was Madame Marie's Temple of Knowledge. Madame Marie was a fortune teller who supposedly told Bruce that he was going to become famous. Although, according to Bruce, all musicians in Asbury Park received the same fortune, just not always with the same level of accuracy. She was mentioned in "Sandy" as being arrested for telling fortunes better than the police. Her shack, of course, was not open, nor was there any trace of Madame

Marie herself, other than the faded lettering on the white walls of the building, which couldn't have been more than about eight feet by eight feet. But we had once seen a picture of Bruce standing right in front of that spot. Laura traced a finger over the lettering on the side. She looked disappointed. I think she had expected Madame Marie to be sitting inside, waiting to tell our fortunes.

We had lunch at the Convention Hall. There was an outdoor bar set up on the balcony that ran along the beach and the few people who were in town seemed to be congregated there. "Glory Days" was blasting on a stereo and if you didn't look out toward the town or the rotting Casino, you could almost forget where you were. But that meant keeping yourself to a pretty narrow field of vision. We ordered hamburgers and beers and tried not to think about how depressing the town was. The next song on the album came on and Laura and I looked at each other. We both started to laugh.

"It's too cheesy," she gasped finally, between giggles. "Playing Bruce in Asbury Park. And *Born in the USA*! It's worse than wearing a Bruce shirt to a Bruce show!" A woman at the table next to us looked up. I glanced over. She was about forty-five and immaculately put together. Laura's look was rich, but casual rich. This woman looked Long Island rich. She was wearing jeans and a black, stretchy v-neck t-shirt, but with gold bracelets, a huge diamond on her hand, and two that weren't much smaller in her ears. She had shoulder length hair, straight, but sprayed so heavily that it didn't move in the breeze coming off the ocean. It was brown with the perfect blonde highlights, subtle enough that they might have been natural, but weren't. Laura had taught me that the nails were a dead giveaway for women from Jersey and New York. In the DC area, most women kept their nails shorter and natural. In Jersey and New York, the longer and more fake looking, the better. Following that rule, this woman was definitely from the area, but she certainly didn't look like she belonged in Asbury Park.

"Are you here to see Southside tonight too?" she asked. Her accent was definitely New York, but not annoyingly so. The man sitting with her looked over, interested as well. He looked a little older than her, with graying hair and glasses. They were clearly a couple, as she reached over as she spoke and put her hand on top of his as it rested on the table.

Laura smiled. She didn't usually warm to strangers, especially women, this quickly. "Are we that obvious?" she asked.

The woman smiled broadly and said, "Only because I heard you mention Bruce."

"Are you tramps too?" Laura asked. We hadn't really met any before. We had seen familiar faces at shows and made a little small talk. But we had just driven to Asbury Park to see if Bruce might happen to show up one night. This was hardcore Bruce territory.

"Since 1975," the man chimed in.

"We met at a concert in 1978," she added, smiling across the table at her husband. "The *Darkness* tour." A shadow crossed Laura's face, but was gone so quick that I knew I must have imagined it.

"Wow," she said, genuinely. "That's awesome."

"I'm Ellen," the woman said, reaching across the gap between our tables to hold out her hand first to Laura, then to me.

"Jeff Gorman," the man said, following his wife's handshakes with his own. Laura and I introduced ourselves as well.

They had gotten married in 1980, we soon learned, and arranged their honeymoon around Bruce's tour dates so that they would be back in time to catch the first of the *River* tour shows, but could still use the excuse of their honeymoon to have time off of work to go to them.

"My parents still think we're nuts for that," Ellen added.

"You've really been doing this for twenty-five years?" I asked.

Jeff turned to Ellen. "Has it really been that long?" he asked her and she nodded at him, her eyebrows raised. "Feels like less," he said, "but I guess that's right. I always justify it by telling people, we don't drink and we don't do drugs. This is how we get high." Laura nodded when he said that. Although we definitely drank.

"How many shows have you been to?"

"What are we up to, two-hundred-twenty?" Jeff asked.

"You've been to two-twenty-six," Ellen said. "I've been to two-nineteen. I'll hit two-twenty on July fifteenth."

"Were those seven before you met?"

"Two were," Jeff said.

"The other five, I was eight months pregnant and it just wasn't going to work." Laura and I both laughed.

"She let me go anyway," Jeff chimed in. "That's how you can tell she loves me."

Ellen shrugged. "It was our second kid. And he wasn't playing with the E Street Band. If I had to miss an E Street show, Jeff wasn't going either."

"That's true love," I said, still laughing. Laura shot me a sharp look. I hadn't thought about the conversation that we had on the night of the engagement party when I said that, but I did when I saw the look on her face. She looked back to our new friends quickly, but I had definitely seen that look that she gave me, and I didn't like it.

"So," Ellen began. "How long have you two been together?"

"We're not—" Laura said quickly.

"Um, no, it's not—" I said at the same time, but Ellen interrupted us quickly and smoothly.

"Sorry, my mistake, my mistake," she said, her eyes going first to Laura's face, then to mine. "When did you start following Bruce?"

I explained that I had started on the Reunion tour with my dad, Laura said she had started with the *Rising* tour and she told her version of how we met, beginning with "Backstreets." I didn't correct it.

Jeff's phone rang, and he got up from the table after looking at the caller ID. "Excuse me," he said so politely that you would think a ringing cell phone was a crime. "I need to take this one." He walked away toward the far end of the balcony away from the music.

Ellen chatted with us while her husband was on the phone. They had driven in from Long Island and expected a few more of their concert friends to show up today.

"Do you think Bruce will actually be here tonight?" Laura asked quietly, leaning in toward Ellen, who held a finger to her lips.

"Shhhh," she said conspiratorially. "If we talk about it, we'll jinx it." Laura and I were both enthralled. Over the next few months, I would think a lot about the relationship we formed with Ellen and Jeff that day. Laura didn't have a mother or a role model. As far as I knew, she didn't have any female friends either. She didn't seem to trust women. And I couldn't necessarily blame her. I had seen the scalding treatment that the girls had given her at Mel and Eric's engagement party, and the way that Katie had responded to her at the beer store that one night. Mel had been nice to her, but that probably had more to do with me than with Laura herself. And Laura almost hadn't known how to respond to that treatment. With the girls who were openly catty, she fought back so smoothly that the girls she went up against didn't stand a chance. But she couldn't seem to trust any girls who weren't like that either. Then again, despite her protests to the contrary, I knew that Mel didn't really like Laura all that much. But that was based on my birthday, and I didn't think that was fair. There was something about Laura though that turned girls off. I wondered again what had happened to Laura to make her turn that hard. Had a friend betrayed her somehow? It couldn't have been by stealing a boyfriend, because there was no way that anyone could steal something that Laura actually wanted. But then again, I wasn't exactly an impartial observer.

If Laura wanted a mother, I think she found some of what she was looking for in Ellen. In those first five minutes, she identified Ellen as a kindred spirit. She did the same with me within a couple of minutes as well. But it felt more drawn out with me because I had seen her so long before we started talking. I watched Laura bonding with Ellen and, for a somewhat embarrassing moment, I felt jealous, because it was like Laura had been completely mine up until then.

I looked from Laura to Ellen and realized she had seen me watching Laura talk. Her eyes were sympathetic and I wondered how much of what I was thinking had been visible to her.

The jealousy couldn't last long, however, because I was nearly as caught up as Laura was. To me, Ellen seemed to offer a glimpse of what Laura could be. It was a feeling that came from being around both of them. She was like Laura, but unguarded. And she gave me hope. Because if Laura could attach herself to someone like Ellen, there was still a chance for me.

Jeff returned to the table and joined our conversation. "Everything all right?" Ellen asked.

He nodded, and apologized to us for having to take the call. "Business," he said, shaking his head slightly. "There's no rest for the wicked."

"Since when are your clients wicked?" Ellen asked.

Jeff smiled at her. "I meant us."

Ellen laughed. "Well, that's why it's a damn good thing that you're a partner." She turned to us. "How did you two get out of work?"

"Called in sick," I said.

"Bruce fever?" Jeff asked. Laura laughed at that but Ellen shushed him.

"You know the rule," she said. "Between you and these kids, he's probably not coming now!"

"Southside is one of his best friends and the band is on a month-long break from the tour. And he lives twenty

minutes from here. You know him. He's got to be itching
to play. He's coming."

"Twenty bucks says he doesn't show." Ellen stuck her
hand out across the table and Jeff shook it.

"You're on," he said. I loved it. They were old enough
to be our parents but they acted like they could have been
our age. I glanced at Laura. She was every bit as into this
as I was.

We sat with them for almost two hours before they
said we should go over to the Pony to wait for them to open
the doors. They entertained us with stories of shows from
the tours that they had been following well before we were
old enough to really be aware of music. They had both met
Bruce a handful of times, including a few times at the Pony.
In 1984, Ellen had been one of the lucky girls pulled on
stage to dance with Bruce during "Dancing in the Dark."
Jeff told us about the decline of Asbury Park, as well as
about some of the Bruce-related sites that we hadn't known
about. He was impressed that we figured out the Flamingo
Motel connection.

Jeff, we learned, was from Philadelphia, and was
introduced to Bruce's music by Ed Sciaky's radio
broadcasts in the early-and-mid 1970s. He started driving
all over Pennsylvania, New York, and New Jersey to see
this skinny kid who had learned to make his guitar talk.
Ellen's introduction was a little different. She started
dating a boy in 1975, mostly because he upset her very
conservative and very rich parents. He drove a motorcycle,
had long hair, and a pierced ear. And he loved Bruce.
Ellen was seventeen, but by the end of the first show that
he took her to at the Bottom Line, right before *Born to Run*
was released, she was hooked. She had broken up with her
rebel by 1976 and had started going to shows with her girl
friends.

"What show did you meet at?" I asked. I wondered if
they had the bootleg of it, like Laura and I did. Ellen and
Jeff beamed at each other. You would never guess that

they had been married for almost twenty-three years. They could have been newlyweds.

"It was May 26, 1978," Ellen began.

"First night of two in Philadelphia, at the Spectrum," Jeff chimed in.

"I had just finished my sophomore year at the University of Pennsylvania."

"And I had just graduated and was starting law school there in the fall."

"I camped out for tickets and was in the third row."

"I was in the second."

"And I went to the show with my roommate, Susan."

"And I looked behind me and saw the most beautiful girl I'd ever seen." Jeff winked at Ellen, who smiled back at him. "So I thought fast. I—"

"He introduces himself to Susan, then asks if she wants to trade seats with him to see better!"

"We've been over this. It meant that I'd get to be next to you for the whole show."

"But you could have let *me* into the second row."

Jeff turned to me. "Twenty-five years later and she still hasn't forgiven me for not letting her be two feet closer to Bruce."

I laughed. "Laura, would you forgive me if I did that?"

"Absolutely not," she said without missing a beat, then laughed as well.

"Anyway," Jeff said. "She came with me to the concert the next night, and we drove to Boston for the next three shows, then down to Maryland for the one after that."

"I knew I was going to marry him by the time Bruce played 'Born to Run' that second night. So I lied to my parents. I told them I was staying down the shore with Susan."

"Liar," Jeff said with a smile.

"Second-row seat giver-upper," Ellen retorted. "But I mostly forgave him for not letting me into the second row, and we got married two years later."

Jeff checked his watch. "Ellie, honey, we'd better head over there." Ellen looked down at her watch and Jeff motioned to the waiter to bring the check.

"Oh, you're right, I lost track of time," Ellen said. She turned back to me and Laura. "You should come with us." Laura said we would love to.

"I've got their check too," Jeff told the waiter when he came over, indicating us.

"No, I've got it," I protested, but Jeff had already handed over a credit card.

"Wait," Ellen said to the waiter, digging into her purse. "Will you take a picture of the four of us?" She handed the waiter a small digital camera. Laura was a little surprised and Jeff looked amused.

"She does this all the time," he explained. "She needs a picture of everything."

"And you love it, so be quiet and smile pretty."

"Yes, ma'am."

Laura and I leaned in to the shot. It dawned on me that I had never seen Laura on this side of a camera. Even when I had offered to take her picture in front of Madame Marie's, she refused to hand off her camera. Ellen took the camera back and turned toward me and Laura.

"Now one of just you two." Laura and I looked at each other for a second. This was couple-y, and a little weird as we had just met Ellen and she wanted a picture of us. But Jeff had said that she really did take pictures of everything, which we would later realize was only too true. And I wanted a picture of me with Laura. I realized that I should ask for their email address so I could get a copy of it later.

16

"You know what?" Laura asked as we merged onto the Turnpike later that night. She had tossed me her keys as we left the Stony Pony, and I was driving.

"What?"

"It's okay that Bruce didn't show up. Like it would have been awesome, but today was a really great day without Bruce too." I was surprised. This was, in a way, the closest she had ever come to saying she liked me. I'm not stupid. I know she didn't mean for that to be about me specifically. But it was. She wouldn't have done today alone. And I had really thought that she would have been disappointed that Bruce hadn't shown up. We had been so hopeful up until the end of the show. There was an extra guitar stand on the stage in case he did come. And according to Jeff, Bruce's assistant, Terry Magovern, was there. But no Bruce.

"I think so too," I said.

The night had turned chilly, so we put the windows up and turned on the heat, but left the convertible top down. Which made it possible to actually have a conversation at a normal volume, as opposed to driving on the highway with the top and windows down, when all you could really hear was the music and the trucks rumbling by. I'll probably be completely deaf by the time I'm fifty between all of the concerts and the highway driving that we did that summer with the top down on Laura's car.

Laura was quiet for a few minutes, and I was lost in my own thoughts too. Asbury Park had left me feeling strangely sad and unfulfilled. I knew it was going to be rundown, but I hadn't expected it to be quite at the level of

destruction that we had found it in. It loaned a dark edge
to a lot of my ideas about Bruce and his music. About his
mortality and my own. Bruce was my age when *Born to
Run* came out. Only a couple of months older than me
when he was on the covers of *Time* and *Newsweek* in the
same week. And look how much Asbury Park had changed
for the worse since then. There were scenes from that day
that I would see long after I closed my eyes. And when
Laura developed the pictures she had taken, I asked for
copies. A black-and-white picture that she printed and
sepia-toned for me of the Casino is framed on my desk at
home. To remind me, I guess, of what can happen while
you're not looking.

Lost in my own thoughts about Asbury Park, I was
startled when Laura spoke.

"Remember those girls? The night of the engagement
party?" That was more than three months ago. Talk about
being blindsided when you're not looking.

It took me a second to see what she was asking. They
were the ones who asked her about us in order to scare her
away from their boyfriends. "Uh huh," I said as non-
commitally as possible.

"Never mind," she said suddenly. "Didn't Southside
put on a great show?"

I was confused. Laura didn't usually do that. Yes, she
would parry with a comment like the Southside one, but
that was if I asked her something that she didn't want to
answer. Not when she started it. I had never seen her ask
a question and then back down. Other girls did that all the
time when something was bothering them. But not Laura.
When something bothered her, she either flat out told you
or else she didn't speak to you for awhile, in which case it
would never be brought up again. So I was suddenly very
interested in why she had asked about those girls. Even if
it was going to lead to some kind of a discussion that I
wasn't sure we were ready to have, I sensed this would be
interesting.

"What about the girls?"

"And Ellen and Jeff were just awesome. Maybe we should have stayed with them tonight after all." They had invited us and they certainly lived a lot closer to the Pony than we did. But it would have been much further to get home later and I was planning to go into the office for a few hours the next day.

"Laura," I said, firmly. She looked over with an eyebrow raised at my tone, but I stayed focused on the road. Finally, she looked away from me and I waited for her to talk.

"They were bitches."

I laughed. Obviously that wasn't what she was planning to say about them when she brought them up. But the girl did have more comic timing than anyone as pretty as she was had any right to have.

She laughed too when she saw she had made me laugh, which loosened the whole mood.

"Anyway," she began. "They said you'd been living with some girl right before we met." It wasn't a question. But it was at the same time.

I felt the blood pounding in my head like a drum solo that would make Max Weinberg sweat. I waited. She didn't say anything else. So I finally went for it. Might as well tell her the truth. I would have to tell her about Katie eventually anyway.

"Yeah," I said.

Because I'm just that smooth.

But apparently that wasn't quite enough of an explanation for Laura.

"Was it the girl we met at the liquor store that night?" I nodded.

"Why did you break up?"

That, I thought, *is the $64,000 question.* Then I wondered if that was the right number for that expression because whatever the game show was that the number came from, I had never seen it. But back to Laura's question.

"I don't—I don't know how to describe it without explaining the whole relationship, you know?"

Laura nodded. "I know what you mean." She thought for a minute. "But how long did you live together?" *Too long*, I thought unkindly.

"About five months."

"What about your lease?"

"I paid three extra months worth of rent and she found a roommate. One of her friends had asked if she could rent our other bedroom right before I left because she didn't have anyone else to live with, and we weren't going to do that, but she moved in after I moved out."

"How long were you together?"

"Just over two years." Laura was quiet for another minute.

"So the real question is: why did you move in with her when you were only five months away from a breakup?"

Time for a dodge that would be worthy of Laura herself. "It was really just irreconcilable differences. She left the toilet seat up." Laura threw her head back and laughed merrily.

"Like Selma on *The Simpsons*?" That was the first time Laura talked about watching television other than talk shows for when Bruce would be on and *The Sopranos* for Little Steven. I learned something new every time I talked to her, even though she never flat out told me anything about herself.

"Exactly," I said. "It was either leave or try to kill her like Sideshow Bob would have done." I wondered what the odds were that she would let it drop now and we could talk about *The Simpsons* or something else instead. Anything else. Apparently, the odds weren't in my favor.

"But really though," she asked, once the laughter died down. "Why did you decide to live together?"

I hesitated. "Have you seen *Fight Club*?" I thought back to how Katie hated that movie, and my palms started to feel a little sweaty on the steering wheel. I hoped Laura could understand what I was about to say. She said yes.

"Remember when Brad Pitt is in the bath? And he and Edward Norton are talking about their lives and how Ed Norton says that he went to college, then he called his father and he was like, 'what do I do next?' and his father said 'get a job.' So he gets a job, then calls his father and says 'what do I do next?' and his father says, 'I don't know, get married.' That's kind of what we grow up thinking we should do with our lives. We ask our parents what to do next, and we live the same lives they lived over and over again."

"That's—actually pretty deep," she said slowly, sounding a little surprised. "Did you love her?"

My answer to that one was always yes. To Katie, to Mel, to my parents, to anyone who asked if I had loved her. Clearly I didn't anymore by the end, but I had to have at some point. If nothing else, it made me feel better to think I had. Because then I wasn't just the asshole who got her hopes up by moving in with her then leaving when I saw something I wanted more. But I couldn't quite say that to Laura. The same way I couldn't tell her that I had really been in love when she asked me the night of the engagement party. And the same way I couldn't say even then that I had been in love based on what I felt about Laura.

"I don't know," I said finally. "I want to believe I did. And I definitely cared about her. But I'm not sure that I ever really *loved* her. I know that by the end I definitely didn't. But I also don't think there was a moment when I started falling out of love with her. Which means I don't really know."

"But didn't you realize that before you moved in together? Didn't you realize that buying sheets and silverware and pictures and throw pillows with her wasn't going to make you happy?" There was an insistence in her voice that made me answer her. I didn't want to talk about a chapter of my life that I had completely closed so many months ago, but I could see that she needed me to answer this for some reason. And I didn't get to feel like I had anything that Laura needed very often. Other than someone to go to concerts with.

"Something clicked one day," I said. I hadn't told anyone this really. Melanie knew some. Katie knew some. No really understood it completely except me. But Laura's question about the Pier One element of domestic life made me think that maybe she would. And I realized that despite what I hoped for, I didn't actually have anything that solid with her. Meaning I didn't really have anything tangible to lose by laying it out there.

"I turned twenty-five. That seemed like the age when you were supposed to start getting serious about stuff and settling down. And Mel and Eric started talking about the whole getting married thing. And Katie, that was my girlfriend, Katie, she and I were right on track for that too. That's why you move in with someone. Or why you're supposed to. But I did it because it seemed like the next logical step. She said 'I think we should do this' and my friends were doing it, and I never stopped to ask myself if that was what I wanted. And she made me breakfast one morning to surprise me. She made scrambled eggs. And I'm sitting there, eating the eggs that she made me. And that was really, really sweet of her. I know that. But for some reason, I asked myself, 'did I really feel like eggs this morning?' Maybe a bagel would have been better. Or cereal. Or—or—or anything that I did for myself instead of for everyone else." I wanted desperately to look over at her and see how she was reacting to this, but I was afraid, so I just kept going. "I felt like I was riding in the passenger seat in my own life, and that I should be the one driving. But I wasn't. And Katie couldn't understand that, which was really kind of the last nail in the coffin. She just thought it was about the eggs." I finally hazarded a glance at Laura. And it only took that one quick glimpse to see that she understood what I meant. I wiped my palms on my jeans, one at a time, and took a deep breath. She got it.

She thought for a minute. "Did you tell her about the eggs when you told her you were leaving?"

"Yeah, but I was using that as a metaphor. She kind of took it literally."

Laura laughed. "So she thinks she got dumped over eggs?" I nodded. "That poor girl," she said. "I wonder how much therapy that's going to take to get over."

"Thanks," I said, as sarcastically as I could.

Laura was quiet for a little while and she took a long sip of her Diet Coke. Then she made a face and asked if we could stop at the next rest stop, because her soda was warm. We were crossing the Delaware Memorial Bridge, just over a hundred miles from home.

We climbed back into the car and Laura put a CD in, but kept the volume low, even though the first song on the album that she picked was one of her favorites to sing along to loudly. "It makes sense though," she said. I didn't ask which part. I knew that she meant all of it.

We didn't talk much over the next hundred miles. I don't know what Laura was thinking about. I started to piece together why she might have asked me about all of that. I knew, by then, that it was purely selfish on her part. And it wasn't her sizing me up as potential boyfriend material, to see if I would do something similar to her. The only explanation that I could really come up with was that someone must have dumped her in a similar way. Probably someone who she lived with, because she had focused on that part of my breakup. It would explain a lot. It explained why she was that closed off. Why she didn't want to answer any personal questions. Why she was so cynical about the whole idea of love. Why nothing had happened with me. And unfortunately, I realized as we passed Baltimore, if that was the case, it probably meant that nothing *would* happen with me. Because it meant she had needed a friend when we met. I thought about Katie and how I had probably decimated her plans for happily ever after. And I figured that had to be what happened to Laura. Except—except that I couldn't see Laura going to pieces over—well—anything. Until Bruce dies that is. I could picture her wearing black for years and going to his gravesite in a veil to leave flowers and Asbury Park mementos. It couldn't have been *Born to Run* guy who left her, could it? I shuddered at the very idea. He embodied everything that I hated, just in that one possessive gesture of putting his hand too low on her hip in the Philadelphia parking lot.

Or maybe, I wondered as we merged from I-95 onto the Capital Beltway, she left someone too and was trying to justify it. But no, Laura felt no need for justification. She did what she needed to do, and I was pretty sure that she didn't look back or regret anything she did.

We got to my place and got out of the car so that Laura could drive herself home. I watched as her car pulled away and felt a tiny stab of fear. Yes, I had driven the car home from New Jersey. But was I really the one driving right now or was she?

17

The summer of 2003 was one of the happiest times in my life. I said that about it then and I am doing my best to be able to say that now. It's hard sometimes, because we tend to let the negative things that come later ruin the good memories. But I refuse to let the later drama ruin my memories of that summer. There has never been a summer like that for me and there probably never will be again.

If you're not a teacher or a perpetual student, summers start to lose their fun factor when you graduate from college. College summers mean working some part-time restaurant-type job while spending as much time drinking/at the pool/at the beach as is humanly possible. It's a three-month party with a few hungover work hours in between.

Then you graduate and boom! Summer is gone. If you show up to your real job too often with a killer hangover, people start to talk about you. Your bosses get "concerned" with your work ethic. And even worse, you start realizing that you can't get your work done and are too tired to go party all summer anymore.

In short, it sucks.

But that summer, I broke all the rules.

Between July 15 and September 20, we went to twenty-five shows. I'll say that again to let it sink in. *Twenty-five shows.* Assuming the average time spent at each one was three hours, although it was always more than that, that's more than three full days spent at Bruce concerts. And Laura and I spent way more than three days traveling to those shows, waiting in line to be in the pit, and staying over wherever we were when there were multiple night stands. We saw all ten shows at Giants Stadium, including the two when it rained for half the night. We went to Boston and Chicago and Philadelphia and Chapel Hill and Canada. She started to bring me running with her in the mornings. But we were comfortable together by then. If I was too tired to run, I wasn't afraid to say no to her. And she didn't mind when I said no. She would laugh, call me a slacker, and wake me up when she got back. Then wake me up the next morning to see if I wanted to run with her then. We didn't talk much on those runs. We both had music of course. But we didn't need to talk. We could just be together.

We both quit smoking that summer too. I only ever did it when I drank anyway, but I couldn't keep up with Laura and all the running if I was still smoking. Laura pulled out two cigarettes at a tailgate for one of the shows and held one out to me, but I shook my head and told her I was quitting. She tilted her head and thought for a second, then tossed the whole pack in the trash. "That sounds like a good plan," she said. I told her she didn't have to quit just because I had, but she shrugged. "Eh, I didn't like it that much anyway. I just did it because it gave me something to do with my hands." I told her I could give her something to do with her hands and she laughed at me. I loved that I could make her laugh.

I used up all of my vacation time, plus all of my sick leave. I worked out some flex time with my bosses to make up the difference, meaning that I worked on my laptop from hotel rooms some nights after shows, and I was at the office just about every Saturday and Sunday that we didn't have a show. And every weekend minute that I spent at the office was worth it because it was another minute that I would be able to spend on the road with Laura.

We had a group of friends by then. Tramps like us. Jeff and Ellen, whom we had met in Asbury, were at about fifteen of those shows with us. Ellen had started an email correspondence with both of us and invited us to stay with her and Jeff for all of the Giants Stadium shows. We only stayed with them for four nights, not wanting to infringe on their hospitality. But we joked with them and called them "mom and dad" whenever we talked to them or about them. They brought their kids to night six at Giants Stadium. And as Jeff and Ellen's children, they were exactly what we expected. Rachel and Matthew were the most well-behaved and awesome kids we had ever met. They knew when to throw their fists into the air during "Badlands" and when to wave their hands during "Born to Run." Rachel, who was fourteen years old, politely requested that the two women who were talking during "Empty Sky," which was about September 11, be more respectful of those who had died. Laura hugged her and called her "little sister," which Rachel loved, especially because Laura had, with Ellen's permission of course, done Rachel's makeup and nails before we left their house for the show. Laura really surprised me. I hadn't expected her to be good with kids. She didn't strike me as the maternal type. And she wasn't maternal with them exactly. But she instinctively knew how to talk to kids and it was clear that within minutes of meeting Laura, both Rachel and Matthew simply worshipped her. And even more surprising, she seemed to adore them just as much.

Jeff and Ellen had a whole group of friends from the concerts over the years and we were welcomed right into the fold. Well—no, that's not entirely true; we were welcomed immediately by Jeff and Ellen and the men among their friends. Claire and Barbara were a little less than kind to Laura, but neither of them would be openly catty enough to cause real problems. Both were in their late forties or early fifties and both had clearly started their descent into the land of Botox. Claire was twice divorced and had no intention of making it to three times. She was nicer to Laura overall, but being Barbara's best friend, she couldn't show too much interest in anything Laura said or did. Or in me, for that matter, but I didn't care. Barbara, however, was just finishing up divorce number one and was none too happy with having a gorgeous, thin, twenty-five-year-old girl stealing any of her spotlight. Which made sense when Ellen explained that Barbara's husband had just left her for a very leggy twenty-seven-year-old girl. Any conversation involving the two of them therefore ended fairly quickly, with them treating us like we were two babies who were being allowed to stay up past our bedtime as long as we remained well-behaved and quiet. But Ellen always stepped in before anything could get ugly. Laura and I said more than once that if the United Nations needed a new peacemaker, Ellen would be perfect for the role. Maybe if they had hired her, the whole situation in Iraq would have gone a bit smoother.

The men of the Springsteen followers, though, had some of the coolest stories we had ever heard, and they genuinely enjoyed having me and Laura as a rapt audience to listen to them recounting tales that everyone else they knew had heard many times by then. A couple of them had been around since before Bruce had a record contract. They told us stories about how the whole band used to have ongoing Monopoly tournaments onstage during the show, which meant the band members would take their turn on the board as soon as their part in whichever song they were playing had a little break. They would bring incredible bootlegs with them to the tailgates, shows that were nearly impossible to get, even for Laura, and they always sent us home with CDs and sometimes DVDs of old shows.

We met Susan, Ellen's college roommate, who Jeff had swapped his second row seat with in order to meet Ellen. She was there with her husband, Paul, whom she met a couple of years later through Jeff. Susan told us her side of the story from the night that Jeff and Ellen met, but in her version, it was like the scene in *West Side Story* when they first saw each other; everything on the borders was blurry and Jeff and Ellen could only see each other. She laughed at Ellen's protest that she didn't know she was going to marry Jeff until the second night. "You're just saying that so you won't sound easy," she told Ellen and leaned in close to me and Laura to tell us that Ellen "was a goner from the second she saw him. And Jeff? Give up second row seats for anything? He was worse off than she was!" Laura said it was the most romantic thing she had ever heard. And Laura wasn't exactly big on romance.

There was never a set group of who would be at the tailgate, but Ellen let us know that they always parked in the same area, and there was always a crowd of people there, sharing food and beer and music and stories. Jeff had a game that we played before every show, in which we would bet on which rarities would be played. He had a full set of rules and everything. But he had started it ten years earlier, meaning that there had been plenty of time to work out all the kinks. It was a dollar per song guess. He suggested that the price go up to five dollars a couple of times, but Ellen said no and he didn't argue. I got the feeling that she wanted to make sure that Laura and I could still afford to play. Not that a hundred dollars would have been too much for Laura, but I was a little short on cash that summer.

Ellen had her camera at every single show and the only physical mementos that I have of that summer other than ticket stubs and concert shirts are thanks to her constant picture taking. And Ellen had quite the eye. She never cut off anyone's head in a shot, not even when she'd had a little too much to drink. (We only saw that once, in a bar after the first night at Giants Stadium. Ellen and Laura ordered second margaritas, which were very strong and served in glasses that would hold about three beers. They wound up singing "Sherry Darling" together, loudly and off-key. But Ellen's pictures from that night didn't suffer.) She took pictures at every opportunity, both when we were prepared and posed and when we didn't know she was taking them.

I have a few favorites, all of which are from when she caught Laura in unguarded moments. Laura always hated those. She liked the ones where she was posing and looked glamorous. I loved the picture where she was painting Rachel's nails and giggling with her like they were the same age. I loved the one of us at a tailgate, although I can't remember which show it was now. She was laughing, it looked like at something I had said, with her head thrown back and one of her arms looped through mine. And the shot of her arguing with Jeff's friend Pete over which bootleg to play next, because she looked so serious. Like she was fighting over a matter of life and death.

But my all-time favorite is the one that was taken just a few seconds before Laura's all-time favorite picture of the two of us. We were sitting on the back of her car, with the top down of course, and I could remember which song was blasting out of it. We played much of the tailgate music out of Laura's car, because as she said, with the top down, her car was basically just a giant boombox. We had each just taken bites of our hotdogs that were too big for our mouths when Ellen wandered over with her camera. And we both tried frantically to finish chewing before she could take a picture, but then we started laughing and Ellen took a picture of that. Laura's favorite picture was a good one too, with the food stashed out of the shot, my arm around her, and her head leaning on my shoulder. That *is* a great picture, but it was posed. And Laura does look incredible in all posed shots.

But, in my mind, there was never anything on this planet like the spontaneous Laura and I'm still grateful to Ellen for being able to capture a few of those moments on film for me.

18

Even now, after everything that's happened, if you asked me to make a list of the best days ever in my whole life, I would put August 11, 2003 at the top. It was one of those perfect days, in which nothing can go wrong. Maybe it wasn't as good at the time as it seems looking back on it now, but in the end, it's the memory, not the reality that stays with you. And my memory of that day is that it was exquisite.

Of course, you don't know that you're going to have one of those days when you wake up. I woke up pretty miserable. It was a Monday morning, which is never good for anyone, and it was the night of the third show in Philadelphia. But I woke up in my apartment, not in Philly.

Laura and I had gone to the Friday and Saturday night shows, but I reluctantly told her that I couldn't afford to miss another day of work to stay over for Monday's show. I had an important staff meeting Monday afternoon and it just wasn't going to work. I told her to go without me, praying she would say that no, it wouldn't be the same without me. Eventually, she relented and, realizing that I was serious about not being able to go, she said we could watch the setlist at my apartment to try to recapture some of the excitement of the show we were missing. It was a poor substitute, but it was better than sitting at home alone, drinking beer and watching TV.

So, despondent at the prospect of a new week at work and having to miss a show that was within driving distance, I trudged off to the office.

And I've never spent a longer day there. Every second that ticked by felt like an hour. And even though I was busy, this little voice in the back of my head kept nagging me that maybe I really *could* have taken the day off and gone to the show. I can't explain it. I had been to more than forty already in less than a year, but with each subsequent concert, I felt like I had to be at the next one or else I would be missing the experience of my lifetime.

But at 1:53, just as I had finished the PowerPoint presentation for that afternoon's meeting, I heard the most beautiful sound drifting in from the outer office. It was Laura laughing. It couldn't be, and I knew it wasn't *really* her, but I went to my office door to look anyway. And there she was.

She was sitting on the low wall that separated the reception area from the offices, impossibly cool in denim capris and a black tank top, with the requisite summer day sunglasses perched on her head. Not remotely appropriate office attire. But Laura could blend in at a black tie affair in sweats. It was always all about attitude with her.

Two of the senior partners from my office were standing near her, Bill leaning against the wall, Scott opposite her, and she was laughing at something one of them had said. Coral, our nosier-than-nosy receptionist was still at her seat, but was peering around her computer in a way that said she had clearly given up on even trying to pretend that she wasn't listening to every word that was being said. Phil and Grace, two of my coworkers, had left their offices and were standing in the space between their two doorways observing the conversation as well. You would have thought that we had never had a client here before. But then again, Laura didn't fit the mold of our usual clientele. Nor had I ever seen anyone sit on that wall. Or both Bill and Scott come out to talk to anyone who wasn't wearing a suit.

"There he is!" Laura cried with delight when she saw me and she hopped off the wall, with a hand on Bill's shoulder to steady her descent. She threw her arms around my neck and kissed me lightly on the lips in greeting. I was too surprised to move. It was just a peck. But it was on the lips. I had no idea what was going on. Then she turned back to Bill and Scott, who were smiling indulgently. "You're sure it's alright?" she asked, looking a little worried. I was floored. Laura never asked permission for anything. Ever.

Bill nodded but Scott spoke. "Of course, sweetheart, go and enjoy."

I turned to Laura. "Go where?" She smiled and pulled two tickets out of her back pocket.

I was amazed. We had sold our tickets on Saturday night when we decided we weren't going to the Monday show. And somehow she had gotten two more GAs. And not only that, she had gotten my bosses to tell me to leave work early to go.

"How—?" I started, but she cut me off.

"Ticket drop. Now come on, we're going to have to speed to get there in time to get in line for the lottery!" She had to be lying. If she had gotten the tickets through a drop on Ticketmaster, she would have had to pick up the tickets at will-call at the venue. That was how tickets worked on the day of the show. There wasn't any way to get tickets the same day except at the venue, which meant that she had clearly gotten them somewhere else. But I didn't ask her. Accusing her of lying would have seemed fishy to my bosses. And she wouldn't have answered me anyway.

I looked questioningly at Bill and Scott. "I'll do your presentation if the PowerPoint is done," Bill said. I told him it was, and he told us to leave so we could make it in time.

I emailed the presentation to Bill and got my keys and briefcase. Laura took my hand as we started to leave, but Bill stopped us as we walked out. "That's some girl, you've got there." Laura beamed up at him and he smiled back. "You kids have a good time tonight!" And somehow, it didn't even sound patronizing when he said that.   I normally would have been pissed to be called a kid at the office, where I tried as hard as I could to act like a professional. But he sounded like he could have been her dad telling us to have fun on a date.

In the elevator, I asked how she had done it.

"Easy," she said, pulling her hair up into a ponytail. "I just asked to speak to the partners and I told them that I was your girlfriend and it's our six month anniversary today and I'd gotten tickets to tonight's show as a present for you. They actually seemed thrilled to get rid of you," she said, with that wicked smile I loved.

I couldn't help it; I pulled her to me and hugged her. I half-expected her to squirm out of it. But she didn't.

Because I took the Metro to work most mornings, we didn't have to deal with having two cars, and it was such a beautiful day that there was no question about whose car we would have taken anyway. It was a convertible day if I had ever seen one. But crossing the garage to her car, I realized we would have a timing problem anyway.

I checked my watch. It was 2:14. We really needed to be in the parking lot by 4:30 to have a shot to be in the pit, because of the lottery system, which had replaced the fan-run list the earlier shows on the tour, and it would take us two-and-a-half hours to get there from my office in DC. Maybe, if we drove like demons right now we would have the smallest chance of making it in time. But even that was unlikely. And I was dressed for work.

"Shit," I said finally.

"What's wrong?"

"We're not going to make it in time."

"Sure we will. As long as we hurry."

"I've got to change; I can't go like this and I don't have clothes with me."

Laura smiled. "It's a good thing I'm a genius," she said, batting her eyelashes at me. She pushed the button on her keys to open the trunk and she pulled out a small pink Adidas duffel bag, which she tossed at me.

"What's this?" I asked, opening it. In the bag were my shorts, which she had mentioned the week before that she had grabbed by accident when we stayed in Jersey after one of the Giants Stadium shows; my favorite Rolling Stones t-shirt, which she had stolen months ago to sleep in; and the old sneakers that I had forgotten in her trunk, when we changed to dry shoes after one of the rain shows. For the second time in fifteen minutes, I didn't know what to say.

"I washed the shorts," she said. "They smelled like smoke."

"You?" I asked with a smile. "You did laundry?"

"What's wrong with that?" she asked. "I'm quite domestic." Then she started laughing. "Whatever, okay, fine, I'm not domestic at all. But I *do* know how to do laundry!"

I didn't thank her. It's one of those tricks I had learned in the past nine months. She could be ridiculously sweet and thoughtful. That was, in fact, the real Laura. But she hated being called on it. And thanking her made her realize that she wasn't keeping up the act. She would pull back when I did that, which was, of course, a setback in whatever our odd relationship was. And as odd as it sounds, I liked the duality of her. It kept me on my toes. It had taken me a long time to decide which parts of her were real and which weren't, and I still screwed it up frequently. But not that day.

I changed in the car while Laura drove, and a bootleg from the third Giants Stadium show saw us the whole way there. We had made the same drive on Friday night, but this was better because it was so completely unexpected. Better because it was such a beautiful day. Better because we were playing hooky from work. It felt like we were kids skipping school. Laura, in fact, pointed out that that was exactly what we were doing when we got to the line about it in "Rosalita."

When I think about Laura, I think about her that day. It's how I want to remember her. Never the fighting that would come later, or the loss, or the pain. Not even kissing her or waking up next to her. But only as she was on that one perfect day. She was so completely alive. The sun hitting her shoulders and the gold in her hair, bleached there by her refusal to put the top of her car up when it wasn't raining that summer. And maybe a little un-discussed help from her hair stylist. I want to remember her laughing and singing, loudly and badly with the music. Throwing her fist into the air during "Badlands" and "Born to Run," and insisting that I do the same, which prompted odd looks from the other drivers around us, which turned into knowing smiles from other drivers as we got closer to the venue. Maybe she really was that beautiful that day. Maybe I just thought she was because I loved her. Maybe I just think she was now, looking back. But it doesn't matter, because it's how I remember her.

The clouds started threatening us once we crossed into Delaware. They had been chasing us since Baltimore. But around Wilmington, the first drops of rain started to fall.

"Should we pull over and put the top up?" I asked, finally, as Laura eventually turned on the windshield wipers. A look of concentration crossed her face as she studied the horizon.

"No," she said. "If we keep moving at this speed, we won't get wet," which was true, as the wind resistance keeps rain from falling into the car until you stop. "And I think we can get past the clouds first." I smiled. She looked over and smiled back at me and the speedometer crept past 80 miles per hour. And as always, she was right.

We beat the clouds around the Pennsylvania state line. Of course, they would catch up to us later, but there was a certain thrill even in just outrunning the rain. Nothing could stop us. And we not only beat the rain, but we made it in plenty of time for the pit line. And our luck held with the ticket lottery because we wound up in the front, right near Little Steven and Patti. Laura's favorite side if we couldn't be dead center. We stuck with Jeff and Ellen as we walked in and wound up next to them in the pit.

We had all huddled for shelter in the parking lot when the rain started, but it had stopped by the time we were filing into the stadium. No real tailgating on pit nights, because you could get out of the pit if you had to go to the bathroom, especially during "Mary's Place," when Bruce extended the song to twenty minutes and did the band introductions; but if you gave up a spot at the front, you were never getting it back. We had entered, what Laura called, "Camel Mode" before we even got to Pennsylvania. We would take bottles of water into the pit, because we would need them desperately by the end of the night, but no drinking until we started sweating. Laura's rules. We even figured out a system for the water bottles, because at Giants Stadium, and a few other venues, they only let you bring water bottles in with you if you didn't bring the top, and they took the tops off the bottles they sold there as well. Laura kept extra caps in her purse, which we would put on our open bottles as soon as we were inside.

But unlike Friday and Saturday nights, which were swelteringly hot, the rain had cooled the temperature down to a comfortable seventy-four degrees, according to the new Eagles stadium's scoreboard, by the time the show started. The sun was still out when Bruce followed the band to the stage.

Laura grabbed my hand and squeezed it as Bruce came out and said into my ear, "Here we go." I loved the excitement level. We had done this a million times. But every time was as exciting as the first. For me as well. I cheered and yelled "Bruuuuuuuce" with the rest of them like my life depended on it. And I waited for the opening notes of whichever song Bruce would play to start the show. While it was sometimes predictable, such as "Who'll Stop the Rain," when it was raining, waiting to recognize the first notes of that first song was intense and exhilarating. And Laura and I played a game of seeing who recognized the song he opened with first.

But that night, that recognition didn't come. I had never heard the song that Bruce opened with. And based on the look of mixed confusion and elation on Laura's face, she had never heard it before either. She turned to me finally. She wasn't going to ask what it was, so I asked her. But she didn't know.

I turned to my right and saw that Jeff has his arms around Ellen and they were singing along. How on earth was there a song that even Laura didn't know? I caught Jeff's eye. I wouldn't have asked him what it was during the song, as that would be a breach of concert etiquette. But he volunteered the answer anyway. "'From Small Things,'" he shouted. "*River* outtakes. Dave Edmunds covered it." I yelled back my thanks and turned to tell Laura what I had learned.

"Has he ever played it before?" she asked. I relayed her question to Jeff, but Ellen answered.

"Just in clubs a couple of times. Never on tour."

A huge grin spread across Laura's face. "History in the making," she said and turned her full attention back to Bruce.

He jumped from "Lonesome Day" into "Night," a moderately rare song off *Born to Run*, which I loved. It was about how you force yourself to survive your days in a job that you don't like because your real life starts at night. It reminded me of the life I had with Laura, even though it wasn't one of her favorite songs.

Next came another new one to us. "Be True," which he hadn't played in the US on this tour yet. If you've never been to a Bruce show, I'm not sure I can really explain what came over us at the beginning of that song. We danced, we sang along, we threw ourselves into it like he was playing it just for us. Yes, we knew he was playing it because he wanted to and he was playing it for Philadelphia, just like he played "Atlantic City" next because it mentions Philly. But when you're there at one of his shows, no matter how many other people are around you, be it a thousand or a hundred thousand, he's playing for you. And when you're in the front of the pit, he's less than ten feet from you, playing a song he almost never plays, just for you. So when he tells you to show some faith because "there's magic in the night," you know what he means because it's true. You're seeing that magic right then.

As if to prove my point, after some of the requisite songs from *The Rising*, Bruce heard people yelling for "Thunder Road" and he played it, even though he had already played it there Friday night. And we screamed as he pulled out his harmonica and we sang the song right back to him, just like every audience has since 1975 when he started telling us to.

The band retreated off stage as the main set ended. We weren't worried; they were coming right back. The norm was two encores, and for the last show in Philly, there was no doubt that those encores would be incredible. I wrapped my arm around Laura's waist during this and pulled her closer to me. She was damp with sweat and I was too. It may have been a cool night, but the pit is always hot. "If you could hear anything in the world next, what would it be?" I asked into her ear. She leaned into me and closed her eyes, deep in thought. Then she twisted her neck up to say it into my ear.

"Incident."

He had played it a handful of times, but never at a show we had been at. But when Bruce and the band came back to the stage, Bruce asked for requests, which I had been pretty sure he would do after seeing him listen to the requests for "Thunder Road." I yelled "Incident" as loud as I could. He heard someone else first, but didn't catch what they had said and joked with them, asking for "something we know." Jeff had heard me and he and Ellen joined in requesting the same song, as did several other people who had heard me and agreed.

And Bruce nodded, then told Roy, the piano player, to start. At the opening notes, Laura tore her eyes away from Bruce and turned to me. She didn't say thank you, but then again she never did. And she didn't have to. It was in her eyes. She turned back to the stage, but she took my arms and pulled them tighter around her waist. I glanced to my right, at Jeff and Ellen, who had seen that. Ellen smiled at me and I grinned broadly back.

I could have held her like that forever. The smell of her perfume coming off her hair, Bruce a few feet in front of us, one of the most beautiful love songs ever written being sung for us, at our request. Remember in *Field of Dreams*, when the kid asks if he's in heaven and Kevin Costner says, "No, it's Iowa"? It was like that. We were at the Linc! I hate the Eagles and I was standing on their field. But heaven is where you find it. And we had found it.

We broke apart to dance when Bruce played "I'm Goin' Down" for the guys holding up request signs about twenty feet behind us. We had seen the signs earlier in the night, and Jeff had warned us before the show started that he would be shocked if Bruce played that, even in Philadelphia, because he hadn't played it since the *Born in the USA* tour. And when he started it, Bruce confirmed Jeff's position as more of an expert than Laura, by saying that the band hadn't played the song since 1986. Jeff laughed and shook his head. The E Street band wasn't on tour in 1986, and Jeff knew that. We laughed when he said that he didn't even know which guitar to play it on. And we danced and sang along. And cheered Little Steven on, even though he clearly got a little lost in the middle. And our faith was rewarded, because Steve kissed his guitar pick and tossed it to Laura when the song ended. She blew him a kiss and he blew one back at her.

"Think he recognizes us yet?" Laura asked. I told her he had to, as she pocketed the pick.

It was the most incredible show we had been to on the tour.

But instead of going straight into "Rosalita" after "Land of Hope and Dreams," Bruce started something else. We heard Ellen and Jeff screaming, and Ellen jumped up and down like Laura, a girl half her age, had at "Be True." Jeff saw us watching and smiled. "He used to play this as an intro to 'Rosie' in the seventies," he explained as he held

Ellen and swayed with her. "Hasn't played it since the *Darkness* tour."

Laura smiled and closed her eyes. She leaned back into me and I put my arm around her waist again. We had heard versions of Bruce covering Manfred Mann's "Pretty Flamingo" on bootlegs, but never live, as he hadn't played it since the year after we were born. Then again, my parents had gone to a couple of shows when my mother was pregnant with me. Maybe I had heard it before after all.

As the last note hung on the air and the first note to "Rosalita" clung to it, opening the song, Laura turned and kissed me.

In real time, I know that it must have been less than thirty seconds, because the kiss had ended by the time Bruce started singing. But if I didn't have the bootleg of the show to prove that it was that short of a time, I would believe it could have been forever.

I had never decided that I loved someone before having kissed them before. Well, okay, excluding my fourth grade teacher. But you know what I mean. To be honest, before it happened, I couldn't really imagine how it could. We had come so far past the point where I could have plausibly made a move that I figured that if it was ever going to happen, it would be because we were ridiculously drunk. Although nothing had happened yet while ridiculously drunk. And even if it did, we would have probably ignored it the next day. Because she didn't feel the way I did. I'm not stupid. Once you're in the friend zone, it's up to the girl to make a move if she wants something to happen. Very few guys have girl friends who they wouldn't sleep with if the occasion arose. So if a girl, who really *is* a friend, wants more from a relationship, she's the one to take it there. And if she doesn't want to, she keeps you at arms length for the sake of the friendship. And while Laura could be affectionate, she was like a cat. It was when she wanted it, and *only* when she wanted it. If I tried to pet her when she wasn't in the mood, there was no chance of it happening. While I had spent months aching to make a move, I never found the right time when she would have allowed it. And I knew her well enough to know that if I did it too soon, I would lose her altogether. And that wasn't a risk that was worth taking. Even if we could never be more than friends, having her in my life at all made my life better. And I would have done anything that it took to keep her in my life.

But she kissed me.

I think.

I know I didn't start it consciously. So it must have been her.

But that didn't matter.

Girls make a bigger deal about kissing than guys do. There's that awful Cher song about how you can tell everything you need to know from a kiss. I don't believe that's true. But for the first time ever really, I started to believe that there was a chance for us. Somewhere in her, she wanted to be with me too. And that night, I believed I could wait forever if that was what it took.

By the time Bruce started singing, she had turned back to the stage. She was watching Bruce and dancing to the music, but Little Steven had seen the kiss and winked at me. It's stupid, I know, but I treasured that wink as Laura would treasure the guitar pick he had thrown her and the kiss he had blown to her. Bruce's guitar player and right—er, left-hand man as it were, approved of my choice of girl. And I didn't question what would happen next, because I knew it wouldn't be anything else that night. And that night, it didn't need to be. It was perfect as it was.

We weren't planning to stay over in Philadelphia, and I had to be at work the next morning, although Laura's appearance at my office would mean if I came in late, no one would question it. But we didn't rush to leave the sports complex's parking lot. It had been cool right after the rain, but the night had turned warm and muggy. The air was so thick and heavy that the sweat we had worked up refused to evaporate, and Laura's hair along the hairline was damp. We walked slowly off the field and out into the parking lot, unwilling to let the night end.

Most of the crowd seemed to be doing the same thing. We had parked deep in the lot, which meant that we weren't getting our car out for a good half hour anyway, so we walked down the steps of the Linc with Jeff and Ellen, discussing the show.

Laura was glowing. She kept dancing a few feet in front of us and spinning around and coming back to me. Every few seconds, she would recount another favorite moment of the show. "And I can't *believe* he played 'I'm Goin' Down!'" she would yell suddenly. Or just "'*Incident!*' He played 'Incident!' Full band and everything!" She started singing "Be True" as we walked toward the parking lot. Jeff and Ellen were as amused by her as I was. This was one of my favorite times with Laura, after a great show, when she was happy. After some shows, she became quiet or sullen, because she knew there wouldn't be another one for a little while. But when she was like this, there was no one in the world like her.

We reached her car and Laura hit the remote button to put the top down before we got there, but tossed me the keys. She never asked me if I wanted to drive home, or if I was tired, or if I minded driving her car (although no one in their right mind would turn down the chance to drive that car). It was one of those things between us that was so special. She might not let me touch her camera, but she always let me drive her car. If I made a list of reasons to believe she loved me, that would be on the list. Of course, the reasons not to believe it list would be longer. But, no matter what the circumstances, as Bruce would say, "people find some reason to believe."

I started to get in the car, but Laura stayed by the trunk. "Pop it, will you?" she asked and I obliged. She pulled out a small cooler, shut the trunk, and climbed on top of it. "Wanna put on some tunes and have a beer?"

I put the same Giants Stadium bootleg that we had been listening to on the way up to the show back into the cd player and climbed onto the trunk next to Laura. We had done this a few times after being in the pit. Post-show tailgating.

We didn't talk for a while. We just sat there, soaking up the night and watching the crowd. Adam and Jen, a couple we had met at the Meadowlands, were walking a few rows over and Laura called to them. They were about our age and we had hung out with them for the first two Philly shows, but then told them we weren't coming to this one. They sat with us and helped us lighten our beer load a bit. Eventually, we realized that it was just the post-gamers like us in the parking lot because it was past midnight. Adam and Jen were driving home to New Jersey, and we decided that it was time for us to leave as well. I realized, as we pulled out of the now nearly deserted parking lot, that this would be our last Philly show on this tour. It could be the last Philly show for years. The first time we had talked to each other had been in this very parking lot. Everything had changed since then. And I was sure that so much more would change before we would be there again. But that was ahead of us, and that night, I wasn't thinking all that much about the past or the future.

Once you get onto I-95, it's pretty much a straight shot home from Philly. A quick dodge around Wilmington on 495 and then one road home until the Capitol Beltway. I could have done it in my sleep. But I was wide awake that night. The air was so thick that it felt like being underwater. But that couldn't matter. It was cooler with the top down on the car at least. Laura switched from the CD player back to the XM radio and cranked the volume way up.

One of the first songs that Laura found was by Journey. She started to laugh as soon as the station landed on it. "It's your song," she shouted over the music.

"Shut up," I said.

"No, come on! Sing along! I know you know the words." I turned a fake glare on her. But I couldn't keep it up. I just shook my head.

"Fine," she said, "I'll do it." She reached into the center console of the car and pulled out a hairbrush, then unhooked her seatbelt and got up onto her knees. "Don't stop, believin'," she sang as loudly as she could into the hairbrush like it was a microphone. "Hold on to the feel-ennnnenen." She held the hairbrush out to me. And I joined in.

Normally, we just listened to the music. If we found a song that was really an audience participation number, we would sing, but that wasn't how we usually did it. That night we sang along. Loudly and off key, every word to every song. We didn't analyze. We didn't praise. We didn't discuss. We were completely and totally silly with it. Laura held the hairbrush and alternated it between me and her for chorus lines. When "Livin' on a Prayer" by Bon Jovi came on, Laura squealed with delight and I loved that even though it was one of her guilty pleasure songs, she didn't feel the least bit ashamed of getting excited about it with me.

When we got to my apartment, I parked the car and looked over at Laura. She was leaning her head back against the seat and was looking at me. I moved the littlest bit closer. Should I kiss her again? Her eyes widened slightly and I stopped. It wasn't the right time. And suddenly, even the idea of kissing her was completely ridiculous. Maybe because it was almost 3am. Maybe because it had been such an incredible day. Maybe because it had all been so unexpected. Maybe because I wanted to prove that it was real. But just the thought of it all made me laugh. And once I started, Laura did too.

I finally got out of the car and Laura followed. She punched me playfully on the arm, still giggling, as we crossed in the headlights' beams. I slapped her just as playfully on her behind as she passed me.

I fell asleep that night remembering the smile that she flashed at me before she drove away.

19

"You know you lucked out on the date, right?"

"You know that's the hundredth time you've told me that, right?" Mel retorted without missing a beat. I was at her apartment helping her seal, stamp, and mail her wedding invitations, and Bruce had just announced the last shows of the tour. Mel and Eric had selected the night of the Wisconsin show, which Laura and I had already decided we weren't going to anyway, meaning that I had no conflicts for either the rehearsal dinner or the wedding itself. I would miss the setlist watch, but hey, Mel was my best friend; I would manage to suffer through it.

Would I have gone to a show with Laura instead of the wedding if there had been one closer that night? Probably not, because Mel would have never spoken to me again. Laura was, at that point, referring to her as "Bridezilla," although I would never tell Mel that Laura had said that. Then again, if I had, Mel would have been able to give me another insight into Laura, as she would have informed me that Laura probably read *Cosmopolitan*, something that Laura would never have admitted to. Anything that would give beauty and "how to please your man" tips was not exactly Laura's style.

As I put the stamp on what seemed like the millionth envelope, I tried not to think about whether I would be bringing Laura to the wedding or not. I hadn't asked her yet.

My name finally jumped out at me from the pile.

"Hey, it's me!" Mel just smiled indulgently as she continued to stuff envelopes. "Why waste a stamp? I'll just take it home." I started to pull it out of the pile.

"No!" Mel shrieked, startling me.

"Whoa, calm down." I put it back into the pile and leaned down to pick up the envelopes that I knocked all over the floor when Mel screamed. "Why can't I just take it?"

"You're my barometer," she said, like she was talking to an exceptionally slow child. "I need to see when you get yours to know when other people should expect to get theirs." It seemed dumb to me, but I just nodded and kept stamping envelopes.

"So I got the invite for Mel and Eric's wedding the other day," I said as casually as I could to Laura as we were leaving the eighth of the Meadowlands shows. "It's the night of the Wisconsin show. The one we're not going to."

Laura shrugged and walked a little ahead of me. "You knew that already. Besides, you'll miss the setlist watch."

"Well either way, I have to go; I'm one of the groomsmen."

"We all have our priorities," she said with a smirk and a coy look over her shoulder. I didn't say anything back immediately. I wanted to grab her arm, spin her around, and just tell her she was coming with me. Cut through the bullshit. But she would never go for that. She would laugh at me and say no. So I caught up with her and walked next to her as we wove our way through the parking lot. We made it back to her car and she tossed me her keys. I unlocked the doors with the remote and climbed into the driver's seat, marveling as I always did, that her legs were as long as mine and that I didn't need to move the seat like I did with every other girl whose car I had ever driven.

It was a nice night, unlike the third and fourth Meadowlands shows, when it had rained on us for two hours, so I put the top down. As I did, Laura nodded her approval and began to pull her hair back into a ponytail. She was unusually quiet. She knew what I was going to ask, and she was waiting for me to get it over with so that she could say no.

It took about twenty minutes to get out of the parking lot. We waved and made small talk with the other drivers we knew by that point. Finally though, it was the four of us alone on the road: me, Laura, Bruce (on the stereo of course), and the unspoken question.

We were staying with my brother in Philadelphia that night, and then with Jeff and Ellen in New Jersey for the next two nights because we were going to all of the last three shows at Giants Stadium. I had been working whatever weekends I could to make up for all the time I was missing at the office. My bosses weren't thrilled, but they hadn't been able to say anything official about it to me yet, as I was getting my work done, just not during a time frame when they could usually discuss it with me. And after they sent me off to the last Philadelphia show with Laura, they didn't have a whole lot of room to complain about me going to more shows with her.

As we passed exit eight on the Turnpike, the exit that we would take if we were going back to Asbury Park, I realized that Laura still hadn't said anything about the concert. He had played "Be True" and "From Small Things," both of which he had played at that third, incredible Philly show, and still she hadn't said anything. God, she was frustrating! She was turned away from me, looking out into the Jersey night. She knew what I was going to ask. She was sitting there waiting for me to do it. I could throw her for a loop and not ask. But I wanted her there. Desperately. But she would say no if I asked. I decided I just wouldn't. Why bother getting rejected?

Fuck it. "Will you come with me?"

She turned her face back to me and asked sweetly, "To what?"

I sighed. When she did this, I found myself asking if she was really worth all the crap that she put me through. Up until then, I had always said yes. But I still found myself asking that question when she behaved this way. "To the wedding."

"As your date?" Shit. Do I say yes and have her remind me that we're not a couple? Or say no and have her ask why I don't want her there as a date and still have her say no?

"As my 'and guest.'"

"Why?" *Because you're a pain in the ass but for some reason I think I'm in love with you.* But of course, I wasn't about to say that. I wondered if I should drop it until after the last of the Meadowlands shows, when it wouldn't be as awkward if she turned me down flat. But I had already come too far for that.

"'Cause I feel like you'll clean up well and it'll make my friends jealous," I said with a grin that was only a little too tense. It was the one answer she might accept.

But no.

"I see," she laughed. "Good answer. But I think I'm going to have to pass."

"Oh come on. Why?"

"Weddings just aren't my scene."

I was irritated, but tried to play it off with sarcasm. "Do you do bar mitzvahs then?"

She just smiled. "Invite me to one of those and you'll find out." She changed the CD to put on a bootleg of "Open All Night," which Bruce introduced as being a song about that "golden roadway of the east: the New Jersey Turnpike," and leaned back in her seat. "Seems appropriate tonight."

I gave up. "Getting 'From Small Things' again was pretty unreal," I finally said, tired of being rejected. Because the third Philly show was the first time he had played it, we didn't know what we were hearing then and we therefore didn't fully appreciate it. This time we knew all the words and while it wasn't as special, it was more fun. I knew she would agree about that at least. And she did.

20

Laura never once mentioned the guy in the *Born to Run* shirt from the first Philadelphia show. As I thought more and more about the first time I had seen her, I started to believe that she had been with him in DC as well, but I wasn't quite sure. When I looked back on the first time that I saw her, I could picture him standing next to her. But I also knew that it could have been someone else, and I could have just been putting *Born to Run* guy's face on him. He never popped up in conversation, and I never asked about him. I knew better than that from the start. If she wanted me to know anything about him, she would have told me.

By the second DC show more than a year later, I had basically forgotten all about him. I knew by then that Laura's money came from what her parents had left her, based on a drunken and bitter sounding comment about "mommy and daddy's money" one night, and that she had never needed a sugar daddy like I had originally thought. *Born to Run* guy must have been someone she had once worked with, or a family friend. Maybe an uncle, although she claimed to have no family at all, in which case I thought that maybe he was the executor of her parents' estate. He was about that age after all. Way too old for her to want to hang out with otherwise. And with the money issue out of the way, I no longer saw him in as threatening of a light. I forced myself to forget the familiarity of their behavior when I had seen them together in Philadelphia. I had been imagining things, I told myself over and over until I almost believed it. His hand had been perfectly appropriately placed on her waist.   Nothing out of the ordinary after all.

The second show in Washington was a huge event.   It was just two days after the two year anniversary of September 11, and everyone knew he must have picked DC for that show on purpose.   We hadn't lost nearly as many people as New York of course, but DC had definitely been hit in the terrorist attacks, and we didn't get the ten-night stand at the Meadowlands to sustain us like New York did. To only play two shows in the entire DC area seemed unfair; Philly had three on this leg of the tour, four total, and the closest shows to DC had been Richmond in March and Philadelphia in August.   We knew we were due for something spectacular.

Laura and I felt like the hosts of that tailgate in a sense. Yes, everyone brought their own food and beer, but this one was on our home turf as opposed to all of the Meadowlands shows.   It was a beautiful early fall day, Laura was at her charming best, Bruce was playing in our hometown, and we had GA tickets. Life was good.

The tailgate started early and, as we always did, we ate and drank only enough to sustain us through a hot night, because too much to drink would cost us our place near the stage.

"'Paradise' is a given," Jeff said, starting the pot for the setlist. "It's about DC. The real question is, what rarities are we going to get?"

"'Incident'" I said, smiling at Laura.

"Nah," Jeff said. "I'm voting for a Johnny Cash song and a B-side like 'Janey.'" This was the first show since Johnny Cash's death, making that a really good guess, but I stood by my choice.

"Laura, back me up here!" But Laura wasn't paying any attention to me.   She was hugging a man who looked a little too familiar.   He wasn't wearing the *Born to Run* shirt, but it was definitely the same guy.   Better looking than I remembered. Taller. Less old. Holding Laura a little too close. Kissing her on the cheek.

She eventually pulled out of his embrace and touched his face, studying him closely. She looked genuinely happy to see him and he was clearly only too delighted to see her.

"It's been forever!" she said as I strained to hear her.

"Too long," he agreed. "I've missed you, kid."

Laura nodded. "I missed you too."

"You look great though. Happy." A flash of something unrecognizable crossed Laura's face. A memory of something that didn't quite agree with her. Then it was gone.

"I am, I guess."

"You guess?"

"Well, yeah. I guess I am." And she smiled that slow smile that melted me every time I saw it. I hated her smiling it at him. In the year that I had known her, I had never been so jealous. Without *Born to Run* guy, I was clearly the man in her life. Other than Bruce, of course. I knew that couldn't last forever, but I didn't want to see it end then. Ellen saw where I was looking and gently touched my arm.

"No worrying," she said with a conspiratorial wink. "He's got to be older than me." I forced a small, grim smile as I looked down at her. She smiled back at me reassuringly. "I'm on it," she said, walking toward Laura. I tried to look away. But I just couldn't quite do it. It was like a train wreck.

Ellen jumped smoothly into their conversation and introduced herself. With anyone else, Laura would have completely blown her off. She didn't allow anyone to move in on her territory, especially women; I had seen that at Melanie's engagement party. But Laura couldn't and wouldn't do that with Ellen, and Ellen knew that. Then Ellen invited *Born to Run* guy to join our tailgate. Not exactly my idea of taking care of the situation. Especially when she steered him and Laura directly over to me.

And then she vanished.

So it was me, Laura, and the guy. I guess that was Ellen's plan though, because it meant that Laura had to introduce us, which also meant that Laura had to give me a little bit of information about who he was. But before Laura realized what she had to do, there was an awkward silence that felt infinitely long.

"This is Charlie Owens," she said, after introducing me. Pause. "I met him when I was doing some freelance work at *the Post* and he actually got me started with the stuff at *Rolling Stone*." I nodded, at a loss for words.

I wasn't really paying attention to the conversation after that. Instead I focused on the body language between them. Laura seemed perfectly at ease with him, touching his arm, laughing, smiling a lot. It was exactly how she was with him when I saw her in the Philadelphia parking lot. And it was completely indecipherable. I couldn't begin to guess the relationship.

I was saved by the intervention of Claire and Barbara, who had clearly not yet gotten the message that Laura was irresistible. Charlie was polite, but very definitively not interested in either. Eventually, he said that he should get back to the people he had come with. Laura walked him to the edge of our group and I offered to take over at the grill for a few minutes. It meant my back was to them, but I was closer and could therefore inconspicuously listen to what they were saying.

"So are you with this guy?" he asked her.

"No," Laura said, honestly, but not in a flat, ruling everything out way. To my ears at least.

"What's the story there?"

I could picture her shrugging. "I don't know."

He laughed. "Well until you figure it out, feel free to give me a call any time. For tickets or," he paused, "anything else."

"Same old Charlie," Laura said laughing. "If you were about a million years younger, you would make a great boyfriend."

"Still younger than Bruce and always will be. Remember that babe."

"Yes," she said, "but Bruce is timeless. You, my darling, are not quite there yet."

"Fair enough," he said. "But I'm serious. Call me if you ever need me. For anything."

"I will," she said. I knew that tone of voice though and I felt more relief than I thought possible when I heard it. She wasn't going to call him. Whatever had once been between them was over now.

"Take care of yourself, kid."

"You too," she said.

A minute later she was talking to Jeff and putting her money on "Bobby Jean."

I guess I was a little quieter than usual on the way home from the show, which was our shortest drive home yet. Less than twenty minutes. We got to my place and Laura turned off the car. We had post-gamed it with the tailgate crowd but it wasn't even 1am yet. "Invite me in for a drink?" she asked.

"Of course."

I had spent the entire evening trying to figure out what I had seen earlier. I knew that asking her would be idiotic. Especially after her response when I invited her to Mel's wedding. If Laura wanted to tell me something, she would tell me, but not if I asked about it. Clearly I could not ask her. I was definitely not going to ask. Nope. Not going to ask. No way. No how.

"So who was that guy earlier?" She had just settled onto my sofa, her shoes kicked off and her feet tucked up under her as she took her first sip of beer. *Idiot*, I thought. *I shouldn't have asked.*

She calmly finished her sip, set the beer down deliberately on the coffee table, placed her hands in her lap, and looked at me completely innocently, as if she had no idea what in the world I was talking about. "What guy?"

"That Charlie guy."

"Ah. Charlie." She reached over to her beer and took another, longer drink, but I think she was buying herself time to figure out what to tell me. She couldn't have thought that I would ask about him. I mean, I would have to be pretty stupid to do that. Which apparently I was.

"I already told you, he got me into doing a little freelance work at *Rolling Stone*."

"What's he do?"

"He's part owner of a whole bunch of publications. Investor kind of. Also involved with a record company." She looked directly at me. "Anything else you'd like to know?"

Why were you with him at the Philly show? I wanted to ask. But that would be too much. Wouldn't it? I shrugged finally. Time for a slightly different tactic. "You've met all of my friends. He's the only person—er—friend, I guess, of yours who I've met."

I hadn't realized how stiff Laura's posture was until she relaxed it. It was usually dumb luck with her when I wound up saying the right thing, and that was definitely the case this time. "He's been kind of like a dad to me, I guess," she said eventually. "I've known him for years now." She stopped, contemplating what else to tell me. "He got me into listening to Bruce last year." Another pause. "He took me to my first few concerts." Pause. "And whenever I had trouble getting tickets, he was always willing to make a phone call or two and find us some GAs."

"Us?" I asked.

"Sometimes. That's how I got our third night in Philly."

"Didn't you say you got those in a drop?"

"Well, they were tickets that were *going* to be released in a drop, but Charlie got them for us first."

"Oh," I said, for lack of anything better. I still wanted to ask if there was more between them. But I knew that I had pressed my luck enough already for one night.

We settled into a mildly uncomfortable silence. There was still so much I didn't know, so much I couldn't know, about her. As the silence stretched on, I started to wonder what would happen when the tour ended. I hadn't really thought about that yet, but it would be over in another three weeks. We were going to a few more shows, including the last three at Shea Stadium in New York, but what would happen then? I wanted to think that after the tour ended, Laura would realize that she wanted to be with me. If we hadn't kissed in Philadelphia, I'm not sure I would have thought that was possible. But as we sat in my living room, looking anywhere but at each other, I started to wonder how that could happen. She would eventually have to open up to me more, that much was obvious, but would she? Could she? Was that who she was? And if not, I realized that I might be in trouble.

The next night's show was in Chapel Hill, then just six more because we were skipping Colorado and Wisconsin. Seven total. Then the moment of truth.

And suddenly, I was terrified.

21

"Do you have a date to that wedding yet?" It was a typical Laura phone call. No hello, no goodbye, and no need to identify herself.

I grinned, but tried to keep the smile out of my voice. "Nah, I was gonna go stag."

"Do you still want me there?"

I tried to pause long enough to not sound ecstatic. I'm not sure I succeeded. "Definitely."

"Then I'll go."

"Okay. It's at seven-thirty on the twenty-seventh. I've got to be there early though, so if you want me to pick you up, it'll have to be around six."

"Six on the twenty-seventh. Got it." And she was gone. I leaned back in my chair with what had to be a ridiculously dopey smile on my face. I had honestly not expected that. Then again, very little with Laura was expectable. But something changed after the show in Philadelphia, after we kissed. We hadn't talked about it at all, and nothing was awkward except for when I asked about Charlie. But somehow the lines of our relationship had blurred. The day of the last Philadelphia show was the first time that I actually let myself begin to realistically hope that Laura felt the same way I did. She wasn't quite there yet, but that kiss was a step. Telling me about Charlie had been a step. And calling to ask if she could come to the wedding was a step. Baby steps maybe, but as I sat there grinning moronically and still holding the now beeping receiver, I could see how those baby steps might eventually get her to the same place that I was at. And for her, I thought I was willing to wait as long as I needed to.

"I-can't-mind-my-own-business" Coral, as I now mentally called our main office receptionist, walked by then, paused to look in my office, and stopped completely when she saw me lost in thought with a dead receiver in my hand.

She tapped her obnoxiously long nails on my door and, although I had clearly already seen her, she squeaked out a totally unnecessary, "Knock, knock." I dropped the receiver and straightened up in my chair. "Everything alright, hon?" she asked, leaning into my door.

"Just fine, Coral, thanks."

"Were you talking to that girlfriend of yours? The one you go to all those concerts with?" *None of your goddamned business*, I thought as she took a couple of steps into my office and a wave of her overpowering perfume reached me.

"No," I said coolly. "Just a friend." I looked desperately at my desk to find something so urgent to do that it would require her to leave. I finally landed on the phone and realized that I did have to call Mel to let her know Laura was coming. She would be annoyed, as it would mess up her table arrangements, but she'd get over it.

"How come you don't have any pictures of her in here?" she asked.

I sighed. "I've got to make a really important call actually, Coral. I'm sorry, but—you know."

"Oh, no problem," she said in a tone that clearly implied that it *was* a problem for her to leave my office. "I had some more filing to do anyways."

"Thanks, and can you shut the door?" She slammed it behind her, but I was too happy over Laura's call to be annoyed with Coral. She could meddle in my love life another day. That phone call was enough to make up for every single show that we hadn't been able to go to. Enough to make up for so much that had happened in the past ten months.

22

"I hear your girlfriend is coming tomorrow night."
Fuck. I should have dealt with this before the rehearsal dinner.

"Eric, buddy," I started. "She's not my girlfriend. And she'll freak if you say that. So don't." Eric just laughed. He had to be the calmest groom ever. "I'm serious, you can't say that!"

"Okay, okay. Jesus, I'm the one getting married and you're the one who's nervous!"

I grinned. "Well at least it's open bar tomorrow night. That'll calm me down a lot."

Eric shuddered slightly. "That did it, now I'm nervous."

I smiled at him and put my hand on his shoulder as Mel began her practice walk down the aisle. "Me too, pal. Me too."

I pulled into Laura's driveway at 5:53. I remembered picking her up for Mel and Eric's engagement party, when I first discovered that Laura ran late when she was nervous. Of course as I later learned, Laura ran late when she was comfortable too. Or tired. Or happy. Okay, Laura always ran late. Except for concerts. But when I was nervous, I ran early. Not a good combination. I drummed my fingers on the steering wheel and glanced at my reflection in the rearview. I had shaved as closely as I ever had in my life and gotten a haircut the day before to make sure that I looked good. I don't know what I expected. But between that and the rented tux, I looked sharp. Despite the heat. Who the hell planned a late September wedding in DC anyway? It was always still ridiculously hot and humid.

Four more minutes, I told myself. I had to wait; I didn't want to surprise her before she was ready. Then a quick fluttering motion at her blinds caught my eye and I realized she had looked out and seen me there, so I started to get out of the car. But before I was halfway up the driveway, she walked out her front door.

"*Wow.*"

She smiled shyly and tucked a dangling lock of hair behind her ear. Her dress had a black background, but with enormous turquoise, magenta, yellow, and fuchsia flowers almost obscuring the background completely, it was anything but a little black dress. It had an uneven hemline, the shortest part catching her at mid-thigh and the longest just a couple of inches above her ankles. The straps were so thin that from far away it looked like they weren't even there, and the dress moved with her like it was part of her body. Her hair was up in a messy, yet elegant twist, with some pieces left out on purpose to frame her face, and she had dangling earrings that glinted so brightly in the sunlight that I assumed they had to be real diamonds. The requisite high heels, which were always the final touch to Laura's outfits, weren't black, but turquoise with thin straps and impossibly narrow, tall heels, and they were perfectly matched to one of the colors in her dress. Her tan skin was absolutely luminous and with her hair up, my eyes kept lingering over the curve of her thin shoulders, the line of her neck, the hollow of her throat.

"You too," she said softly, and then cleared her throat slightly.

"You look beautiful."

"I'm even on time."

I smiled at her. "You're early. I'm impressed." I held out my arm to her. "Ready?" She nodded and took my arm, leaning into me more than usual.

I opened the car door for her and went to shut it as she sat down, but she reached out and touched my arm. She looked like she was about to say something, but she stopped herself.

"You okay?" I asked. I didn't want to ask if she was nervous, because I could see it. In all the time I had known her, I had never seen her looking this vulnerable. It was endearing. Laura was always so tough that I was amazed whenever I saw a tender moment in her. It made me want to protect her, and it made me feel like I was strong enough to do it. I didn't know why a wedding had the power to make her feel that way, and I didn't question it.

Finally, she smiled, a much tenser smile than usual, but still a smile. "Yes," she said firmly. "But I could use a drink or nine." I smiled back.

"Open bar, baby, just make it through the ceremony." She dropped her hand daintily into her lap and I shut the door.

I know that it was Mel and Eric's day, but I won't lie, I wasn't concentrating on them during the ceremony. I was sneaking as many looks at Laura as I could. Luckily, Mel was a little too preoccupied to notice.

Laura seemed to be trying to concentrate on anything but the ceremony itself. She was easy to spot, not just because every other young person in the church was wearing black (and for some reason all older women wear cream-colored dresses to weddings), but because she was the only one who was not focused on the ceremony. She observed every aspect of the church. The stained glass windows. The ceiling. The pews. The walls. Then she looked around at the other people there. The man sitting next to her whispered something to her at one point, and she responded in a whisper, but without turning to look at him. When she had exhausted all of her other options, she studied her hands. Once, I caught her looking at me, but she looked away quickly. I wondered desperately what she was thinking.

Finally the ceremony ended and, after we finished the seemingly unending wedding party photography session, I found her where she was waiting for me so that we could drive to the reception, which was at a swanky hotel about ten minutes away. When I got to her, she was talking to an older couple, who I didn't know. They turned out to be friends of Mel's parents.

"It was just such a beautiful ceremony," the woman was saying, her hand on Laura's arm. "The flowers at our wedding were very similar. When you get married, this is the best time of year. It's not as hot as July but you can still get the summer flowers." Laura clearly had no response for this other than a murmured "mmhmm," and like a gentleman, I came to her rescue. I put my arm around her waist and introduced myself.

"Well don't you two make a handsome couple!" Mrs. Crowley exclaimed. "How long have you been together?"

"No, we're not—" I started to sputter as I felt Laura tense under my arm, expecting her to protest with me, as she had whenever someone made that mistake, but she interrupted me.

"Oh, about nine months now," she said.

Mrs. Crowley looked delighted. "And how long before we see the two of you walking down the aisle?" Laura giggled and held a finger to her lips.

"Shhh, you know boys. You don't want to spook him." She turned to me and planted a kiss on my cheek. "Right, honey?" It was all I could do to nod. She never failed to surprise me.

Safely in the car, I asked, "Where did that come from?"

Laura shrugged slightly. "I didn't think she'd get it if I said we were tramps." I just laughed.

As soon as we got to the reception, we made a beeline for the bar, where Laura immediately introduced herself to the bartender, which of course ensured that she got first service for drinks no matter how many people were waiting that evening.

By her fourth drink, she had loosened up and was more like herself. I hadn't realized just how tense she was until I saw how many drinks it took to get her acting normal. I didn't quite get it. She had asked to come, and she had met my friends before. But there was something strangely endearing about her being worked up over it. Except that she set out to get drunk. I drank a little early in the reception, but I was the one driving that night, and I had no intention of needing to take a cab home.

Once she had a few drinks in her, Laura charmed everyone at the wedding. She hugged Mel in the receiving line and told her she looked "absolutely gorgeous." Mel, who was usually a little put off by Laura, smiled and was completely genuine when she told Laura that she was happy she had been able to come. She whispered something to her and Laura laughed conspiratorially with her, kissed her on the cheek, and congratulated her.

"You look beautiful, Mel," I said, kissing her. Mel just winked at me.

"Have fun tonight," she said with a sly lilt in her voice.

Three minutes into a conversation with us, Eric's brother, James, asked Laura to dance. I watched her moving to the music with him and didn't even notice when Dave and Brian, two of my friends from college who had also been talking to us, started laughing at me. Apparently I hadn't been following their conversation. At all.

"Go cut in," Dave said finally. "James doesn't deserve a girl that hot anyway." I smiled my thanks and took his advice.

Laura and I had danced at concerts. But that was different. This was slow dancing.

Somehow dancing with her was more intimate than that first kiss was. More intimate than sharing a bed with her. I held her and touched her in ways I hadn't been able to before, but it wasn't about that. It was about just being with her in a situation where she was completely mine, and everyone around us could see that.

A couple of dances, a couple of drinks, maybe a stop at our table for a quick bite. It was her pattern for the night. She was no lightweight when it came to drinking, and I wasn't worried. Even at her drunkest, Laura maintained more dignity than most sober people. And everyone at the wedding just loved her. She was more charming than I had ever seen her, but it wasn't—well, it wasn't her in a way. She had needed a whole lot of alcohol and all of her energy to be that delightful to everyone at the wedding. No one but me and maybe the bartender realized how much was behind that. I thought I had seen just about every facet she had to offer, but I learned that night that there were still hidden sides to her. And something, behind one of those sides, was driving her to be the life of the party at that wedding.

James came running up to me toward the end of the evening. He had just abandoned the girl he had started dancing with after I took Laura away. Laura was in the bathroom with Mel and her sisters, who somehow in the course of the evening had found time to adopt Laura as their new best friend.

"What's up?" I asked, giving him half my attention while I watched the door to the reception room, waiting to see Laura walk back in.

"So are you guys together or what?"

'Huh?"

"You and Laura. Is it serious?"

I looked at him with some amusement before I turned my attention back to the door. "Nah, we're not together."

"Then I can ask her out?"

"Absolutely not."

James frowned. "Good thing I like you, man. Otherwise, you know, I'd try to steal her." I turned to look at him as Laura finally re-entered and headed straight for me.

I laughed. "Go ahead and try. And may I be the first to say good luck." Laura slipped her arm around my back and kissed me on the cheek. A sober Laura usually only did that in saying hello and goodbye. Call me an opportunist if you will, but I was in no way about to object.

"Good luck with what?" she purred. I smiled and put my arm around her waist as well.

"James here had a question for you. I told him to ask it." She turned to face James.

"What's the question?" she asked, leaning her head in until it was touching mine. The gesture wasn't lost on James.

"Um—uh—" he stammered. "Nothing." His shoulders sagged as he walked away, defeated. He squared them back again as he re-approached his consolation prize girl from earlier, and he again began to sway with her on the dance floor.

Her head was still leaning against mine and I could smell her perfume. "Wanna dance?" I whispered.

"Mmhmm." She took my hand and led me out to the floor.

The band was finishing a song as we approached and when the singer saw us coming, he looked at me questioningly. I nodded. He turned back to the band and said something inaudible as I put an arm around Laura's waist. The drummer started a beat and Laura looked up at me, startled.

"Was this you?" she asked, her eyes wide with surprise.

I just nodded. President Jackson and I had spoken with the singer while Laura was off bonding with Melanie. And luckily, he and the band knew "Tougher than the Rest." The singer was no Bruce. But it was the song Laura had told me on that first day in Charlotte, before rapidly changing the subject, that she wanted to dance to at her wedding. And I figured it probably wouldn't be me who she would be dancing that dance with, but at least I could dance with her to that song at *a* wedding. We had heard it live in Philadelphia on the second night. Bruce's first, and certainly not last, love song to Patti.

She smiled at me so completely heartbreakingly. I wanted to say it right then. To tell her how I felt. If there was ever a moment when she would say it back, that was it.

But I hesitated and the moment passed as she leaned her head against my shoulder and I held her closer. When the singer began the last verse, she pulled her face back a little so that it was closer to mine. "Thank you," she whispered, her eyes shining. I honestly don't know who moved in first or most. But by the time the song ended, we were kissing.

I don't know how long we stayed like that. Eventually, it was clear the festivities were winding down. Melanie threw the bouquet, the cake had been cut, and the bride and groom said their goodbyes as the crowd started to leave.

Laura didn't let go of my hand until we were at the car, where I kissed her again. Her arms were around my neck as she pressed her breasts against my chest. I had waited so long for this.

"You okay to drive?" she asked when we were both in the car. I said yes. She laughed softly. "Good. Because I'm, um, definitely not."

We didn't talk much on the way to her place, but I got out to open her car door and followed her up her front steps. She didn't say anything.

This was it.

She had her back to me as she fumbled to get her keys in the lock. I put an arm around her waist from behind, pulled her to me, and started kissing her neck, beginning at the top, right below her earlobe, and tracing a path down to her shoulder. She moaned softly and abandoned the keys in the door, turning around in my grip to kiss me again.

It was about to be the culmination of the ten months we had known each other. I had wanted her for a year now and somehow this was the first real opportunity that I'd had. It felt so completely right, and although during the wait, I'm sure I wouldn't have agreed with this, but waiting so long made it all the more satisfying. There was no hurry, I could savor the feel of her against me, the heat of her body, the taste of her mouth on mine. I reached behind her to open the door but stopped before I had fully turned the key.

Taste.

I wasn't just tasting Laura, I could taste all the alcohol too.

Who cares? I thought. *We drink all the time.*

But I was sober. And she was a whole lot more than a little tipsy. I tried to quickly count how many drinks she'd had. But I couldn't. And she had told me that she was drunk in the car. Laura never admitted to that unless she had drank so much that I couldn't understand how she was still conscious.

Shit.

I forced myself away from her. "Not like this," I said softly, kicking myself, but knowing I had to do it. "We can't do this like this."

Based on what I had seen of Laura up until then, she should have gotten mad at me. She hated to be refused when she offered something, and she was offering herself here. Of course, if she tried to convince me to change my mind, I knew it wouldn't take very much at all. I mean, I'm human. If she looked at me the right way at that moment, I would have gone inside with her anyway. But I had to at least say it.

She didn't answer at first, but just looked at me, her eyes naked and open. And while she so often chose to misunderstand things deliberately, there was none of that tonight. She knew why I stopped. She knew I was right. And looking into her eyes on her front step, I saw that I could have had her that night, but I would never have been able to *have* her if I did. I saw respect in her eyes. And I saw hope for a future between us.

"You're right," she said eventually, still looking into my eyes. Words that *never* came out of Laura's mouth sober. "It was—it was just the situation. We were acting like a couple all night. It was bound to happen." I nodded, my heart racing. She didn't mean that. She couldn't.

"Exactly," I said, my mouth feeling dry. "I shouldn't have had them play 'Tougher.'"

But Laura shook her head. "No, it was sweet." She paused. The girl who always had something to say had nothing to say. Finally, after an eternity of silence, "No being weird tomorrow. We've got the last three shows this week."

"Of course," I said, meaning anything but that. How was I going to be completely normal, knowing that I could have slept with her if I had just been able to keep my mouth shut? But I would have to be. It was the only way to give myself a chance to be with her in the end, and that was what I wanted most after all, or I never could have stopped myself.

Being the good guy really sucks some nights, I thought as I walked back to my car and drove home to my empty bed.

23

Laura and I didn't talk about what happened after the wedding. We didn't even talk to each other that week at all, except in emails, until we left for New York. The last three shows of the *Rising* tour were held at Shea Stadium during the first weekend in October. October 1, 3, and 4. We went to all three. Our email correspondence during the days preceding the shows arranged what time we would leave, but we also talked about how we would handle the shows emotionally. And yes, I know that is probably the dorkiest thing that you've ever heard in your whole life. But we actually had to discuss how sad we would let ourselves be over the tour ending. It felt like a breakup. Not between me and Laura, but between us and Bruce. We talked about the need to remember the good times and reminded ourselves that we still had our bootlegs, and we told each other over and over again that it couldn't *really* be that long before he toured again.

It was the end of something huge and we both knew that. It was the end of the summer. The end of our time with Bruce. The end of us having a reason to hang out other than that we enjoyed each other's company. It was so much easier with the concerts as an excuse. Therefore, it was also the end of us being able to pretend that we were together so much because of the concerts, which neither of us was quite ready to do. For Laura, the end of the tour was the end of something that had been sustaining her, although I couldn't know how much or why until later. All I knew was that it was also the end of my definite time with Laura, which was the end of something that had been sustaining me.

But in reality, it was scary to both of us. It could actually be years before the next tour. Would concert bootlegs get us through until then? We could start going to other shows, but there wasn't another group that could hold our interest in the same way. And we always drank a lot more when we weren't going to shows. Was there enough alcohol on the planet to help us survive until the next tour? Could our livers hold out that long? We both dreaded the end of the night on October 4, but neither of us said that. We talked about how it was sad, but we had to be strong, and we couldn't let ourselves get too upset about it.

Yet when I thought about the rest of the year, October 4 seemed to be the edge of the world, and October 5 was already the abyss.

Am I being too melodramatic?

If you're not a rabid Bruce fan, the best way to explain it is to say that we were looking at a span of possibly years without something definite to look forward to. And I honestly didn't know if Laura would stick around with me when we didn't have that.

We stayed with Jeff and Ellen for the three shows, and they brought Matthew and Rachel to the last night. It was cold, even huddled together in the pit, which was extra crowded that night, and we were wearing layers. Laura wore gloves and I wished that I had brought some too.

After Bruce opened the show, he welcomed us to "the last dance," as the bootleg for that show would become known. And he pulled out all the stops. Lots of rarities that even Jeff had not been able to guess, including guests Gary "U.S." Bonds for an encore performance of his hit that Bruce covered often in the 1970s, "Quarter to Three," and, in a move that left us speechless, Bob Dylan for an almost intelligible version of "Highway 61 Revisited." I snuck a look at Laura during "Bobby Jean," even though I hadn't seen a single hint of tears in all the times we'd heard that song, and the first night that I saw her in Washington was the only time that I had ever seen her react to it. She bit her lip at one point, but that was the only thing that gave her away as having an emotional connection to that song. I thought about how far she had come since that night when I first saw her. And about how far I had come since then. That was over a year ago. I was still living with Katie then, and I had thought I was happy. Then I saw Laura cry and the whole world changed.

Laura's crying has marked four distinct changes in my life and that night was one of them. The end of the tour. The end of the happiest time that I have ever known.

Bruce's last song, "Blood Brothers," was what set her off. Not just because it was the last song, but more because of us. And I will never have to hear Laura say it for me to know that. If Laura had been crying for the end of the tour, she would have been inconsolable. I put my arms around her, expecting to hear the album's line in the song about not knowing if any of this matters anymore. And when Bruce changed the words and sang "I close my eyes and feel so many friends around me," Laura looked up at me, through the tears that were streaming down her cheeks and tried to smile. She hugged me back as I wiped her cheeks and kissed her forehead. This wasn't a moment about us as lovers, but us as friends. And somewhere, in the last year, she had become more than a girl who I had fallen in love with. She had truly become a friend.

I think that, in a lot of ways, that realization was one of the first actual grown-up emotions of my life. Because my past girlfriends and I weren't friends. I know that sounds weird. But there was always a distinction. There were girls I wanted to date, girls I wanted to sleep with, and girls I wanted to be friends with. And I realized, as I held Laura, my chin on top of her head, our arms around each other, that she was the bridge between those two worlds. And that made the end of this chapter in my life feel okay. Because suddenly I could see that it was possible for another chapter to start, and that this chapter *had* to end in order for the next one to begin. It wasn't definite, because I couldn't completely know yet what Laura would want from me when Bruce wasn't around. But I knew then that it was possible for the next chapter to be even better. And that was enough.

24

"You're not pregnant yet, right?" Mel swatted at me from the passenger seat. She and Eric had just gotten back from their honeymoon, and I had picked them up from the airport. They were both tan and looked ridiculously happy.

"I am *not* pregnant," she said. "God, why would you even ask something like that?"

"Seems like something you'd do; get pregnant on the honeymoon and start popping out babies."

"I'm not popping anything out any time soon." Eric grinned from the backseat. He started to say something, which I knew would be ridiculously dirty, but Mel turned around and said, "Don't you even think about it."

He just smiled and said, "yes, dear," in his best husband voice.

"So you had a good time?"

"Totally," she replied with a huge smile back at Eric.

"Did you see anything other than the inside of your hotel room?"

Mel giggled a bit. "Not really."

"Then I'd take a pregnancy test like first thing if I were you. Want me to stop at a drugstore on the way home so you can get one?"

"You're an idiot. You can't just take a pregnancy test whenever you feel like it; you have to wait until you miss your period. And I haven't, and I'm still on the pill, so shut up already."

I laughed. "Geez, you're still kind of a bitch, too."

"Hey now," Eric said with a mock menacing tone, "that's my wife you're talking about. If anyone's going to call her a bitch, it's going to be me. As in 'bitch, go make me some dinner!'" Mel and I both laughed, although she warned him that if he ever said that for real, he would find himself single again very quickly.

"So I've been dying to know all week," Mel began. "What happened with you and Laura the night of the wedding?" I knew that I had to wait for her to ask. She was just coming back from her honeymoon, and I couldn't start talking about my dysfunctional relationship immediately on the heels of that. Which meant that if she didn't ask, I wasn't going to be talking about it to her at all for a few days. Besides, I wasn't even sure that she had noticed anything going on at the wedding. She was a little preoccupied after all. But I loved her for asking. And not just for asking, but for actually wanting to know. She had been in the car for less than five minutes, making it pretty clear that she was telling the truth when she said she was dying to know.

I explained about what almost happened and why I didn't make my move then. "Good," Mel said, with a sigh that sounded a little too relieved for my taste. "I'm proud of you."

I grimaced slightly. I wasn't sure why, but her saying "good" just didn't seem like a good sign to me. "Why?"

"Because you did the right thing. It's like you're growing up." She saw the look on my face and added quickly, "That's a compliment."

"Thanks, I guess."

"You're welcome. And to be honest, you've definitely got a better shot with her now because you didn't sleep with her."

"I guess."

"Has anything else happened since then?" I told her about the end of the tour. I didn't mention that Laura cried, but I did tell her that I was worried about what would happen to us now.

"You hung out even when Bruce was in Europe and when he had a month off from the tour and all though."

"Yeah, but this is different. There might not be any more shows for years."

"And does that change how you feel about her?"

"Of course not."

"Then why would it change how she feels about you?"

"You're assuming that she actually really feels strongly enough about me to want me around when there's no tour to follow."

"She does," Mel said. "That's not the issue here." I hoped she was right. Eric's cell phone rang and, because it was his mom, he took the call. "You know," Mel said, lowering her voice to avoid disturbing Eric, "I was thinking about it, and I think I finally really get what you see in her."

I let out a pretty bitter laugh. "Really? Because I'm not always sure that I see it."

Mel gave me a sympathetic look. "Exactly. Because she's a lot more like you than you realize." I glanced over at her.

"What do you mean?"

"I mean you're both looking for the same thing."

"What are we looking for?"

"Can I be totally honest?"

"Could I stop you?"

Mel smiled and glanced back at Eric. "Better men than you have tried."

"Then go for it I guess."

"It's the same reason you both love Bruce so much. It's what all of his songs are about. His music is all about questioning if there's more to life than just going to work every day. His characters aren't sure of what it's going to take to make them happy in life, and they all want to get out there and find whatever that really is. But they don't know what they're looking for, which makes that really hard. And they kind of suspect that it might be love, but they haven't really seen anything yet that proves that to them. And they're all terrified of not finding anything at all and winding up just like their parents. And that's exactly how you are."

Sometime during that conversation, my mouth must have dropped open, because when Mel finished talking, I realized it was gaping. I shut it. "Wow," I said quietly. "That's—," I hesitated. She was right and wrong. And right. And not wrong. And right. "That's really true about the music and really harsh about me."

"I don't mean it in a harsh way."

"I know that," I said quickly, and I did. It was why Mel and I were best friends. And why a lot of girls thought she was a heinous bitch. She told it how it was, even when people didn't want to hear it. And she didn't always take it all that well when people did the same back to her, which could make her seem pretty hypocritical if you didn't really know or understand her. But at the same time, she wasn't capable of misleading or lying to her friends, which in my eyes made her the least hypocritical person I knew.

"I'm saying that I like that about you."

"Thanks, I guess."

"No, really. It means you're not going to settle. You're not going to quit until you find what you're looking for. And it doesn't have to be the same thing that everyone else is looking for either. I saw you at the wedding. If it had been you and Katie there, you'd have been miserable. You had that kind of trapped animal look in your eyes after the two of you moved in together. I mean, you weren't happy, it just took you awhile to figure that out. But you *did* figure it out, and you did something about it. And that makes you a lot braver than most people." She paused here and looked at me. "I just hope you and Laura find what you're looking for in the same place. Because if you don't, she's going to break your heart."

I used a Laura-like conversation shifter. I wasn't ready to talk about that eventuality yet. "When did you ever listen to enough Bruce to make an observation like that about his music?"

"Are you serious?" she asked. "How long have we been friends?"

I counted in my head. "Eight years?"

"So how many times do you think I've heard *Born to Run*? And *Darkness on the Edge of Town*? And *Tunnel of Love*? And *The River*? And hello, you burned *all* of his cds for me junior year of college when you decided that I had no taste in music! And how many conversations about Bruce have I sat through with you, just because you sat through me talking about boys? I could write a book on Bruce at this point, you dummy."

She had a point. I felt a little cheated to be honest. When people asked why I followed Bruce, I said that his music completely expressed what I felt. But I couldn't characterize it much more than that. I described his concerts as religious experiences, but I could never have verbalized what Mel said as accurately as she did. And it made sense too. His later work, once he found Patti and had kids and was writing about being ridiculously happy, was among my least favorite of his music. The songs I loved the most were about still looking for that thing that would make me complete. I saw myself in those songs. And so did Laura. And like in "Born to Run," when Bruce asks if love is real, his characters don't know if love is the answer to what they're looking for in life, and they have a sneaking suspicion that love alone might not be enough. And I was the same way. And so was Laura.

I thought back to that conversation months later, when Laura was gone. And I wished I had been as smart as Mel was that day. Because I would have seen it coming if I was. And I would have been able to run away from her before she ran away from me.

25

I was telling Mel the truth. After the last show at Shea, I didn't know what would become of my relationship with Laura. Would we spend more nights like we used to, listening to old albums and drinking? Would we stop seeing each other? Would we find that it was more than Bruce that held us together?

At first, Laura would show up at my door as she had during off nights on the tour. And we continued that way for that first month. But it was waning. For both of us, although I think more for her than for me. Listening to bootlegs when there wasn't a tour going on just didn't have the same appeal. It was like it was too hard to listen to Bruce when we didn't know when our next real show was coming. It just reminded us of what we didn't have. We listened to other old albums in those weeks. Usually on vinyl. But it didn't have the same energy to it.

Laura practically went into mourning over the shows ending. You would have thought she had lost a loved one, which I guess, in more ways than one, she did. I had wondered before what Laura had been like before the tour started. If she'd had that same vibrancy and passion. I didn't honestly believe that she went to her first concert and just suddenly came alive. She must have had something before Bruce that made her get out of bed in the morning. But in those weeks following the tour, I began to think that maybe there hadn't been anything. She smiled and laughed less and there were times that it was just too painful to look directly into her eyes. I wanted to help her, but I didn't know how. I didn't know what she needed, and she wasn't telling me. Something inside her was hurting, and I couldn't get to where that was.

I've said before that the concerts were like a drug. But for us, all of a sudden, the drug was gone. Not a conscious choice to quit, but a forced version of cold turkey. And soon we both realized we needed our next fix. That was when we turned to local live music, which helped for a little while.

I discovered the joys of the Washington metro area concert venues when I was still in high school. You could see a decent show at Nissan Pavilion, or the MCI Center, or even Constitution Hall. But if you care about music, you know that the small clubs are the best. Seeing a big-name band at the 9:30 Club or The Birchmere is practically life altering. It's what it must be like when Bruce shows up at the Stone Pony in Asbury Park. Laura wasn't interested in the big groups though. They were too hard to get tickets for and not worth the effort that she expended in getting Bruce tickets. And if you ask me, it was easier for her to be blasé and criticize the unknown groups as not being up to the Bruce standard. But at the same time, it was the atmosphere that we went for, and for a maximum ten dollar cover, it became our new favorite thing to do on weekends. Laura quickly befriended bartenders at our usual haunts and by the third time we went to any club, our tabs would only have one or two drinks charged on them at the end of the night. Hanging out with someone as charming as her was certainly cheaper.

It must have been her idea to start going to local shows, but I can't remember when she suggested it. I would say that it was my idea, but I know that if I had proposed seeing a band other than E Street, she would have just laughed at me, so it must have been her idea. Or maybe we never discussed it. It was hard to tell sometimes, what had been said and what hadn't. After all, some of our best nights ended with us passing out on my floor in a haze of beer and occasional marijuana. But one Friday she didn't come in, just told me to grab my coat, and we headed out to find a show.

For two months, the local shows became our new drug of choice. No, it could never equal the shows of the past year and a half, but it gave us something to do, something to look forward to. A rough week at work was okay because I knew I would be at a concert at the end of it. A Monday meeting that seemed to drag on for forever was bearable because the beats from Saturday night were still echoing in my ears; I could remember the way Laura looked in the dimmed club, and the way she pressed against me to make herself heard over the music. Life regained a pattern similar to that of the previous year, minus all of the drive time and the extreme highs of the shows we had been going to. We almost never listened to bootlegs at home anymore. Live music, even when the bands aren't the best in the world, is still better than a stereo in most cases.

Of course, looking back, I probably wasn't making the best choices for me then. Two of my coworkers asked me if I was still seeing Laura while I was pouring myself a cup of coffee one day. I was caught off guard, and she had been a little distant over the past week, so I said that we were still friends, but we weren't involved anymore. Which got me a lot of sympathetic looks at work, but it also meant a few of them had girls who they wanted me to meet. I found excuses about why I couldn't go. I knew I wasn't getting anywhere with Laura, but the idea of going out with someone else? It just seemed like a huge waste of time. I met girls on the Metro and at the gym, but no one could compare to Laura, and I refused to settle. I still saw one of my hook-up buddies when I felt the urge. But I couldn't imagine actually attempting to become even the slightest bit emotionally involved with anyone other than Laura.

Did Laura date then? At the time, I couldn't have told you. I hoped not. I spent more time than I should have convincing myself that she didn't, because she spent her weekends with me. But I didn't really know. By the time I found out that she hadn't been, it didn't matter anymore.

And I guess it wouldn't have mattered if she had been dating then. But at the time, I was so totally infatuated with her, that I couldn't stomach the idea of any other guys being with her. Always in the back of my mind was the image of her with that Charlie guy from the DC concert, but he never came up again and I never brought him up again. There were things I couldn't know yet. But I also knew that there were things I couldn't ask her.

26

I can honestly say that I disliked Mark Houston before I had even heard of him. That Friday night didn't begin like all the others, and it was the difference in Laura that immediately made me dislike him. Normally, our decision about where to go for a concert was based on if any big groups were playing in town, in which case we went wherever they weren't. The weekend before that one, Blink 182 played at the 9:30 Club, so we went into Georgetown. We had some favorite smaller bands by then, who we would make an effort to see when they were in town, like Mike Rocket, Jesse Malin, Ari Hest, and Redline Addiction. But I hadn't heard of any of the bands playing anywhere local that weekend, so I assumed that it would be a random selection. Laura always asked me who was playing where, and I figured she didn't bother looking up the bands. But she is nothing if not full of surprises.

"Should we start at the Black Cat?" I asked, mainly because it had a five dollar cover until 10pm and we had left early.

"No. The 9:30 Club tonight." She said it with such finality. Normally, if I asked where we should go first, she would shrug slightly and leave it up to me.

I turned to look at her as we headed into the Metro station. "Okay," I said, shrugging slightly as I pulled out my farecard. "Who's playing there?" I didn't expect an answer, but I knew something was up.

"Mark Houston."

I was suspicious. Why had she heard of this guy if I hadn't? "Who's he?"

Now Laura shrugged. "Some guy. I heard he's good." It sounded like an unfinished thought, but she closed her mouth and turned away. She stepped onto the escalator and whipped her thin scarf around her neck, although it couldn't provide much protection from the biting air. She was looking down at the platform instead of at me as I followed her.

I could have dropped it, but I didn't. I knew what it meant when she stopped talking like that. She didn't want to explain. She had done that enough times that I knew this game. She never said the words "This conversation is over," but looking away and not looking back until the subject was changed was just as clear as if she had said that. Normally, for the sake of keeping the peace, I let it go and figured she would just tell me whatever it was when she was eventually ready.

"Who'd you hear that from?" No response. "Laura?"

"People," she replied finally, looking at me defiantly. I felt a surge of anger at her for being so secretive. Later, I would piece together that Laura really *did* care which bands we saw and probably spent no inconsiderable amount of time researching them. But all I could think then was that *someone* had told her about this guy, and that was enough to make me hate that someone else, whoever he was, because I knew that it was a he, and for me to also hate the singer that he had turned her on to.

We waited on the platform in silence. After a few minutes, Laura took my arm and wrapped it around her shoulders as she leaned her back against my chest to get warm. It was as close to an apology as she could come and I knew that. Laura never got cold, nor did she hug, but she would use the cold winter air as a way to tell me she didn't want me to be mad at her. And I consented. But nothing could make me feel good about this musician that we were about to see.

Yet when Laura smiled, everything in the world was all right. We went inside and checked our coats, for free, as she had charmed Evan, the coat check guy, weeks earlier.

She got us beers and we staked out our spots, to the performers' left side of the stage, which meant we would be near the bar as well. But I couldn't imagine that it would be that full if I hadn't heard of any of the bands playing.

Mark Houston was the last act on the bill, and it began to take the guise of a normal evening. We were regulars at that point, and we talked to a few of the other people who were there often. The opening two groups were decent, but not memorable. It was more crowded than usual for no-name bands, and as the evening wore on, the female population doubled any that I had ever seen there. I don't claim to be the best of judges, but I didn't see anyone in the first two bands to account for this feminine flurry. When the second group finished their set, I excused myself to return some of the beer I had borrowed that evening. When I came back, he was already onstage.

At first, I thought the club had emptied a bit, which made me feel better. Then my eyes readjusted. All of the girls, who had been spread out earlier, were now tightly packed around the stage, trying, as only girls in late adolescence can, to get the lead singer's attention.

Mark Houston, the lead singer and guitar player, also the writer of all of his band's songs, as I would later learn, was, in the overheard words of one girl, "gorgeous." That was fine. I could deal with that. I'm a good-looking guy. I work out. Laura looked just fine on my arm. And I knew that his looks weren't what drew Laura here either. She could have had her pick of good-looking guys. Even good-looking musicians.

But he was good. Really good. This wasn't pop or alternative, which is all that most young bands are capable of. This was real, genuine rock and roll. The music had fresh beats, staggering guitar riffs, and lyrics that could have been read as poetry. They were the perfect words for each note of the music, and every line flowed seamlessly. And he played to the crowd. The scene from Bruce's video anthology of him singing "Rosalita" in 1978 popped briefly into my head, but I forced it out to concentrate on this music. Before the first song was over, it was clear to me that this group, or at least the singer, was going to make it big. Soon.

I stayed in the back of the club for a while just listening before I made my way back to Laura. And despite myself, despite that I already hated Mark Houston for attracting Laura's interest, I felt drawn to the music. And I knew immediately why Laura had wanted to be there. No one told her he was good. She had heard at least one of his songs. Laura knew before we went out that night what I was discovering then. Just as Bruce had been called the new Dylan back in 1973, *Rolling Stone* could fairly easily tout Mark Houston as the new Springsteen. The music was in no way based on Springsteen's, but the influence was clear. Of course, other influences were equally clear, including Dylan and the Counting Crows, with a little Tom Petty thrown in, but I had no doubt in my mind that this was an artist who also loved Bruce and grew up listening to the same albums that I did and dreaming my same dreams of musical stardom. Only I grew into other dreams and this guy, who couldn't have been older than me, was living exactly what I wanted when I first listened to the whole album of *Born to Run*.

Eventually, I looked over to the bar, expecting Laura to be just as enthralled as the rest of the girls, if not more so, as I knew she would recognize the influences in his music and see the obvious comparison to a young Bruce. But I had to laugh when I saw her. She was leaning with her back against the bar, facing the stage, with her arms crossed contentiously, and she was glaring disdainfully at the band. I laughed because she looked like a child who wasn't getting her way, but more at myself for believing she would be like all the fawning girls. No, my Laura would never be reduced to crowding the stage for attention because of good looks and a couple of good songs. As I walked over to her, a man approached and tried to speak to her. I couldn't hear him, but she gave him a scowl so contemptuous that without her having to utter a word, he quickly decamped and ordered himself a drink at the far side of the bar, peeking over occasionally at Laura as if he was afraid. I laughed again, feeling a million times better. I had seen this mood before. She wasn't looking for anything from anyone tonight. Including, I thought, Mark Houston.

I got back to her side and copied her position by crossing my arms and making an angry face. Then I nudged her with my elbow and leaned over to say into her ear, "Why are we glaring at the stage?" She looked up at me and I exaggerated my look to pure rage. She glared slightly at me, but her frown shook as she tried not to smile, then broke as she started to laugh. I loved her so much in that moment. I loved that I knew how to make her laugh. I loved that she had sent that other man packing without a word. I loved that she was mine. We had kissed twice, nothing more. But she was mine because I loved her, and she was mine because I knew that I could make her smile when absolutely no one else could. And in that moment, I realized, really for the first time, that she must love me too. She wasn't one to put up with anything that displeased her, and that included people. And maybe in her mind it was because I let her have her own way so often, but I knew better. I don't pretend that I fully understood her, and even now, knowing so much more than I did then, I'm still not sure that I do. But I understood how to be with her and, to an extent, she understood how to be with me. And that's rare.

"You'd think he'd be more worried about that guitar being out of tune than which one of those girls he's gonna let blow him tonight," she said with more venom than I expected and resuming her scowl. "He's not serious about the music."

I shrugged. "It's not that noticeable."

"It's not good enough for him to make it."

"I don't know," I said, surprising myself by taking up for him. But with Laura unimpressed, I felt like I had room to like him. "I think he's got it." The song he was playing ended, although we only realized that because of the girls' screaming, which would have drowned out any music that was being played anyway.

He held his hands up in the air. "I need a little quiet folks," he said into the mic and the girls quieted down.

A lone girl yelled out, "We love you, Mark!"

A shy smile crossed his face and he looked down, flushing slightly. "I'm a little out of tune," he explained into the mic, ignoring his boisterous admirer as he tightened his strings and strummed his guitar to check the sound. I snuck a look at Laura out of the corner of my eye. Her mouth opened slightly when he announced his reason for stopping, then she shut it quickly, and looked over at me, probably to make sure I hadn't seen her surprise. She kept her arms crossed, but when she resumed looking at the stage, the look she was directing at the band had shifted subtly. It was softer; skeptical instead of disgusted.

"It sounds good to us!" another girl shouted, to some applause and agreement. He ignored this and the girls quieted down as he made another adjustment on his guitar.

"There," he said when it was perfect. "Ready for another?" he counted off the beat and the band resumed.

Laura stayed focused on the music. I could tell by her body language that she still wasn't sure, although I couldn't say of what at the time. Surely this singer could never supplant Bruce as a favorite, and she had no problem liking other bands, so I didn't know what to make of this attitude. But I thought I knew her. And what I thought I knew was that she would tell me if it was important, or else it would blow over and not matter. So I said nothing, and let the music wash over me. And God help me, I liked him. I wanted him to succeed. I wanted, years from now, to say I'd seen him at a little club before he had an album out. Before he was signed. Before he had made it.

I watched the reactions of the girls watching him as well. Laura was wrong. He was playing to the crowd, but not to the girls specifically, despite their anxious attempts to attract his attention. I started to see them as an ocean, with each girl's individual undulations as waves. They danced to the music, trying to keep the beat of songs they were unfamiliar with, some succeeding better than others. But their heads stayed focused, their eyes gazing up at him. The more experienced flirters kept their heads lowered slightly, so that they could make the most of looking up at him. They played with their hair, ran their hands over their bodies to draw attention to their individual assets, and they smiled as much as they could, desperate to be the one girl who could really catch his eye. Yet none of them did. Which must have taken serious work with a few of those girls.

Three songs later, Mark held up his hand for quiet again and both the crowd and band obeyed. "Anyone have a request for our next song?" he asked. Silence. "It doesn't have to be one of ours." A few people named songs that I assumed were songs of his because I had never heard of them, and the crowd began to buzz.

Then Laura's voice rang out, crystal clear over the crowd.

"Thunder Road."

It was less a request than a direct challenge.

Mark held his hand up to the audience for quiet again, then moved it to shade his eyes from the glare of the stage lights as he tried to see in our direction. It was obvious who had issued this dare, as when he turned to look, everyone else around us did the same. Laura kept her arms crossed and watched him carefully, everything about her saying that she expected him to be unable to perform to her standards. And of course she would be right. What were the odds of this band, no matter how influenced the singer was, knowing this song, which had to have been written before anyone in the band had even been born?

"Thunder Road?" he asked softly and Laura nodded slightly, defiantly. He let out a short, impressed whistle, and then his face split into a large grin. "One of my all-time favorites. I saw the Boss doin' it in Philly this summer." He turned to the band, "You ready, boys?" Keeping his eyes on Laura, he spoke. "This one's for that girl back there with the awesome taste," he grinned at her again. "Just keep in mind that the 'you ain't a beauty' part sure wasn't written about you. Alright, Jimmy, start it off!" and they began the song. They didn't have a harmonica and had keyboards instead of a piano, but they pulled it off. Mark unhooked his guitar and let his other guitar player take the lead, then took the microphone out of its holder to walk around the stage while singing.

Laura watched his every move. She hadn't smiled under his flattery, but she did when he yelled, "sing it if you know it!" before the line he had warned her about. Only a handful of people knew what to sing, but those who did shouted it out. Except Laura, who just smiled. And except me. I watched the way she was looking at him and I saw it change. And fear started to kick in.

The girls in front cheered louder than they had earlier when he finished the song, mostly to prove that they knew it and wanted it too, because he had said it was one of his favorites. Laura didn't cheer, but then again, she never did for anyone but Bruce.

"Did I do it justice?" Mark asked, as the girls screamed louder still, but he was looking at Laura. He had barely taken his eyes off of her during the song. She tilted her head to the side and shrugged a little, but smiled. "Well I don't normally like to do two covers from the same band in the same set, but this is always a good one to end on." He said something inaudible to the band, winked at Laura as they played the opening notes, and began to sing: "Spread out now, Rosie...."

And I knew. In that moment, I knew. I had just lost her.

The rest of the night was hellish, although to Laura, it was the beginning of her very own real-life fairy tale come true, complete with a Prince Charming and everything. Mark finally stopped watching Laura to sing "Rosalita" and played again to the whole crowd. He had the girls in front jumping to the chorus and the energy behind his performance certainly rivaled the times that we had seen the song performed. After the second chorus, there's a small instrumental break in the singing. Mark tossed the microphone to someone who was right off stage, motioned to the girls to clear some room, and when they did, he jumped down mid-song and ran up to Laura. He whispered something to her and she smiled and nodded. He kissed her on the cheek, and ran back up in time to sing the next line.

I leaned over to Laura. I couldn't stop myself. I knew what he had said, and the rational part of me didn't want to hear her repeat it. But I asked. And of course, being Laura, she kept her eyes on the stage and just shook her head.

I wanted to leave. Just tell her to fuck off and be done with the whole situation. I had spent so much time with her over the last year, and I was like a toy to her that she could discard when she found a better one. I was angrier than I could ever remember having been in my whole life. As strongly as I had loved her ten minutes earlier, I hated her in that moment.

But I didn't at the same time. It wasn't just that I wanted her. If that was what I wanted, I probably could have had that long ago and then walked away. But I wanted to be with her. Maybe I wouldn't want that for forever, but when you want it, it always feels like it will last forever. She drove me crazy and I accepted that, but there was so much more. I wanted to make her laugh for the rest of our lives. I wanted her to bestow that most special smile of hers on me. Just me. And I wanted to know what it was that made her look so sad when she thought that no one was watching. I knew that I probably couldn't fix whatever it was, but I wanted to try. And the part of me that knew all of this also knew that I was in way over my head with her. But I was in for good, one way or the other. I wouldn't leave until she made me, which right then I realized could actually happen. And soon. All of my certainty of earlier left me. If she was in love, even if she was scared, would we be here? I couldn't answer that. But I knew enough. She came here for a reason tonight. And as always, everything was going exactly her way.

27

After Laura met Mark, I knew it was just a matter of time until she left me. Until she ran away. She loved me. I knew she did. But there just wasn't any way to keep her anymore.

I pieced together what I could about why she was too scared to stay. As best I could figure it, Laura had fallen in love at some point, probably a long time ago already, and gotten very badly burned. Combine that with whatever residual issues she had from her parents dying and she was terrified to let herself love anyone. I didn't know anything at all about her parents, except that they were dead and that they had left her with a substantial amount of money. I guess I thought that she had lost her parents sometime around college and the love affair had ended more recently, not long before I met her. It would explain the sadness I had seen in her eyes at times. And if the two had happened in rapid succession, well, it was understandable that she would be afraid to love someone. It meant that everyone she had ever loved was gone now.

She never talked about her parents. I speculated it was a car crash or something, but I also kind of toyed with the idea of them having been two of the September 11 casualties. It would have fit with the time frame I had in mind; also, it would explain her fascination with *The Rising*, as the album that the tour was supporting was inspired by that tragedy. I did a quick search of her last name among people who died that day though and didn't find any leads, which brought me back to the car crash idea. Or maybe they had died separately but in a short time span? Did one die when she was young, one more recently? Both when she was young? Maybe she never knew one of them and then the other died? There were endless possibilities. But there are some things you just don't ask when someone clearly doesn't want to talk about it.

One time, I started to ask her what they had done before they died. Laura shot me such a murderous look that even if she hadn't said anything, I would have never asked again. "I do not want to talk about them," she said sharply. And after that, they ceased to exist.

There were no pictures of parents anywhere. I mean, there were seldom pictures of Laura around, except that one of her in front of the Eiffel Tower. And I only knew that had to be her because she spoke fluent French. She once told me she dreamed in French sometimes, which I thought meant that she had probably spent time in France when she was little. No pictures of friends or exes either though. She never talked about past boyfriends, but she was twenty-five; she had to have had them. I was often amazed, when my friends would ask about her, at how little I really knew considering how much time she spent talking. But I guess you can talk a lot without really saying anything.

When Mark came on the scene though, I was pushed into the background. I wondered for a little while what would have happened if we hadn't gone to his show at the 9:30 Club that night. But much later, I came to realize that she would have found another way, any other way, to get away from me. That's not exactly a consoling thought, even when it means that someone actually does love you. But Laura wasn't ready for a real relationship, and I was just too real for her right then. And you can't ever tell someone to get over something. There are some mistakes they will always have to learn on their own. Mark was Laura's mistake. And Laura was mine.

Someone from *The Washington Post* was at the 9:30 club the same night that we were and he reviewed the show. His review of the two opening acts on the bill was tepid. His review of Mark Houston, of course, was stellar. Mark didn't have a record contract yet, but according to the reviewer, it was coming soon. And he was right of course. Mark was a tremendous musician with a lot of charisma. He would go far.

She brought me to a couple of his shows before I chose to stop going. She still wanted me there, but was also obviously uncomfortable having me there. She knew what she was doing to me. Laura would never admit it, but she knew. And more proof that she loved me: she cared. With anyone else, Laura might have been able to be cruel. But with me, she felt bad. And so I spared her that, although she didn't deserve it, and I stopped going to the places where he would be.

The first night that I went to a show with her once they were together, I felt like a parent in the room. Like I was an unwanted chaperone. Afterwards, backstage, Laura was sitting on his lap and I had no idea why I was there. But when I tried to leave, she asked me to stay.

And I just didn't know what else to do.

28

Two weeks after Mark and Laura met, he was playing at Jammin' Java, a little coffee shop in Vienna, Virginia. She convinced me to come along. God, how I wanted to find the perfect thing to say to make her realize that this wasn't right.

But it was too late. I knew I had already lost her and I knew why.

I went to the show with her. I think I was still in denial about it. That I wanted to see them together and find something that would prove that the feeling I had about them wrong. *Or at least get some closure before it's too late*, a tiny little voice, which I tried to silence, told me. I had to know if I had lost her for good. I knew, but I had to know irrevocably before I could let her go. Not that I was sure that I could let her go. But, I realized after they met, I just wasn't going to have a choice in the matter.

Would anything have changed if I had told her how I felt? Not by then, obviously. Then it could change nothing. But what if I had told her earlier? Even just a week or two earlier? Would she have been with me instead of him then?

Not that it would have really mattered. Because I would have lost her eventually in that case anyway. We would have been together for a little while. But I could picture what her eyes would look like if that happened. It wouldn't be the Laura I had fallen in love with behind them. It would have been the look that Mel said that I had when I was living with Katie. And I didn't want her like that. She had to find out on her own what it was that she needed.

We got there late, whereas for any other show, she would have insisted that we arrive early. She gave her name to the woman holding a list at the door and we were allowed in immediately, without paying any cover. Instead of going to find seats in the miniscule venue, which is what we usually did, she led me through the crowd to the wall opposite the side of the stage where there was a small bench. Big enough for just the two of us, with a tiny ocean of space in between. The opening act was just finishing up as we got there. The guitar player looked over at Laura as he played the last notes of their second-to-last song and dropped his pick. Laura didn't notice. She wasn't paying any attention to the band but was looking around the coffee shop instead. It was a strange venue, with a small stage, about ten rows of seats packed closely together, and tables filling the rest of the shop. It probably sat 300 people at most, maybe more when they took out the tables and filled the rest with seats, which they sometimes did there. But it was packed. And judging from the amount of conversation going on during the first band's set and the polite, but disinterested applause, the crowd wasn't here for the opening band.

Laura and I barely spoke as we waited for Mark to take the stage. Laura observed the positioning of the instruments and flashed a smile at the scrawny boy with dirty, scruffy hair who was making sure that everything was in place. He smiled warmly back and waved to her. She had clearly already charmed her way into the hearts of the roadies. Probably the rest of the band as well. My slim hopes that she would be branded a Yoko Ono disappeared.

Finally the band emerged from the small door in the back of the stage and when Mark came out, he glanced immediately to where we were sitting and winked at Laura. I felt about two inches tall. A few people noticed this and turned to scrutinize Laura. I don't think there was any wondering about who she was, based on the looks they exchanged. "Who is that chump sitting next to the singer's girlfriend?" was probably the only question in anyone's mind. Girlfriend! It had been less than two weeks. She hadn't said the word girlfriend yet. But some things are too obvious for words and unfortunately this was one of them.

"I wanna thank you all for comin' out here to see us tonight," Mark said warmly to applause from the audience after his first song. His fan base seemed to be growing rapidly. I recognized several people as having been at the other shows that Laura had brought me to. "One person in particular," he said with a smile at Laura. She smiled faintly back at him and everyone who hadn't turned to look at her before did now. Mark launched into his second song and eventually people turned their gazes from us to him.

I looked over at Laura. She closed her eyes for a few seconds as Mark's voice washed over us. Just looking at her, nothing had to be different. She hadn't dressed up more or done her hair or makeup with any more care than usual. She didn't need to. I wondered how someone could look exactly the same and be completely different from who she was just a matter of days ago. Then again, I was already different from who I was that same number of days ago. Mark had intruded into our lives, and neither of us could be the same.

I wanted to go home. What was I doing there? I felt completely and utterly out of place. Laura leaned across the chasm between us and whispered, "Isn't he phenomenal?" I nodded miserably and replied with as noncommittal a "yeah" as I could muster. She glanced at me sharply. "You okay?"

Another yeah and miserable nod. She looked at me questioningly, saw I wasn't looking back at her, shrugged slightly, and turned her attention back to Mark.

Part of my misery was that he really *was* that phenomenal. I would love to say he was awful or even just that he wasn't anything that special. But I would be lying. I wasn't remotely surprised when he turned up at Laura's door waving a signed record contract a few days later. And if he hadn't been the one who took Laura away from me, he would have been an immediate new musical favorite of mine too.

After a set similar to the one he had played at the 9:30 Club, minus the Bruce songs, Mark thanked the crowd and walked off the stage. About a minute later, he was back for an encore. "Two more," he said, holding up his hands for quiet. And of course, with another look at Laura, he launched into "Thunder Road." She beamed up at him. I could picture it now; this would be their song. Ours was "Backstreets" of course, which fittingly enough was about a breakup that was probably never even a real breakup because they were friends, and the girl leaves with another guy. And "Thunder Road," on the same album, is about a guitar-carrying guy picking up his girl and "pulling out of here to win." I wondered miserably if it was supposed to be the same girl in both songs. One was Mary and one was Terry and the order on the album was wrong in our case, but both were Laura right now. They would play "Thunder Road" at their wedding. Which I, having been discarded long before, would not be at.

I started to get angry. Looking back now, it was a little irrational, but made sense at the time. How dare he not only take Laura from me, but take one of my favorite songs and make it theirs? Technically, Laura had done that, by requesting it at the 9:30 Club. But it was theirs now, not mine, and that wasn't fair. Would I ever be able to listen to it again without thinking of them? I would obviously never be able to hear it without thinking of her, but that was true now of most of Bruce's songs, and I desperately did not want Mark intruding on that. I didn't want to have to think of him and the looks she gave him when I heard those opening notes. It wasn't fair.

He finally finished the song that he stole from me and introduced his last song. "I just wrote this last night," he said, with a sheepish grin that brought squeals from some girls in the crowd. "So hopefully you'll like it," but he looked at Laura as he said that, and it had to have been clear to everyone there that he wrote it for her. I could have stood up and told the whole room what it would be about before he started singing. It was pretty obviously about finding love where you didn't expect it. I could have written a similar song (if I could write songs or read music, I suppose I need to add that caveat there) after I met her in Charlotte. Or after I saw her at the first DC show for that matter. But I think his worst crime of all, even worse than taking Laura from me (because, in all honesty, even I know that I never completely had her), and worse than taking "Thunder Road," was this new song. Because it was that good. It would be his first single. I knew that. And a few months later, I was proven right. To take Laura and be able to give her what I never could, while I was sitting right there, was unforgivable.

They both tried to convince me to stay after the show. Mark was genuinely nice about it too. As nice as someone has to be when he understands the position that he is in. He was someone who I probably would have wanted to be friends with if not for Laura. He knew, in finding her, what she had to mean to me, just as I knew, in knowing her, exactly what he had seen and instantly fallen for in her. He tried to talk Bruce with me a bit, proving that Laura had, at least in the vaguest terms, told him who I was.

But I said I had to get up early the next morning, and I left. Laura said she would call me. Not the next day of course, because it wasn't like Laura to say when she would do anything. Calling me could mean fifty years from now. Although I knew that I would hear from her within a couple of days, and she would still try to bring me to Mark's next show. He was playing in Philadelphia in a week, and she would probably want me to go with her. But I couldn't do that. She and I had a history in Philadelphia and I wasn't going to let Mark's presence ruin some of my happiest memories. So I said goodnight and went home in defeat.

29

I knew something was up when Laura called before she came over. A normal Friday night before Mark entered the picture entailed Laura showing up unannounced. We would either decide on something to do or else sit around rummaging through bootlegs of old shows, trying to find new favorite versions of old songs and getting progressively drunker until we fell asleep in my bed. If we were sober enough to get there. On the sofa if we weren't. A couple of times on the floor. But always together, arms and legs and torsos tangled up like a game of Twister gone wrong.

And after she met Mark, a normal Friday involved me not hearing from her at all.

But that night, she called. "It's me," she said, and I could hear her wincing as she said it. She was committing one of her top five pet peeves. "I was thinking I'd stop by in a bit. Is that okay?" I was scared. Something was wrong. Big wrong. Not only had she called, but she asked if it was okay if she came over. Laura never asked. That was part of the beauty of her. She just showed up. And I knew right then that I wouldn't see her after that night.

For the first twenty minutes, nothing. She sipped her beer. She was quieter than usual. She didn't fidget. I, on the other hand, couldn't sit still. I wanted to shake her and yell at her to get it over with. But I just sat there. Waiting for that inevitable other shoe to drop.

She took a deep drink from her bottle and finally said it. Slowly and deliberately. As if she had practiced. She probably had. "Mark asked me to go to California with him." She was looking at me, but I didn't look at her. I stared down at the carpet. Neither of us spoke for a long time. Finally, I got up and walked over toward the stereo, keeping my back to her. I just didn't want to look at her right then.

"And you're going." It wasn't a question. I knew her too well. There wasn't any question to it. It was what she had always thought she wanted. She would be his Patti. Mark wasn't Bruce, but he would have, at the very least, moderate success. And he had certainly already fallen hard for her. But then, who wouldn't?

"Yes," she said softly. "I'm going."

I looked at my CD collection for awhile, none of it registering. Then, anger set in. Not just anger, but rage. I was angrier than I had ever been before in my life. I had to do something or I was going to explode. The CD rack got too tempting. In one motion, I hit it hard enough to knock it off the shelf and most of the CDs bounced off the wall in an explosion of shattering plastic as the cases broke.

"*Jesus!*" She yelled, crossing the room in two seconds, her face inches from mine, her eyes abruptly blazing. "What the fuck is your problem?"

"My problem? Oh no, it's not my problem. It's your problem!"

"What are you talking about? Have you completely lost it?"

"I'm talking about you being an idiot!" I slammed my hand down on the shelf. I was beyond reason, beyond courtesy, and way beyond tact. And I wasn't thinking any more. It was all just going to come out, and now, looking back, I don't think I could have stopped that deluge if I had wanted to. But I didn't want to.

"*I'm* being an idiot? You're the asshole who's getting mad and smashing shit when you should be *happy* for me!"

I laughed a very bitter, humorless laugh. "Oh, I would love to be happy for you, Laura. But you're not happy for yourself. And you want me to tell you that you're doing the right thing so that you can go off and not feel guilty. But fuck that, you're doing the wrong thing and I'm not going to lie to you this time!"

"Look, sweetheart," she said, the endearment sounding anything but endearing, "this is what I want and you *know* that."

"No, this is what you say you want because you're scared."

"Bullshit." She started to turn away but I grabbed her arm.

"*You*'re bullshit, Laura! But I can see through you."

She tried to yank her arm away but I held on tightly, probably too tightly. "You can't see anything!" Her voice rose higher and higher as she struggled to free her arm, and she sounded almost a little panicky. "Let me go!" She had still been holding her beer with her other hand, and when I didn't let go, she hurled it at the floor, where it broke into a million little shards of brown glass floating in a sea of foam on my carpet. I dropped her arm and she retreated a couple of feet. For the first time, she looked afraid, although she had to know that I would never actually hurt her.

The fear in her eyes made me lower my voice. I could never hurt her physically, but I did want to hurt her. I wanted her to hurt like she was making me hurt. I wanted her to feel it too. I wanted to know that she was feeling *something*. Anything. As long as it was real.

"Don't go," I said finally, struggling to keep my voice low. "Please."

"I have to go," she said, holding the arm that I had grabbed as if my hand had burned her. She was talking softer now too. "I have to go," she repeated, "because I love Mark. I love him."

The anger flared back up. "You are such bullshit!"

"What the hell do you know about it?" she yelled back.

"I know you don't love him!"

"You don't know *any*thing!" She started to turn toward the door. "And I don't have to fucking prove anything to you!"

"No, but apparently you have to prove it to yourself! You don't love him and you know it!"

"I do!" she yelled at me shrilly, unwilling to let me have the last word in the matter. "And besides, it's *my* business, *not* yours!"

"It *is* my business!" I punctuated this by punching the wall, although I wouldn't feel the pain in my knuckles until days later. "It's my business because—because—" But I couldn't finish the sentence.

She had jumped when I punched the wall and taken an involuntary step backwards, but when I fell silent, she crept slowly closer. "Why?" she asked softly. She wanted to hear me say it. She knew what I was going to say, but whether she could admit it or not, she needed to hear it. She came forward until she was almost touching me. "Why?" she asked again, anger gone, her eyes wide.

"You know why, Laura. You already know."

"Why, Ben?" Not darling or sweetie or angel. Only my name. I took a deep breath. Fine. If she wanted to hear it, I would say it. I had to know it wouldn't change anything, but I didn't have any other cards left to play.

"I love you, Laura. Because I'm in love with you." I reached out to touch her face, to pull her close, to hear her say what I knew she felt too. For an instant, she swayed slightly closer, leaning in to me. But then, just as quickly, she pulled away and shook her head violently.

"No!" she exclaimed. "You do *not* love me. You just— you—you don't even know what you're talking about."

"I know that I love you and I know that you love me." Now it was her turn to laugh.

"You seem to know an awful lot," she said, "for someone who doesn't actually know anything at all."

"Laura."

"No!" she said, backing away further. "I do not love you. Look, I'm sorry, but you're wrong."

"I'm not wrong and I know that you don't love him! You love what he is! You've spent the past I don't know how long dreaming about being Patti Scialfa and now you think this is your big shot! Well wake up, Laura, he's not Bruce and you're *not* Patti and you never will be!"

"You don't have any idea what I want or why I want it!"
She was moving closer again, but this time it was part of
the fight. She was getting into my face, moving in for the
kill. "And if you think you can love me without knowing
any of that, well, honey, you're wrong, because that is *not*
how love works!"

"Oh yeah, so you're the expert? Well let me tell you
what I know. Somewhere along the line, some guy hurt
you, and now you're terrified of letting anyone in, but I *am*
in and you can't just cut me out now! And you found Bruce
as a substitute for making a real connection with anyone,
but you can't have Bruce, so you're trying to get away and
live the life of some other rock star's girlfriend, because
then you don't have to let anyone in too far. And if it
doesn't work out, you can always write it off to the lifestyle
because even Bruce wasn't perfect and cheated on his first
wife! But you can't live someone else's life, Laura!"

Her mouth dropped open slightly as I was talking. She
shut it quickly and didn't respond right away. "You think
you know so fucking much," she hissed with venom, her
eyes hard and cold, "but you don't know nearly as much as
you think you do."

"Whoever he was Laura, let it go already. Just let it go.
He's not worth ruining your life over just because he left
you!"

"You don't know what you're talking about," she said
calmly and started to walk away again.

"Then tell me so I can know! If it's not some guy who
left you, then what the hell is it? Because I don't believe for
a second that isn't what happened!"

She turned back to me. "You want to know?" she
asked, her voice positively dripping with poison.

"Yes."

"You really want to know?"

"I said yes."

"You were right. He did leave me. But what you didn't
figure out, Sherlock, is that he was my husband." This time

it was my mouth that dropped open. Her husband? She had been *married*?

"That's right," she said, registering my shock with a smile that didn't come close to touching her eyes, which were still icy and hard. It both broke my heart and made me terrified to hear what she was going to say next.

"We got married right out of college. Big ceremony, white dress, six bridesmaids, the works. Honeymoon in Hawaii. Even bought a little house." She stopped there.

"What happened?"

"He 'went out for a ride' and he never came back," she quoted. Finally she sank down on the sofa. She seemed exhausted, like the act of telling me that had worn her out. She had her head down and was studying her hands.

When it was clear she had no more to say, I walked over to her and knelt down by her feet. I covered her hands with mine. "I'm so sorry," I said. But it was the wrong thing to say.

She jumped up and walked away toward the stereo, but at least she wasn't heading toward the door. "I don't need your pity," she said harshly, her back to me, "and I certainly don't want it."

I waited. Nothing. I moved from my knees into a sitting position on the floor. Finally, I realized that she wasn't going to give me any more information unless I asked. I had to say something. "When?" She didn't turn around or answer me. "Laura."

"Last June."

June. Two months before the first time I saw her. *June.* Suddenly it clicked. In the past year and a half, I had seen her cry twice. The second time, when Bruce sang "Blood Brothers" at the end of the tour, I could explain. Now I could explain the first. I didn't mean to say it and had I been able to stop myself, I would have. But as soon as I made the connection, the words popped out of my mouth.

"That's why you were crying during 'Bobby Jean.'"

She turned around slowly, her eyes narrowed. "What did you say?" she asked quietly.

I didn't respond. All I could think was that I had just fucked up. Big time. She was about to leave. *Fuck.*

She walked closer. "I never cried during 'Bobby Jean,'" she said, her voice still low. "Which begs the question of why you would say that." Her eyes were no longer narrowed, but her brows had come together.

I looked up at her, but now I was the one who was tired. I couldn't play this game with her. If she didn't want to admit it, fine, but I had seen it and now I knew why. That was why she was mad. She had told me what she was willing to let me to know, but she had no idea that I had seen something that she wasn't ready to share, which made her vulnerable. She couldn't have known that I would be able to see into how she had felt right after her husband left her. Laura liked to be the one who surprised other people; she hated it when anyone figured her out without her permission. Normally, I played along. But I couldn't anymore. It was too late for that.

"Because I saw you. At the first DC show. You were there with that Charlie guy. And you were crying when Bruce played 'Bobby Jean.'"

"What do you mean you saw me? You didn't know who I was until the Charlotte show!"

"No, but I remembered you."

"This is bullshit! All of it!" She moved toward the door. "I'm so out of here!" She didn't even look at me. "Fuck you and fuck all of this! Don't tell me you saw me crying in DC months before we met a year-and-a-fucking-half later!" She crossed behind the sofa to avoid being within my reach. But I couldn't just let her leave. Not like that.

I jumped up and yanked on her arm, spun her around, and grabbed her shoulders. She squirmed in my grip but I held onto her. "Let me go!"

"No! Not until you've heard me out! You can walk out on everyone else, Laura, but not on me! Not yet!" She kept trying to get away and I tightened my hold on her.

"I remembered you because there was no way not to! You were the most beautiful girl that I had ever seen and I had to find out what could make you cry like that! You didn't even wipe the tears away! You didn't even look like you knew you were crying!" She kept struggling against me, although she wasn't trying quite as hard as before.

"And when I finally met you, I figured you were insane. You had to be, but I kept coming back for more because I couldn't get enough. And I didn't want to, but damn it, Laura, I fell in love with you. And you love me too. And I refuse to lose you just because you're too scared to handle this!"

"I do not love you." She said each word with the finality of its own sentence. As if she were talking to a child who wouldn't listen. But she had stopped struggling. Which was all the encouragement that I needed.

I brought my face closer to hers. "Prove it then," I said quietly. When my lips were an inch from hers, I whispered it again. "If you don't love me, then prove it." And I kissed her.

For a couple of seconds, which felt like a lifetime, she didn't respond.

And then she did.

Her arms, which had struggled to free themselves from my hands, went easily up to my neck. I buried one hand in her hair and wrapped my other arm around her narrow waist to pull her closer. I'm not sure how we got to my bed, but we were there. Her body, which I had seen so many times, from so many angles, in so many different stages of dress and undress, was new tonight. The feel of her body next to mine, her skin under my skin was familiar but not. There had never been a night like that before and I didn't see how there could ever be a night like that again.

I was afraid to fall asleep. Part of me thought it was a dream and if I fell asleep, I would have to wake up to the reality of my life without her. Part of me knew she would be gone in the morning if I lost consciousness at all. But she pulled herself up off of my chest and kissed my eyelids closed. "Sleep," she whispered between kisses. And who was I to refuse?

30

I woke up because I rolled over and realized, even asleep, that she was gone. Panicked, I sat up. And then I heard her laughing. She was sitting in my chair, which she had dragged over until it was directly under the window, and she sat in the light like a cat. She looked so little sitting there with her feet up, her chin resting on one upright knee, the other leg tucked under her, an unlit cigarette dangling from her hand. I hadn't smoked in over six months and as far as I knew, neither had she. She had pulled on one of my concert shirts and her hair was messy, but her face was clean; she had washed her makeup off sometime in the night.

"Think I wouldn't still be here?" she asked when she stopped laughing. I was so relieved I couldn't even speak. I just nodded. She smiled at me and it was the most beautiful sight that I had ever seen.

"What are you doing over there?" I finally asked.

She shrugged. "Couldn't sleep. Didn't want to wake you up though."

"You should have."

"Nah," she smiled again, almost shyly this time. She looked so sweet. I was amazed. I had known her for over a year now and was seeing a side of her that I had never imagined existed. Then she stood up and brushed a piece of hair out of her face, abandoning the normal head toss that she used to remove errant locks. "Come on," she said, holding out her hand to me. "I'll make us some pancakes." I got up and took her hand as she started to lead me to the kitchen.

"I don't have any pancake mix," I said. "But I can make us some eggs."

"No," Laura said with a laugh. "Definitely not eggs." I smiled at her. "Do you have milk and flour?"

"Yeah."

"Then I can make pancakes. Mixes are for people who can't cook." A year and I had never seen any indication that she could cook, let alone that she would know a recipe for making pancakes from scratch.

While Laura was cooking, I tore myself away to put some music on. I wasn't planning to clean up the CDs or the broken beer bottle yet; I didn't want to be away from her for that long. But when I went into the living room, the CDs were back on their rack and the only trace of the bottle was a damp spot on the carpet where she had tried to clean up the spilled beer.

I couldn't really explain the change in her. Except that it was like the mask was gone. The girl who I had seen at odd times in her eyes, when she was tired or forgot who she was supposed to be trying to be, was here, with me. Yes, it was the free spirit that attracted me at first, but it was the girl behind that who I had fallen in love with. The girl who had cried at "Bobby Jean" without knowing that anyone saw it. The girl who had organized her glove compartment so carefully. The girl who automatically burned an extra copy of her bootlegs for me. The girl who had remembered our "Springsteen-iversary" on December 8. That was the girl I loved and now she was here. And that was the girl who loved me too.

Sometimes I wasn't sure that the next two days really happened, especially over the following few months, when I would wonder if I had imagined the whole thing. But the days were real, as were the nights.

Laura was—well, she was Laura, but without the shell. We made love all over my apartment. We didn't go more than a few minutes without touching each other in some way. We ate together, we showered together, shared every thought, we couldn't get enough of being with each other. I had been starving for her for months and months and now that I had her, I couldn't let go. But incredibly enough, Laura was the same way. She returned caress for caress and kiss for kiss. It made me wonder how nothing more had happened the two times we had kissed before.

Mark didn't exist anymore. I didn't mention him, and neither did she. But the wall that he had become between us was suddenly gone.

31

Our second night, as we were lying in my bed, Laura rolled over so that her back was to me, and she sighed. But not a happy sigh, as her others of the day had been. I moved behind her to put my arms around her, exhausted and ready to fall asleep, but she edged away and rolled back to face me.

"Ben," she said, her eyes brimming with more pain than I had ever caught in them even in her most unguarded moments.

I couldn't breathe.

"I—I didn't tell you the full story last night." I almost laughed in relief. Had she looked less miserable, I probably would have.

"Then tell me," I said with a smile, stroking her arm lightly.

"I can't." Her eyes started to fill with tears.

I moved my hand to touch her face. "Then don't," I said. "It's up to you. If you want me to know, tell me. If you don't, it's fine." I was telling the truth. Yes, I wanted to know everything about her. But if she didn't want to tell me, it didn't matter because I had her now.

Laura just shook her head. I tried another tactic. "Why can't you tell me?"

"Because you won't love me anymore," Laura closed her eyes briefly and let out a quiet, choked laugh. "That sounded a lot stupider out loud than it did in my head."

I smiled as encouragingly as I could. "There's nothing you can tell me about your past that will change how I feel about you now."

Laura took a deep breath then let it out. "When Justin—my hus—my—ex—my ex-husband, when he left, I didn't know until a couple weeks later. But I was pregnant." She paused here and looked at me. I didn't know how to respond to this, so I didn't say anything. I didn't think I was expected to.

"When he left, I—it just killed me. I didn't know it was coming. We hadn't fought, he hadn't seemed unhappy, it was the same as it always was with us. We were married for two years and we had been together for five-and-a-half. He didn't even tell me. He left me a note. A fucking note." She paused again, and again I said nothing.

"He didn't say why, or where he was going. Just that he didn't want to be married anymore. I was frantic, I called all of our friends but they told me they didn't know where he was either.

"My best friend was supposed to be in Italy the week that he left. I called her as soon as she was supposed to be back in town. And he answered her phone.

"That killed me. I just—I didn't know what to do. I mean, they were my whole family. And a couple weeks later I finally realized two things; he wasn't coming back and I was pregnant." She stopped again, for longer this time.

"What happened?" I asked finally. For as long as I live, I will never forget her eyes at that moment. They were naked, and looking into them was like drowning.

She just stared at a point over my left shoulder. "Well clearly I didn't have it."

What do you say when the girl you love tells you that?

It explained a lot, actually. Because she honestly thought that I wouldn't still love her once I knew that. She hadn't forgiven herself. And how could she expect anyone else to love her if she didn't think that she deserved to be loved?

I have always described myself as being pro-choice, but not necessarily pro-abortion. I don't think I can decide what a girl should do in those circumstances, because I can't be in that position. That doesn't mean I necessarily think abortions are right either. I'd never really had to think about it before though.

So how could I both reconcile myself to that and find something to say in a reasonable amount of time for a reaction to what she had just told me? Well, I thought about how I had felt the night before, when I realized that she was leaving. I thought about how I would feel if she left the next day. Could I promise not to do anything rash, anything I might regret later?

I guess I didn't respond quickly enough because Laura spoke again.

"I know this changes things." A tear slipped down her cheek and she wiped it away hastily with the back of her hand. "But that's part of why I said you didn't really love me. You couldn't, not without knowing that. And you can't now, knowing it." She had misinterpreted my silence and sat up, gathering the sheet around her. But I had already processed it and sat up with her, putting one arm around her and using the other hand to turn her face to mine.

I kissed her on the forehead, then lightly on the lips.

"Is that the best you can do?" I asked with a smile. "Because it'll take a hell of a lot more than that to get rid of me."

A second tear crept down her cheek and I kissed it away. And she whispered, for the first time, that she loved me.

32

I had slept in the same bed with Laura dozens of times. I say that I slept, not that we slept, because I had never actually witnessed Laura sleeping. I knew she was an insomniac and just about the lightest sleeper in the world, and I think I would have known that even if I had never slept next to her because of the circles that permanently resided under her eyes. If I woke up in the middle of the night, sometimes she would still be in bed, but she was always awake. Most times, she wasn't in the bed. If we were on the road, Laura was always sitting somewhere else in the motel room when I woke up. Usually staring out the window. If there was enough light to see by, she would be reading. I sometimes thought about getting her a reading light so she wouldn't worry about waking me up. But if Laura wanted one, she would have bought herself one. And at my place, Laura was always gone by the time I woke up.

But that morning was different.

I woke up before she did.

And I lay there next to her for nearly two hours until she woke up, just before noon. I had never seen her so peaceful. I felt such relief. If she could sleep with me, really sleep, it showed how much she cared. She couldn't leave me then.

She stirred a little before she actually woke up. Her eyelids fluttered and her breath caught slightly. She opened her eyes, blinking, and saw me looking at her. First, she looked surprised. Then she smiled, but it was a little guarded. Next, she yawned and stretched her arms out over her head. I liked what I saw. I decided that I wanted to be able to watch her wake up for the rest of our lives.

"What time is it?" she asked eventually and I told her. "Wow."

"I'll say," I said, pulling her to me. "I didn't think you ever actually slept."

She snuggled in close to me. "First time for everything, I guess."

But when I woke up the next morning, she was gone.

Later, I felt like an idiot, because I didn't even worry at first. I assumed she was in the kitchen or the living room. When I realized that she wasn't in the apartment, I thought maybe she had gone out for a run. Even though I knew she didn't have her running gear with her. When I saw her car was gone, I figured she had gone home to get clothes, or maybe she had gone to pick up food for us. I thought it was a little strange that she didn't leave a note, but it wasn't Laura's style anyway, and clearly she must have thought that she would be back before I woke up.

But she didn't answer her cell phone. Maybe she had the music up really loud in her car. That happened all summer; she never heard her phone when she had the top down. But it was about thirty degrees outside. She would definitely have the top up on her car. Then again, she hadn't charged her phone in days; maybe the battery was dead. But it rang. It hadn't gone straight to voice mail like it would have if it was turned off.

An hour later, there was still no sign of her. I took a shower and got dressed. I tried to tell myself that she would be back soon and she would laugh at me for having worried. But the problem with lying to yourself is that you always do know that you're being lied to.

At three, I decided to drive to her place. Just to see. Because what if she had been heading there and had an accident? What if something bad had happened? I just had to see if she was there. I started to write a note to leave on the door. But what should I say? "Went looking for you, stay here if you beat me back?" No. I didn't like that. I had to keep it light. "Ran out to get us more food, call me when you get back?" I looked at it on the paper. I didn't love it. She hadn't left me a note. Plus, if I left that and then came back without food, she would know something was up. I crumpled it up and started a new sheet of paper. "Ran out for a few, be back soon." Perfect. It didn't say what I was doing.

I started to drop the first note in the trash when a similarly crumpled sheet of paper off the same pad caught my eye. I hadn't written another note.

Cringing a little, I fished it out of the trashcan. It had to be nothing.

But it wasn't.

"I wish I could, but I can't," it read in Laura's handwriting, scrawled across the top of the page and crossed out heavily. She had planned to write more, then quit. And apparently she stopped for good because there were no other papers in the trash and no other note left for me anywhere. I don't remember sitting down, but later I realized I was on the floor.

Now that I have a little distance from the situation, I feel sorry for her. Which I guess does mean that I also forgave her sometime in the last year. Poor Laura. She threw away her shot at any real happiness with that scrap of paper. Yes, she was living out her fantasy by following Mark, but it was just that: a fantasy. And looking now at what she did, I understand why she did it. Who wants reality when your fantasy is offering to become real? But the beauty of a fantasy is that it isn't real. It dies when it becomes real. Laura clearly didn't know that. Even Bruce couldn't have made her happy if she was living the day-to-day reality of life with him. And maybe I couldn't have either. But she would have had a better shot of it with me than with anyone else on the planet, and she was too scared to say yes to that. So she said no.

It did take me the better part of a year to be able to feel sorry for her though.

I didn't bother going after her. It wouldn't have done any good and I wasn't about to beg. If nothing else, by not chasing her, I had my dignity. Yes, she had left me without the courtesy of even actually leaving a note, let alone telling me. That was worse than what Justin had done to her. But clearly she would expect me to go after her, and in not doing that, I got to feel a little like I had been the one to decide. Had I thought even for a second that going after her would have gotten her back, I would have gone. But I knew better.

More than hurt, however, I was angry for a very long time. I learned how completely and utterly scorned love can imitate the purest hatred. Leaving when she did was so much worse than if she had actually left me the night that she came to tell me she was leaving. No one was stupid enough to repeat that bullshit about it being better to have loved and lost to me, because I think I would have punched anyone who even started to say that to me during that period. I told myself that people who can believe that cliché are the stupidest people to ever walk the earth. Maybe it was different when the person you love dies. But when she does what Laura did to me, it's pretty fucking hard to justify the waste that your life has become.

33

Prior to my experiences with Laura, my advice to friends had always been that the best way to get over a girl was to get under another one. I had followed that advice myself quite a few times in college. And after Katie, before I officially met Laura. Although to be fair, I didn't really have anything to get over after Katie. And that advice didn't always work perfectly, but sleeping with someone new is a great way to create some closure for yourself when you didn't get enough from a breakup. I mean, yes, sometimes you feel like shit afterwards, but in general, at least you're feeling like shit about someone new instead of about the girl you just lost.

That advice, however, never once crossed my mind in the weeks following Laura's departure. For the better part of two months, I didn't go out. I went to work most days. I only went to the grocery store when absolutely necessary. But you would be surprised how long you can survive on stale crackers and random refrigerator stuff, like olives. I stopped shaving most days. A couple of times, I woke up determined to get my life back on track. I would shave, actually iron a shirt or two, maybe even make a real meal. But that initial preservation instinct would be worn out by the end of those two or three activities, and I would sink back into the stupor that had consumed me since she left. Post-Laura Syndrome.

I only told Mel what happened when she forced it out of me. I hadn't answered anyone's calls, including hers, for two full weeks. So she showed up at my door.

Laura, I thought, jumping up when I heard a knock. I hesitated in the hall for a second. I hadn't shaved in a week. My shirt was dirty. My socks didn't match. But it was Laura. I ran the last few steps and flung the door open, the first smile on my face in weeks.

It died when I saw Mel standing there.

"Glad to see you too," she said, the sarcasm in her voice telling me just how annoyed she was by my expression. "Now that I know you're alive, I guess I can go home." She turned to leave, stopped when she realized that I wasn't going to call her back, and then she walked back to take a good look at me. "Jesus," she sighed. "When did she leave?"

I told her most of the story. I left out the parts that I knew Laura would never forgive me for telling. Because I still thought she was coming back. Mel was sympathetic. She didn't say "I told you so" or anything that would make me feel worse. But she wouldn't tell me that she thought Laura was coming back either. Mel always was smarter than me.

Mel called me with ridiculous frequency after that. I took the calls if I happened to have my phone with me, but I didn't call back when she left messages. I only checked my messages to see if maybe Laura had called me and it somehow hadn't showed up as a missed call on my cell. When I heard Mel's voice, I deleted the messages without listening to the rest. Eric called a couple of times to see if I wanted to go to the gym, but I didn't answer calls from anyone but Mel. And I think she spread the word that I was hiding out because no one seemed to be questioning my sudden drop off the face of the earth.

"I know you're going through a rough time right now," Mel began gingerly as she surveyed my living room. "But that's not an excuse for living like this." I looked around. And as much as I hated to admit it, she was right. I knew it was getting messy, but I hadn't really noticed how bad it had gotten, and that was actually kind of scary. But I was too tired to do anything about it now. Laura had been gone for five weeks.

I sat down without noticing the empty beer can on the chair. I pulled it out from under me and tossed it onto the floor. Mel sighed and went into my kitchen, reemerging with a trash bag, a bottle of Lysol that she must have smuggled in with her in her purse, and a roll of paper towels. She opened the trash bag and handed it to me, then started gathering the beer bottles, cans, and other assorted trash.

"Listen, Mel," I began, but she cut me off.

"No, you listen. I've listened for a long time now. You need to cut this out. I'm going to help you clean this place up and then you're going to go out tonight." I sighed and she turned around to look at me. "It's been long enough."

"It hasn't been that long."

"It's been a year and a half."

"No, I mean since she left."

"I know what you meant. But you've given her too much of your life already. Way more than she wanted or deserved. And I'm sorry if I sound harsh right now, but you need to hear this. She's not coming back." I didn't respond. "She's not coming back," Mel repeated slowly.

While I was in the shower, Eric and Chris showed up with a bottle of Jagermeister and six packs of both Red Bull and beer. Mel let them in and I heard them laughing as I toweled myself off. I stepped into my bedroom and saw that Mel had laid clothes out on the bed for me. She picked out the shirt I had been wearing that night when Mark played at Jammin' Java and I had to sit there next to Laura while he played the song he had just written for her. I buttoned it, wondering if I should buy a wardrobe without a memory. But then, as I sat on the edge of my newly-made bed, which probably also had freshly-changed sheets thanks to Mel, I realized if I was going to do that, I would have to buy practically everything new. Everywhere I looked, there was the ghost of Laura. She had slept in this bed with me, walked on this carpet, curled up in that chair, lain on my sofas, sat at my table, cooked in my kitchen, breathed the air of my apartment. If I closed my eyes and inhaled as deeply as I could, I thought I could still smell the faintest hint of her perfume.

Maybe I should move.

But how would she know to find me when (*if*) she came back?

She's not coming back, I told myself firmly. *Not ever*. I sighed and put on my shoes. I didn't want to be a downer tonight. Not in front of this consolidated effort to get me out. Not to Mel. Not in front of Chris and Eric. I put on aftershave to mask the perfume smell that I was now positive was still there, even though I had been sure it had completely left the apartment a week ago.

I took a deep breath and walked out into the living room. "Hey!" Chris and Eric called loudly, raising their bottles of Miller Lite. I looked at the remaining four beers in the cardboard casing on the coffee table. Laura used to bring Miller Lite. Mel caught my look and seemed to understand it. She gave me a warning glance before taking one of the beers for herself.

"Yo, those are for pre-drinking only." Chris said menacingly. "We've gotta get a buzz going before we go out." Mel looked at him sweetly.

"Gee, then maybe I should go with you too?"

Chris laughed. "That's okay, honey, you just drink as much as you want right here."

"Thanks, *honey*," Mel replied, with a quick smirk at Eric, who just laughed.

"Jager Bomb time," Eric said before I could sit down. "We need shot glasses and beer glasses." Mel started to get up, but I said I would get them.

"Are you in?" I asked her. She said no, so I carried three shot glasses and three pint glasses to the sofas. Chris poured the Red Bull, Eric the shots, and I did my best to try to look like I wanted to go out with them as we dropped the shots of Jager into the Red Bull, then drank as fast as we could. Chris burped loudly and looked defiantly at Mel, who surprised all of us by burping herself.

"Sick!" Chris yelled.

"You hypocritical asshole!" She retorted, laughing. "You burped way louder and way grosser than that."

"I'm gonna have to side with Chris here, Mel," Eric said. "That's not sexy."

"Geez, I can't win," she said winking at me and taking another swig of her beer. "I act like a girl and get yelled at for being too girly, I drink a beer and burp with you guys and get called sick."

"What are you going to do tonight?" I asked her. She had already said she wasn't coming with us.

"Going out with my girls," she said. "But we're just going down to Dupont Circle, so Adams Morgan is all yours tonight." I nodded. Mel looked at her watch and handed the rest of her beer to Eric. "I've actually got to run if I'm going to get home in time to shower and all." She kissed me on the cheek, then kissed Eric, whispering something to him that sounded like, "take care of him tonight," and started to put her coat on.

"What, no sugar for me?" Chris asked. Mel turned around and shot him a sexy smile. She swayed a little closer, stopped, looked at him coyly, and slowly gave him the finger. We all laughed. "Any time, baby, any time," Chris said as Melanie laughed and walked to the door.

"Have fun tonight, boys," she called sweetly as she shut the door behind her.

"Time for another Jager Bomb," Eric announced. We downed the drinks again and leaned back on my sofas. The first one hadn't done much for me. My tolerance had certainly gone up during my time with Laura.

"So what's the plan for tonight?" I asked, knowing full well that Mel had dictated exactly what we had to do tonight, probably including where we should go.

"Have another drink, then go to Adams Morgan," Eric said at the same time that Chris said, "Get you laid."

I looked at Chris. "Did Mel actually say that?" He said yes at the same time that Eric said no. I shrugged finally, twisted the top off a beer and drank the entire bottle in four long gulps.

"Now this is what we've been missing! You're one of the guys again!" Chris exclaimed. "Let's do another Jager Bomb then go pick up some girls."

By the time we left my apartment, I was starting to feel better than I had in a month. Three Jager Bombs and a beer in fifteen minutes will do that. That's the beauty of the Jager Bomb. The Red Bull part of it makes you feel fantastic. At least until the next morning when you only want to live long enough to find the guy who created Jagermeister and kill him. But in the moment, it's a great high.

Mel was smart, I thought as we walked to the Metro. She knew I had never been to Adams Morgan with Laura. She knew there would be no memories of her there.

I wondered how well she had primed Eric and Chris. She must have been pretty thorough. I had known Chris almost as long as I had known Mel. On a good day, he had the tact of a four year old with Tourette's. He should have been screaming stuff like "fuck that bitch," and calling Laura all kinds of disgusting, foul names. Usually, that was a good thing after a nasty breakup. But, especially with a few drinks in me, I might have decked him if he called her anything too bad. I don't have any idea what Mel said to him, but he was on his good behavior. With anyone else, I would have been pissed off by that level of interference. But with Mel, it showed just how worried she was. She had to have told him that I was just about suicidal or else threatened him with castration to get him to not mention Laura. Or both. I told myself that I would really try to have a good time that night because of how hard she had tried for me. It wasn't going to be easy. But maybe Mel was right. Maybe this was actually exactly what I needed.

I was starting to sober up by the time we made it down to TomTom, where one of our old frat brothers was working as a bartender. That's the trick to going out in DC. Get to know a bartender very well—it means it doesn't cost a million dollars or take nine years to get a few drinks. Laura had been the expert at that.

We started off upstairs. Chris and Eric began pointing out girls to me. And I found something wrong with each their choices. There were pretty girls there. Lots of them. A few of them were even shooting me looks. But they weren't Laura. I tried to tell myself that it was good that they weren't Laura. It didn't work. One girl "accidentally" bumped into me by the bar and did her best to strike up a conversation, which would have worked, except I just didn't have anything to say to her. My tongue felt too big for my mouth. She was beautiful. But she didn't have Laura's grace. She was quick with her replies, but not as quick as Laura. When she smiled, one corner of her mouth went the littlest bit higher than the other. I couldn't talk to this girl. Eventually, sensing my disinterest, she walked back to her friends. I saw her shrug her shoulders as the girls gave her questioning looks. One looked appraisingly over her shoulder at me, then shot me a look that so completely asked who I thought I was to reject her friend. I sighed. I wasn't interested. Was that a crime?

"Dude," Chris began, "what the hell is wrong with you? That girl was amazing!" I shrugged. I knew that saying she wasn't Laura would make me sound like a total pussy. "Fine," he said, finishing his drink and slapping the glass down on the bar. "I'm going over there." I watched as he strolled over to the group of girls and put his arms around two of them. "Ladies," I heard him say. "How are we doing tonight?"

Down to me and Eric. "Another drink," Eric said, turning to Andy to order them. He handed me a glass that looked and smelled like it was pure bourbon.

"Whoa," I said, recovering from how strong that first sip was. "Did you just order me a shot in a tumbler?"

"Drink it," Eric said over the noise of the bar. "You need to loosen up." Two more of those and I was finally loose enough to not care. About anything. I don't remember a lot of what happened next. I was talking to a blonde girl at one point. She didn't look anything like Laura. She was short, with wavy hair and Irish features, which was about as far from Laura's looks as it was possible to get. She resembled Katie a bit, if anything. Definitely my old type. Eric gave me a thumbs up from his spot by the bar. Then we were dancing. She pulled herself very close to me, her round body pressing seductively against mine. She smelled different from Laura, more citrusy than spicy. Eric brought over two drinks for us. It was hot in the bar, and I was sweating. Her hair was damp right at the base of her neck and curling into little corkscrews. She tasted like rum when I kissed her, and I remember noticing that her lips were thinner than Laura's, her tongue more insistent. But another bourbon cured any complaints I might have had.

Before I really woke up, I realized something wasn't right. I was aware of a heavy weight on my arm. The sheets weren't mine. The light from the window was on the wrong side of the bed. For half a sweet second, I let myself think I was with Laura. But I definitely knew I wasn't. I peeled a painful eyelid open. Oh fuck.

I was in a strange room on pink flowered sheets. And the weight on my arm was the girl from last night. I couldn't see her face. I leaned up to try to see her, but her hair blocked much of the view. The blanket only covered one of her naked breasts. Fuller than Laura's. Pinker.

All of a sudden, I thought I might throw up. I didn't want to be touching this girl. I didn't want to be anywhere near her. Beads of sweat broke out on my forehead. I didn't remember her name. *I have to get out of here. Now.*

But I couldn't just leave. Right?

Okay, I told myself. *Baby steps. Step one: get your arm back.* I appraised the situation. She was definitely asleep. The light through the window was so faint that it had to be really early or else really cloudy out, so if she had anywhere close to as much to drink as I did last night, she could still conceivably be passed out. I wasn't even sure that anything had definitely happened. I mean, yes we were both naked, but there was no guarantee that I had managed to pull anything off. In fact, I would be pretty damn impressed if I had, considering the amount of alcohol that it would take for me to not be sure if we had done anything or not. But that was something to worry about later. The first problem was my arm.

I think I took a full ten minutes getting my arm out from under her. I moved as carefully as if my life depended on it. I was not even close to ready to talk to this girl.

I eased myself out of bed, careful not to pull my weight up too quickly or make a sound. I looked around. There were three doors across the room. A closed one on the left that clearly led to the rest of the apartment, as the middle door opened into a walk-in closet and the open far-right door revealed a bathroom. Bingo. I realized I was still pretty drunk as I stumbled across her floor, which was good, because it meant she might still be drunk too and therefore stay asleep until I got myself together enough to talk to her. I stepped on something crinkly and it stuck to my foot, but I kept moving as quietly as I could, putting my weight on the heel of that foot to keep from making noise as I dodged the piles of clothes, books, shoes, and other random messy room bits and pieces. I got into the bathroom, shut the door as quietly as I could and turned on the light. Then I reached down to pull whatever I had stepped on off my foot. It was a condom wrapper. I felt nauseous, but it could have been worse. I could have stepped on the actual condom. I shuddered at the thought. There was another empty wrapper on the bathroom counter. How the hell we could have gone through two of them after that much booze, I may never know.

The counter was grimy and the floor had a coating of blonde hair on it. A pair of stockings was hanging over the shower rod and the toilet bowl looked like it had seen better days. I looked at myself in the mirror. Red eyes glared back at me. My hair was sticking up all over the place and I had scratch marks on my shoulder. I sat down on the fuzzy toilet seat cover, refusing to let myself think about how dirty the bathroom was. God knows I'm not a neat freak, but bathrooms and kitchens should stay clean.

Okay. I can't just leave. I actually have to talk to her. I thought. *But I don't know her fucking name!* Panic started to set in. I could look in her wallet! Assuming I could find her purse in that mess. But, Jesus, what if she woke up while I was doing that? That wasn't going to work. I sat there for a little while trying to come up with a game plan. Finally, I decided that I would just wake her up, tell her that I had to leave, and give her with my phone number. Then, if she called, I wouldn't answer my phone, she would leave a message, and at least then I would know her name. *But I don't want to talk to her.* That doesn't matter. Giving her my number is the non-asshole move. Taking hers and never calling after sleeping with her, that's the asshole move. *I can't be that asshole guy.*

I took a deep breath and walked out of the bathroom. She was still asleep. It really didn't make any sense to wake her up before I put on my clothes, so I found my jeans under hers and put them on. Shirt too. I only found one sock, but I decided it was easier to do without the other. It was just a sock. I didn't need it badly enough to dig through the mess of her room to find it. And above all, I didn't want her to wake up until I was ready to go. Until I was ready to talk to her.

After what felt like a year, I was finally dressed except for the missing sock. My wallet was still in my back pocket, now minus the two condoms that I vaguely remembered Chris and Eric slipping me right before I left. Cell phone and keys in the front pockets. Okay, that was everything. Now it was just time to wake the girl up and say goodbye.

Just walk over there, lean down, and do it.

Any time now.

Any time.

I started sweating again. My mouth felt fuzzy. I wanted to brush my teeth desperately. I wanted to take a shower. I wanted to do the right thing.

But I needed to get the fuck out of there.

I opened her door as quietly as I could and tiptoed out. I didn't shut the door fully behind me because I couldn't risk the noise. A roommate or a friend was passed out on the sofa in the living room. Her head popped up as I walked past her. "Who are you?" she slurred sleepily.

"No one," I said miserably and continued to the front door. Safely in the hallway, I leaned on the wall and took a deep breath.

I couldn't believe that I just did that. I had just walked out on a one-night stand without even saying goodbye or leaving my number and with no pretense that I would call her. Oh God. What would she think when she woke up? How awful would that be? What would I do to a guy who did that to one of my friends?

I had to get out. I found the stairs and ran down them, desperate for fresh air. Thankfully the apartment was only on the second floor. I made out of there and threw up on the lawn outside of her building. Miserable and retching, I sat down on the curb. When my head finally cleared, I looked around to see where I was. Still in DC, but the neighborhood didn't look familiar. Brick walkup buildings and parking on the street. The road at the top of the street seemed busier than the one I was on, and I stumbled up there to try to get my bearings. I followed the direction that the cars were coming from and found myself on Wisconsin Avenue, not all that far from the Tenleytown Metro Station. Probably under a mile away. I checked my cell phone for the time. The Metro would be opening soon. But the thought of a subway ride made me feel queasy again. If there was ever a time to splurge on a cab ride home, this was it. Disgusted with myself, I flagged a cab down and agreed to the exorbitant fee that the driver told me he would charge me to take me home.

I watched the city go by from the back of the cab. *How did I get here?* I wondered, leaning my forehead on the cool glass of the window. Apparently the cab driver didn't like my looks. He kept watching me in the rearview mirror.

"You are okay?" he asked thickly.

"No, not really," I replied. Did I look so pathetic and wretched that even the cab driver could see it?

"If you need puke," he said through his almost unintelligible accent, "you tell me, I pull over. No puke in my cab. You puke, you walk." I leaned my head back.

"Don't worry, sir," I said, surveying the McDonalds bags, Whopper wrappers, and Dunkin Donuts coffee cups piled up in the backseat. "I'm not going to throw up." He watched me suspiciously through squinting eyes in the rearview mirror.

"No puke in cab," he muttered. I closed my eyes and kept them closed until he reached my street. I had never felt so disgusting and dirty in all my life. I could smell stale cigarette smoke on me; sweat, both mine and hers; along with her perfume, which had appealed to me last night because it was different from Laura's, but which today smelled cheap and foul.

When I got home, I took the longest, hottest shower possible. I scrubbed my skin until it was raw. My whole body was bright red from the heat of the water by the time I got out nearly an hour later. I brushed my teeth three times and gargled with Listerine for five full minutes, until my eyes watered and my mouth burned. I got into my bed and still felt dirty and humiliated. I stayed in bed for the rest of the weekend, leaving it only to take two more showers. I didn't sleep. I didn't answer Mel's or Eric's calls. Mel finally sent me a text message saying: "Just write back and let me know that you're alive and I'll leave you alone if you don't want to talk." I wrote back: "Living, but not alive." She wrote back one more time, telling me to call her when I was ready.

I couldn't imagine ever being ready for anything again.

34

But everything fades eventually.

And it's easier to be miserable while it's still cold outside.

When Laura left me in February, I thought the world was going to end.

My first awful post-Laura foray into the world of sex was in early April. By the end of April, Mark had a single in the top ten on the charts. It was the one that he had written about Laura and played that night at Jammin' Java when I was there with her.

By mid-May, he had three music videos playing constantly on MTV. I didn't even think MTV still played videos until I discovered that I couldn't escape from his. One of the videos was for Laura's song. She was in that video.

Eventually, I started going out with my friends again by choice. Once the weather gets warm, it's hard to sit inside and mope. It's much easier to go out and try to forget how wretched you feel. And there's always something to do in the spring.

My friends took me out for my birthday. And got me drunk enough that I could try to forget that Laura wasn't there that year. They were getting very good at making sure I got that drunk early in the evening. I will probably owe Mel for that for the rest of my life. She took care of me without ever making me feel like I needed to be taken care of.

I had yet to make it through a day without thinking about Laura at least twenty times. Every time I saw a tall brunette or a red convertible, I stopped breathing for a second. And I still felt like crap pretty much all the time. I wasn't doing well yet. Or even okay. But I was starting to see how maybe it would be possible for me to get to okay at some point in the future. Doing well still seemed like a stretch. But okay was a good goal for right then.

In June, however, everything exploded.

Mel saw it on television before I found out and didn't tell me until later. I think she was hoping that it would all blow over before I could even hear about it. Or maybe she was trying to figure out the right way to tell me. Or maybe she was hoping that I wouldn't care anymore. All she said, when she found out that I knew, was that she was sorry she hadn't told me when she first heard. I eventually saw it on a tabloid cover and couldn't stop myself from reading it.

The tabloid had a series of pictures on the cover. One of Laura and Mark that was taken directly from the music video that she was in. Another was a shot of them at some concert or something, and then a photo of an older couple. The man looked vaguely familiar and when I saw his name, I recognized him as a director. The woman was Sophie Landau, the actress whom I had once, early on, told my friends that I thought Laura looked so much like. The headline read "Socialite Daughter Finds Love with Music's Hottest New Hunk." My first thought was that it was bullshit. Laura's parents were dead. She had told me that.

But she never said dead. She said gone. I had assumed that meant dead, but with Laura, it could mean anything from dead to down the street buying a gallon of milk.

Holy shit.

I had decided to take off work early to enjoy the nice day and run some errands. I had barely missed any work since the tour ended in October, and there was no one left in the office by the time I left that Friday anyway. I was in line at the grocery store when I saw it, but I wanted time to really read the article carefully. So for the first time in my life, I bought a tabloid. I didn't even make it home with my groceries; I read it on the hood of my car.

It was unbelievable.

According to the highly esteemed journalists at *The Star*, Laura was, along with several Academy Award-winning movies, the product of a 1975 marriage between actress Sophie Landau and director Andrew Calder. When she was born, they'd opted to give her her maternal grandmother's maiden name in order to allow her to have a private life. It explained why I'd never found anything interesting when I'd Googled her until she met Mark. But according to the tabloid, she had been born in France and lived there until she was six. It was no secret that her parents had had a child, but Laura had been very deliberately kept out of the public eye her whole life until she brought herself into it through her connection with Mark. And her parents were the kind of celebrities who kept a low enough profile in their personal lives by avoiding messy affairs and scandalous parties that they could manage to stay under the normal radar of the tabloids. Until this.

The article talked about Laura's failed marriage. They had gotten Justin's name and a picture of them from their wedding. He was handsome and Laura was radiant. It must have been a beautiful wedding. Her parents still lived in Europe and according to the article, she was sent to boarding school when she was very young and hardly ever saw them while she was growing up. Then I saw the last picture in the series. It was Laura, "sharing an intimate moment with publishing and music mogul Charles Owens." They were standing on a street corner in New York City, with him in a suit and tie, no *Born to Run* shirt to be seen. She was wearing a dress and the predictable, impossibly high heels. They were both wearing sunglasses and had their arms wrapped around each other, Laura leaning up even higher than her shoes required as she kissed him. According to the article, they had enjoyed a "brief but torrid romance immediately following the end of her marriage." I was sweating when I finished the article.

I got in the car and sat behind the wheel, the keys in my lap. I didn't know what to think. It made a ridiculous amount of sense in a way. It explained the money. It explained the parents who were never there. But was it true? Could it be? Did she still have that big of a secret left?

Born to Run guy. Charles Owens. She had called him Charlie. He was the only clue I had to finding out if this was true. Tabloids made up stuff all the time, didn't they? Like Bat Boy and Hillary Clinton having sex with aliens and all. One cover of *The Weekly World News* definitely had Osama Bin Laden and Saddam Hussein getting married, complete with a picture of the two of them riding off for their honeymoon together on a camel and Bin Laden wearing a wedding dress. They could have made up who her parents were. Except I knew they didn't. It fit. In absolutely every way. But I had to know how much of the rest of it was true. Charlie was the only person who I had really met from her life. And somehow, I knew that he would know the truth.

Thank God for Google. I don't know how people lived without it. I found a phone number and an office. But I couldn't do this over the phone. Knowing full well that he wouldn't be there and that I would need an appointment anyway, I MapQuested his office address and drove into DC to try to find out what he knew.

I didn't know what I should say, nor did I know what might come out of my mouth when I saw him. I didn't like this guy. No, okay, that's not fair. I didn't know this guy. But I did *not* like him. Even before I had seen the "intimate moment" that they had shared in the tabloid photo, I knew they must have had some kind of an affair. I remembered how his hand rested just a little too low on her hip when he touched her in Philadelphia. And the way he told her to call him for "anything." She said he had been like a father to her, but what kind of father figure could he really be? And she said that she had known him for years. Was she sleeping with him before Justin or after? Could she have cheated on Justin and not told me? What justification could he possibly give me for her relationship with him? Would he even be willing to talk to me?

But I also knew that he had gotten more from Laura than I had. Physically, if not emotionally. Because no one could ever characterize what we had as a "romance." Why had he gotten to have that with her when I couldn't? What was it that he had that I didn't? Other than money, which couldn't have been the deciding factor, because she had enough money of her own. He was old enough to be her father. Was that why she was with him? If so, she had gotten it out of her system by now because Mark was our age. So was Charlie a friend of her parents? Now that I knew that they were alive and well and living in southern France at the moment, if they weren't at one of their villas on Lake Como or in Greece.

His office was on the sixteenth floor of a gaudy and pretentious-looking building downtown. No, I was wrong. Apparently his office *was* the sixteenth floor of the building. An extremely attractive receptionist greeted me warmly as I stepped out of the elevator, and I was suddenly very self-conscious, even though she did not acknowledge in any way that I was not appropriately dressed for such a posh office.

"What can I help you with today, sir?" she asked in a way that made me feel like she genuinely wanted to help. Whatever he was paying her, she was worth every penny.

"I need to see Charlie Owens. As soon as possible." She hesitated and looked at me, a mildly confused expression crossing her pretty face.

She apologized for the pause and explained by saying, "I've only ever heard one person call him Charlie before." She seemed to be waiting for me to say something, but I didn't. "Do you have an appointment?" she asked.

"No, but I think he'll see me."

"I'm really sorry, sir, but I can't let anyone through without an appointment." I realized that I knew how to play this game. Thank you, Laura. Although I wouldn't be here demanding to see some sketchy millionaire in the first place if I didn't have to know why you had slept with him.

"Was the person who called him Charlie a girl named Laura Mercer?" The secretary eyed me skeptically. I took this to be a yes. I gave her my name and asked her to tell "Mr. Owens" that I was there about Laura.

"Just a minute," she said and she delivered my name and who I was there to discuss to another secretary through an intercom. After about thirty seconds, I got my response and was led through a hallway that ended in another office, which seemed to belong to a personal secretary, and finally I was admitted into Charlie's office.

He was seated behind a massive mahogany desk in a room bigger than my entire apartment. It was open and airy with huge windows looking out onto the city. He rose from his chair and walked around the desk to shake my hand, then gestured for me to take a seat. He was wearing an exquisitely tailored suit and looked like the millionaire that he was, not the concert-going, lecherous older man I took him to be in the Philadelphia and Fed Ex Field parking lots. Had I passed him on the street, it would never have occurred to me that this was the same man as my *Born to Run* shirt nemesis.

"I thought I might hear from you," he said, half smiling, "although I admit that this was sooner than I expected."

"Really?" I didn't quite know how to respond. I felt very uncomfortable sitting across from this man. He was too smooth. He didn't seem like a real person. Laura and Bruce were the only common elements between our worlds.

"If you've already figured out that I leaked the information to the press, then yes." I stared at him in surprise. "Well, I suppose that secret is out now, isn't it?" he asked, interpreting the look on my face correctly.

"You?" I asked finally, unable to comprehend how he could have done that if he cared about Laura. If a tabloid had called me about her, even after everything that had happened, I would have given a polite "no comment" and hung up.

He nodded. "I'm a large shareholder in a few publications and when Laura decided to put herself in the public eye, it was bound to make headlines somewhere. She knew that and quite graciously allowed me to sell the first scoop." He smiled wryly. "But no interview. She's a sharp kid. Giving an interview to a tabloid would have been poor planning."

"Then it's true?"

"Every word of it." He flashed me a wide smile of very white, even teeth. "Reads just like a fairy tale, doesn't it?"

I didn't know what to say to that. I hadn't really thought out this whole barging into his office thing. I also hadn't actually thought that I would get into his office today to see him. And I had no idea how much he would be willing to tell me. All I knew was that any information that I wanted to get about Laura was hanging in the balance of those next few seconds.

I wanted to hate him beyond anything that I have ever wanted. I wanted to hate him on the same level that I want to breathe. But he took pity on me. He knew that I couldn't ask the questions I needed to ask without his help. In my mind, he was completely without merit. Just a cold, heartless, albeit rich, older man who had somehow taken advantage of Laura. But Laura wasn't like that. And she would never involve herself with someone who wasn't basically kind. Then again, there's a pretty wide gap between pity and kindness, and I will not—cannot—confuse what he offered me that day in his office with kindness.

"Have you heard from her since she left for LA?"

I shook my head.

"Really?" I didn't respond. "That's surprising."

"Why?"

He hesitated. "Well, maybe not that surprising." He got up and walked over to a small bar that was set up on the side of his office, where he began to pour two drinks. He came back and sat down behind his desk, holding out a tumbler to me. "You might need this," he said. I took it, but didn't drink. "And I think I might need it too.

"So," he said. "Tell me why you're here."

I realized my only chance was the truth. "I need to know," I said plainly. "She said her parents were dead— well—not dead, she said gone." Charlie smiled and shook his head.

"She's a master equivocator. Never a lie, but never the truth either."

I nodded. "I thought I finally knew the whole story. She told me about Justin. I figured she left me because she was just scared of getting hurt again." I paused. "I remembered meeting you," I said. "And I saw you with her at the Philadelphia show." He raised his eyebrows but didn't say anything. "You're the only one I know about who could tell me anything else."

He looked at me for awhile. Deciding I guess.

"What did she say about me?" he asked eventually.

I didn't want to talk about him. I wanted to talk about her. But I would play the game that he wanted me to play. "That you were like a father to her. That you helped her get work at *Rolling Stone*." Pause. "And that you introduced her to Bruce. Which is how I met her."

"Like a father," he repeated. "Well that's not exactly how I want to be remembered. But it's better than being forgotten." He watched me as he asked his next question. I knew the look, because I had learned to watch Laura that way when she answered questions. He wanted to see if I would tell the truth. "Did she say anything else about our relationship?"

"No," I said. "But I figured it out. Before I saw the pictures today, I mean. I thought you were together the first time I saw you, in Philadelphia."

Charlie nodded thoughtfully. "How much are you looking to find out?"

"As much as you'll tell me." He thought about this for a minute, then got up and stood by the window, looking down onto the street. Finally he turned back to face me. He had sized me up and somehow I had passed his inspection.

"Alright, kid. I'll tell you as much of the story as I know. Part of me wants to tell you to get out of my office and not come back. But she didn't look happy again until she was with you. I couldn't make her look like that and God knows I tried. So maybe if you know all of it, you'll be able to keep her looking that happy when she comes back."

I gripped the edge of his desk, my knuckles turning white. "When she comes back? You think she's coming back?" I latched onto this desperately. He had been in touch with her. Did he really know something?

But he just gave me a condescending smile and said, "One thing at a time, kid. One at a time." I pried my fingers away from his desk and forced myself to assume a more relaxed pose. I couldn't have been doing a very good job because he indicated that I should have a drink, which I finally did. Laura called people kid. Not usually me, but she did. I wondered if she had picked that up from him or if he picked it up from her. What had she and I picked up from each other?

"Laura said she met you when she was working for the *Post*," I said, trying to make sure he started at the beginning.

Charlie nodded and swirled the scotch in his glass. "About three years ago," he said, leaning back into his chair. "She was living in New York and was down here about some freelance work she was doing in DC. I was visiting a friend of mine who is an editor at the *Post*, and she walked into the newsroom. Everyone stopped working to look at her, even the women. You know what it's like when she walks into a room.

"I could see she didn't trust me at first. Richard, my friend at the *Post*, introduced her to me and I asked to see some of her photos. I told her I had some contacts at *Rolling Stone* and that I could probably pull a few strings to get her some work there. She was interested, and we went out for a drink to talk about career opportunities." He stopped and looked at me.

"I could lie and say that was why I took her out for that drink," he said. "But I won't. She was one of the most beautiful women that I had ever seen, and I've seen a lot." He was watching me for a reaction, but I really didn't want to give him one. I didn't have much of anything to say to that anyway. And I knew why he wanted to take her out for a drink before he told me. I'm not stupid.

"So she met me with her portfolio and we talked shop for awhile. And then I asked about the ring on her finger." He paused. "You said you knew about Justin?" I think he expected this to have been one of the big bombshells from the article.

"Yeah. She told me all about that." He looked mildly surprised for the second time but didn't comment.

"She lit up when she talked about him. I said she was awfully young to be married. And she kind of bristled at that and said she was twenty-three, which wasn't too young for anything except retirement. I agreed with her.

"I spent about half the time that I was with her that first day just trying to figure out who she reminded me of. Finally, I told her that I would swear she was Sophie Landau's kid, if Sophie had ever had a baby. I never for a minute thought it would be true. In fact, I expected her to ask me who Sophie Landau was, but she just looked down and didn't respond for what felt like a decade. You must know how it is when Laura turns her light off." That much I knew. "'That's a compliment,' I told her."

"And she snapped at me and said, 'I'm sure you think it is.'" Charlie turned in his chair and looked out the window onto the city. "I didn't know quite what to make of her," he said quietly. "I was about to give up. She was married and clearly I had just offended her, although I didn't have the first clue how. I've never had a woman, even a married one, reject me that summarily. So I was going to walk away, beautiful girl or not, when she asked if I could keep a secret.

"I told her yes and she didn't say anything for another minute, then told me quietly that Sophie *was*, in fact, her mother.

"Well, I was stunned when I heard that. I knew her mother back in the seventies, before she married Andrew. We ran with the same crowd from time to time. But I had no idea that she had ever had a baby. Laura said that they kept the whole thing quiet, because Sophie hadn't wanted to ruin her image as a sex symbol. Back then, if you were a mommy, you didn't get the siren roles anymore and that's what she was known for."

"But wasn't she a big star back then?" I asked.

"One of the biggest," Charlie replied.

"Then why wasn't it all over the tabloids that she'd had a baby? I mean, when any celebrity gets pregnant, it's all over the front page of everything."

"It wasn't like that back then. There was no *People* magazine. When Bruce was on the cover of *Time* and *Newsweek* in the same week, it was the first time that anyone other than a world leader had done that. And it was common knowledge that Sophie and Andrew were living in France for a few years while Sophie took a little break from acting. That meant that when they came back on a private jet with a baby, there wasn't any paparazzi following her. They hired a long succession of nannies and spent their time making movies.

"According to Laura, they were never exactly active in her life. She hardly talks to them. The only things they ever really gave her were her mother's looks and a big pile of their money."

I felt relieved in an odd way, hearing this. I knew she had been involved with Charlie and there wasn't much that would make that sting less, but at least that wasn't where any of her money came from. It was a little worse in some ways, I guess, that she had decided to be with him for non-financial reasons, but at least I could assume that he had been completely out of her life by the time I came into it.

"They didn't even come to her wedding," Charlie added. "They were on location somewhere in South America and they sent a huge check, but she said there was no one to give her away at the ceremony." Here he hesitated and thought for a moment before he continued.

"She never said it, but that's why she got married that young. She never had a family, so that was what she wanted more than anything. The money never mattered to her; she just wanted someone who was actually going to love her. Her mother is a beautiful woman. And can be a lot of fun to be around. But warm and loving she is not. And her father was always well-known for being completely and utterly absorbed in his work. I can't begin to imagine why they ever decided to have a baby in the first place, if she wasn't an accident, but it was pretty clear that they got tired of being parents quickly. They shipped her off to boarding schools as soon as they could, and any holidays that she couldn't spend there, she spent with nannies."

It made sense. And it made sense why Justin's sudden and unexpected abandonment with the second closest person in Laura's life would turn her so hard. But I still couldn't quite see how Charlie fit into the equation before I entered it.

"After that, Laura and I became—well—friends, I guess. I admit; I was waiting the marriage out. But I did play the daddy role there for a while. It was what she needed then, and she was too special to let go. But I never met Justin. She knew he wouldn't like our relationship, and I knew from what she had told me that he would prevent her from seeing me if he had any idea what my intentions were. So I played the part that she needed me to play and I waited. I saw her when I was in New York and when she came to DC.

I went to New York more often than was strictly necessary in those months, but Laura didn't know that.

"Then I didn't talk to her for a couple of months. I was out of the country for awhile, and I was seeing this model and I just lost touch with her. When I came back to the city, I called her and said I was taking her out to lunch.

"She immediately said she couldn't make it and I could tell something was wrong. But I told her I wasn't taking no for an answer because I couldn't even remember what she looked like and that I would have a car at her place to pick her up in an hour.

"I knew, of course, what had happened the second I saw her. She walked into the restaurant and was a completely different person. She's always been thin, but she must have lost about fifteen pounds. She could have just stepped out of Auschwitz. And she just looked at me with these eyes that were so dead. And I tell you, right then, I could have killed that little asshole for making my girl hurt like that.

"She didn't say anything. She just looked at me. 'Justin?' I asked eventually. She nodded. 'Left?' I asked. She nodded again and she looked for a second like she might cry, but she got herself under control and didn't." He paused here. "I've only seen her cry once," he said.

"'Bobby Jean,'" I supplied.

"Excuse me?" Here he was alert. I had told him that I saw them together in Philadelphia. It was the same reaction Laura had to finding out that I had seen her cry in DC. He was sharp. He knew I wasn't in the picture yet when she cried in DC.

"She cries when Bruce plays 'Bobby Jean' sometimes." It was a Laura-like equivocation. She had done it once, and she looked like she was close to tears when he played it at the last show on the tour, even though she was emotional for other reasons that night too. Still, I could therefore say that she did it sometimes without actually lying. I couldn't fully explain what I had seen that night and what it meant to me. Not to him.

He looked at me warily, but I again passed the test because he eventually resumed his story. "Yes," he said. "That was the one time I saw her cry.

"So I told her I wasn't going to let her be alone right then, and lunch turned into afternoon drinks, which turned into dinner, which turned into more drinks, which turned into a walk through the city, and by the time I took her home, she looked more like my Laura. Her eyes still had that look in them, but she could smile by the end of the day." He turned away from me at that point, which I was thankful for. I felt such a wave of revulsion when he called her his Laura, and if he had looked at me, he would have seen that disgust written all over my face. He looked out the window again and I was grateful that I didn't have to look at his face while he told me about what came next.

"I didn't mean for anything to happen that soon. And maybe that was my mistake. If I had waited for her to rebound with someone like you, maybe I could have kept her. But I had waited more than a year, which is longer than I've ever waited for a woman."

He didn't tell me how it started. But I could picture the whole thing. He took her home that night and by then she was more than a little drunk. Like the night of Mel's wedding, I thought with a sickening feeling. Like what could have happened if I hadn't walked away that night. But he wouldn't have walked away. Not this guy. He would have kissed her lightly on the lips to say goodnight. Just once. Then one more time. Then a real kiss. And then they're in her house. I drained my glass of scotch, which burned slightly as it went down, to try to get rid of the image of his hands on her body, removing her clothes, touching her.

Charlie continued to look out onto the street long enough for me to imagine the whole seduction. By the time he spoke again, I was in danger of crushing the empty glass in my hand and stabbing him, then possibly myself with the shards.

"I fell in love with her," he said slowly. Almost like he was just admitting it to himself. "I would have married her," he laughed softly at this. "Don't they say fourth time's the charm?"

"It's third time," I said, trying to keep the murderous tone out of my voice.

"The third time certainly wasn't for me, but if Laura was the fourth, I think that could have been it." He sighed and drank the rest of his Scotch too. "She moved here to be closer to me. But that was never really why. She wanted a fresh start and she didn't have a way to do that living where she had lived with Justin, going to the same places and seeing the same people.

"It didn't last long. About two months. I took her to those first couple Bruce shows. I dragged her to the first one and she was hooked. She begged to go to the next two. And there wasn't anything in the world that I was going to refuse her. But she was done with me by the fourth." He was looking into his empty glass and I could almost feel bad for him. I was still at the stage where I believed you couldn't completely recover from Laura leaving. Not ever.

"I can't even remember the last time I lost a woman to another man." I looked up at him. Did he mean me? Could that even make sense?

But he saw the look on my face and laughed. "No, kid, not you. Bruce."

"She left you for Bruce?"

He shrugged. "She didn't need me anymore once she had him. It was kind of funny actually, at the time. She absolutely ransacked my music collection. And she knew immediately what she liked. And what she hated. But that's how Laura is about everything. All in or all out. And absolutely nothing in between." Didn't I know it?

"It made sense though, her fascination with Bruce. Because I was listening to *The Rising* then, which was, of course about September 11, so it was all about dealing with loss and moving on. And that's exactly what Laura was trying to do. I saw that, so I gave her *Tunnel of Love* next, which really hit a strong note with her. Then *Born to Run* and it was all over. She was completely addicted.

"But it couldn't last with me, and I think I knew that even then. I was the last remaining trace of her old life. No, I wasn't really part of that life, but I was close enough to it that she couldn't stay with me. She cut out everything from her past when she came down here. She bought all new furniture even. For all I know, that house in New York is still hers and completely the same as it was the day she left. She stopped dancing and started running instead. She used to teach ballet to little girls in New York. She still says she's a photographer, but she's barely touched a camera since then. At least not for any real work. She cut out all the people she used to know too. I don't think she's spoken to a single one of her friends from New York. And she had a lot of them at one point." I wondered if Charlie knew Justin had left her for her best friend. I wasn't about to supply that information if he didn't already know, but it made me realize that he too could be leaving out part of the story. I also thought about how Laura had run out so quickly on my birthday. It was because she used to be part of a group. And seeing us all together reminded her that she wasn't anymore. That was why she was so weird about going to Mel and Eric's engagement party. And their wedding. She'd been there. She'd done all of that. And watching other people do the same things that she had done reminded her of what she had lost. And she was willing to do almost anything to avoid remembering that.

"We stayed in touch a little bit, as I'm sure you know. I would put money on my being the only person she still talks to who knew her before her marriage ended."

"What was she like?" I asked. "Before, I mean."

He smiled sadly at me and paused between each word that he used to describe her. "Softer. Younger. Innocent. Happier. She lost a lot when he left. I gave her some of it back, but I know Bruce gave her more." He hesitated. "And I suppose you gave her some too. The next time I saw er looking as happy as she did with him was when I saw the two of you at the last DC show."

I realized all of a sudden that he didn't know about the baby. Not that he necessarily would have told me if he did. But he couldn't know about that and blame the whole metamorphosis that occurred on Justin leaving. He would understand completely if he knew about that. He wouldn't have told her to call him for "anything" the way that he did when I overheard them talking in DC if he really understood. But then again. If he really did love her like he said he did, and if he really did think that I was someone who could make her happy, he would tell me everything that he knew. Because if he could have been the one to make Laura happy, I would have hated him; but I would have told him what he needed to know. And I think he was telling me all that he knew. Which meant that I was the only one who knew that about her. And I realized that she couldn't have told him about the baby, because she had told me that I couldn't know that and still love her. If Charlie knew and loved her, she would have known that couldn't be true.

It was one of those realizations that makes no difference at all, but also makes all the difference in the world. When I stormed into Charlie's office, it was because I needed to know what he knew that I didn't. I thought it was the secret about her parents that mattered. But I suddenly understood that what I actually needed to know was what *I* knew that *he* didn't. Laura didn't tell me about her parents because they weren't in her life. She could say they were gone and mean it. And she hadn't lied about the money either. Her parents had left her with as much of it as she could ever need.

But even though I knew more about her past, Charlie knew more about her present. And he said the happiest he had seen her since she was with Justin was when she was with me.

"You said you thought she was coming back? Did she actually say she was coming back?"

Charlie shook his head. "Does she ever say anything like that?" He watched me carefully. "When do you think she'll come back?"

I thought about it. I had imagined her coming back, but I don't think I believed it could actually happen, so I had never really examined the question of when as a logic problem. Maybe that was one of my big obstacles with Laura. From day one, I had held her apart as defying all logic. But now that I had all the pieces in front of me, the Laura problem suddenly looked fairly clear. Of course, I couldn't be positive that she would follow the same rules that had governed her behavior before, because there could still be another couple of variables that neither Charlie nor I knew about. But assuming that Laura acted the way that Laura always had, Charlie was right. She would be back.

"When she realizes that running away with a musician doesn't actually solve any of her problems."

Charlie smiled at me. It was a little bit of a sad smile. I think he wanted to hate me as much as I wanted to hate him, and therefore he wanted me to get it wrong.

"Or when Bruce tours again," I said. "And she has to choose between following him or following Mark." Charlie laughed at this. I laughed too, but not at my joke. It suddenly struck me as funny that I was sitting in *Born to Run* guy's office, having a drink, talking about Laura, and that I was composed enough to make a joke that would make him laugh. The me of a year ago would never have believed that I could be in that situation.

35

My conversation with Charlie was both the best thing that could happen to me at the time and the worst. Well, other than Laura coming back, I guess. That probably would have been much better and much worse.

I felt lighter after talking to him. Calmer. Still miserable, but he planted a seed of hope there, which blossomed over the next six months.

Laura would come back.

I felt awful that she wasn't there then, but it didn't matter. Because she was coming back.

Knowing that meant I could function with some semblance of normalcy in social situations. I wanted to be around people again. And being around people took the edge off Laura not being there yet.

Especially during the summer. There were twenty-five days that summer that were anniversaries of shows that we had been to. If Laura had been with me, those were twenty-five bootlegs that we would have listened to together, reliving the moments of our shows. That was what we did with the one-year anniversaries of all the shows that we had been to. So I listened without her. Wondering if she was doing the same thing on that day. Knowing it was only a matter of time until I would be spending a summer listening to them with her. And who knew? Maybe Bruce would be touring again by the time she was back. Maybe that one phenomenal summer didn't have to be an isolated occurrence.

At first I mentioned her name a lot. "Laura and I always did this." "Laura loved it when that happened."

"That's Laura's favorite drink." "Laura and I went there."
She popped up so frequently in my thoughts that talking
about her felt natural. But my friends started giving each
other worried looks when I did that. They thought I didn't
notice, but I did. And Mel pulled me aside one night and
told me to stop it.

"You're making everyone uncomfortable," she said.
"No one knows how to respond when you say stuff like
that."

"What do you mean?"

"I mean, she's gone. And when you mention her like
she's around, it sounds like she's your imaginary friend. If
you need to talk, call me and we'll talk. When you talk
about her like she's your girlfriend around everyone,
people get weirded out."

So I tried to keep it under control.

And I knew that Laura wasn't sitting at home thinking
about me. She was in LA with Mark. So I went out with
the guys every weekend. I went out most Thursday nights
too. I went to happy hours all over the city. I wasn't ready
to date yet, but I started flirting again. I didn't follow
through with the flirting that often, but I did eventually
start going home with girls. It always seemed like a better
idea that night than it did the next morning, and I always
woke up with a wave of panic, remembering that first night
that I spent with a girl after Laura. But I never got as
drunk as I did that night. If I didn't know the girl's name, I
asked her or else I didn't go home with her. I made sure
that they got my phone number before we went to sleep.
And I always woke them up before I left. Not because I had
any desire to talk to them once I was done with them, but
because then I didn't have to feel bad about myself. I told
myself that the girls were in it for the same thing I was. No
one took a guy home from the bar looking for true love.

Of course, I didn't answer or return their calls.

That was asking just a little too much of me at that
point.

The problem was that because Charlie had said Laura was coming back, I didn't work on getting over her. If I thought she wasn't coming back, I wouldn't have let myself think about her. I would have been more miserable in those months, but I would have started healing.

Instead, I let myself think about Laura all the time. She was my first thought when I woke up in the morning, and I fell asleep every night picturing what it would be like when she came back. I had the whole scenario worked out in my head. She would show up at my door one night, unannounced, like the old days. And while the actual conversation that I imagined us having varied from night to night, the basic gist of it was the same. She was sorry and she had run away because she was afraid. And she loved me.

I started watching "Entertainment Tonight" to see if there was any mention of trouble between her and Mark. I Googled her at least two or three times a week. I checked the Mark Houston message boards to see if there were any rumors about the two of them being on the rocks.

There never were.

But I had hope.

No one understood why though, not even Mel. And I finally stopped wanting to talk about Laura with anyone, because I kept having to explain why I thought she was coming back, and no one ever understood what I meant. And worse, everyone who I tried to explain it to looked at me with these frustrating looks of pity. Like I was the one who didn't understand. So while it was clear to *me* that she was coming back, it became easier to not tell people that. They all thought I was wrong. But I knew better.

When her name came up, I started telling people that I was over her. Because it was easier. It wasn't remotely true and I wasn't making any attempt to get over her. But it was easier to tell them all that.

36

"You know, I've been thinking." Whenever Mel said that, I knew I was in for some analysis of my character that I probably wouldn't want to hear.

"I do that sometimes too," I said cautiously.

"Not often enough."

"Thanks."

Mel grinned over her beer bottle. "Any time. But seriously, it's time to stop thinking about Laura."

I groaned. I wanted to say that I hadn't been thinking about her. But Mel knew better. I thought about saying that it would be easier to stop thinking about her if people stopped bringing her up to me. But that wasn't true and Mel would know that. It wouldn't shut her up anyway. And I probably needed to hear what she had to say. But telling me to get over her was like rubbing salt in the wound. In my mind, there was no way to get over Laura because she was only gone for a little while. And there was no point in trying when I knew that she would be back.

"Isn't there a Shakespeare quote about that? 'Tell me how to not think' or something along those lines?"

"It's from *Romeo and Juliet*. 'Teach me how I should forget to think.' But you just made my point for me. He's not talking about Juliet when he says that. He's talking about that other girl. Rosaline. The one who he realizes he's not in love with as soon as he sees Juliet."

"So I'll find my Juliet, forget about Laura, and then kill myself by the end of act five? Wonderful."

"Shut up," Mel said. "I'm serious."

"Okay, go on Ms. Shakespeare."

"Mrs. Weston, actually. You were in the wedding, if you recall. But thank you." I did my best to smile at her. But it felt like I was smiling at the executioner as the axe was on its way down. "My point is that I think if you really loved her, you would be with her right now and she wouldn't be out in California with that other guy."

"You mean if she'd loved me."

"No," Mel said. "I mean if you had actually really wanted to be with her. If that was the case, I think you'd be with her now."

I heard Laura's voice asking if I had ever been in love the night of the engagement party. And I remembered how I couldn't say yes. But that wasn't my problem now. The next time someone asked me that, I would be able to say yes, without a doubt. But I felt like the bottom had just dropped out too. Because Laura had believed that she had been in love with Justin when she asked me that, and she had still said that love didn't exist. And no matter what I thought I would respond when the question wasn't being asked, would I be able to say yes when someone really did ask? Is unrequited—no, it wasn't actually unrequited because I knew Laura loved me too—is unfulfilled love really love? Can it be? Is that possible? *Why is Mel doing this right now?* I wondered. *Why is she questioning if I really loved Laura when the question she should be asking is if Laura really loved me?*

My voice was colder than I meant it to be when I finally replied. "Then you mean I subconsciously did not want to be with her and therefore screwed it up myself and it's my fault?"

Mel looked at me sharply and hesitated. I knew her looks. She was hovering between wanting to tell me not to use that tone of voice with her and not being sure if she had actually crossed a line that she didn't know about.

"I didn't mean for that to sound the way it did," I said. "Tell me what you mean." The worry line between her eyebrows went away.

"I mean, if you had actually, really, honestly wanted to start spending the rest of your life with her, you would have."

"How do you figure?"

"How long did you know her before you kissed her?"

I sighed. "A while."

"How long?"

Two-hundred forty-five days, six hours and about twenty-three minutes. "About eight months."

"And how long before you actually told her you loved her?"

"Over a year."

"And how long before you slept with her?"

"The same night I told her I loved her. But I could have the night of your wedding." Mel raised an eyebrow. I was making her point for her by bringing that one up. Damn it.

"Do you remember that guy from my Econ class who I had a crush on after you and I dated. Right before Eric and I got together? Nick? He lived in over in Easton Hall?"

"The one who you used to study with?"

"Yup."

"Yeah, I remember. What about him?"

"Do you remember how I used to come into your dorm room, throw myself onto your bed and be like, 'I really like him! But he's not making a move! Should I just tell him I like him and see what happens?'"

I smiled. She probably played out that exact scene about a thousand times over one semester. In fact, she and Eric first got together the night that she found out Nick was dating one of the University of Maryland cheerleaders. Funny how a bottle of tequila can result in marriage sometimes. "Of course."

"What did you tell me?"

I stopped smiling. "This isn't the same situation."

"What did you tell me every time I did that?"

"It's different."

"What did you tell me?" she repeated again and I sighed.

"I said to wait. Because if you're flirting with a new guy and he likes you, he'll eventually make a move. And if he doesn't make a move, it means he just doesn't like you like that. And then you would get all upset and want to know why he didn't like you like that and I would say it was because he was an idiot." Mel smiled.

"Well, he *was* an idiot, which was a damn good thing because it meant that I got Eric. But do you see the point I'm making here?"

"But Mel, seriously, it's not like that with Laura. There just wasn't a right time to make a move."

"Did she flirt with you?"

"Yes—I think so. Yes. Sometimes. I mean—well—yes."

"Are you saying you didn't make a move because you were scared that she didn't like you?"

I didn't want to say yes to that. But it was the best I had right then. So I tried to say it. But I met Mel's eyes and the word stuck in my throat. I was quiet for what felt like an eternity as I wrestled with and finally gave up on the word. "Pushing for something like that before she was ready would have scared her off," I said finally. "Remember, she was in a rough place."

"But you didn't know that then."

"I knew she had issues."

"Please, we all knew that. Her issues were visible from outer space."

"Thanks," I said.

"Regardless, you did know that someone had dumped her pretty badly before she told you about it." I nodded. "Were you really that terrified of her telling you that she didn't want to be with you? That it was better never to know than to make a move?"

I couldn't say yes to that one either. I had told myself for months that if I had the opportunity, I would take it. I remembered the way Laura was close enough to kiss in Asbury Park when I told her that Bruce would probably be there. I remembered falling asleep next to her in countless hotel rooms. Why didn't I ever make a move? Yes, I had been afraid she would laugh at me or stop seeing me. But was it really me who kissed her in Philadelphia? Or had she kissed me? I didn't know. Okay, I had gotten the band to play the song she wanted to dance to at her wedding at Mel's wedding. But I knew what Mel would say if I tried to use that as evidence of my having actually made a move. It was ten months into our relationship at that point and all I did was slip the singer twenty bucks to play a song that I wanted to dance with Laura to. That didn't count as a move. What had really held me back?

Mel was watching me mull this all over. "So what's the point you're trying to make here? That I'm a coward?"

Mel smiled softly at me. It was a pitying look, but a kind one. "No. I'm saying if being with her was really what you wanted, you would have tried. Because by the time you tried, you knew it was too late." I wished that I hadn't gone to happy hour with her. I had no idea that Mel calling me up, saying that Eric was working late, and asking if I wanted to get a drink with her after work would be an ambush like this. Why reopen those wounds? The ones that hadn't healed yet and still felt like they never would completely. Why not let me forget the parts that I wanted to forget?

I knew the answer, of course. She was a good friend. And good friends do what they need to do in order to help you really recover, not just forget the pain. She knew I was glossing over the rough parts so that I could imagine a happy reunion, even though I hadn't told her any of that. And she knew that would cause me more harm than good in the end.

"Maybe you're right," I said, looking down into my beer. "But that doesn't mean I can't still regret losing her."

"I know that," Mel said, putting her hands on top of mine. "And I'm not starting this conversation to upset you." I would have been angry at anyone else who said that because anyone else would have been telling a blatant lie. And Mel could be just as malicious as the next person. But not to the people she loved, and I was in that group.

"I know," I said. "But what is this conversation going to change?"

"I just want you to start thinking about what you actually do want," she said. "Because if Laura had said, 'Okay, I love you too, I'll stay,' and you two had started settling down together, I don't think that would have been enough for you yet. I mean, can you honestly say that you would have been happy a year from now planning a wedding with her?"

Yes, I wanted to say. *Sublimely, ridiculously, ludicrously happy. Happy on a scale that would make you and Eric look miserable.* But I didn't know that. I wanted to know that. But I didn't. And if Laura had stayed, I don't know what would have happened. I believed that I felt more for Laura than I ever had for Katie, of course. But when Katie and I first got together, I believed that I loved her. Could actually having Laura have changed how I felt about her?

"I think that's the worst part right now," I said. "I never got the chance to find out what would have happened."

Mel nodded. "I know. But you two played this out the way you both had to. Because you really are a lot alike in that way. Neither of you quite knows what you're looking for yet. And if you don't know what you want, how can you know when you've found it?"

"You're saying that we're both alike in that neither of us actually wanted to be with the other person? The only real flaw in that logic is that Laura isn't sitting at home wishing I would come back to her."

"If she's not, I think she will be, when she figures out what she wants. But I think it'll be too late by then." I felt that prickle of anticipation. The same one I felt when Charlie had said she was coming back at some point. But I couldn't get into that with Mel. She would think I hadn't understood the whole conversation if I turned it back around to hoping that Laura would come back. "In a sense," Mel said, "this situation *is* what both of you were looking for."

"Being miserable without each other because we were both too stupid to figure out that we wanted to be together?"

Mel's lips twitched like she was trying not to laugh. "Well, think of it this way: if Bruce were to write a song about the two of you, he'd be plagiarizing himself."

I tried not to laugh. I honestly did. I wanted to be mad at Mel for that because it was a low blow. But she saw the look on my face and started laughing and then I couldn't help myself. She was right. It would be some mishmash between the angry and sad songs about someone walking out and the songs about leaving someone because you couldn't quite handle what you had together.

When I finally got the laughing under control, I said, "Except the real problem with your logic here is that with her being the one walking out, I'm the 'wife and kids in Baltimore, Jack' from 'Hungry Heart.'" Mel smiled at me.

"Well, honey, that *is* the other reason I wanted to talk to you without the guys here tonight. This moping around over someone leaving you thing is awfully girly after all. Aren't you just supposed to go out and screw a lot of random chicks and then be over the whole situation?"

"Thanks, Mel."

"Anytime," she said with a smile. "And you listened so well to what I had to say that the next round is on me." I agreed and she bought our next beers.

She was right though. It was time to go figure out what I wanted so that I would know what to do with it if I ever found it again.

I couldn't fall asleep that night. I kept running the conversation with Mel back through my head. And it kept getting stuck at the same place. Would I have been happy planning a wedding with Laura a year later?

That was taking it a little far, wasn't it?

But then again, where did I expect it to go if Laura had stayed? My mind hadn't ever, in the past year and a half, really made it past the threshold of her realizing that she loved me and us finally being "together."

I remembered watching *When Harry Met Sally* with Katie. It was her favorite movie, meaning that I sat through it about ninety-seven times with her. Billy Crystal's character says something at the end about how when you realize how you want to spend the rest of your life with someone, you want the rest of your life to start right then. Katie cried at that line every time. And toward the end of our relationship, when I was starting to feel as trapped as Billy Crystal's character looks right after he and Meg Ryan's character sleep together, Katie would touch my arm and look up at me with those big blue eyes and say something about how that line was so true.

But was it? I mean, maybe when you're in your thirties and you want to settle down and stuff. But I couldn't see how it could be true in my life.

Laura was what I wanted. Probably forever.

Except something had held me back for the whole year and a half that we spent together.

And I had a sneaking suspicion that it had something to do with that word. Forever.

At twenty-six, forever was the scariest concept that I could imagine.

I don't think of myself as a person who is typically afraid to go after what I want. But that doesn't mean that it's easy to say "I'm done now" with everything you've known for your whole life, even when doing that means getting exactly what you've been building toward and working for.

There wouldn't be any way to explain that to Mel, I realized as I lay there in the dark. Mel couldn't understand what I was feeling because she had shut that door years ago, long before Eric even proposed. She wasn't looking to hold on to her youth because she wanted to move on to the next stage in her life and be a real grown up with a family of her own.

When you're a kid, twenty-six seems like it's a real grown up age. Even in high school. Our twenties seemed like some great precipice of adulthood. We would be married and start having kids by then. But twenty-six sneaks up on you really quickly. It felt like I was in high school just a couple years ago. Then college. But I was four years out of college already, I realized. When I started college, part of me kind of thought that I would meet the girl I was going to marry there. And maybe I had met girls I could have married, but I wasn't ready for any that, despite what my parents did, and what Mel and Eric were doing, and what Laura had done, and what anyone else might want to do. For me, twenty-six was still just too young. And I wearily realized that that was okay and that it was okay that I had waited so long to make a move on Laura. Because it was okay that I wanted to spend my life with her but wasn't quite ready to dive into serious adulthood.

I wondered briefly if Laura was lying awake somewhere too, staring at the ceiling of whatever room she was in. Probably next to Mark. But I doubted she was sleeping. My grandmother used to say that when you're thinking of someone, it means they're thinking of you too. If that was true, then Laura would definitely be awake. Of course, if that was true, she was thinking of me pretty much all the time, and I doubted that was true.

She was the only person who would actually completely understand why I had been so afraid to make a move toward that next step. Because she had taken that step and had it crumble beneath her. She was just as scared as I was. And maybe that meant we could never have gotten our acts together enough to be together. Maybe at least one person in a relationship needs to be emotionally mature enough to handle it. But I felt an intense pang of loneliness and longing for her as I realized just how deeply she would have understood and been able to sympathize with what I was feeling.

If she had only been there to hear it.

37

It was the hardest thing I had ever attempted, but I tried to stop thinking about Laura. Not just because of Mel, but because I realized that I had to. Yes, Laura would come back. Someday. But if I was sitting around and waiting for her in the exact same place that I had been in when she left me, we still wouldn't work. We couldn't work. So I tried to figure out how to forget about what we had been. I stopped Googling her. I stopped watching any entertainment shows, and I changed the channel when the legitimate news shows had entertainment segments. When they came on at the gym, and I couldn't change the channel, I turned my music up louder and looked anywhere else. It was impossibly difficult. I still glanced at the magazine covers out of the corners of my eyes in checkout lines. When I heard his name, on the radio, at the record store, or anywhere else, my ears still perked up. I wanted to know what was going on in their lives. But I had to cut myself off if I had any hope of getting over her.

I read an article online one day that said they had torn down the Palace in Asbury Park. It was one of those icons of the Jersey shore, immortalized in "Born to Run." I couldn't help thinking about Laura when I saw that. The Palace was one of the big sites we had wanted to see when we went to Asbury. She took a million pictures of it. Later that day, Ellen took pictures of the two of us standing together in front of it.

The article's headline read "Beyond the Palace: Jersey Shore landmark demolished for Asbury Park redevelopment." It talked about how the Palace had been built in 1888 and described all the changes it had gone through as Asbury Park boomed and then declined. It outlined the plans for the site and the plans for refurbishing Asbury Park overall. And of course, it mentioned Bruce and his efforts in the campaign to restore Asbury Park to its former glory.

There was something tragic in the idea of it being gone. True, it had been vacant for over a decade and condemned for years. It was faded and peeling and, to anyone other than a diehard Springsteen fan, it was a tremendous turquoise eyesore. But it was an eyesore that represented a town for 116 years, through success and through ruination. It didn't seem right to tear it down. Not with so many other buildings in Asbury Park in just as bad, if not worse, shape. Why not renovate and reopen it? Why couldn't they fix it up and make Asbury Park into the town that it had been so long ago?

But that was the point, I guess. You can't go back to exactly the way things were. It just isn't possible. Ever. Restoring and renovating the Palace wouldn't bring the people back to Asbury Park. It's a rundown town full of crime; a big green arcade with rides and swan boats isn't going to make the family crowd come back. And what Asbury Park was in its heyday isn't what the family crowd even wants anymore.

The only way to get the people back to Asbury Park is to tear down, to rebuild from scratch. To go beyond what it had sunk into recently and create something new. Something different. It couldn't be better than what it was in its prime, because there's no way to compare the two totally separate entities. It was okay to mourn what was lost, but it was also time to look ahead.

For Asbury Park and for me.

The good times of Asbury Park were behind it, as were the good times that I had spent with Laura. Laura and I could no more go back to what we had been than Asbury Park could go back to what it had been. It was time to stop looking back and time to start looking toward the future, with something new and different. And just like Asbury could, through tearing down and giving itself a new beginning, develop into something that would eventually attract the family crowd back to its shore, if Laura came back, we would have to tear down what we had been and create something original, something different. That was the only way. Because anything that we tried to build on the old foundations that we had built together would have to crumble. There was just too much damage done in the past year. We would need something fresh. And so, like Asbury Park, it was time for me to demolish what I had held dear since she left me. To make room for the possibility of the new.

We were all beyond the Palace now.

38

Every night, I went to bed hoping to wake up the next morning without thinking about her. And every morning, I was still disappointed. I had completely stopped letting myself think about her during the day, and I had gotten good at that, but in those first few seconds after I woke up, I couldn't quite stop myself.

But I was finally past the point when I thought that every out-of-area phone call was from her. Past scanning my mail for her handwriting. Past jumping up with her name on my tongue when someone knocked on my door. I no longer glanced at magazine covers. Not looking was a habit already. I didn't have to remind myself anymore. I switched the radio station automatically when Mark's songs came on. There was no point in listening. It would just make life harder. I never watched MTV or VH1 anymore. I thought those retro "I Love the '80s" shows were harmless, but they had interviewed Mark for one of them, and I decided it was better to stay away from those channels overall to be safe.

Bruce did his small run of Vote for Change shows in the beginning of October of that year. A few people asked me if I was going, and it was easy to say no. I couldn't face that. Not without her. Not yet. I told everyone it was because I wasn't the target audience for the shows. I didn't live in a swing state, and I was already planning to vote the way he wanted to convince people to. But even when he announced a show in DC, I stayed away. It would have been too hard. And secretly, deep down, in a dark place inside of me, I knew that I couldn't go. In case she was there. With him. There was no incentive on this earth that could have enticed me to go anywhere that seeing them together was even in the realm of possibility.

Another two months passed. I knew it was December, of course. I knew, but I was able to forget that it would have been our second "Bruce-iversary." It didn't even occur to me that it was the eighth until I opened the package.

I had started going to the gym just about every day after work. That was probably the best part of her leaving. I was spending enough hours at work to totally erase my coworkers' memories of all the time that I took off when I was with her. And when I wasn't at work, I was logging serious time at the gym. It meant that I was in the best shape of my life, and that I slept at night, because apparently the only thing Laura had left me with was her insomnia. So when I finally got home that particular day, it was long since dark out, and all I wanted to do was take a shower, eat some dinner, and climb into bed. I literally tripped over the package that was outside my door and banged my elbow hard against the door frame.

Cursing, I bent down to pick it up. It was a large cube, about fourteen inches on all sides. It rattled a little, softly, as I shook it, but it was too dark to see the return address and I was too tired to be that curious. I went inside, dropped my gym bag by the door and walked into the kitchen with the box. I flipped on the light switch and my heart started racing.

There was no mistaking the handwriting. It wasn't exactly neat or messy, but distinctive. As if she had studied how other people wrote and decided she needed something totally different. Like she had done with everything else in her life.

I put it on the kitchen table and studied it. No return address. Of course. That would mean I could find her.

Not that I would. But it wasn't Laura's style to put a return address anyway.

Just my name, my address, and a California postmark. Los Angeles. December 6, 2004. December sixth? That was two days ago. That made it the eighth when I got the package.

Throw it out, the rational part of my brain told me. *Don't open it. All it can do is hurt you.*

I forced myself to get up and walk away. And I almost made it to the door. But I had to know. I didn't want to know. But I had to.

I took it into the living room and sat down on the sofa with it, then ripped into the box. And in that second before I looked, I let myself hope. I don't even know what I was hoping for. It wasn't big enough for her to be inside. But maybe it would hold something that would mean she was ready to come back.

Covered in about a zillion packing peanuts, was the album *Born in the USA*. Autographed. Not the CD, but the record. Because Laura knew I had my dad's old turntable and that everything sounds better on vinyl. We had listened to every album we could get our hands on in vinyl on that turntable. It was one of those Laura touches that was both sweet and heartbreakingly cruel at the same time.

"Ben—Listen to the second song on side two, for an old friend. –Bruce Springsteen"

My heart sank. I didn't need to flip it over. I knew what the second song on side two was. I didn't want to listen to that song. And for a second, I actually thought I might throw up. But Bruce had never told me personally to do anything before, so I walked over to the stereo and pulled out the record. A piece of paper came out with it and fluttered to the floor. I glanced down and saw that it was a page torn out of a magazine, with an ad for Absolut Vodka on it.

I dropped the second side of the record on the turntable, took a deep breath, and put the needle at the groove for the second song. Then I sat down on the floor and looked at the other side of the magazine page. It was torn out of *People* magazine and had shots of a bunch of celebrities at different events. And circled there in red sharpie, as if she didn't stand out on her own, was Laura. She was standing between Mark and Bruce. Mark had an arm around her waist and Bruce had an arm around her shoulder. Patti was on Bruce's other side. Even without the red circle around the picture, she was impossible to miss. Nicole Kidman, Halle Berry, and Brad Pitt were all on the same page, but it was Laura whose face shone out of it. It was her dream come true.

As I stared at the face that I had tried to avoid seeing for most of the past year, the song that I first associated with her blasted out of my speakers. I listened to Bruce sing and I studied Laura's face, right next to his.

The song was "Bobby Jean."

It's a song about saying goodbye to the only person in the world who ever really understood you. The only person who ever really will. And how, even though he knows he can't make her come back or do anything to change her mind, he's saying that he misses her and goodbye, and that he hopes she'll remember him whenever she hears this song.

I remembered how she looked when I first saw her, when Bruce sang those words and she cried. And I remembered that perfect night in Philadelphia. And dancing with her at Mel's wedding. And I remembered waking up next to her.

It was her goodbye to me, because she had left me without one all that time ago. It was her way of saying she remembered me. That she was still thinking of me. She picked this song on purpose and asked Bruce to tell me to listen to it very deliberately. It also meant that she forgave me for not telling her that I had seen her crying to this song. It meant she missed that I knew what I knew about her and could still love her, because she didn't have that with Mark. It meant that she would still think about me every December eighth.   But I realized that it also meant she wasn't coming back. Not ever.

She hadn't gotten *Born to Run* signed, or *Darkness on the Edge of Town*.   It was this album, one of my least favorites, because it had this song on it.

I knew that it was the last time I would hear from her. No matter how desperately I might want to believe that she would come back, I knew then that she was gone forever. Even if she and Mark broke up, she would never come back. She had gotten everything she wanted. And it wasn't me.

For the first time since she left, for the first time in years, I think, I put my head in my hands and cried.

I don't know how long I sat there. I guess I was there until after the album ended, because I don't remember shutting it off, but there was no time that night. Eventually, I got up, and I took a shower, and I set my alarm clock for the morning, and I went to sleep.

It's strangely liberating to give up all hope. I was free suddenly, because I wasn't looking for her anywhere anymore. When the phone rang, I didn't even wish that it could be her.   I wasn't constantly scanning faces everywhere I went. I actually wanted to go out with the guys again. I wanted to meet people. I wanted to meet a new girl. I asked Amy, a girl who had been shooting me looks and smiles at the gym for weeks, out on a date and actually had a good time with her. And so I called her again and went on a second and third date.

I could think about Laura objectively by then. I wasn't even angry. I could see that we just hadn't worked out. And I really didn't think about her much any more at all. I heard a couple of weeks later that she and Mark had gotten engaged. It was on the radio and I saw it in a pop up ad that came up when I logged into Instant Messenger one day at work. I shrugged when I heard. *Good for her*, I thought eventually. *I hope she can be happy now.*

Sending me that album was cruel, but it was also the kindest thing that Laura ever did for me. Because it set me free.

39

I ran into Katie at Mel and Eric's New Year's party. I was in the corner, chatting up Cara, Mel's older sister, when Mel rushed over to us, clearly alarmed. "I had no idea she was coming," she exclaimed breathlessly. "She's here with one of Eric's friend's from work. They're dating. I had no idea." She looked at me expectantly. *Laura?* I wondered, confused and not even knowing how that could be possible. But who else would send Mel into such a panic? I turned slowly toward the door and glanced over my shoulder. *Oh shit*, I thought. *This can't be good.* I turned quickly back to Mel.

"Does she know it's your party yet?"

Mel turned to look at Katie, who spotted her, looked surprised, then waved hesitantly. "She does now," Mel said out of the side of her mouth through the smile she forced at Katie. "If you cause trouble, I will kill you."

"Should I talk to her or avoid her?" I asked. Mel, of course, would be perfectly content to tell me exactly what to do, and I had no problem following her directions. That way, if Katie had a meltdown, I would be far less to blame.

"Go talk to her," she hissed. The guy Katie was with took her coat and walked it to the bedroom while Katie went into the kitchen where a makeshift bar was set up on the counter. I excused myself from Cara and followed Katie. I turned back briefly and looked to Mel for guidance, but she just moved her hands in a shooing motion. *Here we go*, I thought. I hadn't seen or heard from her since the night that Laura and I ran into her at the beer and wine store, which was well over a year-and-a-half ago. She was standing by the counter with her back to me as she poured two glasses of wine.

"Hey stranger," I said. Her shoulders tensed slightly then lowered.

"I didn't know it was Mel's party," she said without turning around. "I would have told John that we had to go somewhere else tonight if I had known."

"It's okay that you're here."

She turned around and looked at me. "I don't need your permission," she said. She sounded tired.

I was a little surprised. Katie didn't usually talk like that. "I know," I said, then paused. I didn't really have anything to say. "How have you been?" I asked finally.

She took a slow sip of her wine. "Wonderful, actually," she said with an eventual smile. But it was a hard smile. It didn't reach her eyes. It was familiar, but it wasn't Katie. She didn't volunteer anything else and she didn't ask how I was. It's cruel when girls do that. Don't they know how hard it is for us to keep a conversation going without their help?

"So how long have you been with—" I struggled for the name she had just said. "John?"

"A little over a year," she said, with a softer smile.

"Wow, that's great," I said lamely.

"What about you?" she asked eventually. "Still with Laurie?" I hated that trick. I had made sure to get her boyfriend's name right and I knew she messed up Laura's on purpose. But I was not about to let her get to me tonight.

"No," I said, refusing to even give her the satisfaction of correcting Laura's name. "We were never together." I looked her right in the eye as I said this. I had nothing to hide and nothing to be ashamed of. And I was not going to be the one to look away first.

"My mistake," she said airily, clearly not believing me. "I thought you were together for quite a while." I shook my head. "Well, then," she said coolly. *She's not the reason we broke up,* I wanted to scream. But I needed to let Katie think what she needed to think. And who even knew why we broke up anymore? Maybe in some weird cosmic way, Laura *was* the reason. Maybe Laura leaving me would, in the same way, be the reason I was able to find someone else. I thought briefly of Mel's sister and had to hold in a smile. She was clearly not the girl for me, but she could be a lot of fun later. If I managed to make it out of this situation alive.

"Is it serious then with you and John?" I would be lying if I said I wasn't tempted to say "Joe" or some other wrong J-name. But I wasn't going to play her games. I didn't care about the answers enough to toy with the questions. But if I could get her to say that she was in love with him, then that meant that she had to be over me enough to be mature tonight. And my primary goal in this conversation was to keep Mel from getting mad at me over Katie spoiling her party.

Katie held out her left hand. "We're engaged," she said simply as the diamond picked up the fluorescent lights. Moderately-sized ring. Smaller than what Eric had given Mel, but perfectly suited to Katie's taste.

"Congratulations," I said earnestly, without having to try. "I'm really happy for you."

"Are you?" she asked flatly. I stared at her. That tone. She could have been channeling Laura. I think my mouth dropped open. She stared right back at me, her eyes unchanging, her brows drawn together ever so slightly with the question.

"Of course I am," I managed finally, my brain spinning.

"If you say so," she said softly, neutrally. The change in her was suddenly totally apparent. With what I had loved about her so completely gone, I could now remember what had drawn me to her all those years ago when we first started dating. It had been her innocence, her sweetness, her inherent goodness. But that was gone now. She was harder now. Tougher. Stronger. I looked at her, trying to see some outward sign of the change that had occurred as I worked this out.

"John!" she exclaimed as her fiancé walked into the kitchen and a little of the light returned to her eyes. I didn't think it was as much as there was when she was happy with me, but it was clearly enough for him. She kissed him with her eyes closed as he slipped an arm around her waist. He turned to look at me and it became apparent to both of us that Katie was not planning to introduce us.

"John Baker," he said, extending his hand easily. I shook it and introduced myself. He looked for a second like he was trying to place the name, then it clicked. "Ah," he said finally, his smile fading as he looked slowly from Katie to me. "Very nice to meet you."

I congratulated him on the engagement and excused myself as quickly as I could without being rude. I grabbed a beer and headed out to Mel's deserted balcony to be alone for a minute. It was too cold for anyone else to be out there, even the hardcore smokers.

My mind went back to Katie's voice when she had asked if I was actually happy for her. It was so cold and detached. It was Laura. The look in her eyes. Was that really all that it took for a girl to become like that? Could Laura have been like Katie used to be? What did it take to turn a really sweet, happy girl into someone like Laura? How could a breakup do that much damage to the core of who she was? And how would I react to Laura if I ever saw her again? Would it be with that same hurt detachment that Katie had just shown me? Why did we let ourselves be open to something that could do that to us? I wasn't sure that there was any reward that could be worth that risk.

I wanted to run inside and grab Katie and say I was sorry. Tell her not to let me be the reason that she became like that. But I saw her laughing with John through the sliding glass balcony door. She wasn't mine to save anymore. I had been the catalyst for the change in her, but she had picked her own path. So had Laura. So would I. I drank my beer and looked south toward the city on the horizon.

Eventually, Cara came out and snaked her hand around me and into my back pocket. She had brought me another beer and she shivered as I put my arm around her shoulder.

"What are you doing out here in the cold?" she asked, leaning close into me. I had drank that last beer very quickly and was starting to feel it. Her hair smelled delicious. I glanced cautiously over my shoulder into the apartment, but Mel was nowhere to be seen. Oh fuck it. I could always blame it later on the alcohol and finding out that Katie was engaged. Besides, Mel *did* tell me that I should be more of a guy about the whole situation.

"Waiting for you," I said, as smoothly as I could.

She laughed. "How did you know I'd come out here?"

I shrugged. "Because you know Mel won't like you being out here with me."

"We're just talking," she said in a little girl voice that was anything but innocent and looking up at me with "fuck-me eyes," as we called that look in college. I leaned down closer to her.

"We don't have to be just talking," I said quietly when my mouth was close enough to hers to leave no doubt about what I planned to do.

"What did you have in mind?" she asked, bringing her mouth even closer.

"We could play board games," I said with a smile. "Or make prank phone calls to the party." I was going to make her make the move. This was a version of Laura's old game. And I could see why she played it. It was fun. "Unless you've got a better idea."

I brought her home with me that night. Neither of us ever told Mel.

40

That mystical entity of "they" always says that you see someone you have been dying to see when you finally stop thinking about them. When you no longer expect to see them. When you no longer care if you see them. And as usual, they are right.

I hadn't thought about Laura, even in passing, in at least a week. I hadn't even felt bad when I found myself singing along with a catchy song while driving to work and then heard the DJ say that it was a Mark Houston song. I just shrugged, acknowledged that the song was good, and went on with my day. I smiled more than I had since the last Springsteen tour. I started checking online again to see if there was any news about a new tour or new album coming soon, although I wasn't sure what I would do about concerts when Bruce toured again. I assumed that I would go to a few. I was pretty sure I'd be ready for that by the time it happened. In short, I actually was okay again.

So when I was getting ready to go over to Mel's place for dinner on a Friday night, I didn't even think about it when I heard a knock on my door. I had just finished shaving. Normally I wouldn't bother when I was just going to Mel and Eric's apartment, but I had just broken it off with Kelly, the girl who I had been seeing for the past two weeks. And Mel's best friend from high school, Alyssa, was going to be at dinner. I had always thought she was cute, and she too was newly single, so I figured what the hell. Mel would object of course, but if anything happened, well, I would tell her that it was her fault for inviting the two of us over on the same night. It was a dangerous game I was playing, especially after sleeping with Mel's sister just a month earlier. But I was having trouble caring. I wouldn't make things awkward as long as the girls didn't.

I wasn't even sure if I had actually heard someone knocking or if I was imagining it because I had music on. I muted the stereo and listened again, then went to check.

And there she was.

Her hair had a lot more blonde in it and was pulled back into a long ponytail, with bangs, which were new, off to one side of her face. The circles under her eyes were a little heavier, which she had clearly tried to hide with makeup. But she looked the same. The leather jacket, jeans, and spiky-heeled boots were all new, but the general idea was the same. A different thin scarf was looped once around her neck. Sunglasses perched on top of her head, even though it was dark out by then. Long red nails. No engagement ring. Instead she had a silver skull ring on the middle finger of her left hand. She looked like she had stepped out of a fashion magazine or a music video, which, actually, she had.

I didn't say anything. I didn't know what to say. I don't think I even had anything to say at that point. I just looked at her. It was like seeing a ghost.

"Hey," she said eventually, quietly. I couldn't get a read on her from that. She didn't kiss me hello, which she had always done in greetings. She was looking at me and I realized that I hadn't responded. But I still had nothing to say.

"Oh, invite me in already," she said, attempting to laugh. "It's too late to slam the door in my face." She started to give me one of her usual coy looks, but saw immediately that it wouldn't work and looked at me pleadingly instead. "Ben—?"

I still couldn't say anything to her. I just didn't know what to say. It struck me as mildly funny that I had started our relationship tongue-tied, but for far different reasons. But I needed to hear what she had to say. Even though I, at the same time, didn't want to. Unable to either tell her to leave or invite her in, I moved slightly to the side and held the door open. She walked into the hall and toward the living room. I felt a sudden and intense urge to just walk out the door and get away from her, but I resisted it, and instead shut the door and followed her.

I deliberately avoided the sofa and chose the chair. I didn't want her next to me. She watched me sit down.

"You look good," she said. "Been working out?" I nodded. I had to say something soon, and I knew it. "Look, I know you're mad, but—"

"Why are you here?"

She paused. I knew she wouldn't answer that yet.

"Do you hate me?" she asked. But I knew her games by then and for the first time in the more than two years since we had met, I was in charge. And I wasn't letting her get away with that avoidance crap.

"I asked my question first."

Laura sighed and crossed the room to sit on the edge of the sofa nearest to me. She looked into my eyes and I looked right back. She looked away first.

"Did you get the record I sent?" I remembered some of the anger from the last time we had a conversation in this room. The night she told me she was leaving. I wasn't about to get into this with her again.

"You've got about thirty seconds to start talking before I leave. I'm not interested in the bullshit anymore." My voice sounded flat and far away. I wasn't even sure why I had let her in or asked her what she was doing in the first place. I really just did not want to be in the same room as her right then. A few months ago, I would have killed for that opportunity. But too much had happened since then.

"I—" her voice wavered. She stopped, got control of it, and continued. Then quietly, "I miss you." She looked up at me and saw I hadn't responded. I think she honestly thought that saying that would make everything okay. I felt a mild desire to laugh. Even a five-year-old kid knows that saying you're sorry isn't always enough. As she looked at me, her eyes started to shine.

"I'm sorry," she said, her voice shakier than I had ever heard it, even in the few times that I had actually seen her crying. "I'm so sorry. I know I shouldn't have even come here, but I had to at least see you. I had to at least know—" she stopped and again tried to get control of her voice. "I had to at least try to explain and try—just try." She was twisting the ring on her finger and looking at me pleadingly. My chest felt tight.

She looked down and took a deep breath. She opened her mouth but no words came out. Another deep breath. "I had to tell you that you were right. Because I never told you that. Not once. And you were always right. About everything." She was watching me, but I still didn't respond. The words started to pour out. "You were right that I left because I was scared. I was so scared. I—I was terrified. I did love you. I loved you so much. More than I'd even loved Justin and, I mean, I *married* him. And you said you loved me. You saw me at my worst and you still said you loved me. But I didn't think it could last because there was no way that you could keep loving me. I would screw it up. I'd have to screw it up. And I did. I actually did because I was scared that I would, and I know that I did. And I'm so sorry. I'm so, so sorry." She started to cry in earnest as she repeated the last part. Hearing her say all of that should have meant so much. But it didn't. It couldn't by then.

"Aren't you engaged now?" My voice surprised me. I felt far away, but my voice sounded extremely sharp. Like Katie's did that night at Mel's party. But I couldn't worry about the implications of that right then. Laura looked up, the tracks of her tears cutting through her makeup.

"I was," she said thickly. "But I couldn't do it. I broke it off. Did you hear his last single? It's about me. It's mean, but I deserve it. I know I do." I thought back to that song I had been hearing on the radio without realizing that it was Mark's song. I hadn't even thought about the lyrics.

It had just been catchy. But she was telling the truth, it was about a girl leaving him.

"It was actually Bruce, believe it or not, who made me realize that I couldn't do it. If you got the record, you saw the picture. I met him in October. He was doing all that campaigning for Kerry after the Vote for Change shows, and there was this benefit that I knew he would be at because I'd been calling Mark's people at Columbia like every day to find out. So I went out and found a copy of *Born in the USA*. I knew exactly what I wanted to do. But I couldn't bring it into the actual benefit because there was all this security. So when I met him, I asked if I could stop by his hotel later and have him sign an album for me and he said yes. I mean, that wasn't the whole conversation. Mark told him what a big fan he was, that we both were, and he told him about how we—he and I—met and all.

"Then the next morning, I went to his hotel room. And I told him the album wasn't for me. I told him about you. About how you and I met and about all the shows we went to. And he looked me right in the eye and asked what I was doing with Mark and not you.

"I tried to laugh it off. I said it wasn't like that, but he knew I wasn't telling the truth.

"'I know we've all gotta make our own mistakes,' he said, 'but if you've found that one person who you can make that connection with, that's what it's all about. And if you're smart, in some fashion, you're going to realize it's time to stop being afraid and start going after that one thing, that one person, who can really make you happy.' He said that, word for word." After so long with her, I could tell immediately when Laura was making stuff up. This was real. She kept going.

"I told him Mark was that guy. But I knew he wasn't. I just wasn't ready to admit that yet. And Bruce told me to remember what he'd said. I mean, like I could ever forget it!" She laughed a little. "You know, it's funny. I felt like I really knew him so well after so many concerts and listening to his songs so many times, and then when I actually met him, it was him who understood me better than anyone in the world. Except you."

She looked at me for a long time before she continued. "And I sent the record, I guess, to say that I was sorry. I almost didn't send it. Part of me hoped you'd forgotten about me. Because I wanted to forget about you. I wanted to be happy with Mark. So much. It was everything I wanted, I mean, it was—it was everything. Everything I was so sure that I needed after Justin. Because—and I know it's stupid—but I had tried a normal life and it didn't work. So this—this was what I thought would work. And he loved me. He did. He asked me to marry him. And it was perfect, it was at one of his shows, and it was so, so romantic. And I said yes. But I kept thinking about you and about what Bruce said." Another tear ran down her cheek. "He played 'Tougher than the Rest,' when he proposed. And I said yes, but I thought about you. When we danced at the wedding. And that whole night. And how you didn't push me for anything when I wasn't ready. Or maybe you didn't actually want to. I don't know. But you didn't push. And I felt like such a liar saying yes to him. But it was everything I'd wanted, and I didn't know why it didn't feel like enough all of a sudden. All I knew was that I couldn't stop thinking about you."

I admit that a teeny, tiny, little part of me wanted to go sit next to her. To put my arms around her. To kiss her. And tell her that everything would be okay. But the majority of me would never let that happen. I had simply come too far to go across the room to her.

It was too late, and I knew it. It was just too late to be with her. To do that now, I would have to forget all the hurt of the past year since the tour ended. Forget the emptiness that had been threatening to consume me. Forget what seeing them in magazines had done to me. Forget what I had felt when I saw her in his music video for the song he had written about falling in love with her. Some of that I might have been able to overlook. Some of it I wouldn't be able to put behind me. Not completely. Not ever.

I knew that every word of what she had just said to me was the truth. No equivocations this time. But it was just too late.

I think I wanted to still feel what I used to feel for her. And when she told me what Bruce had said about us, I wanted to say okay. Bruce had told her to be with me; who was I to say no to that? But I couldn't do it. I just sat there watching her. I wanted to stop her too. I didn't want to hear what would come next because I knew that I couldn't say yes to her. And at the same time, I didn't want to know what effect hearing it might have on me.

But I couldn't stop her either. The same way that I had to open that package, I had to hear what she had to say. Maybe that meant that I still loved her. Maybe it meant I wanted closure. I still don't know.

"We were engaged for less than a month," she said, looking at the carpet and still twisting her skull ring. "I couldn't do it. It was my dream, but it wasn't what I wanted anymore. I guess I thought that if I could get someone who was like a young Bruce, we would have this perfect life and he could never leave me and it would be right. But it wasn't right. It just wasn't right. So I told him I couldn't do it. And he said 'Okay, we'll wait,' and I had to tell him that I couldn't ever do it. That I couldn't be with him. And it was awful. I didn't just leave; I stayed and I told him. It was so hard, but I didn't want to do what I'd done to you. I didn't want that on my conscience again. It was what Justin did to me and it wasn't right.

"Then I called my mother." I guess I looked surprised at this part because she nodded at me. "I had told her when we got engaged because she had called me when she heard that I was in the tabloids, and I guess I was hoping I could start to have some kind of a real relationship with her. So I called her when I left Mark and told her that it was over. And she asked me why and I told her that I just couldn't do it. And she asked me—" Laura choked a little at this part. "She asked me—"

"What did she ask?" It popped out of my mouth before I could stop myself.

"She asked how many times I had to ruin my life before I could be happy." Laura broke down into sobs at this, her thin shoulders heaving, and it was at least a minute before she could even go on. I wanted to comfort her. At least pat her hand or *something*. But no. I pitied her. The Justin thing hadn't been her fault, but the mother who hadn't even gone to her daughter's wedding couldn't see that. And I guessed her mother wouldn't have known about the baby, so she couldn't have known how hard she was really hitting her daughter by saying that.

"I started to cry then too," she finally continued. "And she told me to call her when I'd calmed down. But I realized that the only time that I'd actually been the one who ruined anything was with you." Her wet eyes looked into mine, but this time I looked away first. She sighed slightly.

"So I drove home. It took me six days all alone. And then I wanted to come here, I wanted to come see you. But I was too scared. I've been home for almost three weeks. I didn't know if you would even talk to me. I drove over here almost every day, but I couldn't do it."

She got off the sofa and knelt down by my feet. She put her hand on top of mine. I wanted to snatch it back, but I couldn't. My whole body was tense. The moment of truth. What was I going to do when it came down to it?

"Ben," she said softly. "I love you. And I know how much I hurt you. And I wish I could take it back. But I'll do whatever it takes to make you forgive me." I didn't say anything. I was afraid to open my mouth. Afraid I'd say yes. Afraid I'd say no.

"Please," she said. "Tell me you still love me and I'll make it right. I'll—"

"Stop." I disentangled myself from her grip, got out of the chair, and walked over toward the stereo, unconsciously mirroring the dance we did the night that I told her I loved her. "Just stop." I wasn't sure that I could look at her and still have the nerve to say what I needed to say.

"I did love you, Laura. You know that. And I know you loved me as much as you could. But I just can't do this. It's too late for us." I heard her crossing the room to me.

"I know you're mad," she said, touching my arm tentatively.

I turned to face her. "No. I'm not mad. I'm just—I'm tired, Laura. Exhausted in fact. It's just too late." She was crying again.

"But—" she looked up at me, her eyes begging.

"Don't do this, Laura. It's not you." I kissed her on the forehead and she closed her eyes as another tear slipped past her lashes and ran down her cheek. "You're going to be okay. And I am okay." *Am I?* A little voice in my head asked. "It's not anyone's fault anymore. It's just too late," I repeated again. I took a deep breath.

"Now you need to go home because I have plans tonight." They were harsh words, but I said them gently. She wiped her eyes with the back of her hand and squared her shoulders slightly. *Am I doing the right thing?*

She nodded at me. "Okay," she said softly. "Okay."

"Maybe I'll see you further on up the road," I said as she walked away for the last time. She turned and smiled sadly at me over her shoulder, her lower lip trembling slightly.

"Maybe," she said. And was gone. I sank down shakily on the sofa, still able to smell her perfume.

41

Two more months went by after Laura came to my apartment.

They were quiet months, but they went quickly. It didn't feel like that long at least. It's hard to characterize the change that occurred after she came back. I didn't see her again. I didn't even know if she was still in town. She could have been traveling or have moved to a new city. Or even back to New York.

It didn't matter if she was in town or not. Because, in a sense, I finally had my closure that I had spent so long trying to find. I felt lighter. It was like my head had been held underwater for the past year, and I had finally managed to get it back up and was able to breathe again. Or like when you run, as far and as fast as you can and your lungs start to burn. But when you stop, and you get your breathing back to normal, you feel free and so completely alive. That's how I felt.

The boulder on my shoulder, to quote Bruce, was gone.

Except the problem was that I kind of missed that boulder. Because Laura had finally given me the ability to put the hurt behind me, I could remember the good times when I thought about her. I didn't need to remember the bad parts anymore. It was over. And suddenly, everywhere I looked, I could see things that reminded me of her. Of the happy times. I heard "From Small Things" on the radio, and remembered how amazing that day was in Philly when Bruce first played it. A red BMW convertible zipped by me on the highway, and I remembered driving her car home through the hot, Jersey shore nights. A girl on the Metro sat down next to me one day; she was wearing Laura's perfume. Of course, the girl on the subway must have thought I was a total pervert, because I leaned in a little too close and smelled her. She stood up at the next stop and got off the train, shooting me a completely disgusted look as she exited my car. It was just little things that reminded me of Laura, but they made me miss the good times that we'd had.

And sometimes, when something like that would happen, I asked myself why I didn't just call her.

But I never did.

Almost two months to the day after I last saw Laura, Bruce tickets went on sale. He was doing a solo tour, without the E Street Band, and he was playing in small theatres. Venues that sat less than ten-thousand people, some as small as two thousand, which was tiny after seeing him with sixty-thousand other fans at Giants Stadium. But for the first time in years, I didn't buy tickets.

I thought about it. I really did. And unlike the Vote for Change shows, I actually wanted to go. But I knew she would be there. I wasn't not buying tickets to avoid her, but I didn't think it would be good for me to go back. And I felt so much older than when the *Rising* tour started. Too old to be chasing a rock star around the country. And without Laura, could the concerts be the same? Yes, I followed him before I met her. But after I met her, how could I go back to shows without her? I just couldn't do it. I woke up to buy tickets and I logged onto Ticketmaster, but I couldn't quite hit the purchase button. I wasn't the same person that I had been the last time he toured. And this person would still listen to Bruce's music, but wasn't driving all over the place to see him live anymore.

The first show was scheduled for Detroit and he wasn't even coming to the East Coast until the tenth show on the *Devils & Dust* tour, which helped because it meant that not buying tickets didn't even feel like it was that big of a deprivation. Without Laura, I really had no desire to leave my concert comfort zone of DC, Philly, Jersey, and Virginia. Drive more than three hours for a concert? No, thank you.

But then they announced rehearsal shows. In Asbury Park. The first one on a Thursday night, the second on a Friday afternoon. And tickets were going on sale just a few days before the shows. A chance to finally see Bruce in Asbury. Like we tried to do the day that we went there. The day that we met Jeff and Ellen.

No, I wouldn't go.

I couldn't go.

God, how I wanted to go.

I was on edge all week. No matter how many times I told myself that I didn't have any desire to be there, I wanted to go. I needed to go. It was like every particle in my body was humming. Everywhere I walked, my feet beat out the tune of "Born to Run." My keyboard seemed to be banging out "Badlands" as I sent emails at work. I heard "Glory Days" on the radio in the shower, and when I was in the car, the DJ on one of the XM radio stations played "Incident on 57th Street" straight into "Rosalita," just like on the album that they songs are on. I switched channels after those two songs and landed on "Tunnel of Love."

The final straw came at work. One of my coworkers had music on. I thought I was imagining it at first. But I walked by his office a few times. It was a CD. And it was *Born to Run*. That was it. When I heard the opening notes to "Backstreets," I pushed the power button on my computer to turn it off without exiting Windows first, scrawled a note to my boss who was out to lunch, and practically sprinted out of the office. I pushed the button for the elevator, but it was too slow, so I ran to the stairs, which I took two at a time. I raced home, changed my clothes, and, less than an hour after I left my office, I was on I-95 speeding toward New Jersey.

I didn't have a ticket, but I didn't care. I knew I would find one.

And that didn't matter.

I tried not to think about her. But it was no use.

I didn't know what I would say. I didn't know if she would be there. Yes, I *knew* she would be there, but I still couldn't be sure. Maybe she had found something else and had stopped needing Bruce. Maybe she figured that it wouldn't be the same without me there and had decided not to go. Maybe she would be there and I wouldn't even see her.

Except I knew that she would be there. And I knew that if I wanted to, I would see her.

Maybe Laura was right when she was in her cynical moods, and maybe love isn't real. Maybe I was on that road because I didn't want to spend the rest of my life alone. I guess I don't know the answer to that one.

I got onto the Turnpike and took the exit for the shore. And I thought that maybe I should just turn around and go home. But no. I couldn't now. I had come too far to ever go back. One way or another, I had to come today and I have to see her. I thought back to the last time we were in Asbury Park. And that perfect day in Philadelphia back in August 2003.

I don't know what I will say if she is here, and I don't know what I will do if she's not. All I know is that I am here. I'm showing that little bit of faith. And now it's time to see if there really is magic in the night after all.

Acknowledgments

Thank you to my parents Jordan and Carole Goodman, for supporting me and believing in me through the whole process of writing and self-publishing this novel. To my father, I owe my love of music and my first Springsteen concerts, without which, this book would not exist. To my mother, I owe my love of reading. You have always been my first audience with everything that I have written, and without your support, I would not be writing today. Thank you to my brother, Adam Goodman, who helped me keep my narrator's voice male enough, who was always willing to talk a scene through with me when I couldn't figure out where it should go, and who was the first one to tell me, "hey, this book is *really* good!"

Thank you to my uncle, Michael Chansky, who brought me to two of the concerts that became pivotal scenes in this novel, for letting me be his successor as the family's biggest Springsteen fan, and to his family, Stephanie Abbuhl, Andrew, Peter, and Ben, for allowing me to use their shore house, where most of this was written. Thank you to my grandparents, Charlotte and Bert Chansky; my aunt and uncle, Dolly and Marvin Band; my cousins Allison and Andy Levine, and Ian and Kim Band for always believing in me, supporting me, reading early versions of my work, and being tireless cheerleaders for my success.

Thank you to Kevin Keegan, my high school journalism teacher, mentor, and friend. I still learn from you every time we talk.

Thank you to my friends, Jennifer Doehner Lucina, Lisbeth Nielsen, Sharon Kim, and Neil Mutreja, for being the inspiration for so much of my work and for taking me out when I needed a break! Thank you to my best friend, Ary Kim Bays, for absolutely everything.

Thank you to my former students and first editors, Nora Belblidia, Angela Chiang, Patricia Glinkowski, Susan Hwang, Parisa Karimi, Emily Stelling, and Grace Yee, for being brave enough to edit your teacher's book! Without your insightful edits, this book would not exist. Thank you to Katie Crockett, for being one of those first editors, this book's biggest fan, and for becoming one of my closest friends. Thank you to Kora-Lynah Abelard, Shrey Tarpara, and Riley Wilson for doing the last round of edits. Thank you to Felicia Roopchand, for giving me that last little push to self-publish. Thank you to Natalia Morrison, for helping to design the book cover.

A very special thank you to Lowell Kern, for reading it closer than anyone else, fixing all of the Bruce-related mistakes, and yelling at me when I needed to be yelled at.

Thank you to Bruce Springsteen, for writing the music that has shaped who I am today.

And last, but certainly not least, thank you to my uncle, Julius Goodman, who gave me a typewriter when I was eight years old and told me that I should become a writer. None of us will ever forget you.

Made in the USA
Lexington, KY
03 October 2010